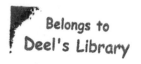

CALL ME HENRI

Call
Me
Henri

a novel by

LORRAINE M. LÓPEZ

CURBSTONE PRESS

Printed in the U.S. on acid-free paper by Berryville Graphics
Cover design: Susan Shapiro
Cover artwork: Photodisc/Veer

Connecticut Commission
on Culture & Tourism

This book was published with the support
of the Connecticut Commission on Culture
and Tourism, National Endowment for the
Arts, and donations from many individuals.
We are very grateful for this support.

NATIONAL
ENDOWMENT
FOR THE ARTS

Library of Congress Cataloging-in-Publication Data

López, Lorraine, 1956-
  Call me Henri / by Lorraine M. López.— 1st ed.
    p. cm.
  Summary: Faced with family problems, difficulty in school, and gangs in
    the barrio, Enrique dreams of reaching the "other America" depicted on
    television some day, while sympathetic teachers help him cope by
    supporting his fight to study French instead of ESL.
  ISBN-13: 978-1-931896-27-6 (pbk. : alk. paper)
  ISBN-10: 1-931896-27-5 (pbk. : alk. paper)
  [1. Family problems—Fiction. 2. Gangs—Fiction. 3. French language—
    Fiction. 4. Middle schools—Fiction. 5. Schools—Fiction. 6. Mexican
    Americans—Fiction. 7. California—Fiction.] I. Title.
  PZ7.L876363Cal 2006
  [Fic]—dc22   2005035790

published by
  CURBSTONE PRESS   321 Jackson Street   Willimantic, CT 06226
      phone: 860-423-5110   e-mail: info@curbstone.org
                http://www.curbstone.org

Acknowledgements

The author wishes to thank the following people for inspiring the work, reading the manuscript, and caring about this project: Sandy Taylor and Judy Doyle, and all the devoted Curbstonistas, who have validated my work with their care and attention; Sara Baker, Lauren Cobb, Sheri Joseph, and my closest friend and kindest editor Kathryn Locey; David Horvath and Lisa Sánchez, whose insights have strengthened this book; my mentor and *compañera*, Judith Ortiz Cofer; the wonderful teachers and unforgettable students at Pacoima Middle School whose stories triggered ideas for me, especially Kerry Skoczylas, María Arredondo, Carlos Loya, and Josanne Wayman; all of my nieces and nephews on the López and Siegel sides of the family, thinking of you as I wrote this kept me on my toes; Jasmine Parham and Nicholas Bennett, to whom I will soon read this book; and above all others, Louis A. Siegel, my husband, my inspiration, and my wise and careful editor.

In 2003, an excerpt from this book appeared in *Once Upon a Cuento* (Curbstone Press), edited by Lyn Miller-Lachmann, to whom I am also grateful for seeing the promise in this work.

For Nick and Marie, with love

CALL ME HENRI

Chapter One

Call me Henri, Enrique wrote after begging a pencil from his seatmate, Cake Angie. She broke her only pencil in two, giving him the splintered end with the eraser and keeping the sharpened half for herself. Enrique felt lucky the teacher, Ms. Byers, passed out paper. Otherwise he would have had nothing to write on. *I want to learn French.* Ms. Byers had asked the students to write a paragraph about themselves, what they liked to be called, favorite foods, music, hobbies…

Hobbies? This triggered a brief discussion among the students. Marvin Alfaro, who spoke English better than most of the others, asked on behalf of the group: "What is hobbies?"

Marvin's grandmother walked to school with him daily ever since he was jumped by the gang called White Fence last fall. His grandmother glanced up from her needlework, as she did whenever Marvin spoke in class, and smiled proudly. Enrique liked the old woman very much, though she had no teeth.

"Well, pastimes," the teacher explained, "like collecting things, building models."

"Past time? Like in the past?" Marvin asked.

"Things you do to pass the time," Ms. Byers said. "Things you do to relax and enjoy yourself, like the sewing your grandmother does." All heads swiveled toward Marvin's *abuelita* at the rear of the room, stitching. She looked up again and grinned.

Though his grandmother took pride in whatever

Marvin said or did in school, Marvin didn't seem especially pleased to have his grandmother pointed out during class.

Cake Angie raised her hand. "Like baking?" Cake Angie was given her nickname because she liked baking cakes and bringing them to school as assignments. Book reports, science experiments, social study projects, anti-drug slogans—everything could be done on a cake. Enrique's stomach rumbled as he remembered the relief map of California she had done in fudge marble with four different colors of frosting.

Angie scored high marks with her cakes, and the class always got to eat her projects. This should have made Cake Angie more popular with teachers and students than she really was. But there was something about Cake Angie and her fascination with cakes that made her seem strange and hard to get to know.

"Yes, baking," agreed the teacher. Enrique hoped Ms. Byers would encourage Angie to bring in a cake soon. It had been a long and cake-less summer for Enrique. His mother didn't like to bake even when the weather was cool. He pictured the shelves in Cake Angie's kitchen crammed with cake mixes and ready-made frosting containers—all waiting patiently for her next school assignment. "But creative things, too," Ms. Byers continued, "like drawing, painting, writing stories."

Enrique could tell Cake Angie wanted to argue that baking cakes *was* creative. Politeness kept her silent until she agreed to break her pencil, so Enrique could write his paragraph.

My favorite foods is French, wrote Enrique, who did enjoy french fries and french toast, too, come to think of it. *My favorite music is French.* Here, he fibbed a little, never having heard any French music that he could recall. *I go to visit Paris for the vacations.* He figured another lie wouldn't hurt. Besides, how could the teacher check? *My hobby is French,* he decorated the "F" in French with a few vines and leaves. Enrique counted six sentences and decided they were enough for a paragraph, yet he finished with a question: *Why cannot I take French instead of ESL?*

Maybe this new teacher would figure out how to get him out of the two-hour English-as-a-Second-Language class and into Beginning French. He felt sure he could learn French faster than English. From the books he checked out of the library, he could see French was very close to the Spanish he spoke, read, and wrote from an early age. And there was something about the French— the way it sounded—that attracted Enrique, like familiar music he longed to play.

Enrique was just writing *Merci!* Under his paragraph when his friend Francisco Valles stepped into the classroom with Mr. Toro, the vice principal. Enrique sat up, alert and interested. Francisco, though an "A" student and a well-behaved boy, created unusual situations wherever he went. He was much less dull than people expected a serious and studious boy to be.

From the redness around Francisco's nose and eyes, Enrique knew his friend had been crying. Francisco often wept when he was upset or frustrated or when others disappointed him. His feelings were easily wounded. The only thing that saved Francisco from being teased for this was his size. Francisco was bigger and stronger than most adults. He could punch anyone he wanted into next week. But he rarely wanted to punch anyone. He didn't have to. All he had to do when people picked on him was to stand up and say: "Could you repeat that, please?"

"This student," Mr. Toro said to Ms. Byers, "was mistakenly assigned to a beginning ESL block."

"I already had ESL-1." Francisco extended his hand for a handshake. "My name is Francisco Valles."

"I'm Veronica Byers." The teacher shook his hand. She seemed startled by the sudden appearance of the vice principal and this large, red-faced student.

"Where would you like me to sit, Ms. Byers?" Francisco scanned the room for an empty desk. "*Buenos días, Señora Alfaro.*" He waved to Marvin's grandmother.

"How about over there?" Ms. Byers pointed out an empty seat at the back.

"I usually like to sit in front," Francisco said with a smile. "But I'll sit there for today."

"There have been mix-ups with scheduling all day," Mr. Toro told Ms. Byers on his way out. "This here is a great kid, but he was upset to find himself back in Mr. McGrath's beginning language arts."

Whew, thought Enrique, no wonder. He would have wanted to burst into tears too, if they'd sent him back to McGrath. He turned to give Francisco a sympathetic look. But his friend was arranging his pencils, pens, and notebook paper.

Ms. Byers quickly explained the assignment to Francisco and held a short discussion with the few students who were willing to talk, like Marvin, Cake Angie, and now Francisco, while the rest of the class listened. Because it was the first day of school, no one fooled around too much. But Horacio Díaz was already starting to make a few silly faces. When the teacher turned to write on the board, Enrique crossed his eyes and stuck his tongue out at Horacio in return.

Enrique had a firm policy of never taking part in class discussions, but he was not against whispering and horsing around when he thought he could get away with it. Francisco had many serious talks with him on this subject. Ms. Byers passed out a few sheets for the class to fill out, then she collected everything when the bell rang. The school was on a half-day schedule because of the intense September heat. Many of the classrooms were in new mobile units that were not yet air-conditioned. Temperatures climbed past a hundred by afternoon under the aluminum roofs of these units.

Enrique liked to be one of the first ones out of the classroom, and Horacio usually beat him. Horacio was already lounging against the lockers past the breezeway as Enrique stepped out the door. On his way out, Enrique noticed that Francisco was still writing his "paragraph." He had already filled a few sheets. No matter—Enrique would catch up with his friend at recess.

"Hay labio jabón lechuga," Horacio said to girls who strolled past him. He didn't care if they were fat or skinny, tall or short, shabby or well-dressed. Horacio greeted them all with the same nonsensical phrase that

sounded like *I love you—I won't let you go* in English. Translated, it meant: *There is lipsoap lettuce.*

As Horacio explained it, he could never get in trouble saying this to girls, in case they turned out to have jealous boyfriends or protective brothers, or if the girls themselves turned out to be tattlers. What harm was there in declaring the existence of lipsoap lettuce after all? And every once in a while, he claimed, some girl would smile and talk to him when he said this to her. Sometimes, he said with a wink, they would even "go out" with him. Enrique had his doubts about this. Who would want to be seen with the guy known for announcing the existence of lipsoap lettuce?

Horacio just liked any kind of silliness. This saying was just silly enough to suit him, so he said it over and over, pretending to be a *mojado*. Though Horacio didn't have to pretend all that much.

"Hay labio jabón lechuga," Horacio said as Enrique approached.

"Oh, yeah," Enrique said. "I love you too. How about a date?"

I wasn't talking to you, idiot, Horacio switched to his comfortable Spanish.

There's no one else here, Enrique pointed out. The other kids had scattered to their next classes. *We better get moving.* The school allowed only short breaks between classes to discourage fighting.

What do you have next period?

Sanchez. How about you?

Sanchez, too. Come on.

Enrique divided teachers up into two categories:

those who got on his nerves and those he didn't mind that much. Mr. Sanchez fell into the second group. Enrique didn't mind the burly, bearded ex-marine, who was really more interested in his own wife and three daughters than in how World War Two was won. Sometimes full class sessions would be given over to Mr. Sanchez's plans to convert his garage into a family room. Students heard a lot about the problems of installing dry wall and paneling. Enrique didn't mind that too much.

Once, Enrique arrived at school early by accident. On his way to homeroom, he caught Mr. Sanchez sitting alone in his pickup truck with the radio on. Though all the windows were rolled up, Enrique clearly heard the music to "Lonely Girl" throbbing from the cab. He'd shot a glance at his teacher. Mr. Sanchez had worn a dreamy look on his dark, hairy face, like he was remembering something from a long time ago. His lips had moved with the lyrics, as he swayed slightly from side to side. For a while, Enrique hadn't been able to decide whether or not he minded that.

Horacio whistled. Cake Angie crossed the breeze-way to the lockers. Enrique imagined she might be planning her next confectionery masterpiece.

"*Hay labio jabón lechuga!*"

"Got a cake in there?" Enrique asked when she pulled open her locker door.

"Shut up," she said and slammed her locker shut.

"But, *hay labio jabón lechuga,*" Horacio insisted.

Chapter Two

Peralta Middle School reminded Enrique of some low-to-the-ground creature, like a crab or a complicated lizard that had been dissected and laid out in an orderly collection of segments. Rows of bungalows spiraled out from the main office building as joint sections might from the squat central body. The metallic trailers that radiated beyond the bungalows shimmered like tentacles in the sun. And there was something reptilian about the gray-green industrial paint that covered every building, challenging graffiti artists with its dark slickness.

A small patch of grass off to the side of the trailers made up the recreation yard. Beside it, the lunch area was marked by a series of picnic tables under a shelter. As small and crowded as the play yard seemed to Enrique, an airplane tried to land on it some years back, killing three students who were playing kick ball below. In memory of those students, the P.T.A. erected a bronze plaque, which stuck out like a grave marker in the grass. Almost every day, one kid or another stumbled on that plaque on his or her way to the lunch area, but no one could pull it out or move it because it was embedded deeply in a cement plug.

At recess, Enrique carefully stepped around the memorial scanning the faces under the shelter for Francisco. Unless he was sitting, Francisco was usually easy to spot in the herd of short, dark-haired kids. At first, Enrique didn't see him. He spotted Horacio leaning against a shelter pillar. *Hay labio jabón lechuga,* he could almost hear him saying. There was Cake Angie again walking with Drunk Angie. Drunk Angie got her name when she drank so much wine at her cousin's *quinceañera* that she vomited on the dance floor. Enrique didn't know if she ever drank wine again, but after that incident she was always known as Drunk Angie.

There were just too many Angies at Peralta Middle School. The nicknames were necessary to keep track of them all. If you were an Angie, you had to be careful about how you behaved and looked because there were always people around waiting to give you a nickname. Watching Drunk Angie talking with Cake Angie, Enrique felt lucky there were only two or three other Enriques.

Enrique finally spotted Francisco sitting at one of the picnic tables. He was patiently explaining an idea to Mr. Bolton, the technology teacher. Bolton was one of the younger teachers, who liked to wear tight-fitting jeans that showed an inch of his white socks at the hems, short-sleeved shirts, and clip-on ties. It was clear to Enrique that the man had no idea how goofy this looked. Mr. Bolton even picked comical ties to add to the effect. Today he was wearing a tie printed with the "Brave Little Toaster" from the cartoon Enrique remembered watching years ago. Enrique thought he would stand to the side until Mr. Bolton moved on. Unlike Francisco, Enrique didn't want to be seen talking to the teachers.

"It works with sound-activation," Francisco was saying, as he twirled a finger in the air. "It's like 'the

Clapper.' You know. Clap on. Clap off." Francisco clapped his large hands to demonstrate.

"'The Clapper.'" Mr. Bolton nodded, rubbing his chin. "Turns lights on and off."

"Right, same principle, but I call this 'the Barker.' Let's say a *ladrón*. How do you say...?"

"Thief," offered Enrique, in spite of himself.

"Let's say a thief comes in the yard to steal from the house. Well, some dog always barks, right? When the dog barks, the porch light goes on and the thief runs away."

"Hmm...," Mr. Bolton murmured. "I think they already have something like that, though, Francisco. They have lights that go on when people come close to the house."

"I know," Francisco said, "but this is better. You see, the thief *hears* the dog, and then the light goes on. He *thinks* the dog got the people up. The other way, the thief just thinks it's the step light and keeps coming."

"Let me think about this one, Francisco." Mr. Bolton rose from the table with his Donald Duck mug. "Let's talk about this later. I've got to run and get my coffee now."

"You could even rig it to a sprinkler system and wet the thief," Francisco added.

"Why don't you write out the idea, so I can have a look at it on paper?" Mr. Bolton noticed Enrique and gave him a friendly wave before heading for the cafeteria. "*Bonjour, Henri!*"

"*Bonjour*," Enrique said, surprised that news of his attempts to get into French class had reached as far as the Tech Lab. He wasn't sure he wanted someone who wore ridiculous ties and drank out of a Donald Duck cup knowing about his desire to learn French.

"What do you think of my idea?" Francisco asked Enrique.

I preferred your other idea, Enrique answered in Spanish. *Remember, the one about the video game channel? This one seems a little stupid.*

"Speak English," Francisco said. "I need to practice. What's wrong with 'the Barker'?"

"Well, we got so many dogs in my street the lights won't never go off. You hook it to the sprinklers and drown everybody. Stay with the video game channel."

Last week Francisco had a terrific idea for starting a channel that would broadcast interactive games—new and old—for subscribers to try out, a different game every half hour. But the catch was, people only got the game for half an hour before another game popped on the screen. Kids could try out new games or play an old favorite for thirty minutes. If they wanted more time, they would have to pester their parents into buying the games.

"I haven't worked out the technology for that one yet," Francisco admitted.

"Fight! Fight! Fight!" A wave of kids swept past the two boys nearly knocking Enrique down with its force. The crowd swelled and surged toward the center of the play area.

Francisco stood and lumbered after the wave. He usually stopped fights if no teachers were around.

"Who is it?" Enrique asked. "Who's fighting?"

"It's Horacio and that Ricky dude," some boy told him as he rushed past. Horacio and Ricky? Enrique tagged after the crowd. Horacio and Ricky had been tight all summer, hanging around the neighborhood together and spending time at one another's homes. There must be a mistake, thought Enrique.

But when he pushed to the inner circle, Enrique saw Horacio, blood streaming from his nose, rearing up to charge at the other boy. Ricky stood, weaving with his fists clenched like a professional boxer. Enrique only caught a few words in all the noise and confusion. One of the boys shouted "thief!" and "I ain't no thief!" a couple of times, but he couldn't tell who said what.

Ms. Byers stepped between the boys as Horacio lunged. She took a fist in the chest, a solid blow, thumping like a bat against a softball.

Francisco jumped into the center of the ring of greedy faces cheering the struggle. He grabbed Horacio by the collar of his flannel shirt and hefted him off his feet. The smaller boy's khaki covered legs kicked angrily, but uselessly, several inches from the ground.

Ms. Byers wrapped her arms around Ricky's shoulders and pulled him away. He was shorter than Horacio, so she dragged him off without too much difficulty. He even seemed relieved to have the fight interrupted, though he shouted and cursed for appearance sake all the same.

"Hey, let me go! Get your stinking hands off me!" he hollered at the teacher, but his struggle against Ms. Byer's embrace was feeble. "My mom is going to sue you, you touch me!"

Enrique rolled his eyes. Ricky was one of the *norteamericano* kids, born in the United States. He spoke Spanish poorly, and, like many of the U.S. born kids, he threatened to sue people whenever he had the chance. Like some judge was going to sit there and listen while Ricky accused Ms. Byers of pulling him out of a fight.

The crowd groaned in disappointment when the fight ended. Mr. Toro jogged over looking like a chunky badger, his megaphone bumping against his chest, to yell at the kids and get them to class.

Enrique shot a last glance at Francisco still clutching Horacio and wearing a confused look on his face. His friend couldn't decide whether to hold onto Horacio, who still seemed angry, or to obey the vice principal's command and set him down to head for class. Enrique shrugged sympathetically, but pivoted to head toward the gym for his favorite class. When he pulled open the heavy glass door to the gymnasium, he could still hear Horacio complaining that Ricky was a thief.

In the gym, the P.E. coaches had made the students sit cross-legged on the basketball court while they took roll and issued lockers and gym clothes. Experience taught Enrique to be first on hand when gym stuff was passed out. Because he had been absent the first day of school, he'd spent all of last year running and exercising in shorts without elastic in the waistband and a t-shirt with cigarette burns on it. Enrique had been a top runner, and he often thought he might have been the best if he hadn't had to run clutching at his loose shorts to keep them from falling.

Just as Enrique began to rummage through the large bin of shorts and shirts, Coach Sharp, the teacher in charge of the gym caught his elbow. "Enrique Suarez?"

"Yes."

"You are to report to the Counseling Office this period."

"Me? Why?"

"Don't know." Coach Sharp shrugged and examined a slip of paper on his clipboard. "Alls it says here is you are to report to the Counseling Office right away."

"Okay, just let me pick some shorts first." Enrique got his hands on a newer pair that looked to be his size.

"No can do." Coach Sharp shook his head. "Says here you are to report immediately. No time to issue you regulation wear. Don't worry; there'll be plenty to pick from tomorrow." He took the shorts from Enrique.

"Can you save those for me?"

"No can do. First come, first serve." The coach tossed the shorts back into the bin. Another kid snatched them out before they had even settled on the soft mounds of worn clothing.

Chapter Three

Enrique thought the reason he had been summoned was something to do with the fight. As he sat on a hard bench in the waiting area of the Counseling Office, he could see his face reflected in the darkened glass of Mrs. Schubert's office, behind the reception area. Mrs. Schubert was the counselor assigned to him, but she was out having a baby. He waited to see Dean Hardin in her place.

Enrique tried raising an eyebrow at his reflection. Dean Hardin was known for her slowing arching eyebrow, which could bring tears from some of the meanest gang-bangers on this side of the Valley. Dean Hardin, herself, was so tough that she reminded Enrique of the leather dog chews he sometimes bought for Boy, his Chihuahua-mix.

Hardin had been at Peralta Middle School since before the airplane crash into the play area. Before she became a dean she was a P.E. teacher. Some girl once brought her mother's old yearbook to school and showed Enrique a picture of the unsmiling Dean Hardin taken nearly twenty years ago. She had exactly the same hairstyle she wore these days—straight and short, like the Dutch kid on the can of cleanser Enrique's mother bought.

Dean Hardin stepped briskly into the wait area, examining a sheaf of papers on a clipboard. "Enrique Suarez, step into my office."

Enrique stood and followed her into the office. He

thought he should say something like "Hello," or "How was your summer?" Francisco would have had no trouble finding something to say that would break up the embarrassing silence hovering over them like a cloud.

"Sit down." Dean Hardin pointed at a chair and took a seat behind her desk. "Do you know what this is about?"

"The fight?" Enrique said, his voice squeaking. At critical moments, he could pretty much rely on sounding like a cartoon character when he spoke.

Dean Hardin didn't seem to notice. "Tell me about the fight," she said, and she arched her famous eyebrow.

"It wasn't no big deal," Enrique said. He had the idea this was the first she'd heard of the fight, and he didn't want to get Horacio in any more trouble than he already faced. "Just some kids in the yard. Ms. Byers was there, and Mr. Toro too."

"Mr. Toro took care of it?"

"Ms. Byers broke it up, you know, but he was right there afterwards. I don't know who it was fighting, just some kids."

"Actually, Enrique, this is about your program of study. You put in a request to Mrs. Schubert last year to take French instead of English-as-a-Second-Language, is that correct?"

Enrique nodded. "She said I couldn't take French until I had two more years of ESL."

"Then you wrote a letter to the principal, asking for an exception."

Enrique was stunned. In Beginning ESL, Mr. McGrath had given the class an assignment to write a business letter. Unable to come up with anything else, Enrique had written a somewhat unfriendly letter to the principal for permission to take French in place of ESL. He remembered addressing an envelope, but he had no idea that McGrath would put a stamp on it and mail the letter. The man was mean enough to do it, though.

"I didn't mean to send—"

Dean Hardin put up her hand and continued, "This morning, Ms. Byers told me you are still asking to take French. Is this true?"

Whew! Ms. Byers must be an even newer teacher than he suspected. Enrique usually waited weeks before his teachers got around to reading and grading his work.

"Yeah, but—"

"I have one question for you, Enrique. What's wrong with learning English?"

Everything! Enrique wanted to say. Why should he have to study an ugly language like English (and to his ear nothing sounded worse than English) for two hours every school day? Why should he have to sit in those babyish classes and practice words and phrases he already knew? It was stupid. They say this is a free country, he wanted to tell Dean Hardin, but they make you learn a language you don't want to know. It's like Spanish and French aren't good enough. Someday he would move to France or Canada and only speak the language he wanted to speak.

"Well?" Dean Hardin asked.

"I already know a lot of English," Enrique said, finally. "I like French. I like the way it sounds. It's close to Spanish. I think I could learn it fast."

"The primary language in this country is English. The law states you must complete all three levels of ESL before you can take an elective if you have limited English proficiency."

Teachers and counselors were always jumping on the law, as though it were a real reason for doing something, like rain causing you to open an umbrella.

"I already speak good English," Enrique insisted.

Dean Hardin shuffled through the papers on her desk. "You speak pretty well," she said. "But your writing and reading scores are not what they should be."

"I could learn to read and write good in French."

"In this country, we speak English. Now, what would happen if everyone decided, like you, to speak any language they felt like speaking?"

Enrique shrugged. "People here would learn a lot more languages."

Dean Hardin shook her head. "Enrique, you can't be approved to take French this year because you are only starting Intermediate ESL. If you do well, maybe we can cut you back to one hour of Advanced next year and let you take one hour of Beginning French. Do you know that the stronger you are in your other languages, the easier it is to learn a new one?"

"I guess."

"So, then, work hard with Ms. Byers. Do well in the class and take French next year." She unclipped the papers from her board and slipped them into a file sleeve. "You'll come to me if you have any other problems while Mrs. Schubert is out."

"Okay," Enrique said. Things must be pretty slow the first day of school for Dean Hardin to call him in like this. She didn't solve anything, really. But she did try to understand the problem. He tried to come up with what Francisco might say in this situation. "How are you feeling these days, Dean Hardin?" he finally blurted.

"Not well, Enrique." She frowned. "Thank you for asking, but I'm not doing very well these days."

"I'm sorry," Enrique said. Though he longed to step out the door, something kept him rooted before her desk.

"It's brain cancer," she said. "The principal is already looking for my replacement."

Enrique sucked in a deep breath. "I'm sorry. That's terrible."

"I don't think I'll be here after the winter break."

"I'm really sorry." Enrique felt stupid saying the same thing twice. He wanted to touch her liver-spotted hand or put a hand on her shoulder, but he'd never touched a teacher before, let alone a dean.

"Now, you're going to be late for your next class if you don't hurry. Here's a pass in case you don't make the second bell." She handed him a slip of yellow paper on which she had scrawled the time and date.

"Okay, thanks." He took the pass and bolted out of the office.

Chapter Four

It turned out that Enrique didn't need the pass. He was in time for his next class, math. The teacher, Mrs. Burwell, was a bit famous at school because her husband, who had been a radio traffic reporter, was killed in a grisly helicopter wreck. Mrs. Burwell had been interviewed on television about the accident, making her into something of a celebrity for a while.

Enrique had never had a class with her before, but he had heard that she was prone to losing her temper for no reason since her husband's death. Horacio had taken Basic Math with her last year, and she had even scared the clowning out of him, even. *Man, that's a mean one,* Horacio said when he saw Mrs. Burwell's name on Enrique's schedule that morning.

Worse than McGrath?

Horacio thought about this a moment. *I'm not sure.*

The first day of class, Mrs. Burwell had the students take a test that took the whole period to get halfway through. Because of the intense heat in the bungalow, Mrs. Burwell set up a tremendous fan that sounded, well, like helicopter blades whirring right beside her desk. Despite the fan, most students were sweating pretty hard. Some, like Enrique, were counting on their fingers under their desktops. Others had used up so much scrap paper that they had to scribble on the desk surfaces, rubbing out the pencil marks with their fingertips as they went.

Many students drummed fingers or jiggled their

ankles nervously. All Mrs. Burwell would have to do, thought Enrique, is pull the grate off the fan and bump a kid in with her large hips. She was small, but solid. Since her husband's death she had given up dyeing her hair dark and a cap of snowy curls crested over the top of her head, making her look a bit like a bald eagle. She hardly smiled. Mrs. Burwell just sat at her desk, staring out at the class like some terrible bird of prey until it was time for her to collect the unfinished work. "You will finish the test tomorrow," she said, narrowing her eyes at the class. No one dared to groan.

Enrique had serious trouble even counting, let alone working out multiplication and division problems. Even the basic rules for arithmetic evaded him when he grew tense, and Francisco, placed in gifted classes for math and sciences, was never around to help him understand the lessons. Math class was never fun for Enrique, and this one promised to be the worst ever.

Earth Science, Enrique's last class, turned out to be very lame. The teacher, another new one, made everyone play a ridiculous name game and then something called "Hello Bingo." During this activity, the students had to walk around the classroom finding people to sign squares on a mimeographed grid the teacher had provided. Different squares required different people to sign. For instance, one square asked for someone who was left-handed, another asked for someone who had a dog.

Luckily, Horacio was in this class too, and Enrique had the chance to ask him about the fight. *Did they suspend you?*

No. There was no one at my house to come get me from school.

What about that Ricky?

His mother got him.

How long?

Just today, I think.

What happened?

He's a stinking thief. Last time he came to my house, he stole ten dollars from my mother's purse and took my colognes. Remember those colognes I had?

Why did you wait until now to get him?

I didn't know it was him until today.

The teacher drifted over, and the boys switched to English.

"Are you a vegetarian?" Enrique asked, pointing out a square for Horacio to sign.

"What's that?"

Enrique shrugged. "Don't know."

"A vegetarian is someone who doesn't eat meat," the teacher said and smiled.

Enrique frowned. How could anyone not eat meat?

"Give me another one," Horacio said.

"Have you been to the ballet?"

"The *what*?"

Horacio finally signed Enrique's box for left-handers, and Enrique signed the square for someone who speaks Spanish. Then they separated when the teacher lingered nearby.

Enrique wanted to hear more about the fight, and he was sure that eventually he would get the full story. Stealing money from someone's mother was pretty low,

Enrique thought, but he probably wouldn't want to get in a fight over it. As for the colognes, Ricky had probably done Horacio a favor by taking those. They were the cheap kind from the discount dollar store, and they reeked worse than roach killer.

Marvin Alfaro won "Hello Bingo" and his grandmother clapped. He had gotten a diagonal row of signatures. No one had a "black-out" because of questions like the vegetarian and ballet ones. The prize turned out to be a pencil eraser. Big deal, thought Enrique. But Marvin presented the bubble-gum pink rectangle to his grandmother with a flourish. She wrapped it in a tissue and tucked it into her handbag.

After class, Enrique and Horacio headed to the cafeteria for lunch. School had ended for the day, but the cafeteria ladies remained to serve lunch to the kids with meal tickets. Most students qualified for the free lunch program, and many would stay to eat, though they were free to leave at noon. Only a few, like Francisco, went home to eat.

Enrique liked his lips, remembering the times he'd been invited home to have lunch with Francisco. His friend's entire family managed to get home for lunch almost every day. Francisco's father owned an upholstery shop, which he left in the care of his assistant from noon until two, so he could drive home for lunch. Francisco and his brother walked the short distance home from school at mid-day. Enrique didn't blame them; he would have taken two buses and trudged several blocks in blasting heat to get to Francisco's house for lunch, the way Francisco's mother cooked.

She'd load the table with rice and beans and chicken and vegetables that didn't taste like vegetables, but as good and sweet as fruit. Every day she made fresh tortillas and salsa from the tomatoes, chili, and cilantro she grew in her garden along with corn, green beans, lettuce and whatnot. Enrique couldn't even name all the stuff she grew. She knew exactly how to cook everything, too, so it tasted better than any food Enrique had ever had. He easily understood how Francisco and his younger brother had gotten to be over six feet tall, not fat, but what the *norteamericanos* called "buff," while both of Francisco's parents were small and stringy.

Remembering his last lunch at Francisco's, Enrique felt more than usually disappointed by the cold, tough pizza bagel the cafeteria lady thunked on his Styrofoam plate alongside a drippy scoop of salad. He knew better than to complain, though. Those ladies in hairnets could whisk the food away ten times faster than they could dish it up.

I thought you and that Ricky were such great friends, Enrique said to Horacio, standing beside him in line.

I thought so, too. That's what makes me so angry. I had him over to my house. My mother even took him to the movies with us. And he takes money from her purse, steals my colognes!

What happened? Did you get him mad or something?

No! It's like this. He was making a lot of trouble for his mother. Remember last year? He was always in trouble.

Yeah.

24

She wanted to send him to live with his father up in San Bernardino. He thought he was moving up until the last minute. I even invited him to sleep over that night before he was supposed to leave. That's when he took the money and my colognes.

He thought he would just take off with it? He thought he would get away with it?

Yeah, I guess so, Horacio said. *But it turned out his father didn't want him after all, and he stayed. He didn't come over for a few days. I thought he was just ashamed that the old man didn't want him.*

Did you try to talk to him?

No, man. Every time I asked him to do something, he acted like he was busy. Then I noticed my stuff missing, and my mother asked me if I took the money. I thought it might have been these cousins we had visiting us from Mexico.

You didn't know until today?

I didn't know until I smelled the thief at nutrition, and then I just started swinging. I got him good too.

You got busted in the nose, Enrique pointed out. *And you almost got suspended.*

I don't care, man. It was worth it. Nobody steals from my mama, takes my cologne like that. I thought he was my friend. That's the worst part.

But you've got to feel sorry for the guy. His own father doesn't want him.

Look, you feel sorry for him. I want my stuff back.

Enrique had never even seen *his* father. He'd left Enrique's mother before Enrique was born. She never kept a picture, so Enrique didn't know what the man looked like. Still, he believed if he could find him, his father would want to be with him. Enrique had many pleasant daydreams about meeting a man who looked just like him, but bigger, stronger, and older, and he would *know*, just *know* this was his father without even being introduced.

The two boys sat under the shelter, chewing their pizza bagels. Enrique stabbed a plastic fork into his limp salad. *Hay labio jabón lechuga*, he said, holding up a milky forkful. "This is the real thing, man. This is what you been talking about all along—lipsoap lettuce, in person!"

Chapter Five

After school, Enrique hung around the outside basket-ball courts behind the gym as long as he could. He found a discarded lunch bag with an aluminum soft drink can in it, which he balled up and used to throw into the net. He competed against himself in a game of "Horse."

Horacio had left with his uncle for an appointment with the Health Department. As poor as Horacio's English was, he often had to translate for his entire family—uncles, aunts, cousins, grandparents—when they had such appointments. Enrique's stepfather spoke English pretty well, so Enrique didn't have to lead his mother around on such errands.

The aluminum can began dripping through the bag, tearing it and making it hard to use as a substitute basketball. Luckily, Francisco soon appeared on the courts with his regulation basketball. The two boys played "One-on-One" and "Horse" until they could no longer stand the afternoon heat.

Enrique knew Francisco, a terrific basketball player, "took it easy" on him. But even though the bigger boy slowed down, took risky shots and cut back on his blocking, Francisco beat Enrique easily every time. When it came to basketball, no one in school could really compete with Francisco Valles, who confided to Enrique that he planned someday to become a professional ballplayer and an inventor.

His newest idea, though, wasn't an invention. It was a business. He told Enrique about it as they played,

Francisco insisting they speak English to develop their language skills.

"It's a laundry that is a library and a bakery."

"Like a laundromat or a—what's it called?—dry cleaner?"

"A laundromat where people put money in the machines to wash the clothes, you know, like the one near the Mini-mart. Why not make it a library or a bookstore, too?"

This prompted Enrique to recall that Francisco's family had their own washing machine and dryer on their back porch. "You ever been in a laundromat?"

"People waste so much time waiting for their clothes to get clean. What if they could get some doughnuts and cocoa or coffee and sit in a comfortable place with some books or magazines, maybe some nice music."

"I don't think you know laundromats," Enrique said, picturing the gritty floor littered with cigarette butts, single-load boxes of detergent, soiled diapers, and fast food wrappers. Once he caught sight of a drunk urinating in a waste basket near the super-load machine. And he could never remember anyone reading anything, not even the flimsy magazines the Jehovah's Witnesses stacked on the folding tables. As for drinks, the laundromat had a vending machine that dispensed soft drinks, while Mini-mart offered beer. And how would anyone hear music over the squalling babies and roaring machines? "I think I like your idea for the video game channel best."

"I would call it the Café-Book-o-Mat."

"I even like the 'Barker' idea better."

"You just don't have vision sometimes," Francisco said. "You got to have more vision."

Enrique experienced a sudden vision of getting in trouble for not being home in time to watch the triplets so his mother could get to work. He shot the ball one last time at the hoop. "What time is it?"

"Nearly four-thirty."

"Gotta go." If he ran, he could make it just in time, so his mother wouldn't be late. She was probably getting more than a little nervous by now, though.

"Work on your vision!" Francisco called after him.

Enrique jogged out of the schoolyard, warming up for a burst of speed after the traffic light on the corner. He trotted in place, waiting for the light to change. It was a busy intersection, and Enrique didn't dare cross on a red light. When the light finally turned green, Enrique dashed across the street. Running usually made him feel good. He got into a rhythm of steps, heartbeat, and breathing that was like music to him, almost like dancing. Relieved the only traffic light was behind him, Enrique ran straight through the remaining streets toward the apartment building where he lived with his family. Enrique leapt over broken beer bottles and grassy cracks in the sidewalk, wondering where he might find the *other* United States.

Sometimes when he watched television at night, he noticed the situation comedies he enjoyed never showed places like his neighborhood with its apartment buildings and stores tagged so many times that no one could tell the color of the original paint. Everywhere he looked he saw refuse and mess—bursting garbage bags, discarded furniture moldering on the sidewalk, broken-down cars in the streets.

He wondered if he could reach that *other* United States, the one on the television, by running far enough in the right direction. Would there be some kind of border with patrol officers like the one in Tijuana? Or would the litter and graffiti just gradually thin out, disappearing as the new houses and neat lawns began to appear?

And what would happen to him if he did reach the other U.S.? The police might stop him, he thought. Or maybe a homeowner would shoot him for trespassing. But, maybe he might meet up with one of those big joking families, like the ones in the shows he enjoyed. Maybe he could make friends with one of the kids, and the whole family would take to him. Since they had so many rooms in their house and since they were so friendly and funny, maybe they would ask him to live with them. He would offer to cut the grass, of course, and even wash their cars or take care of the swimming pool in exchange for food and shelter...

Just a few more blocks. He was making good time, but he could do better if he cut through an alley off Paiute Street. Normally, he wouldn't consider this shortcut. The risk of being caught "slipping" scared him. Enrique didn't belong to a gang, but the fact that he lived on a certain street identified him with the tough guys who ruled his neighborhood. And that gang battled the Paiute Street Regulars for every inch of run-down street.

Enrique pictured his mother, probably pacing the

kitchen and checking the digital clock radio, and wondering if she could just leave the babies and trust that Enrique would arrive soon after she left. Maybe she would be dialing his stepfather at the poultry plant. Enrique decided to dash through the alley. Who would be there now to catch him? From the cooking smells, he knew it was nearly dinner time. Even gangsters have to eat.

He bolted over a rust-stained mattress thrown in the middle of the alley. He might try out for the long-jump when track season started. He was probably good enough to make the team, and he saw himself in the red and gold shorts and tank top, when he spotted Israel Jimenez, of the Paiute Street Regulars, strolling toward him and swinging a bicycle chain.

His shock at seeing Israel, or "Itchy," as he was usually called, was deepened by the fact that he hadn't known Itchy had been released from McNulty Hall, the juvenile detention center. Enrique had heard Itchy was arrested for biting off the tip of his older brother's ear. His own mother called the police. And Enrique had seen for himself the older brother's bandaged head at school last spring. Did they let guys out this early for something like that?

"You slipping, dude," Itchy said. It was not a question.

"Slipping?" Enrique stopped and faced the guy; he just might get away if he acted ignorant. Itchy might think him an imbecile and let him go.

"Yeah, you ain't supposed to be here, and you know it too." Itchy stepped closer.

If stupidity wouldn't work, maybe reason would. "I

got to take care of my little brothers, so my mother can go to work."

"So you thought you could take a shortcut through our turf."

"If my mother is late, she might lose her job."

"If my mother is late," Itchy mimicked Enrique, raising his voice an octave. "You sound like a freaking girl."

"I rather be a girl than a dog who bites!" Enrique blurted, pushing past Itchy to run for it. If stupidity and reason wouldn't work, his next choice was speed. And it might have worked, but when he pushed Itchy, Enrique's right hand caught in the bicycle chain. He stumbled, getting it free.

Itchy took the opportunity to punch Enrique under the eye with his free hand. Then he grasped the smaller boy's t-shirt. He wound the chain in his fist and slammed Enrique in the jaw with that.

At first, Enrique didn't even feel it. He was too busy twisting and turning to get free. Finally, he reached a foot around and kicked the back of Itchy's knee causing his leg to buckle. Enrique's shirt ripped when Itchy grabbed for it as he fell, and he jumped free, running like he was on fire. Itchy's curses and threats to kill him rang in his ears even as he shot up the stairs to his apartment several blocks away.

He steadied himself on the landing and smoothed his hair. He hoped he hadn't made his mother late. She wasn't the kind of mother who screamed at him or hit him, but she did get worked up—worried and upset—

very easily. She'd probably freak out when she saw his face banged up and his torn t-shirt. Nothing he could do about that now. He took a few deep breaths and pushed open the front door.

But his stepfather, not his mother, glared at him from the couch. Two of the babies slept on cushions on either side of the man, while he bottle-fed the third in his arms. "You little punk," he said, whispering so as not to disturb his napping sons. "You were supposed to be here fifteen minutes ago."

Where is my mother? Enrique asked. He needed her cool touch on his face; he longed for the warmth of her coffee-brown eyes.

"Where do you think she is? Some people got to work around here." Enrique's stepfather was still wearing the rubber boots he used for working at the plant. His mother must have called him to come home to take care of the triplets.

I'm sorry, Enrique began. *I got jumped—*

"That wouldn't have happened if you'd been doing what you're supposed to do." Juan rose from the sunken couch with the baby in his arms. "Here," he said and handed Enrique the baby and bottle. "I've got to go back to work. Now, I'm supposed to work overtime on account of you being late."

Enrique was still shaky, but holding the baby settled him some. His whole face throbbed with pain.

"I'll deal with you later." Enrique's stepfather grabbed some change from a shelf near the door, and he left.

Boy, Enrique's little dog, crawled out from under the coffee table where he'd been hiding. Trembling and whimpering, he climbed on top of Enrique's gym shoes.

Chapter Six

When the baby in his arms drifted off to sleep, Enrique settled him in his crib. He arranged a barrier of blankets and cushions on the floor around the couch where his other two brothers slept. He would wash up and eat while the triplets were quiet. Enrique didn't risk leaving them on their own to take a shower, but he had to splash some water on his sore face.

He'd let the babies sleep half an hour, he decided, while he ate. Any longer than that and they would be up fussing most of the night. Besides, they were probably wet. His stepfather was not one to change diapers while he watched the triplets, and Enrique didn't like to think of his little brothers lying around in soggy diapers for too long. If they developed rashes, his mother would blame him.

After cleaning up his face and hands, Enrique tip-toed to the kitchen to find his dinner. The one-bedroom apartment was so cramped that he could see the entire living room area and bathroom from the kitchen. Enrique surveyed the sleeping babies one more time before peering into the refrigerator for the food his mother had left him.

The refrigerator, older than his mother, ticked like a time bomb. The freezer compartment on top wept without stopping through the loosely sealed door and onto the shelves below. It dripped icily on Enrique's bowed head while he rummaged through the damp contents of the lower sections. He was glad for the coolness, though.

The worst thing about this apartment, Enrique thought, wasn't its closet-sized rooms or the ticking and dripping refrigerator. The worst thing by far was the busted air conditioner. The summer heat climbed from the lower floors and stayed trapped in the small rooms of this upstairs apartment. No matter how many windows he opened and no matter how high he set the fan, Enrique could not force the stubborn heat out. He pictured it like some kind of enemy that couldn't be evicted, an unwanted giant spread out and sleeping, taking up every room.

Enrique hoped his mother had left him something cool to eat like a salad with hard-cooked eggs and olives sliced on top. Instead, he found two burritos and a shriveled looking ear of corn wrapped in plastic on his dinner plate behind the babies' bottles. He ate his food chilled from the refrigerator shelf as he stood under the plop-plop-plop of ice water on his neck from the freezer. Boy, his tail wagging, stared up at Enrique hopefully. His bulging eyes gleamed in the arc of refrigerator light, while Enrique finished his meal.

After he ate, he prepared the babies' food from the little jars his mother bought. He heated one jar of chicken and rice and another of smushed peas in a boiling pot of water on the stove. He figured they could eat another jar, labeled apricots, cold. He set up the highchairs while the food warmed.

His stepfather's church had donated three of every-thing in the way of secondhand baby supplies to

Enrique's family when the triplets were born. In addition to the three highchairs that collapsed to be stored on the balcony when they weren't being used, there were three cribs crammed into the bedroom his mother shared with Juan, making it impossible to walk like a normal person through the room. Enrique had to slide between two of the cribs, crawl under the third and climb over the double bed when he needed clothes from the closet. The church had even provided a used triple-stroller which was kept in the locked storage cubicle above their vacant parking stall.

Enrique had plans to pull it out later and give the boys a ride in the cool evening air. If he stuck to his own neighborhood, Itchy wouldn't dare bother him. Members of the gang that ruled Enrique's neighborhood had just been waiting for Itchy to be released from McNulty Hall and to show his face on the street. Many would be pleased to catch Itchy slipping into their neighborhood.

Enrique nudged the triplets awake and carried them to their seats—one at a time. Over the seven months he'd been caring for the babies, Enrique had learned a few time-saving techniques for handling all three. One thing he figured out early on was to strike while they were still drowsy. If he changed them and seated them in their highchairs before they were fully awake, for instance, they would be less likely to scream their heads off, throw their dishes, or try to climb out of the chairs.

Another thing he learned was to use their personalities to his advantage. Maclovio, the triplet born last, was the most active, so Enrique always woke him last.

Hilario, firstborn, had a quiet and watchful nature. Enrique sat him in his chair first. Juan, the middle one they called "Yunior," had a bad temper and cried a lot. Enrique gave him a pacifier to plug his mouth between bites.

All three babies liked watching Boy while they ate. Usually, Boy hid shivering under the bed while the triplets crawled around. But Boy enjoyed their company during mealtimes, especially when they spilled food on the floor. Sometimes the little dog clowned for the babies, dancing on his hind legs and waving his tiny front paws in the air.

With Boy's help entertaining them, Enrique fed his brothers pretty quickly. He wiped their faces and trays while he phoned his neighbor, a girl his age named Maricela Cruz and her mother to help him take the triplets downstairs for their walk. He couldn't manage that by himself. Luckily, Maricela was home. She promised that she and her mother would be right over.

Maricela didn't know it yet, but she was Francisco's girlfriend. Francisco confided to Enrique complicated plans for getting to know her better, but he never found the courage to follow through on any of them. Enrique liked Maricela too, as a friend. She was smart and kind, but a little funny looking due to her large pale body, glasses, and crinkly copper-colored hair. Maricela told Enrique she was adopted, which explained why she was so tall and fair, while her parents were dark and almost as squat as elves.

Now, she and her mother appeared in the doorway to Enrique's apartment. They divided the triplets among themselves and carried them downstairs for their walk. Maricela held two of the babies while Enrique pulled the stroller down from the storage space and assembled it.

"You're lucky to have little brothers," Maricela said in English. She didn't like her mother to know she was lonely sometimes, being an only child.

"Yeah, I guess." Enrique scraped an ankle on the stroller brake. "Ouch!"

"I wish I had a brother or sister."

Enrique pinched the skin between his thumb and forefinger in the hinge that released the push bar. "I wish I could give you one of these," he said, thinking of Yunior, who was already beginning to grumble.

"*¿Qué?*" Maricela's mother disliked being left out of conversations. "*¿Qué? ¿Qué?*"

"*Nada, Mamá,*" Maricela told her before turning to Enrique. "You're not serious." She kissed both babies in her arms.

With his neighbors' help, Enrique loaded the babies into the stroller. He thanked them both and released the brake.

"You want me to come with you?" Maricela asked. "I'll ask my mother."

"Sure," Enrique said, "if you come, we can bring Boy."

Maricela got her mother's permission and watched the babies while Enrique bolted upstairs to get Boy and his leash. Boy was so thrilled to see his leash pulled out of the closet that Enrique was afraid the tiny, old dog might have a stroke.

"You walk Boy," Maricela said when Enrique

reappeared leading the dog. "I don't like dogs that much. I'd rather push the babies."

"Fine," said Enrique, who had been hoping she would suggest this.

Maricela struggled with the stroller over unpaved stretches in the street. Enrique walked alongside, feeling light and carefree with only the thin leash to manage. Boy trotted at his feet, darting away to sniff and mark posts and trees with swift jets of urine.

What happened to your face? Maricela asked.

Israel Jimenez happened to my face.

The one they call Itchy?

Yes, Itchy.

I thought he was in jail.

They let him out, I guess. Tell me, does the face look bad.

It looks like you were in a car wreck. You're probably going to have a black eye. Even my mother noticed it, and she never notices anything.

I didn't want my mother to know.

Well, she's going to know all right.

They walked the babies three times around the block. An ice cream truck wailed hopefully at the curb beside them at one point, but they ignored it, and it sped off. In the entry way to one of the apartments they passed, Enrique noticed Pirata and Cobra standing around with some other guys from the neighborhood gang. They were passing a paper bag among themselves and sipping from a bottle in it. Enrique jerked on Boy's leash when he wanted to loiter in front of that building. The dog whimpered.

Do you know those guys? Maricela asked him when they'd moved out of earshot.

Yes, and I don't like to be where they are.

Do they ever bother you? Do they ever try to get you to join the gang?

No, Enrique admitted. *Not yet.*

Sometimes, I think I am lucky to be a girl.

To change the subject, Enrique asked Maricela a question about her classes. They talked about school and their teachers until it was time to go back to the apartments.

With Maricela and her mother's help again, Enrique put the stroller away and lugged the babies upstairs. He bathed them all at once in the tub, played with them, and gave them their last bottles filled with cool milk before settling them in their cribs for the night. For once, they didn't fuss too much, and he was able to watch some television while he looked at a book called *Le Petit Prince* that he had checked out from the library. With the help of colorful illustration and some Spanish-like words, he could almost make out the story. He tried holding his nose to pronounce some of the unfamiliar words in the French way before he grew sleepy and put out the lamp. In minutes, he fell asleep, cocooned in a tangle of sheets on the couch.

It seemed only seconds had flown by when a pan of light splashed in his face and he heard his mother cry, *My God, son, what happened to you?*

Chapter Seven

"Bonjour," Enrique murmured, sleepily. In a few moments, his eyes adjusted, and he could make out his mother in her pink uniform, standing near the couch. He focused on the package of corn tortillas she had tucked under one elbow. Once in a while she brought home tortillas that were torn or too crumbly to sell.

Enrique, what happened to that eye? she said.

Enrique realized then that he could not open it all the way. He fingered the lid. It felt hot and puffy.

Playing basketball, he said. *I fell down.*

On the eye? Though his mother seemed unconvinced, he hoped she would at least stop asking questions. She sighed and set the tortillas on the coffee table that served as Enrique's nightstand. *I'll get some ice.*

You brought me tortillas. He grabbed the sweating bag of fragrant tortilla pieces and followed her into the kitchen. He pressed the plastic wrap to his nose to inhale the moist, mealy aroma. Enrique couldn't remember when his mother started working at the tortilla factory, but for as long as he remembered he associated her with the savory scent of lightly salted *masa*, the aroma of fresh tortillas, sheathed in steam-clouded wrapping.

Let me put ice on that eye. Then I'll heat them for us. She cracked a few cubes out of the battered aluminum tray and wrapped these in a dishcloth to place as a compress against Enrique's cheek. He held the cold bundle to his face while his mother pulled the butter dish and a few limes from the refrigerator. *Where's Juan?* she asked in a casual-sounding voice.

Enrique shrugged. *He said he might work late.* Enrique could tell his stepfather's absence made his mother nervous, especially late at night. Before the babies were born, Juan used to stay out late and drink with the men from his work. But the church he joined helped him to quit drinking, and at least twice a week, he attended meetings with other people who had given up alcohol.

Enrique looked forward to these meetings. He enjoyed having Juan out of the house on those nights. Come to think of it, Enrique realized, it wasn't so bad when his stepfather had been drinking because he stayed out even more then. But when he did come home during that time, it had been worse, much, much worse.

They probably gave him overtime, he told his mother.

You think so?

Of course.

Enrique's mother smiled and flung two tortillas with wedges ripped out of them on the stove burners. These looked like Pac Man and Ms. Pac Man resting above the low blue flame.

You don't know what I saw today, his mother said.

Enrique's mother worked in the mission district, where tourists came to visit the historic church. They would buy postcards and curios from small shops on the cobbled block where the tortilla factory was located. She had a special view into the odd lives of the colorful and noisy *norteamericanos* who came through the mission to snap photos of the deteriorating adobe structures. Sometimes Enrique thought his mother was the real tourist, staring from the window of the tortilla factory, and the *norteamericanos* were the curious sights to enjoy. He longed to buy her a camera one day, so she could capture and collect their images.

What did you see? Enrique asked.

I could not believe my eyes!

What was it?

A dog, she said, her eyes shining, *a bit bigger than Boy, that was in a wheelchair.*

A wheelchair? With a crippled person?

No, no, in its own wheelchair. The back legs were removed.

Of the wheelchair?

Of the dog! It had no back legs, just the front ones. And the owner, a woman in a black car as big as the bedroom, set it in a little metal wheelchair, made for dogs. The wheelchair was low, so the dog could push it along with its front legs. It even had a hole in back for the tail.

Enrique wondered what was so strange about that. If Boy lost the use of his back legs, he would want to provide the dog with some way to get around. A wheelchair would be just the thing. *A dog wheelchair,* he said. It was the kind of thing Francisco might have invented.

And it had an umbrella, a green and white striped umbrella to keep the sun off the dog's face. She laughed. Even on this steamy night, his mother's laughter reminded Enrique of the Christmas bells that Santas in the mission district jingled every winter, calling tourists to drop change in their pots.

His mother served them both plates of steaming, buttery tortillas, salted and sprinkled with lime juice. *What more did you see?*

Well, some Japanese men came through the factory. They took my picture. Watch, now, I'll be famous in Tokyo. The factory's owner scheduled tours through the place for special groups. Enrique wasn't surprised the men wanted his mother's photo. She was so pretty with her pink cheeks and curly black hair that she could be a movie star, he felt sure, if she didn't have to work in the tortilla factory.

I bet they make a poster of your picture and sell a million copies.

Shh.... Hear that? Is that Juan? She froze. Enrique jumped as though he'd been stung by a bee. He dreaded having Juan barge into one of their whispered tortilla conversations. Juan usually behaved as though he were insulted when he caught Enrique and his mother talking together, making Enrique feel somewhat guilty without really knowing why.

They heard a crashing sound from the stairwell and then a drunken voice singing: *Estas son las mañanitas que cantaba el rey David!*

Señor Bocadillo, Enrique said. He and his mother exhaled noisily in relief. Mr. Bocadillo sold hard-roll sandwiches, *bocadillos* stuffed with spicy meat, from a pushcart he rolled through the neighborhood. After he sold his wares, he locked the cart in his storage closet and strolled to the corner bar where he became just drunk enough to be able to stagger home, singing songs in Spanish. Neither Enrique nor his mother knew the sandwich vendor's real name, and the spare white-haired man didn't seem to mind being called Mr. Bocadillo by his customers.

I think Juan is angry with me because I was late this afternoon, Enrique admitted.

What happened? I was waiting and waiting. I was going to be late. Fortunately, Juan came home for his cigarettes during his break.

You didn't call him?

I knew you would come. Why were you late?

I was playing basketball. I forgot about the time. I'm sorry, Mamá.

Son, I have to count on you to help me with your brothers.

I know. I won't be late again.

How was the school?

It was fine.

Did they give you the French class?

That morning, Enrique had complained to his mother about having to take another year of ESL. He bragged that they weren't going to get away with it, that he had his rights, that he would make them give him a French class. He would write a letter to the mayor and to the governor. He would make a picket sign, like the workers at the supermarket, and march back and forth in front of the school with it.

No, maybe next year, if I do well in ESL.

Someday, you will learn French, son, if you don't give up.

Oh, don't worry. I won't give up.

How were the babies tonight?

Fine. I walked them, and I washed them.

Good, I hope they sleep through the night.

They finished their tortillas and washed the plates. Mr. Bocadillo's singing on the stairs reminded Enrique that Juan would soon be home. He hurried to dry the dishes and put them away in the cupboard, so he could get to bed. Juan would be even angrier than he had been that afternoon, if he found Enrique and his mother talking together and enjoying a snack. Even this late at night, he would manage to interrupt their discussion and come up with some chore for Enrique to do.

I hope you're right, Enrique's mother said. *I hope he is working late like you said.*

Enrique dropped the melting cubes from his ice pack into the sink and hung the damp cloth to dry on the balcony. He glanced down at the street and glimpsed Juan walking steadily toward the apartment building.

He's here, he said, and he rushed past his mother to vault over the back of the couch, so he could pretend to be asleep.

How is he walking? she asked.

Straight. He looks fine.

She gave a quick smile, put up the last dish, and dashed to the bathroom to wash up and straighten her hair.

One of the babies, Juan Jr., from the sound of it, began to stir, making the low grunting sounds that signaled the howling that would soon follow. Enrique couldn't decide if he should ignore the grunts and hope his mother emerged from the bathroom in time to get his brother or to pick the baby up himself before his screaming woke the others.

Cursing, Enrique kicked the sheets off his legs and jumped up to get Juan Jr. He hefted the baby out of the crib and held him close, wondering if the little thing was scared, waking up in the dark.

It's fine, he whispered to the baby. *Everything is fine.*

Enrique carried his brother into the kitchen and filled a bottle with milk from the refrigerator. He set this in the pot of water on the stove and lit the burner. He took the grumbling baby out to the balcony while his milk heated. Enrique still worried an outburst of crying would wake the other two.

The baby burned in his arms as though he had a fever. Enrique held him away from his chest, so the night air would cool his small body. Yunior quieted and stared at Enrique with large, wet eyes. He seemed to like being dangled away from his brother's body on the balcony. The cool air calmed his fussing.

Just as Enrique started wondering what was taking Juan so long to climb the stairs, he heard his stepfather's key scrape the lock. Before Enrique could turn around, Juan had raced through the compact apartment and grabbed the baby out of his arms.

"What the hell are you doing with my baby?" Juan shouted. Yunior sucked in a large breath and let out a cry that gave Enrique chills. "You little bastard! You were going to throw him over!"

"No, no!" Enrique realized what the scene must have

seemed to his stepfather. *Yunior is hot. I was trying to make him cool.*

Juan's arm shot out and struck Enrique below the ribs. He reeled into the rickety railing, clutching his stomach. Enrique felt like a balloon that had been popped. All his air gone, Enrique was sick with dizziness.

The baby sobbed, hiccoughing. Enrique slipped to the balcony floor, doubled up in pain. His stepfather stood over Enrique with the baby, as though he meant to kick him if he moved.

Chapter Eight

On the way to school the next morning, Enrique struggled to push memories of the previous night from his thoughts. This hadn't been the first time his stepfather had struck him, not by a long shot. Juan would often push Enrique against a wall or yank his hair when he was angry. Sometimes he would pull off his belt and whip angry welts onton Enrique's legs and arms. Juan always took care to "punish" Enrique when his mother wasn't home. But last night, it was his mother's face that stung Enrique sharper than the blow. True, she had argued with Juan to be sensible. The baby was feverish, she pointed out, and Enrique had seen Juan coming home. Why would he decide to throw the baby off the balcony when he knew his stepfather was on the way?

Still, she wouldn't look in Enrique's eyes as she spoke. She seemed like a stranger to him, with her face turned away as she tried to calm Juan. And when all the babies began wailing, she and Juan tended to them, as if they didn't trust Enrique to put his hands on their babies.

I'll hold Hilario, he had offered.

No, no, his mother said, *you go to sleep. It's late, son.*

Enrique scarcely slept. He kicked and twisted, knotting himself into the sheet. He dreamed of crawling through dark tunnels, searching for the manhole cover so he could climb out into the light. He kept seeing

Juan's head in the shadows, bobbing before him like a slick gray balloon.

Though his ribs ached with every step, Enrique strode swiftly through the quiet streets that morning. He shook his head from time to time to clear away the sleep. He knew he was early. Enrique gave up his struggle to sleep long before the sun came up. And he was so anxious to get out of the apartment that he hadn't eaten. He also hadn't given his hair the kind of attention with a comb and gel that he usually did. Enrique decided to stop by Francisco's house and walk with his friend to school. Francisco's family kept a rooster, an old *veterano* rescued from a cockfight, who crowed at the first streak of sun in the sky. Enrique was sure they would be awake.

In fact, Francisco's mother was fully dressed—her long braid coiled neatly atop her head—when she opened the door for Enrique, smiling. *"Buenos días."*

"Buenos," Enrique echoed.

Francisco is in his room. I am just making the breakfast. Would you like to eat with us, Enrique? Francisco's mother was famous for giving people food, and Enrique appreciated that about her.

"Sí, gracias." As Enrique moved through the hallway with her, he noticed that he'd grown a few inches taller than his friend's mother. This made him feel sad and gentle towards her. He held the kitchen door open for her.

Enrique found Francisco sitting at his desk pulling a piece of string out of an envelope. He looked up at Enrique and grinned. "Reversible envelopes," he said.

"Reversible envelopes?"

"Yes, reversible envelopes." Francisco nodded with pride. "You know how bills and things like that, where you have to write back, always send extra envelopes? I thought if the return address was printed inside the envelope, then people could pull it inside out, like this. Pulling the string attached inside, Francisco slowly inverted the envelope. Of course, the paper got crushed and tore a bit in the process, but he managed to turn it inside out. "And there it is! They could use the same envelope to send the reply or the payment. Think of all the trees this will save."

"Well, it is better than the musical laundromat," Enrique said.

"Café-Book-o-Mat," Francisco said, correcting him. He flattened the envelope with his hand to smooth out the wrinkles. "I really need a softer paper and a peel-off adhesive strip."

"What's this?" Enrique pointed to a series of twisted safety pins with buttons attached to them. These were stabbed into Francisco's corkboard.

Francisco glanced up. "Button pins," he said, "for when people pop out a button. They can just put it on one of these specially shaped pins and stick it right back on until they get home to fix it."

"Now, *that's* a good idea." Enrique had once lost a crucial pants button at school.

"I just need softer metal."

Francisco's mother opened the door and leaned in. *The breakfast is ready.*

Francisco pulled the door wide and embraced his

mother. "Softer envelope, softer metal." He laughed and waltzed his tiny mother a few steps. "But I don't need a softer mother, do I, Enrique?"

His mother smiled and swiped at him with her dishcloth. *Silly, you better come to eat before your brother empties the table into his mouth.*

The dining table held every possible good thing to eat for breakfast, thought Enrique. A yeasty steam rose from the fresh rolls in a basket at the center of the table. This was surrounded by bowls of cut melon and orange sections and fresh wedges of tomato with limes, a platter of scrambled eggs and one of browned potato slices, and then a ring of cocoa mugs capped with whipped cream encircled all of this.

Sit, Enrique, Francisco's father said, entering the dining room with Francisco's younger brother. *We are glad you can join us.* When everyone was seated, he pressed his palms together and said, *Let us give thanks for this food and the people at this table.* They all closed their eyes—all but Enrique, who stared at the potatoes. Silence for a moment, and then the dishes were passed around the table.

Church stuff and praying bored Enrique, but he didn't mind the way Francisco's family said grace, quickly and quietly. He thought of Juan with his long, speech-like prayers thanking God and the church for his sobriety, followed by accounts of his days of drunkenness in dull, yet embarrassing, detail while Enrique's food grew cold.

So, Enrique, what happened to the eye? Francisco's father asked. He lifted a forkful of eggs to his lips.

Francisco's mother shot him a curious look that let Enrique know she had wanted to ask about it herself, but had been too polite to do so.

I had an accident, he said, thinking fast. *I fell off a bike.*

You got a bike? Francisco's brother Jorge asked.

No, I borrowed a bike from my neighbor.

Maricela has a bike? Francisco smiled at the mention of her name.

Not Maricela, another neighbor, a new kid. You don't know him. Enrique wondered how he'd remember which story he'd told to whom and reminded himself to keep his mother from talking to Francisco until after the bruises faded.

I see, Francisco said in a quiet voice, and his mother and father traded a look.

You look like a boxer, Jorge told him.

Francisco's father caught the boy's eye and shook his head.

I have some cream. Francisco's mother rose from her chair and left the dining room. She returned in a few moments with a jar and a soft washcloth. She blotted the sharply scented salve to Enrique's brow and cheek. *Leave it alone, now,* she said. *You can keep the jar. Use it again tonight.*

"*Gracias.*" Enrique slipped the jar into the pocket of his khakis.

It's nothing, just a cream for horses, but it works on people. She smiled and continued eating. Francisco and Jorge emptied their plates first and reloaded them for seconds. Enrique applied himself more seriously to his potatoes, so he would be certain to have another helping before the brothers struck again.

We're going to pick up some fabric in Carson on Sunday, right, Mamá? Francisco's father said. *That's over by the state park. Why don't you come with us, Enrique? We can make a picnic.*

I might have to take care of my brothers, but I'll ask my mother. Enrique would love to go to the state park. He'd had great fun hiking in the foothills with Francisco's family last fall, before the triplets were born. He licked his lips thinking about the picnic basket Francisco's mother had packed. But Sunday was a big church day for Juan and his mother. Luckily, they didn't expect Enrique to go to church, but they depended on him to watch the babies during the long hours they attended back-to-back services.

Mamá, Jorge said in a whiny voice, *Francisco took all the tomatoes. I wanted some. He always takes what I want.*

You didn't get them when they were on the table, Francisco said. *But now they're on my plate, you want them.*

Francisco's parents said nothing. They just stared at Francisco.

He always does this. He doesn't want things until I have them.

Francisco's mother and father kept staring.

Francisco ladled the tomatoes back into the serving bowl. *Here, take them. I don't want them now.*

Jorge didn't make a move toward the tomatoes.

Well? Francisco said. *Take them. I don't want them. I'm full.*

Señor and Señora Valles turned their gaze on their younger son.

I don't want them now, Jorge said. *He's already breathed on them.*

I'll have them. Enrique scooped the dewy wedges onto his plate. *I don't care if they're breathed on.*

After they finished eating, the boys excused themselves to leave for school. Enrique waited, looking away out of politeness, while Francisco and Jorge kissed their father and mother.

"Adiós."

"¡Adiós!"

"Gracias, Señor y Señora."

Enrique, come here," Francisco's mother called after him. She pulled him close and kissed his undamaged cheek. *You forgot. You can't leave this house without a kiss from the mother.*

Chapter Nine

Horacio, as usual, lounged against a pillar in the breeze-way near the lockers while students made their way to their first classes. *"Hay labio jabón lechuga,"* he said with a yawn as Enrique and Francisco approached.

"You need to come up with something new to say," Francisco told him. "How about 'there are ankle-shrinking radishes'?"

"Or hair-straightening carrots," Enrique said. He could tell by the strange shape of his shadow that he really shouldn't have skipped his morning hair treatment. As he passed Horacio, Enrique caught a whiff of something that smelled like turpentine. "Did you get your colognes back?"

"No, my uncle bought me a bottle of aftershave for translating for him yesterday. Like it?"

"Well, I can tell you're wearing it."

"Don't go near any open flames," Francisco said.

Francisco and Enrique headed for class, leaving Horacio in the breezeway. He liked to be the very last to arrive to class.

Enrique took his seat in the back, while Francisco stepped to the front of the room. Earlier, he'd told Enrique he had some ideas for rearranging the desks that he wanted to discuss with Ms. Byers. Enrique glanced around the room. He nodded to Señora Alfaro, who was knitting with fuzzy blue yarn, and he smiled at Cake Angie as she sank into the desk beside him.

"I hope you brought your own pencil today," she said with a frown.

Enrique hadn't, of course, but he said, "Sure, I got one."

Ms. Byers approached his desk and leaned in to speak to him in a lowered voice. "What happened to you, Enrique?"

"I fell off a bike," he said, sticking to the bike story, in case Francisco was listening. "It's nothing."

She put her hand on his shoulder and gave him a sympathetic look before moving to the front of the class to write the agenda on the chalk board.

In a few minutes the classroom filled, and Ms. Byers faced the students still wearing her bright new teacher smile. Her crisp yellow curls danced around her pale, freckle-splotched face, and her blue eyes sparkled behind her glasses. "Today, we are going to start a special project," she said.

Enrique could feel Cake Angie tensing at the word "project."

"We are going to join our intermediate class with a beginning class to form a partnership. We will help them, and they are going to help strengthen our language learning skills."

Enrique had no idea what she was talking about.

Marvin's pudgy hand sailed up like a bird startled into flight. "What do you mean, Ms. Byers?"

"You have heard of 'study buddies.' Mr. Bolton tells me you have them in Tech Lab. Well, you are going to be partners with beginning students in Mrs. Jaramillo's class. In other words, each of you will be assigned a beginning ESL student to tutor in English."

Mrs. Jaramillo? Enrique had heard about her. She was a new teacher last year, and her students said she acted like a kindergarten teacher. He'd heard her speak a few times in that loud, slow voice people use for talking to deaf people. He groaned inwardly.

Cake Angie raised her hand. "Will we do a project? Like a poster? Or like a cake?"

"Not exactly. You will just be helping them learn English by talking with them."

"Could we help them on a project for extra credit? I mean, outside of class?" Her voice rose, sounding whiny.

"Well, I hadn't thought of that, but I suppose you could," Ms. Byers said.

"I think it is a good idea." Francisco nodded in approval. He wasn't in the habit of raising his hand. He just said what he had to say in a calm, adult way. This was one of the main reasons he didn't get along too well with Mr. McGrath in beginning ESL.

"Thank you, Francisco, but next time, please raise your hand," Ms. Byers said, giving Enrique the idea she had been talking to McGrath about Francisco and his habits. "This project will give everyone the chance to make a new friend and offer support to someone who is new to our country."

Marvin's hand shot up again. "This isn't *my* country. *My* country is El Salvador," he said in defiance.

Uh-oh, thought Enrique, here it comes. Marvin, normally a cooperative and conscientious student, was very critical of the United States. Usually, his complaints about the U.S. infuriated his teachers. If not for the presence of his grandmother, Marvin would probably have been beaten senseless with the chart pointer in McGrath's class, and his body stapled to the Current Events board.

Even the friendly Ms. Byers looked upset for a moment, and then she smiled her brave, new teacher smile, revealing a smear of lipstick on her front teeth. "You are right, Marvin. I misspoke. I should have said you are offering friendship to someone who is new to *this* country. Thank you for the correction."

Just then, Horacio stumbled into the classroom like a slapstick comedian ready to perform a pratfall. Many kids laughed. Ms. Byers held out her hand for his late pass. Horacio took it for a handshake and bowed in a formal way. More laughter spilled from the classroom, and Ms. Byers' face burned bright red. "Where's your late pass?" she asked.

Horacio made a show of patting his jacket and turning the pockets of his khakis inside out. "Must have lost it."

"You'll need to get another one."

"But, Ms. Byers, if I get the late pass, they will give me the detention."

"I didn't know that, Horacio," Ms. Byers said, "but you knew it when you decided to come to class late. You knew what to expect. Please hurry and get your late pass."

"Please, Ms. Byers, please, please." Horacio sank to his knees.

"Horacio, get up and step outside with me, will you?" Ms. Byers said in a calm voice.

Horacio wouldn't get up, though he crawled on his knees out the door following Ms. Byers. The class giggled again. Enrique noticed Francisco shaking his head.

"Your friend's a dumbbell," Cake Angie said with a snort.

Enrique shrugged. He had no answer for that.

Ms. Byers returned. She didn't seem too angry as she told the class they would be meeting their study partners the second period of class when they would all walk over to the auditorium to get together with Ms. Jaramillo's class. Then Ms. Byers passed out some folders.

"These are for keeping your journals," she said. "You will see your first journal is already inside with my comments on it. Every day we will write in our journals, and you'll keep them all together in your folders. I will not always be able to comment on your journals. I *will* read them all, and if you have a question you want me to answer, write a big question mark under your journal entry. Sometimes, I'll assign a journal topic, but most of the time you can write about whatever you want. Go ahead and write anything you like today."

Enrique searched the floor for a discarded pen or pencil. He couldn't ask Cake Angie again, and he was too embarrassed to ask the teacher.

"I'll hand out some book club order forms for you to look at when you're finished. Usually, we will read while people finish writing in their journals, but the books I ordered haven't arrived yet." Ms. Byers passed out the book flyers advertising paperbacks students could buy. As she gave Enrique his order form, she slipped him a new pencil, freshly sharpened. He caught her eye and smiled before opening his folder to see what she'd written on his journal: *French is a beautiful language. I'm sure you will speak it one day if you keep trying.*

Enrique wrote six sentences about the little prince in the French book he was trying to read, and then he settled back to look over the book order form. He thumbed through the usual collection of bookmarks, stickers, horror books, and romance stories without much interest. A short section on the last page, though, caught his eye. *Dictionaries and Reference Books.* He examined the synonym, antonym, and spelling diction-aries, the home science experiment and believe-it-or-not books. At last, there it was! Exactly what he wanted —a French/English dictionary! For *six-fifty?* His hopes sank. He was closer to stepping on the moon than to having six dollars and fifty cents to spend.

A loud knock on the door interrupted his thoughts. Maybe Horacio had returned, trying to get even more attention. But when Ms. Byers opened the door, a short, old man wearing glasses and a wilted-looking black cap appeared at the threshold.

"I'm glad you could come," Ms. Byers said.

"Which one is he?" asked the old man.

"Enrique," Ms. Byers called out. "Enrique, there's someone here to see you."

Chapter Ten

"Enrique," Ms Byers said, "this is Monsieur Nassour. I don't know if you have met him. He's the French teacher here at Peralta."

Enrique stood, staring in amazement at the man who not only spoke, but also taught French.

"*Bonjour, Henri.*" The old man smiled and clasped Enrique's hand to shake it. "Please, will you step outside with me? I would like to talk with you."

Enrique glanced at Ms. Byers.

"Go ahead, Enrique," she said.

"It will just be a minute or two," Monsieur Nassour promised. Enrique stepped outside after him, and Ms. Byers shut the door.

Monsieur Nassour checked his watch. "I must be back for rehearsal in a few minutes. You see, I am the French teacher, and I am the drama coach. *C'est la vie,*" he said with a sigh. "That means, such is life. *C'est la vie.*"

"*C'est la vie,*" Enrique repeated, trying his best to imitate the old man's pronunciation.

"*Trés bien! Trés bien!* That is very good! Your teacher tells me you want to learn French, is that correct? But you cannot take the class because you must first learn English, is that correct? You will learn French. You are a fighter, yes? So you will fight to learn." Monsieur Nassour didn't wait for answers. He just kept talking. "I think we can help each other. We have a little French club here at the school. Did you know that? Yes, it is not what they call a 'big deal.' We meet once a week on Wednesday afternoons and practice our French together.

"We take a small field trip and a big field trip. The little trip is to a French restaurant downtown, but the students must not keep asking for bread when we go. The waiters get very angry, and we may not get our discount next time. It is good bread, but one or two pieces are enough." He wagged his finger at Enrique.

"The big field trip is to *Monréal*! Yes, *Monréal*! During vacations. It is so wonderful, I can't tell you. You must come and see it yourself." The old man closed his eyes, smiling. Probably, he was remembering the fine times he'd had in *Monréal*.

Enrique cleared his throat. "Um, how can I join the French Club?"

"*Simplement*. You must be in a French class."

But I can't take French," Enrique reminded him.

"Or you can have special permission from the club adviser, from me."

"Will you give the special permission?" Enrique asked.

"*Mais oui*. Of course, I will. But you must do something for me." Monsieur Nassour's many lines and wrinkles stitched themselves into a sly grin.

"What do you want me to do?"

"You must join the Drama Club. *Oui*, the Drama Club."

"The *Drama* Club? That's acting, isn't it? Would I have to be an actor in a play?" Enrique's heart plunged.

He could barely speak English. How could he act in a play? The audience would laugh him off the stage.

"We have a very small part, a tiny part." Monsieur Nassour produced a jumble of papers from the pocket of his blazer. "Yes, here it is. We need a telephone. Will you play the part of the telephone."

"The *telephone*?"

"Yes, the telephone. You would not even have to step on the stage. You will stand behind the curtain and go like this: *Br-r-ring! Br-r-ring!* Can you do that? Try it out. This is your audition. Don't be nervous, please."

"*Br-r-ring! Br-r-ring!*" Enrique's ears burned with embarrassment, but he thought he sounded more like a real phone than Monsieur Nassour had.

"Perfect! Perfect! I knew it! You are a natural. The part is yours. Now, listen, you must come to the Drama Club meetings on Tuesdays. That is today. We meet in Room B-12 after school. So don't forget. Tuesday for the Drama Club and Wednesday for the French Club— same time, same place. Okay, Henri?"

"*Oui,* I guess," Enrique said.

"I will give you the script at the meeting."

"Why do I need a script if I'm just the telephone? I think I already know the part."

"Ooh-la-la! I forgot!" The French teacher hit himself in the forehead. "The one who plays the telephone is also the understudy. So you must know the whole play."

"Is it a short play?"

"It is *petit* beyond belief. You will learn it like that." Monsieur Nassour snapped his fingers. "Now, I am late. I must go. I will see you, Henri, after school."

Monsieur Nassour moved pretty fast for an old man. He disappeared before Enrique could think to ask him what an understudy was supposed to do. Whatever it was, it would sure be worth it if he got to join the French club and maybe visit *Monréal*. As long as I don't have to get on the stage in front of everyone, he told himself.

He turned to go back into the classroom when he saw Horacio loping back across campus from the attendance office. He carried his tardy slip in his mouth. "Now, I got detention," he said, the tardy slip—stuck to his upper lip—flapping like a duck's bill when he spoke.

"Well, I get to be a telephone," Enrique said.

But Horacio wasn't listening. "Second day of school and I already got detention."

"*C'est la vie*," Enrique said.

"Hey, who kicked your ass?" Horacio said, finally noticing Enrique's bruises.

"My ass was kicked," Enrique began, wondering if he could trust Horacio with the truth, "by a bicycle."

Chapter Eleven

Ms. Byers wasn't the kind of teacher who seemed to mind if kids talked a little in line on the way to the auditorium. But anyone could tell she was new at the game, thought Enrique, because she didn't know she should walk at the end of the line to keep an eye on the kids in front of her. Instead, she led the way, as though it never occurred to her that some kids couldn't help acting goofy every time a teacher's back was turned.

Horacio was a kid like that. Enrique watched him with interest, waiting for the next burst of silliness from him. But Horacio marched along in a meek way. Since returning from the attendance office, Horacio had been silent and serious. Enrique was sure his friend was planning a major episode of clowning. Now, while Ms. Byer's back was turned, was definitely the time.

"What's up?" Enrique asked him in English, in case Ms. Byers should change her mind about allowing them to talk in line. He would say he was practicing his conversation in English.

"Nothing."

"How come you're all quiet?"

"Yes," Francisco said, seeing that it was okay to talk a bit. "Why are you behaving yourself for a change?"

"When Byers took me outside, she said it seemed like I wanted personal attention. Then she said she would give me personal *detention, ese,* if I wanted it, for a month, an hour a day after school." Horacio looked grim. "And I believe it, too."

"Personal detention, that's pretty good." Francisco laughed. He pulled his book order form out of his back pocket and opened the neatly folded sheets. "Eh, Enrique, did you see the dictionary on the last page? English and French? 'Seventy thousand words,'" he read. "'Pronunciation guide and grammatical tables,' it says here. That sounds like something you could use."

"Yeah, but check out the price."

"What? It's only six-fifty."

"Yeah, and I got exactly zero."

"Why don't you get them to pay you for all the babysitting?" Horacio asked. "Every time I translate for my uncles or wash their cars or anything, they give me money, or they buy me something. Even my moms pays me to cut the grass."

Enrique thought about this. Maybe if he asked his mother while Juan was at work or at one of his meetings... Of course, he would have to wait until she forgot he'd been late yesterday.

Ms. Byers held open the auditorium door while the class filed into the cool, dark hall. The auditorium was one of the few air-conditioned buildings on campus. Enrique lingered at the threshold, enjoying the cool gust that greeted him.

Mrs. Jaramillo's class, already seated in one section of the vast room, stared openly as Enrique and his classmates took their seats. Of course, a few wanna-be gangbangers tried to sneer and look tough, but most of the new students looked small and scared in their poorly matched and ill-fitting clothes that marked them as newcomers. They wore tight plaid pants, loud striped shirts, t-shirts with religious sayings—most of their clothing probably came from barrels like those at Enrique's stepfather's church. Enrique felt a pang remembering his mother and Juan digging infant coveralls, pajamas, and t-shirts for his brothers from the stained and faded jumble of clothing.

"Sit down on this side," Ms. Byers said in a loud voice. "Mrs. Jaramillo and I have already matched up partners. Mrs. Jaramillo will read names of the partners. When you hear your name, stand up and meet your partner, then both of you will take your seats in the third section on my right." She pointed to a bank of vacant seats near the emergency exit.

Mrs. Jaramillo climbed the stairs to the stage. Being a short woman, she twisted the microphone to accommodate her height. Then she spoke, but no one could make out what she said because the microphone squawked so.

"Consuelo, I don't think we need the microphone!" shouted Ms. Byers over the racket. Students giggled at hearing Mrs. Jaramillo's first name.

Mrs. Jaramillo switched off the microphone and pushed it away. "Very well, then, can everyone hear me?"

Enrique nodded. Mrs. Jaramillo's loud voice throbbed at his temples. He wondered if her husband owned a good pair of earplugs, as she talked about the project. She explained how "very educational" for everyone it would be. "Very educational" seemed to be her favorite words. Enrique lost count after she repeated them six times. Even though Mrs. Jaramillo spoke

slowly and formed each word carefully, Enrique had
trouble paying attention. He felt like a cartoon character
who stares at a swinging watch while the hypnotist
drones about eyelids growing heavier and heavier.

Finally, Mrs. Jaramillo read the names so slowly that
Enrique's head began to hurt. He was sure it would be
lunchtime before she got to his name. But he hoped at
least he would get a decent partner, a boy like himself,
maybe, who liked running and basketball, and who
wouldn't make fun of him for babysitting his little
brothers every afternoon.

Enrique heard his friend Horacio's name called and
watched him stand to meet his partner, Sandra Flores,
or Changa Flores, as they called her. "The Monkey."
Enrique remembered her from last year. She entered
school late in the year and had to take her last semester
of beginning ESL this year. She was okay, but a bit of a
tattletale. Changa had wispy brown hair like a coconut
and longish arms which earned her the nickname,
Monkey. When Horacio heard her name, he gasped as if
he had just tuned into the worst part of a horror movie.
And Changa's eyes widened as though she were about
to get hit by a car.

Next Francisco was paired up with some kid named
German, a boy Enrique had never seen before. One
glance, though, told Enrique that German—with his
loose, flabby lips and unfocused eyes—was *un poco
loco,* or "mental," as the *norteamericanos* liked to say.
German looked underfed and puny, but he had squeezed
himself into jeans that were even smaller than his narrow
hips by a few sizes. The ragged hems hiked up to his

calves, and he wore no socks. He'd thrust his bare feet into an overlarge pair of deck shoes which slapped the floor like duck's feet when he walked. He reminded Enrique of someone rescued from a shipwreck. He even had dark stubble shading his sharp jaw.

Enrique couldn't read Francisco's expression. If he felt disappointed in winding up with German, he didn't show it. Francisco hardly minded how other people looked or dressed. Francisco, himself, wore whatever his mother ironed for him to put on each day. Enrique doubted Francisco would notice if his mother pressed a clown suit for him to wear. He would probably just step into it. Enrique smiled, picturing his friend striding to school in a ruffled collar and roomy polka-dot pants.

Several more names were called before Enrique heard Mrs. Jaramillo sound out "En-ri-que Su-a-rez" like she was just learning to read syllables. The name she read with his was short, but she dragged that out too. "Fe-lor Ca-ruz." Flor Cruz? Who's that? Enrique stood. A skinny little girl, wearing a mini-skirt and shiny black boots to her thighs, wobbled toward him. Her wavy brown hair reached to her waist. The bangs were long too, and they kept falling over her freckled face and large, bold-looking eyes. She looked like somebody's kid sister playing dress up in borrowed clothes.

Though she looked young, her voice sounded confident, even harsh, when she spoke. "So what's the big deal?" she said when they sat down together. "It's not like you got to marry me."

"You speak English pretty good," Enrique said, amazed. He expected someone who could barely ask for the bathroom, but Flor's English—he had to admit—sounded better than his.

"I watch a lot of television," she explained. "I can talk real good English, but I can't write for jack and I can't read too good neither. That's why they put me in the beginning class. Hey, who's that kid with the old lady?" She pointed out Marvin, whose grandmother smoothed out the blue panel she'd been knitting.

"That's Marvin," Enrique told Flor, watching Marvin and his grandmother join up with their partner, a Vietnamese girl named Sue. Both Marvin and his grandmother seemed pleased as they returned Sue's deep bow and took turns shaking her hand. Enrique explained to Flor about Marvin's grandmother, how she sat knitting quietly in the back row of every class Marvin attended.

"Weird," said Flor, shaking her head, "really weird."

Mrs. Jaramillo finally finished with the names and stepped down from the stage as though she were climbing off an airplane after a long and exhausting flight.

"She looks tired," whispered Enrique.

"Bet you'd be tired too, if you had to talk like a baby all day long," Flor replied.

Ms. Byers took the stage next and gave the assignment. With the remaining time, the Intermediate ESL students were to interview their Beginning ESL partners in English and write a paragraph for homework called "My New Friend." Flor looked at Enrique and rolled her eyes. The Beginning students were supposed to write five interview questions to ask their new partners the next day. "Does everyone understand?" Mrs. Byers asked.

No one, except probably Francisco and maybe this Flor, thought Enrique, fully understood. But only Marvin was brave enough to ask Ms. Byers to explain more, which she did until the students nodded, murmuring,"*Oh.*"

"What d'ya wanna know?" demanded Flor, twisting in her seat to face Enrique. "Where I was born and stuff like that?"

Enrique was really wondering how she got those boots to stay up with such bony thighs. They seemed to defy gravity.

"I'll tell you whatever you want to know," Flor continued. "I'm very honest. I never lie unless it looks like I'm going to get in trouble."

"*Pues*," began Enrique.

"Speak to me in English. I don't speak good Spanish."

"I still don't know why they put you in ESL," Enrique admitted.

"Remember I told you I don't read so good. I'll tell you a secret. Don't ever tell anyone, or I'll kick your butt." She lowered her voice. "I really can't read at all. And I don't know how to write more than my name. My last school, they put me in the dummy class. I hated it. So when my family moved and I transferred to this school, I decided to try ESL. I figure they can teach me to read."

"Why you never learn reading?" asked Enrique. His

mother taught him to read in Spanish even before he started his first year of school in Mexico.

"Fruit," blurted Flor.

"Fruit?"

"Yeah, fruit and lettuce. My family picks fruit—you know, grapes, strawberries, apricots, you name it. I pick too. We always got to move where the fruit is. We're always moving and I got to work a lot. I never got that much school, but we always had television. I love TV. Do you love TV?"

"It's okay," shrugged Enrique, who never thought about loving the television any more than he loved the refrigerator or the vacuum cleaner as it nested, its long hose curled around the canister, under his mother's bed.

"TV is not just okay. TV is the world!" Flor said, holding out her arms to show how much television meant to her. Enrique looked around to see if her startling reaction had attracted attention to him. But the other students seemed too busy chattering with one another to notice his partner's outburst. "Now, you tell me something, who stomped your face?"

Enrique glanced around to make sure Francisco and Horacio were out of earshot. "I got caught slipping," he said in a lowered voice. "Itchy Jimenez caught me."

"That's dumb," Flor said. "You seem smarter than that."

"You think so?" Enrique wanted her to go on.

But Ms. Byers and Mrs. Jaramillo called time and dismissed both classes for recess with reminders about the homework assignments. The students shuffled out of the air-conditioned auditorium.

"Hey," Enrique called after Flor. "You didn't tell me what to write in the paragraph."

"What do you want to know?"

"Where were you born?"

She stopped and put her cool fingertips on his elbow. She cupped her hand to speak into his ear. Her breath smelled like peppermint candy. "I was really born in Fresno, but don't write that. Say I was born in Zacatecas or Chihuahua, okay?"

"You're legal?"

"Damn straight," said Flor, striding to join the horde of students in their slow stampede toward the cafeteria. "You tell anyone, and I'll kick your butt!" she shouted as she vanished in the crowd.

"Nice girl," Francisco said, catching up with Enrique.

"She's not bad," Enrique told him. "What about that German? What's he like?"

"Well," Francisco paused, as though trying to think of the right words. "Well, he needs lots of help."

"You better help him find the bathroom," said Horacio, appearing at Francisco's elbow. "German is peeing on a tree by the parking lot."

Horrified, Francisco bolted after his new partner.

That German is a strange one. Enrique slipped into Spanish comfortably with Horacio who, unlike Francisco, couldn't care less whether or not they practiced their English.

Changa told me these people found him alone in the mountains in Mexico. He was living like an animal, eating rats and birds. They found some of his family

living here, so they put him on a bus and sent him over,
Horacio explained.

Enrique wondered how much of this was true. He
especially doubted that a boy like German could cross
the border by bus. Probably, German was just a poor,
crazy kid, waiting in the regular school until space for
him opened up in the special school downtown.

You like having la changa as your partner, teased
Enrique.

*Ah, she's not bad. She knows everything about
everyone, so she's interesting.*

Bring her a banana tomorrow, suggested Enrique,
meanly. He wanted to get a rise out of his friend.

*I'll bring her a banana when you invite me to the
wedding. I saw you whispering with your girlfriend,*
Horacio chided Enrique. "Oh, Enrique, I lub you zoh
mush!"

"Shut up!" cried Enrique. He should have remembered that teasing Horacio only prompted his friend—
the master tease—to get back at him.

"I lub you. I lub you. I lub you!" Horacio made kissy
noises.

"Shut up! I don't even *like* that skinny thing in
boots!" Enrique turned away from Horacio sharply and
found himself staring into Flor's brown eyes, which were
narrowing into angry slits.

"What about my boots?" she said, holding a
cardboard tray on which a cup of orange juice and an
apple were balanced. Enrique imagined that orange
juice streaming down his face and neck.

"Horacio is-is-is being a *pendejo*," Enrique stammered.

"You don't like me, huh? Well, guess what, Mr. Born-in-Mexico, I got a news flash for you: I don't give a damn about you either." She turned her back on Enrique and stomped off, but Enrique saw her shoulder quiver, just once, and her boots looked shaky from behind.

He shook his head at Horacio, blaming him for the hard words Flor had overheard. Enrique tensed to sprint after the scrawny girl in her shiny boots. He would catch up to her and tell her he was talking about someone else, another girl in boots. No, maybe he would tell her the truth: Horacio shamed him by guessing a secret even Enrique had not realized. He didn't know *what* he would say when he caught up to Flor. Maybe he would just change the subject. He could ask her about her favorite television programs. He would talk about something she liked, something to make her bold eyes bright and her voice thick with joy.

Enrique almost caught up with her—he was about to reach for her elbow—when he felt a rush of wind at his back, then a hard slam that sent him to his knees. He caught himself with his hands before he fell flat. As he turned to stand up, a sharp kick to his rear sent him diving into the cement.

Chapter Twelve

Itchy Jimenez! Before Enrique could get to his feet, Horacio leapt piggyback onto Itchy and pummeled the larger boy on the head and the neck. Itchy brushed the blows off like dandruff. He jerked behind him, grunting, as he tried to pull Horacio off. But Horacio twisted and turned, so Itchy couldn't reach him. The swelling crowd hooted with laughter, as though the boys were staging a comedy skit, a slapstick routine. On his back, Enrique scooted crab-like under Itchy and landed solid kicks at the back of his knees. Itchy folded like a card table with Horacio on top of him, and then he rolled over Horacio and sprang to his feet, something glinting in his fist.

"Knife! He's got a knife!" someone yelled.

Mr. Toro, with his megaphone bouncing and his tie flapping, trotted over in time to pull Itchy away from Horacio. "You again!" he said to Horacio. "And you too. You're on probation, Mister," he told Itchy.

Itchy tried to slip the blade into the pocket of his oversized khakis.

"I already saw it," Mr. Toro said. "Give it up."

A school police officer arrived to cuff Itchy and lead him away.

"You must really like trouble," Mr. Toro told Horacio. He noticed Enrique's torn pants and the blood from his scraped knees. "Were *you* involved too?"

"He just got knocked down when we was fighting," Horacio said quickly. "He didn't have nothing to do with nothing."

Enrique shot Horacio a look, and his friend winked at him.

"Well, get to the nurse's office and get yourself cleaned up. Here's a pass." Mr. Toro scribbled on a slip and handed it to Enrique, who took it and hobbled off.

Mr. Grissom, the nurse, cleaned and bandaged Enrique's knees. "Looks like you've got yourself a shiner too. Where'd that come from?"

Enrique shrugged. "Bike," he said.

"Ah," Nurse Grissom said. "Do you want to call home and see if someone can bring you another pair of pants? These are pretty much ruined."

Enrique shook his head. What would his mother do with the triplets, even if she did have another pair of pants to bring him? She had just bought this pair. They were supposed to last until Christmas. He was to wear them every day to school, change into gym shorts at home, and wash them on Saturday to wear again on Monday. Now, the knees gaped open like bloody mouths.

"We've got some extra clothing in back. Things that have been donated to the school. Would you like to look for another pair or maybe some shorts to change into for the rest of the day?"

Enrique shook his head again. He would rather wear his ripped and stained khakis than somebody else's ill-fitting cast-offs. He had seen that stuff before, and it had been donated for a reason.

"Suit yourself." Nurse Grissom jotted on a notepad. "Where are you headed?"

Enrique glanced up at the clock above the nurse's desk. "P.E."

"I don't recommend you run on those knees. I'm writing here that you should sit this one out, okay?"

Enrique nodded. His knees hurt, his ribs ached, and his eye throbbed. No way did he feel like running around the track or up and down the bleachers for warm-up.

"Here's your pass." The nurse tore the slip from the pad. "Be careful out there, will you?"

Enrique sat on the bleachers during gym, watching the other kids in his class play. Coach Sharp was absent, and a substitute teacher stood in the middle of the basketball court, wearing a confused look on his face and blowing the whistle now and again, while the kids threw balls to one another and shot baskets. The equipment clerk issued Enrique a pair of shorts, a t-shirt, and a locker. It was pure luck that a shipment of new uniforms arrived earlier that day and Enrique actually got shorts and a t-shirt in his own size. He cradled the new gym clothes in his arms, planning to take them home with him until he could persuade Juan to give him money for a combination lock to secure the locker.

He limped through the rest of the school day, his body sore and his head heavy. After lunch, he yearned to curl up on a bed of short grass in the play area and nap for a solid week. If a plane tumbled out of the sky to crash onto him, he wouldn't even roll out of the way, he was that sleepy.

During his last class—science—all he could think about was hurrying home to crawl onto the couch to join the triplets for their afternoon nap. Two times, the teacher called on him, and he had no idea how to answer her questions. What English he knew had deserted him. The first time, she had just asked his name, and Enrique shook his head—he didn't know. Other students snickered, and the teacher had to ask him again, slowly, before he could tell her.

Finally, the last bell sounded, and Enrique stumbled out the door, heading for home. He was about to cross the boulevard when he noticed his arms felt oddly light, like he was missing something. *His new gym clothes!*

That woke him up. He spun around and raced back to the science lab, his knee caps burning like they were on fire. A stitch developed in his side where his ribs hurt and he worried he would run out of oxygen and faint, but he made it back to the lab just as the teacher was locking up.

"I—I—wait a minute," he said, doubling over to catch his breath.

"What is it, Ricardo?" she asked. "Did you forget something?"

"Enrique," he said, and he gasped. "Enrique."

"I haven't seen Enrique."

"*I'm* Enrique."

"Are you sure?" The teacher squinted at him in doubt. "I thought you said your name was Ricardo."

Enrique shook his head, but he wondered if he had given the wrong name. He was so exhausted, he might have said anything.

"Did you forget the homework, Ricardo, I mean, Enrique?"

Homework? Had there been homework? He shook his head, still struggling to breathe like a normal person.

"What is it then?"

"Gym clothes. I left them here."

"Those were yours? I had my monitor run them over to the Lost and Found right after class."

Enrique shot out the door and ran. In a few seconds, he doubled back. "Where is the Lost and Found?"

"In one of the offices north of the classroom bungalows, I think," the teacher said. "I'm not really sure. I'm new here, you know. I don't even know for sure if there is a Lost and Found. I just assumed there'd be one."

Enrique jogged toward the main office.

"Henri! Henri!" someone shouted through an open window as he galloped past a bungalow. "Henri! Henri!" several voices joined in, chanting. Enrique glanced up to see Monsieur Nassour and a group of black students waving him over from one of the classrooms. "Henri!" called Monsieur Nassour. "We are waiting for you!"

Tuesday, he remembered, the Drama Club meeting. "I am looking for Lost and Found," Enrique called back.

"Then I will come to the meeting."

"Henri, we're waiting for you!" the students chanted.

"Lost and Found?" shouted Monsieur Nassour over the din of voices. "Is there such a thing?"

"Henri! Henri! We're waiting for you!"

"I hope so," Enrique said.

"Come to the meeting, my boy. Afterwards, we will find this so-called Lost and Found, *oui?*"

Enrique didn't have the strength to argue. He

climbed the few steps to the bungalow and sank into a seat, resting his head on the desktop.

"Henri is our newest member of the Drama Club. Let's welcome him to our first meeting," Monsieur Nassour told the group.

"Z'up?" said one boy.

"Z'up?" another repeated.

"Z'up?" "Z'up?" "Z'up?" echoed the others. Enrique lifted his head, glanced around the classroom, and smiled. Everyone, he noticed, except for Monsieur Nassour and himself, every single person was African American.

"Why, he's a cute little white boy!" one girl said.

"Nah," some boy told her, "he's Mexican or Cuban or something, aren't you?"

Enrique nodded.

"See, he ain't white."

"Enough, enough," Monsieur Nassour said. "Let's get on, *s'il vous plait*, with the election of the officers. Who wants to be president this year? Dantonio?"

"Yeah," a girl seconded. "You weren't that bad last year, D.T."

"Heck, no!" A husky boy with large green eyes shook his head. "I did it last year, and my mamá said she'd kick me inside out if I do it again. That was too much work, man. Make Howard do it."

"No," a tall thin boy said in a deep voice.

"Why not? I swear you never do nothing," Dantonio said.

"No."

"Come on, Howard, you lazy mother."

"No."

"Who else?" Monsieur Nassour asked.

"I'll do it," said one girl with pretty half-moon dimples indenting her cheeks when she smiled. "I'll be president."

The others groaned.

"You can't be president, Karis," Dantonio told her.

"And why not?"

"You never show up to the meetings. That's why not," someone else explained. "You come to the first one, and that's it."

"Merci, Karis, *mais non,"* Monsieur Nassour said. "Who else?"

"I know let's make the new kid president," another girl said.

Shocked, Enrique shook his head with force.

"Yeah," Dantonio said, "he's never been president before."

"Yeah," Howard rumbled.

"I nominate the new kid," Karis said. "What's his name again?"

"Henri," someone said.

"That's right—Henri. I nominate Henri for president of the Drama Club."

"And I second it." Dantonio held up his hand, as though taking a pledge.

"Those in favor," began Monsieur Nassour, but he was drowned out by a chorus of "aye's!"

Chapter Thirteen

Soon the other students were congratulating Enrique, shaking his hand, and thumping him on the back. Dantonio said he would tell Enrique how to be president, assuring him that it was "real easy," especially in the beginning.

Karis insisted on being vice president. She argued that it never matters if the vice president shows up or not, unless the president dies. Since no one else wanted the job, Karis became Enrique's second-in-command. A quiet boy, Rico, who had been writing everything down in a spiral notebook, nodded his acceptance of another term as secretary. Everyone else wanted to be treasurer, but Monsieur Nassour took the job himself.

"Whatever happened to democracy?" Dantonio asked.

"The same thing that happened to our field trip money two years ago," Monsieur Nassour told him. "It disappeared with our last student treasurer."

"Are we really going to get a field trip this year, Monsieur Nassour?" Karis said. "'Cause if we do, I'll show up for that."

"*Mais oui*, if we do well in the bake sales and the ticket sales, we will certainly have our field trip."

"What play we doing?" she asked.

"Same as always, right?" Dantonio said.

"It's the only one we know," someone else put in.

"We ought to learn a new play," Dantonio said,

"something like *West Side Story*, with the singing and the dancing." He snapped his fingers, humming a tune.

"Then we'd have to learn to sing," Howard put in. "I can't sing."

"Let's stick to our usual play," Karis said. "We all know that one real good."

Monsieur Nassour nodded. "It's a good play, and every time we do it, we get better."

Most of the club members seemed relieved and murmured in agreement.

After some discussion of where the club should go on the field trip, Dantonio said that he had to go to basketball practice. Others started mumbling about having to leave too. "Adjourn the meeting, would you, Henri?" Dantonio said.

"What?"

"Say, 'this meeting is adjourned,' so we can get out of here."

"This meeting is adjourned," Enrique repeated, and Rico glanced at the clock and wrote it down. The club members slung their backpacks over their shoulders and headed for the door.

"*Trés bien*," Monsieur Nassour said. "Very well done. You are going to make an excellent president, Henri. I can feel this."

"The Lost and Found, Monsieur Nassour. Can you help me find it?" Enrique asked.

"*Oui, oui!*" Monsieur Nassour flicked off the lights and hefted his briefcase. "Let us find this mysterious Lost and Found."

The old man shambled alongside Enrique toward the

administrative offices. "Do you think you could talk to me in French?" Enrique asked after a few moments.

"You will not understand me."

"That's okay," Enrique said. "I just like to hear the sounds."

Monsieur Nassour squinted at Enrique, and then he smiled. "You are an unusual boy." He began speaking in French. Enrique couldn't tell what he was talking about, but he listened anyway. He smiled and wanted to tap his foot as though he were listening to music.

When they arrived at the main office, Monsieur Nassour pulled the door handle, but it was bolted shut. They circled around to the counseling office, the clinic, and the textbook/supply room—all locked.

"They must be having an administrative meeting," Monsieur Nassour said. "It is too early for everyone to leave. I'm sorry, Henri, but you will have to look for the Lost and Found tomorrow, unless you want to wait for these people to return."

"What time is it?" Enrique didn't want to be late again for babysitting.

"It is a little after four."

"I better go home," Enrique said. "I got to work." He hoped Monsieur Nassour would think he had a real job in a store or at a gas station. It didn't seem dignified for the newly elected president of the drama club to work as his mother's babysitter.

"All right, Henri, *au revoir*, until tomorrow." Monsieur Nassour shook Enrique's hand. "Don't forget the French club meeting after school tomorrow."

"I won't forget."

"What's this?" Monsieur Nassour pointed to a bundle under the waiting area bench outside the counseling office. Enrique peered under at a wrinkled heap of gym clothes! He reached for them and checked the size on the tag inside the shorts.

"These are mine, Monsieur Nassour! These are what I wanted to find in the Lost and Found!"

"*C'est bon!* What good fortune."

"That monitor must have put them here when he couldn't get in the building. Enrique brushed the dust from the clothing and folded them carefully. "*C'est muy, muy bon,*" he said, "and lucky, too."

Enrique "power walked," the way he'd seen an athlete do on television, all the way home. He didn't care if he looked odd taking huge steps with his elbows swinging like frantic chicken wings. Power walking was faster than regular walking, and he was still too sore to run. Plus, it got him home before his mother had to leave for work.

She was standing at the mirror, tucking her curls into a hairnet, when Enrique came through the door. She smiled at him in the mirror. This was another donation from Juan's church. It was long and narrow with dents in a couple of places. Enrique liked playing "freak show" in it. From where Enrique stood, his mother's reflection made her forehead seem nearly a foot long. Her eyes, nose, mouth, and chin were squished into a tiny fist-sized knot. She looked like one of the "jar babies" on the pamphlets members of Juan's church handed out to protest abortion.

How was school? she asked in a hushed voice that

told him the babies were sleeping in their cribs nearby. *Did anything interesting happen?*

Enrique shrugged.

Those pants! She turned to face him, forgetting to whisper. *What happened to those pants?*

I fell down.

We have no money for new pants.

I know it.

She examined the ripped knees. *Maybe I can sew those when I get home tonight,* she said, but her voice was filled with doubt.

I can fix them, Enrique said, wondering how anyone could repair holes as big as these.

Leave them for me, Son. Were you hurt when you fell?

Enrique's lower lip quirked. A knot burned in his throat and his eyes went blurry. He longed to put his head on her shoulder, breathe her fresh *masa* smell, and feel her soft arms around him like a blanket. *De nada*, he said. *I am fine.*

His mother searched his face and reached out a hand to touch his shoulder, but then she pulled back and turned to adjust her hairnet in the mirror. A few stray tendrils had escaped in the back. Enrique tucked these under the black webbing.

Thank you. She smiled and gathered her purse and keys from the coffee table. *The babies are sleeping, and your food is in the refrigerator. Juan has a meeting tonight, so you will have to put the babies to bed again.*

Fine.

About last night, son, I know you would not hurt

your brother. It's that Juan gets so worried about them. He has never had children before. Sometimes he doesn't know—

Fine.

I'm sorry that he hit you. I know he loves you, and he feels very bad about hurting you.

It is fine.

Is that all you can say?

"Sí."

Enrique's mother jerked the door open, stepped out, and shut it firmly behind her without kissing him or even saying goodbye.

He sighed and sank into the couch. Boy, shivering, crawled out from under the table and jumped into his lap. Enrique fell asleep before he could stretch out on the cushions. When he woke to the babies' cries half an hour later, he was still sitting upright with his head thrown back like a fighter knocked senseless by a powerful blow. Enrique shook himself and yawned. His ears felt plugged, as though he were under water. He couldn't hear too well. And the babies sounded different, not as loud as usual. Or not as many. Enrique bolted to his mother's bedroom. Maclovio and Hilario, twisting and kicking, sobbed in their cribs, but Juan Jr., usually the loudest of the three, was silent.

Enrique ignored the other two to stand over Yunior's crib. The baby lay on his back, completely still. Enrique wiggled his brother's bare foot. The baby didn't stir. Enrique's heart shot to his throat. He placed a hand on the baby's chest, and felt nothing. He was completely still. Yunior wasn't breathing.

Chapter Fourteen

Enrique raced for the phone. With shaking fingers, he jabbed 9-1-1.

"My brother is not breathing," he told the operator, as calmly as he could. "he's just a baby, and he stop breathing."

"How old is the baby?" the operator asked.

"Eight months."

"You are at Terrace View Apartments on Logan and Third? Apartment N?"

"Yes, yes."

"We're sending paramedics out there right now. Is the baby in the room with you?"

"No, he's in the bedroom."

"Can you take the telephone to where the baby is? I'm going to tell you what to do until the paramedics arrive."

"No. It's on the wall." Enrique tugged uselessly at the short plastic coil connecting the mouthpiece to the wall-mounted phone.

"Is anyone else with you?"

"No, I'm alone, but I can get help. Wait!" Enrique set the phone on the table and dashed out of the apartment to pound on Maricela's door across the hall.

She opened the door. "Enrique?"

Help me, please! Yunior's not breathing!

Oh, God, my mother isn't home.

I need you! Enrique grabbed her pale arm and yanked her across the hall. *Talk on the telephone and tell me what I have to do.* Enrique practically flew back to the bedroom. Hilario and Maclovio were hiccoughing now, between wails.

Maricela must have picked up the phone because he heard her say, "Hello...yes...yes, okay."

What do I do, Maricela. What should I do?

Can you feel the heartbeat? she asked.

Enrique pressed his fingers on the baby's chest. He couldn't feel a thing, but with the other babies howling, it was hard to tell for sure. *I don't know!*

"He doesn't know...okay," Maricela said into the phone. *Put the baby on his back!* she called to Enrique.

He is already.

Open his mouth and clear it out with your finger.

Enrique pried the baby's jaw open and scooped a finger through his mouth. A wad of whitish cream came out on his finger. Enrique wiped it out of Yunior's mouth with a blanket. *Now what do I do?*

Pinch the nose closed and blow into the mouth!

Enrique sealed the little nose and forced his breath through his brother's lips. Nothing happened. *Now what?*

Count to five and try it again.

Enrique counted and blew again. Still nothing. *It's not working!* He tried another time and another time. Sirens screeched in the street below. He tried one more time.

Juan Jr. gurgled. More white stuff spilled out of his mouth, and then the baby sucked in a big breath and cried.

He's alive, Maricela! Enrique shouted.

The paramedics burst into the apartment, crowding the small bedroom like huge trees shoved into a closet. They dumped heavy cases on the floor and worked rapidly over Juan's crib. They unzipped his sleeper and tested his heart and lungs with a stethoscope that must have been cold from the hollering it produced in the baby. Maclovio and Hilario finally settled down to stare at the strangers bent over their screaming brother. Enrique stumbled out to find Maricela and thank her while the paramedics examined Yunior.

Maricela stood in the kitchen, still clutching the phone so tightly the tips of her fingers and knuckles had whitened. Her eyes were pinched, red-rimmed. Enrique hugged her. "*Gracias,*" he whispered in her ear. *Thank you. I will never forget this.*

"What the hell's going on here?" Enrique's step-father stood in the open doorway, glaring at the two in the kitchen.

Enrique and Maricela jumped. They pulled apart to face the angry man.

"Why is this door open? And what are you doing necking in my kitchen?"

Maricela's pale cheeks flamed.

"Yunior wasn't breathing," Enrique said. "Maricela helped me when I called the paramedics. Didn't you see the ambulance downstairs? Look for yourself—they're in the bedroom."

Juan didn't answer. He hurried to the bedroom. Maricela and Enrique huddled in the doorway, listening to the voices from the other room.

"How is he?" Juan asked.

"He seems fine now, but we think we ought to take him to Saint Pete's for observation," one of the paramedics said.

"What happened? That boy, did he hurt my son?"

"That boy, Mister," another paramedic said in a gruff voice, "saved your son's life. He gave him mouth-to-mouth when the baby stopped breathing. We got here just as he got his breathing started again."

"The baby was most likely sleeping on his back when he vomited and choked on it," the first voice explained.

"He was sick last night," Juan said.

"Where were you, sir? Where's the mother of these babies?"

"Working," Juan said. "We both work."

"You leave these three babies with that poor kid out there?"

"We have no choice." Juan's voice dropped. Enrique could barely hear him.

"My wife does childcare, sir, in our home. She has a daycare license, and I've got to tell you, I'd never want her to take on three babies by herself at the same time."

"You were lucky that boy knew how to handle a serious emergency like this," the other paramedic added. "Really lucky."

"We're going to take the baby over to the hospital, sir. You can follow in your car."

"I have no car."

"Fine, you can ride along with us. Is there another adult who can help the boy out here?"

Maricela opened her mouth, but Enrique clapped his

hand over her lips. He didn't want his stepfather to know he had been listening.

"I will find someone."

"Go ahead and do that, so we can head out."

Juan shambled back into the kitchen. "Maricela, ask your mother to come over here to help Enrique for a little while, okay?"

"She's at the store, but when she gets back, she'll come over."

"Thank you," Juan said. He turned to Enrique and drew a deep breath, as though he was preparing to say something, but whatever it was it wouldn't come out, and he made his way back to the bedroom.

After the paramedics left with Juan and Yunior, Maricela and her mother helped Enrique feed and bathe the other two babies. Maclovio and Hilario were exhausted by their bouts of crying. They played only a short while after their baths before growing cranky. Enrique heated their bottles and settled them back in their cribs much earlier than usual.

When Maricela's father returned from work, he offered to go out for pizzas to bring to his neighbor's apartment. Enrique and Maricela sat at the kitchen table doing homework and Maricela's mother watched *telenovelas* on television while they waited for the food.

Enrique worked on his paragraph titled "My New Friend" for ESL:

Today I meet a new friend. She is the girl Flor Cruz. She is born in some place in Mexico. She love the television. She has boots very long. I like my new friend.

He counted the sentences. "Six," he said aloud. "That's enough."

"Can I read it?" Maricela asked.

"Sure." Enrique pushed the sheet of paper across the table. Maricela took advanced ESL. She'd be able to help him correct any mistakes.

Maricela took a long time to read the paragraph. Then, Enrique noticed she seemed sad.

"I forgot something," he said. He added one last sentence: *But my old friends are the best!*

Maricela smiled reading that.

"I can't remember what cities Flor said to say she was born in," Enrique muttered.

"What do you mean 'said to say'?" Maricela asked.

"It's a long story." Enrique remembered Flor's promise to kick his butt if he told anyone where she was really born. "Zacatecas, I think." He grabbed his pencil. "Or Chihuahua."

"Chihuahua?" Maricela said. "Enrique, where's Boy? I haven't seen him at all today."

Chapter Fifteen

"He's probably hiding somewhere," Enrique said. He hadn't seen Boy since the dog curled up on his lap that afternoon. The poor thing couldn't take too much commotion and noise. "He gets scared real easy."

"Did you feed him?" Maricela asked.

Scared or not, Boy always liked to eat.

"No, I haven't seen him since this afternoon." Enrique rose from the table. "I'll find him. I bet he's asleep under my mother's bed."

But when he crawled under to peer beneath the bobbed fringe of the bedspread, all Enrique found was the vacuum cleaner with its hose wrapped around it like an anteater curled up in a cave. Enrique checked the closet, the bathroom, behind the television set—no Boy.

"Those paramedics had the door open a long time," Maricela said.

"I'll go look for him outside. How long can you and your mother stay?"

"I don't know. We'll at least stay until my father brings the pizza. When is Juan coming back?"

"He'll probably go to a meeting after the hospital," Enrique said. He glanced at the clock on the stove. It was nearly nine. His stepfather usually returned from his meetings before ten. "He should be back in about an hour."

Mamá, Enrique wants to know how long we can stay.

I do not know. When is his father coming back?

One hour.

Fine, we can stay until he returns.

"I'm going out to look for Boy," Enrique said. "Do you think your mother will mind?"

"She never cares what boys do," Maricela said, with resentment. "She won't even let me go to the corner to mail a letter by myself, but if I were a boy she'd probably let me hitchhike to Tijuana on my own."

Enrique slipped on his shoes. "*Con permiso,*" he said to Maricela's mother. *I have to go out for a few minutes.*

The streets were full of cars and people milling around, talking, smoking, eating, and drinking sodas or beers. Little kids threaded through the shadows between streetlights, shrieking and tagging one another. Babies howled. Boom boxes and car stereos made the sidewalk throb.

Enrique knew Boy would be terrified to be out here by himself. He imagined his little dog cringing and puddling himself in the midst of these confusing sights and sounds. Boy had gotten loose a few times when he was younger. Each time, Enrique found him after a short while, right near the apartment, the pup whimpering as though he'd been wounded. Boy had been unharmed, terrified, but fine.

This time, Enrique didn't find Boy right away. He circled the neighborhood, searching the shadows and whistling his special tune for calling Boy when he had a treat to offer him. When he couldn't find Boy on his block, Enrique walked another block, then another. He went as far as he could without slipping. Enrique worried that Boy might have run into Itchy's territory or the Mission Boys' *tierra*. Dogs don't know about gangs, he told himself. Dogs don't know about slipping.

Enrique peered into a clouded pawnshop window to look at the clock. It was nearly ten. He had to get home, but he made one last sweep of the barrio, calling Boy's name and clapping his hands. What if the dog had been hit by a car or stolen? He'd heard about people from laboratories who swiped dogs and cats for medical experiments. He might never see Boy again.

But Enrique knew it was time to head home. He took slow steps hoping to see the gray and brown dog jump out at him as he turned each corner. Why didn't he remember to shut the door after he went for Maricela. He had been the first to leave it open, not the paramedics.

With heavy feet, Enrique climbed the stairs to his apartment. What if Boy returned while he was out looking for him? Maybe he found his way home and scratched at the door until Maricela or her mother let him in. He might be eating scraps from their pizza dinner or snoring under the coffee table right now.

His heart lifted, and he skipped up the last few steps. He flung open the door to find Juan on the couch, chewing a wedge of pizza and staring at the television screen.

"Where were you?" his stepfather asked without looking up. Only Juan's cracked boots lay under the coffee table.

Enrique felt too disappointed to speak.

"I asked you a question," Juan said and wiped his mouth with a napkin. "Where were you, huh?"

"Boy got out. I was looking for him."

Juan tossed pizza crust onto the paper plate in his lap. "I can't believe you would go out looking for a dog while your baby brother is in the hospital. He almost *died* tonight. And you're out there looking for that bag of fleas."

"How is Yunior?" Enrique asked.

"*Now*, you ask about him," Juan said. "They say he's going to be okay."

"I want to go to bed," Enrique told his stepfather, hoping he would go in the other room and leave him alone. He pulled his sheets out of the closet, while Juan unplugged the television set and wound the cord around it to take into the bedroom and watch with the volume turned down.

His stepfather stood near the door, holding the set awkwardly. Enrique flapped a sheet over the couch. Juan cleared his throat. "They said, those paramedics said, that you saved his life."

Enrique shrugged, kicked off his shoes.

"In my meetings, they say I need to ask forgiveness, you know, to say I'm sorry to those I hurt when I was drinking."

Enrique shook his head. With Juan, it was all about what the paramedics said, what the people in the meetings said... He wondered why Juan didn't just go to bed, if he couldn't say what *he* had to say.

"I guess I'm trying to tell you... I'm not good at talking..."

Enrique yawned. "I'm tired."

"Well, okay," Juan said. "Goodnight." He disappeared into the bedroom, shutting the door behind him.

Enrique undressed. He folded his shirt, but threw his khakis in a ball. He was too tired to sew them that night. He'd wear an old pair of gym shorts to school in the morning. He sank into the couch and slept without dreaming.

Early the next day, his mother had to shake his shoulder to wake him. He opened his eyes to find her standing over him and holding Hilario against one shoulder. *I brought you pan dulce, my son, and cocoa. Wake up. You will be late for school.*

Enrique sat up and rubbed his eyes. The khakis he'd crumpled the night before were neatly pressed and folded atop his knees. He unfurled them. They had been washed and sewn.

"*¡Gracias, Mamá!*"

I did not do that, son. Juan cleaned them and sewed them for you. She smiled as happily as if she had just delivered the news that they'd won the lottery.

Enrique examined the khakis. The rips were closed up and the thread matched, but the long, jagged stitches looked like they had been put in by Dr. Frankenstein to piece together monster skin. Enrique's ears burned from the jokes he would no doubt hear in school about this. *It will be hot today,* he said, *I think I should wear shorts.*

His mother's smile fell. *He wanted to surprise you.*

Enrique sighed. *I'll wear them.* He planned to take his shorts in a bag with the new gym clothes. He'd leave early to change at Francisco's. *But, will I get a new pair soon?* Francisco's parents might get a little tired of having Enrique show up every morning.

I will buy you another pair when I am paid.

I also need a combination lock, he said, remembering the new gym clothes.

We have one. Hold your brother while I find it.

Enrique took Hilario in his arms. The baby blew spit bubbles that trickled down his chin. Enrique wiped the spittle with Hilario's bib, a scratchy thing with plastic backing. He bounced his brother on his lap and tickled his soft, round belly. Hilario grinned and made a gurgling sound. Enrique thought about Yunior in the hospital. Had he been frightened to wake up in a strange place without his family?

Enrique's mother handed him the lock. *Come to eat.*

When is Yunior coming home, Mamá?

Tía Ceci will take me to pick him up in a little while.

Is he going to be okay?

I saw him last night when I got home from work. Your aunt took me over there, and he was sleeping. He looked fine, she said.

I was very scared. I thought he would die.

When you were little, smaller than these three, you stopped breathing once too. I put you in cold water, and that made you angry enough to breathe. She smiled.

Do you think I shouldn't have called for help?

She sighed and sank on the couch beside him. *Enrique, you did the right thing. You saved your brother's life. It's hard for Juan and for me to tell you how thankful we are because we feel bad for putting so much on you.*

What do you mean?

We shouldn't leave the babies with you every day.
We know something dangerous could happen. And it did.
We were lucky that you knew what to do. She pulled a
paper from her pocket and unfolded it. *They gave me
this at the hospital.*

What is it?

*It is a letter. It says they are going to investigate us
for child neglect.*

Why?

*Because we leave you to care for the babies every
day. They say it is wrong. You are too young to do this.*
She refolded the letter. *What if they take the babies
away, son? What if they try to take you away?* She buried
her face in her hands.

Enrique reached over Hilario to pull her close. *They
can't do that.*

I love you. I love you all, she said. *I won't let you go.*

Chapter Sixteen

Enrique had a hard time paying attention to what Ms. Byers was saying the first hour of class. He kept wondering if they *could* take his brothers away, or take him away, from his mother just because they thought he was too young to care for the babies. He had taken on the job of babysitting his brothers from the time his mother went back to work, when they were just wrinkly red creatures that sounded like sheep bleating when they cried. Enrique was proud that he'd helped raise them into plump, strong babies who could already pull themselves up to stand, slobbering on the bars of the cribs. He was training them to walk, and he'd started trying to teach them a few words. And, he couldn't wait to teach them how to play basketball and video games. They wouldn't just take them away. Would they?

And Enrique worried about Boy. He had searched for him as long as he could before school. But the little dog was nowhere to be found. Francisco offered to make a flyer advertising the missing dog in Computer Lab. They'd copy it in the library and post them all over the barrio.

"What kind of reward should we offer?" Francisco had asked, planning the flyer on the way to school.

Enrique shrugged. "I don't have nothing."

"You should offer something," Francisco told him. "Or else no one will want to look for him."

"I don't have nothing. What am I going to give? A handshake? I'm not a rich kid like you."

Francisco hadn't said anything after that, and Enrique could tell from his silence that he had hurt his friend's feelings.

Another problem was that Enrique had no photos of Boy. He tried to draw a picture to copy for the space Francisco would leave on the flyer. But the drawing made Boy look more like a stick insect with bugged-out eyes than a Chihuahua-mix.

Enrique erased to try again. As he was about to start over, he felt Cake Angie's elbow jab his ribcage.

"Well, what do you think, Enrique?" Ms. Byers asked in a tone that told him she'd already asked him the question once.

"Yes," he said. He had no idea what Ms. Byers was talking about, but "yes" was usually a pretty good answer to teacher-style questions. "Yes, *sir*!" had been the only correct answer to give in McGrath's class.

"Yes?" Ms. Byers said. "What do you mean by 'yes'?"

"I agree."

"What do you agree with?" she asked.

"I agree with the question?"

The other students laughed.

Ms. Byers sighed. "Enrique, we were talking about rights and responsibilities in the classroom. I asked what some of your responsibilities are to the other students and to me."

"Yes," Enrique said. "*That* is a good question."

"I can think of one responsibility students have to their classmates and teachers," Ms. Byers said, evenly, "and that is to pay attention."

Later in his journal, Enrique wrote:

Some times you have worrys and the teacher she doesn't know. Like your dog is running away. It is hard to hear the teacher some times with worrys. People have other worrys too.

He counted the sentences—only five, so he added: *Do you have worrys, Ms. Byers?* He set down his pencil.

After the journals were collected, Ms. Byers took up book orders and money to place in a large yellow envelope. Francisco, naturally, had a crisp twenty dollar bill and change for all the books he wanted. Cake Angie ordered a cookbook. Even old Señora Alfaro pulled a couple of limp bills out of her purse for Marvin's order. Enrique wished Horacio hadn't been suspended. He missed his friend. Horacio would surely come up with something funny—maybe something a little mean—to say about the book orders.

Then Ms. Byers herded the class back to the auditorium to meet with their "new friends." Enrique didn't think Francisco looked too thrilled about spending more time with German. On the way to school, Francisco told Enrique how German had not appreciated his advice about not "urinating in public," as Francisco put it. The strange and wild boy had laughed in his face and tried to squirt him with a jet of urine. Next, he gave Francisco the finger and ran away setting off car alarms in the teachers' parking lot.

Enrique pitied Francisco, but he walked with Marvin and his grandmother, instead of his friend, to the auditorium.

Enrique asked Marvin how he liked his new partner.

"Sue is from Viet Nam," Marvin told him. "Her family is Hmong from a little place near Cambodia. She says the Hmong people helped the U.S. during the war in her country, but afterwards they were forgotten."

"Forgotten?" Enrique wondered how it was possible to forget a bunch of people.

"Yes, the *norteamericanos* just left them there to face punishment from the Communists. Sue's family escaped after their village was burned." Marvin shook his head. "This country had no business in Viet Nam. Everybody knows that."

Though they were speaking English and Marvin's grandmother could not understand, she nodded in agreement with her grandson.

In the auditorium, the students paired up to finish their interviews. The teachers planned to have the partners introduce one another on stage during the last twenty minutes of the period.

Ms. Jaramillo assigned Changa to Enrique and Flor, since Horacio was absent.

"Hey," Flor said, smiling under a lock of hair that had fallen over her face. She seemed to have forgotten how angry she was the day before. Her smile was crooked, Enrique noticed, in a way that would have looked goofy on anyone else. She pulled a folded sheet of notepaper from her boot. "I got my questions."

"You wrote questions?" Enrique asked, surprised. He glanced over her shoulder at the paper. It was blank.

"Of course, that was the homework, wasn't it? I always do my homework unless my favorite shows are on TV. Last night, my dad made us watch stupid basketball." Flor caught Enrique's eye and glanced at Changa, shaking her head. She didn't want the Monkey to know she couldn't read or write. "I'll ask you both the questions to save time."

"Okay," Enrique said. "Do you want me to write down the answers? To save time?"

"No, I'll remember. I got a good memory."

"Ask me a question," Changa begged.

"Okay, here goes," Flor said, and she pretended to read from the paper. "Where do you go to have fun around here?"

"*Qué fácil.*" Changa snapped her fingers. "Too easy! I go over to the park. They got a big slide there and lots of swings. I like the swings. I am like a bird flying on the swings." She looked like a much younger kid when she smiled.

"How about you?" Flor turned to Enrique. "Where do you go to have a good time?"

"Well, I go to my friend's house or to the basketball court here at school." He couldn't think of too many places. The park was okay if you were a little kid like Changa, but the last time Enrique went, he got jumped for his bus fare and had to walk more than three miles home.

"Do you go to the movies?" Flor asked.

"Not that much," Enrique said. The movies cost money, which he never had.

"You got to go to the movies!" Flor said. "Movies are even better than TV. I don't mean those action, fighting pictures or those outer-space things. Those are dumb. I mean the kinds of movies that show people falling in love. The ones that make you cry from the music. Those movies are the best."

"They show fighting movies at the Oñate," Changa said.

"Those are all Spanish movies. I like the movies in English," Flor said. "I hate those subtitles."

"Movies are okay," Enrique said.

"They are not just *okay*. Movies are better than anything in my whole, wide life. I bet you never even saw a really good one, huh? I'll go with you to see a good one. My aunt works at the Rialto, and she can get us in for free. They're playing a great one this weekend. I seen it four times. Want to go with me on Saturday?" Flor asked.

Enrique shrugged. Saturdays were the only days he didn't have to babysit his brothers. It might be kind of fun to see a movie for free.

"It's not like you're going out with me or anything," Flor told him. "It's just to the movies. How about it?"

"I guess so," he finally said.

"How about you, Sandra?" she asked Changa. "You want to come?"

Changa shook her head. "Mamá don't let me go no where."

"Okay, next question," Flor said, squinting at her paper. "Do you got a girlfriend?"

Enrique shook his head.

"How about you, Sandra?" Got a boyfriend?"

"You want to know a secret?" Changa smiled and crooked a nail-bitten finger to get them to lean in and listen. "I am getting married next month."

109

"What?" Enrique thought he must have heard wrong.

"But you can't," Flor said. "You're way too young. It's against the law, isn't it?"

"I will have fifteen years next week. In *Méjico*, I can get married, no *problema*. *Mamá* was married when she had just thirteen years."

"Who are you getting married to?" Enrique asked. He wondered if Horacio had played some kind of mean joke on the Monkey yesterday, promising to marry her or something like that.

"He's a nice man from Chiapas. He's a friend of *mi papá*, and he already has some childrens. His other wife died," Changa explained, "so he needs me."

"You're marrying some old guy with kids in Mexico?" Flor's eyes were wide with horror.

"Shh," Changa whispered. "*Cállate la boca.*"

"I don't never give advice," Flor said, "unless I have to, and, Sandra, you really need some advice. So here it is: You got to pack up all your stuff—clothes, toothbrush, everything—and run the hell away from home."

Not a bad idea, thought Enrique, under the circumstances.

"I don't want to run away. I'm going to get married. I'm going to have a cake with five floors on it and coconut icing." Sandra licked her lips.

"Why on earth would you want to get married?" Flor asked. "You're only fourteen years old."

"He has a job," Changa said in a patient voice. "He makes good money."

Later, when Flor clattered on stage, her boot heels

cracking like gunshots, she stepped to the podium to introduce Changa, saying: "My new friend, Sandra Flores, is a girl who likes swinging on the swings at the park. She is really nice, but she has a terrible secret. A secret I can't tell you."

Then she introduced Enrique. "Enrique Suarez is my other new friend. He looks kind of like the guy with long eyelashes that plays Charles's son on *Tomorrow Is Another Day*. He doesn't have a girlfriend. Not yet."

Enrique's face felt like it was on fire. He slid deep in his seat.

Flor gazed out at the audience and gave her big crooked smile. "We're going to the movies together on Saturday."

Chapter Seventeen

After dismissal, Enrique remembered another exit from the rear of the auditorium near the boys' bathroom. He slipped away as fast as he could. He found a discarded folder in one of the trash bins behind the building. Enrique held this to his face to see if it was large enough to shield him from recognition. Maybe he could get through the rest of the day without being noticed. By tomorrow, he *hoped* most of the kids would've forgotten to tease him about Flor.

"What are you doing, young man?" a harsh voice barked.

"Nothing, nothing." Enrique turned to face Mrs. Burwell. Her eagle eyes burned into his. A plume of smoke rose behind her two-tone hair. Was she holding a cigarette behind her back? He held up the folder. "I, uh, I threw this away by accident."

"Your name is Latosha Pritchard?" Mrs. Burwell asked, after reading the name printed in block letters on the cover.

"Girlfriend?" Enrique swallowed hard. "That's my girlfriend's name. She asked me to get it."

"You're not supposed to be back here," Mrs. Burwell said. "This area is off limits for students. Go back where you belong."

"Yes, okay. I'm sorry." Enrique turned to leave.

"Just a minute," called Mrs. Burwell. "Aren't you in one of my classes?"

"Yes, I mean no, *no*. That's my brother." Like Flor,

Enrique usually told the truth unless he thought it would get him in trouble. "We are twins."

Mrs. Burwell gave up pretending she wasn't smoking and puffed on her cigarette. "Enrique Suarez," she said, squinting hard at him. "I remember you." She stabbed the glowing tip of her cigarette in Enrique's direction. "You ought to be in remedial math."

Enrique nodded and then hurried away as quickly as he could without making it look like he was being chased by a bogey man.

The folder didn't prevent Enrique from being noticed, but it did work as a distracter.

"Hey, Enrique, how come you got that folder in your face?" some kid said.

"What's with the folder?" Cake Angie asked.

"My grandmother wants to know if there's something wrong with your face," Marvin said.

No one mentioned his date with Flor, except Francisco, who caught up with him at nutrition. "I don't think a folder is going to give you much protection from that girl."

"*She* asked me to the movies," Enrique explained. "She says her aunt works there and she could get me in free. I didn't ask for no date."

"Well, I'd rather go to ten movies with Flor than keep up with that German. He's getting worse and worse. I just stopped him from eating the angelfish in Mrs. Jaramillo's aquarium. He needs more help than I can give him. And I haven't been able to invent anything since he became my partner." Francisco's voice cracked, and his eyes filled.

Enrique handed him a napkin. "You don't have to babysit him, you know."

Francisco blotted his eyes and blew his nose. "Oh, yes, I do. He's going to hurt himself or somebody else if I don't watch him. I told Ms. Byers he needs a special school. But she told me they can't put him in one because the school psychologist doesn't speak Spanish."

"So?" Enrique wondered what that had to do with anything.

"So they can't place him in a special school because the psychologist can't test him. I told her that German doesn't really speak Spanish either. He just makes noises—grunts and humming sounds. I can't really help him. I just got to put up with him until they get someone over here to test him."

"Do you want to see if we can trade partners?" Enrique offered.

"No, they gave me that German on purpose. They want me to work with him. Besides, I am too tall for Flor," Francisco said. He batted his eyes. "And my eyelashes are probably not long enough."

After that, no one teased Enrique about Flor. It was as if no one thought it important enough to mention. Disgusted, Enrique threw away the folder after nutrition.

As the day wore on, Enrique missed Horacio more and more. He would have teased him about Flor until his ears felt ready to burst into flames. The empty breezeway near the lockers reminded him of his friend. "*Hay labio jabón lechuga*," he said under his breath, wondering what Horacio was doing all day. Earlier at nutrition, Enrique caught sight of Ricky, Horacio's former friend, sitting by himself and chewing on a burrito. He looked lonely, Enrique thought, lonely and bored.

When the final bell rang, Enrique remembered the French Club meeting. Apparently Enrique and Monsieur Nassour were the only ones to remember it. As they sat in the bungalow waiting for the other members, who never turned up, Enrique began talking to the old French teacher.

First, he told him about Boy running away. He explained how long he'd had boy and how he'd trained the dog to do a few tricks, describing how Boy would "dance" for the triplets while they ate. This led Enrique to talking about the babies and what happened to Juan Jr. the day before. He didn't know why, except that the old teacher listened so closely and kindly, but he even mentioned the investigation for child neglect and the possibility of losing his family. To his shame, Enrique even wept, but Monsieur Nassour didn't seem to mind. He just handed Enrique a big, silk handkerchief that smelled of pipe tobacco and peppermint.

He knew that Monsieur Nassour probably couldn't do much to help him solve these problems, but talking about them made Enrique feel physically lighter, as though he didn't have to carry them alone anymore. He glanced at the wall clock and realized he'd been talking over an hour.

"I got to go," he said. "I want to look for Boy again before I have to be home."

"I hope you will find your little dog," Monsieur Nassour said.

"Thanks. I mean, *merci, merci* very much," Enrique called over his shoulder as he headed for the door.

He made another sweep of his neighborhood, whistling and clapping and asking people he met if they'd seen a scared-looking little dog anywhere. But he didn't find Boy, and no one had seen him. When Francisco finished the flyers, Enrique would post them all over on telephone poles, in store windows, and on fences. Somebody was sure to find Boy and return him, he told himself.

Maybe Boy had found his way home on his own, and he'd be in the apartment waiting when Enrique opened the door. But that wasn't too likely. Boy had a terrible sense of direction. The little dog sometimes grew confused finding his way from the bedroom to the kitchen in the compact apartment.

Even so, his heart lofted with hope when he pushed open the door and his mother said, *Enrique, I have a big surprise for you!*

Chapter Eighteen

Seated on the couch, and causing it to dip in the middle from her weight, was one of the fattest women Enrique had ever seen. She seemed familiar in a vague way to Enrique, who had *maybe* seen her before when she was thinner.

Do you remember Leontina, your grandmother?

Grandmother? How did Juan's mother become Enrique's grandmother? To him, she was just an expanded version of the woman he'd met once at the wedding years ago.

Enrique, come give grandmother a hug, the old woman clucked. *"Qué lindo, lindo, lindo."* Leontina held out her lardy arms, the flesh on them wobbling like gelatin. *Come on. Don't be afraid.* She had warts on her cheeks and thick black whiskers under her chin.

Enrique took a deep breath, as though preparing to dive into some pretty murky water, and he plunged into those jiggly arms.

Leontina smelled of mentholated cigarettes and the spray people use to cover up bathroom smells. *Just like my Juan at this age,* she said, finally releasing Enrique to pull a cigarette from her handbag. *He has Juan's hair too.* She flicked her lighter and inhaled smoke noisily. *"¡Ay qué lindo!"*

Enrique wondered why the old woman thought he resembled Juan. Did she think he was somehow related to his stepfather? Besides he couldn't see how his hair was like Juan's unless she meant that they both had dark hair. Enrique had fine brown curls, while Juan's hair was stiff, as coarse as the brush Enrique's mother used to baste chicken.

Leontina is going to stay with us, Enrique's mother said, smiling hard. *She's going to help you with the babies. You don't have to take care of them by yourself anymore.*

Where would the enormous woman sleep? In the bathtub? Surely, they wouldn't both fit on the couch.

As if reading his mind, his mother added that Juan had gotten a folding cot from the church that Enrique would set up in the kitchen. Leontina would sleep on the couch. Before Enrique could ask any questions or form a complaint, his mother grabbed up her purse and rushed off to work.

We are going to have a good time, no? Leontina said, and she pulled a deck of cards bound with a rubber band from her bag. *Do you play cards?*

Enrique nodded. When Juan first dated his mother and was still trying to seem nice, he had taught Enrique to play a few card games.

Leontina shuffled the deck and dealt. Her thick sausage-shaped fingers were surprisingly quick when she handled the cards.

Did Juan Jr. come back from the hospital? Enrique asked.

Yes, they are all three sleeping like angels. When they wake up, you will have to show me how to change the diapers and how to feed them. It's been such a long time. She sighed.

Later, Enrique figured out that whenever Leontina

said that he would have to "show" her how to do this or that, she meant that Enrique would have to do whatever it was by himself.

That afternoon, Leontina won the first game, then the second. *Do you have any money?* she asked, chugging like a locomotive on what must have been her twentieth cigarette. *We could put some bets.*

Enrique shook his head. He never had money, and this was the one time it was a relief that he didn't. Leontina won hand after hand. Enrique couldn't understand it. Usually, he played pretty well, but she seemed to have all the luck. He watched her more carefully, and then he saw it. She was dealing to herself from the bottom of the deck. Old Leontina was cheating!

I'm tired of playing cards, Enrique said, after losing yet again. His forehead hurt from squinting at his cards through the haze of smoke. *I think I will go out and look for my dog. He got away last night.*

Fine, Leontina said, gathering up the cards. *Bring me some ice water, grandson, and something to eat before you leave.*

Enrique headed to the kitchen to pour her a glass of water. He couldn't think what to give her to eat. Then he remembered some Christmas candy—hard, striped ribbons—that not even Boy would eat. He rattled a few of these onto a saucer for Leontina.

Thank you, grandson, she said. *Don't be gone too long.*

I will be home before the babies wake up, Enrique promised.

Enrique leaped down the steps—two at a time—and

wondered how he was going to like having old Leontina around. Not very much, he decided. Still, it was fine to have a bit of freedom to be outdoors by himself in the late afternoon. Not having the triplets' stroller to push or Boy's leash to pull made Enrique almost feel like he had wings.

He decided to clap and whistle for Boy in the direction of Horacio's house. He still missed Horacio, and he was curious how he'd spent the day. On the way over, the people he passed gave Enrique suspicious looks as he called for Boy. Maybe they thought he'd lost his mind and was calling a make-believe pet. Still he continued clapping and whistling, only a little less noticeably.

Horacio, when Enrique found him, was standing outside the Cuban *bodega* not far from his house and talking with a group of guys Enrique recognized from the gang that ruled his *barrio*. There was Stumpy, El Chivo, Cobra, and Pirata, the tall one who wore a black eye patch. Enrique waited across the street, until they performed their special handshake all around and parted before approaching Horacio.

"Eh, where's the babies, *ese?*" Horacio said when he saw Enrique.

Juan's mother is staying with us. She's watching them while I look for Boy.

Boy got away?

Last night.

I'll help you look for him, Horacio said, and the two boys walked together.

What did those guys want? Enrique asked. Seeing Horacio with that group had made him uneasy.

Are you my mother?

No, but I'm just curious.

They were telling me about Itchy.

What about Itchy? Enrique asked. *Did he get locked up for having that knife at school?* Enrique sure hoped so.

Yes, but he's going to get out one of these days.

Not for a long time.

I don't know, Horacio said, scratching his chin. *McNulty's pretty crowded. Pirata thinks they'll only keep him a few months.*

What's going to happen when he's released? He can't come back to school. Enrique remembered Mr. Toro announcing at a school assembly last year that anyone who brought a weapon to school would be automatically expelled.

What's going to happen when he gets out is that he's going to make me into carnitas and eat me for lunch, if I'm still around.

Where are you going?

Stupid, I'm not going anywhere. He put a contract on me, don't you understand. He's got the Paiute Street Regulars after me. That what those guys were talking to me about.

Why did he put a contract on you? He wanted to fight me. Enrique couldn't understand this. *I'm the one who kicked him down. Two times.*

Enrique, Horacio said, turning to grab his friend's shoulders. *Listen to me. You are nobody on the streets.*

Nobody knows you, and nobody cares what you do. You are all the time shut up with those babies. You never come out. I bet Itchy doesn't even know your name.

But I was the one who made him mad.

"It don't matter what you do, *ese*," Horacio said, reverting to English, probably to sound tougher. "You got zero reputation."

What about you? You don't have reputation.

I got uncles, cousins, friends all connected with White Fence. So Paiute Street is coming after me and White Fence. Horacio released Enrique and sighed. He resumed walking with his head bent. *It's really about White Fence and Paiute. They hate each other. They're always looking for some reason to fight.*

What are you going to do?

Horacio shrugged. "I ain't going to hide in my house like some old lady, *ese*. It ain't a 'snuff him' contract. It's just a 'kick his ass' contract. Besides I got protection. I got uncles. I got cousins, friends. I'm just going to wait, see what happens.

Are you going to join White Fence?

Dummy, I am in White Fence. You are too. Every guy who lives in this barrio is White Fence. Those little brothers you got at home, they're White Fence too. We all are. Horacio rolled up the sleeve of his flannel shirt to reveal a tattoo on his forearm—a picket fence with a burning heart in the middle. A ribbon rippled across the heart. *Por Vida*, it read. *That's what White Fence is, all of us. You just don't know it.*

Enrique thought about what Horacio said all the way home. He thought about Maclovio, Hilario, and Yunior, all belonging to a street gang that rolled drunks, sniffed glue, stole cars, and sold drugs. The babies couldn't even walk or talk—they didn't even have teeth yet—but they were part of this thing, this White Fence, according to Horacio. And he was part of it too.

Enrique wondered if he would have a tattoo like Horacio's if he were out on the streets every day. What Horacio had said about Enrique being a nobody because he babysat the triplets rang true. He was no stronger or smarter than Horacio. If guys as scary as El Chivo, Pirata, and Cobra had approached him, he would have officially joined White Fence in a flash.

A couple of weeks ago, a kid in White Fence had been jumped by the Mission Boys. They beat him to death with a tire iron. That could have been me, Enrique thought. He remembered how he forced breath into little Juan's lungs, and then he thought about saving his brother's life another way. *He saved me,* Enrique said to himself, thinking about the dead kid as he mounted the steps to the apartment.

And he didn't mind walking in the door to find Leontina snoring in front of a wrestling match on television, as his brothers screamed in the bedroom. It didn't bother him to change their cod-stinky diapers—one after another—as they squirmed and wriggled to get free. He even liked spooning mashed yams and strained chicken between their smacking pink gums. And when Maclovio spit a stream of apple juice onto his chin, Enrique just wiped his face with a dish towel and laughed.

Juan came home early that night. Enrique figured his stepfather must have skipped one of his meetings when he heard the key scratching into the lock. He was in the bedroom, toweling the babies after their bath when Juan called out, "Hey, I'm home."

After a few moments, his stepfather poked his head in the bedroom. Enrique was struggling to shove Hilario's plump arms into the sleeves of a t-shirt, but he could see it when he glanced up at Juan's flushed face and shiny eyes. He sensed it before he smelled the toxic fog rolling from his stepfather's sweaty body. He knew before Juan slurred another word: his stepfather was drunk again.

Chapter Nineteen

Enrique tossed restlessly on the cot in the kitchen. The lumpy mattress was sheathed in plastic that crackled and crunched so much when he moved that he felt like he was sleeping on a bag of potato chips. On top of this, the kitchen reeked like an ashtray from the cigarette butts Leontina dumped in the trashcan under the sink. And when his mother returned from work, angry voices rang out from the front room, keeping him awake. At one point the babies woke crying, and Enrique had to get up and fold the bed, so his mother could get to the stove to heat their bottles. When Enrique finally dozed, he had the feeling that he was not alone in the kitchen. He shot upright in the cot, causing the steel frame to fold on him like the jaws of a rusted bear trap.

"Boy?" he whispered, struggling to free himself.

Go back to sleep, his mother said. *It's only me.*

She stood in the light pouring through the window from a streetlamp. Though her voice was steady and her shoulders still, Enrique could tell she was crying and that she had been standing there a long time, crying without tears.

Mamá, what is it? He pulled himself out of the cot and rose to put an arm around her. *What do you want me to do?*

Son, there is nothing you can do.

I'm sorry you feel sad.

Go back to sleep. You need to rest for school.

Enrique slept little after that. The entire day, he felt

tired and dull, like his head was stuffed with cotton balls that muffled everything he heard and saw. He snapped at Francisco on the way to school for making the print on the flyers too small. He irritated Ms. Byers by not following directions during a dictation exercise. He was relieved the class wasn't scheduled to meet with Mrs. Jaramillo's group again until Friday. Surely, he would say a few things he'd regret if he had to deal with Flor that day. He didn't have the homework—he didn't even know it had been assigned—in Mr. Sanchez's class, and he lost his math book during nutrition. In P.E., he stumbled in with the last group—the chubby kids and the asthmatics—at the end of the mile, huffing and puffing. Not even Horacio (who was absent again) would have been able to joke him out of this dark mood.

At last the day ended, and Enrique threw his books into his locker and slammed it shut in relief. He didn't even try to remember if he had homework.

"Young man!" A sharp voice pierced the din of raised voices and locker banging.

Enrique glanced up. Dean Hardin stood in the breezeway with her hands on her hips, staring straight at him. "Young man, pick up that litter." She pointed at a candy bar wrapper that had settled near Enrique's feet.

"I didn't drop it," Enrique said.

"Did I ask who dropped it? I told you to pick it up."

"Pick it up yourself." Enrique turned and strode away, ignoring her.

"Young man, young man, I'm talking to you! Come back here!"

Enrique could tell she'd forgotten his name. Did the

brain cancer do that? Make people forget? He told himself it wasn't his fault she was going to die. It wasn't his fault Juan got drunk last night and made his mother too sad to sleep. It wasn't his fault Horacio joined White Fence and had a "kick his butt" contract out on him. Yet, somehow, these things made Enrique feel guilty and responsible, as thought they wouldn't have happened if he had never been born.

Heading home, Enrique stared down at the pavement. He didn't want to see anyone he knew. He had no desire to talk and joke and act cool. All he wanted was to get home, pass the afternoon and evening as quickly as possible, and start again the next day. He picked up his pace to speed through this part of town.

A small old woman tottered in front of him, taking up the whole sidewalk with her shade umbrella. She was leading a little dog on a rhinestone leash, and both of them took short, choppy steps that made their progress incredibly slow. Enrique stepped into the street to pass her. The dog wore a strand of green pearls around its neck with the collar. It was a rickety-looking brown and gray mutt that looked a lot like—

"*Boy*!" Enrique fell to his knees and cradled the dog in his arms. Boy's skinny tail whipped with excitement as he licked Enrique's cheek and chin. His fur smelled of talcum powder and lipstick. "Boy, it's you! I found you!"

"Leave my dog alone," the old woman said, and she jerked on the leash. She was a shriveled-looking white woman, who'd probably lived in the area since before it turned into a *barrio*. She had bright blue eyes like the dolls Maricela kept in her bedroom, and a cloud of thin pinkish hair tacked down with red plastic clips shaped like butterflies. "Leave him alone."

"This is my dog." Enrique stood to face her. "He ran away a few days go. I have looked everywhere for him."

Boy tried to jump all the way up into Enrique's arms. "See, he knows me."

"This is my dog," she said. "This is Simon. Simon, come here." She yanked the leash, pulling Boy away from Enrique.

"Lady, this is my dog, and I can prove it." He unfolded one of the flyers from his shirt pocket. "Look, see this? It's a lost-dog flyer."

"That's not a picture of a dog," she said, squinting at Enrique's drawing. "That's some kind of bug or lizard, isn't it?"

"I can't draw too good," Enrique explained. "Read the writing, though."

"How do you expect me to read that? The print is smaller than fleas." She dug into her handbag and produced a glasses case. She snapped it open and put on a pair of thick glasses. "Why, it's in Spanish. I can't read Spanish."

"The bottom half is English, see?" Enrique began reading: "Lost Chihuahua-mix, answers to the name 'Boy.'"

"He answers to the name 'Simon,' too," she said.

"'Brown and gray fur. Knows some tricks—"

"What tricks?"

Enrique shrugged. "Dancing, begging—"

The old lady snorted. "That's not a trick! Just go

down to the mission district. Everyone knows *that* trick."

Enrique continued, "'Owner Enrique Suarez.' That's me."

"What's the reward?"

"I didn't put a reward," Enrique admitted.

"You must not want your dog back if you can't even offer a reward."

"I don't have nothing to give for a reward."

"Still, this is my dog—Simon. Had him for ten years, and then he ran away. Now, he's come back, and I can prove it."

"No way," Enrique said, reminding himself he probably shouldn't shout at old ladies.

"Come with me. I'll show you. I just live over there." She pointed down a side street.

Enrique hesitated, bouncing on the balls of his feet. He could snatch Boy and bolt. She'd never catch him.

"Come on," she said. "I'm not going to bite you."

Enrique sighed, and he followed her to a small yellow house surrounded by a short brick wall, which was duly tagged by White Fence. Inside the wall, Enrique saw a thick green lawn bordered with purple and yellow flowers, splashes of bright color against the dull brick.

"Those are my pansies," the woman said. "That's Simon's house over there." She pointed out a wooden dog house with a water bowl near the door. "Of course, he sleeps indoors at night. This is just a shelter for when he's outside."

"It's nice," Enrique said.

"Come inside. I have pictures I can show you, pictures of Simon taken a long time ago. I can prove this is my dog."

Enrique stepped into the cool, dark house that reeked of lemon furniture polish. A clock ticked like a heartbeat in the front room.

"Sit down," the woman said, pointing at the sofa, which was covered with plastic. Air escaping under his weight made a gasping sound when he sank onto it. He gazed around at the knick-knacks, bookshelves, and framed pictures, thinking of the few photos of him and the triplets that his mother had tacked up on the walls of the apartment.

The old woman reached under a coffee table for a thick photo album. "Look here, what's your name. What *is* your name?"

"Enrique."

"Enrique, I'm Mrs. Dabrowski, Ethel Dabrowski. My friends call me 'Pixie,' but you can call me Mrs. Dabrowski." She pushed the heavy album onto his lap and sat beside him. In another room, Boy lapped water noisily. "Don't worry," she said. "I always keep the toilet shut. He has a water dish in the kitchen." She flipped through the album's pages, stopping to show Enrique a snapshot of a black Scottish terrier. "See, there he is. That's Simon." Mrs. Dabrowski was also in the picture. Enrique recognized the scowl on her face, but she was a young woman in the black and white photograph. He guessed the picture was taken thirty or forty years ago. She turned to another snapshot of the Scotty dog, posed near a birthday cake. "That was his birthday. I always bake a cake for his birthday."

"Missus, the dog you're showing here is a different dog."

"No, he's not."

"Yes, he is. Look. This dog is black. Boy is brown and gray. Look at him."

Boy trotted into the room, his toenails clicking on the wood floor. He leapt into Mrs. Dablowski's lap. She ran her knotted fingers over his fur. "The pictures have gotten darker over time."

"But it's another kind of dog here," Enrique said. "Look at the little pointy ears and the mouth. Boy is not like that. He's a Chihuahua-mix. They're different dogs."

"Simon ate more when he was younger. He was a little fatter, had a double-chin, didn't you, Simon?" She lifted boy to nuzzle him.

"And look at you. Isn't this you in that picture?"

"Yes, that's me."

"When did you take this picture?"

"1965 or '66, I think, because that's the Impala in the background. We had just bought that car second-hand."

Boy yawned and snuggled against her knee.

"I think that's like over thirty years ago, isn't it? Boy is sure old, but no dog lives that long. This can't be your dog."

The old woman's blue eyes filmed over. She rose, dumping Boy to the carpet. "Are you calling me a liar? Are you trying to tell me I'm crazy? A crazy old woman? Is that what you think I am?"

Enrique agreed, of course, but thought it would be better not to say so.

"If that's what you think, you can get out of here. Take your stupid little dog with you. Get out! Just get out!"

Enrique scrambled off the couch and grabbed Boy. He was out the door before she could find something to throw at him. His heart pounded in his throat, and he was shaking as he ran through the yellow gate. He was nearly home when he noticed the strand of plastic green pearls still draped around Boy's neck. Enrique tried to pull it off, but the beads were tangled in Boy's collar.

As if old Ethel Dabrowski were hot on his heels, he leapt up the stairs, two at a time, and burst into the apartment, where he shut and locked the door behind him.

His mother and Leontina's voices rang from the kitchen

A man needs to be a man, Leontina was saying. *You don't let my son be a man in this house.*

Juan is as much a man as he wants to be, his mother said.

But a man needs to be free in is home. He works hard

I work hard too.

A man is different. He needs to feel he is a man. Men drink. They like to drink. They don't need a woman, like their mamá, telling them they can't drink in their own house!

Leontina, Enrique's mother said in a slow and steady

voice. *Juan has a problem with drinking. He knows it. That's why he goes to his meetings.*

He goes because you make him go. Think how he feels in this house. You won't let him take a little drink after a hard day of work, and you make him go, like a little boy being punished, to those meetings. Think how he feels. I never told my husband what to do. I can't imagine what would have happened if I told Felipe, rest his soul, he could not drink in his own house.

He might still be alive, thought Enrique, standing by the door, listening. The old man had died of liver cancer.

I don't want to be married to a drunk, Enrique's mother said.

Are you saying my Felipe was a drunk?

Enrique looked at Boy and nodded.

I'm not talking about Felipe. I'm talking about Juan. I don't like him when he drinks.

He drinks because you won't let him be the man in this house. You make that boy more the man around here than poor Juan. And that boy is spoiled too. He doesn't wash the dishes—

Don't tell me about my son, Leontina. You don't know anything about my son. The low pitch of his mother's voice signaled her anger.

And you don't know anything about my son. You don't know how to treat a man. You, younger women, don't know how to let a man run his house. That's why they leave and you have divorces. In my day, women knew how to treat men right. We didn't need divorce.

Things are different these days, Leontina. Women

have to take care of the children and work. Men should be able, at least, to take care of themselves.

Except for his mother's tired-sounding voice, the argument reminded Enrique of the *telenovelas* that Maricela's mother watched in the evenings.

I like you, Dora. You're like a daughter to me, Leontina said. *I never said one word when Juan told me he was marrying a woman with a son. I thought there would be problems, but I thought you would try hard to solve them.*

Juan needs to try to solve them too.

Leontina sighed. *This is what I mean. You do not understand that it is the woman's job to make the marriage work. You have not learned anything. Let me ask you this—where is your first husband? Why didn't you make that work?*

Enrique's mother was silent.

I beg you, Leontina continued, *don't make my son's life a misery because you refuse to make this marriage work. Don't drive him away like you did the first one.*

Enrique couldn't take any more. He burst into the kitchen, still cradling Boy in his arms. *Mamá, I found Boy!* He kissed her cheek, tasting a salty wetness on his lips. She stood over the stove, stirring a deep blue-and-white speckled enamel pot of beans. Her eyes were red-rimmed, and her nose looked swollen. Leontina sat at the table, peeling roasted chilis and plopping them into the blender. She had her bare, cracked and yellowed feet propped on a dining chair.

How wonderful! his mother said. *I was hoping you would find him soon. I know how you missed him.*

A dog! Leontina shrieked at the sight of Boy as though he were a sewer rat. *Don't bring a dog in here! Filthy thing! Take it out before I get sick!*

Chapter Twenty

Enrique glanced at Leontina's vein-scribbled ankles and corn-crusted toes, then at Boy's rough, but clean fur and clear eyes. *Boy's not dirty,* he said. *He's a clean dog.*

Take him outside! Get rid of that dog!

You better put him out on the porch for now, son. His mother's voice sounded weary, as though she couldn't take much more.

But he could fall off. Enrique worried that Boy was skinny enough to slide between the rails and fall to the street below.

Then tie him up, son. Just for now.

Not just for now! Leontina said, and she lit a cigarette. *You have to keep that thing out there. You can't have a dog inside the house with babies.* She gulped a lungful of smoke and exhaled through her nostrils like an angry dragon. *It's not good for their health.*

Enrique carried Boy out to the porch. He hooked his collar to his leash and tied that to the door knob. *I'm sorry, Boy,* he said, nearly regretting that he'd removed the dog from his comfortable home with Mrs. Dabrowski. Boy wagged his tail. He cocked one ear and tilted his head, a puzzled look in his soft brown eyes.

You have to stay out here for now, Enrique told him.

Boy wagged his tail a bit slower and yipped.

When Enrique stepped back inside for Boy's water bowl, the little dog began to whine and scratch at the door. He had never been shut out on the porch before. Enrique imagined the height scared him. Boy didn't seem at all interested in the water and bit of cheese that Enrique brought him. He just wanted to get inside. Enrique flashed on the old woman's cool dark house and the little dog house on the thick grass near the pansies in her yard. He bit his lip and shook his head.

"*¡Lindo, lindo, lindo!*" cried Leontina, as if Enrique had just arrived home from school. *Where is my kiss? Where is my hug?* She extended her flabby arms and puckered her lips, which she must have painted with a waxy red lipstick after her cigarette.

Enrique thought fast. *I need to wash. The dog licked me.*

"*¡Sucio!*" Leontina shouted. "*¡Cochino marano, asqueroso, barroso!*" She let loose a stream of words that followed Enrique all the way to the bathroom. He was amazed she knew so many words for filth. As soon as he finished washing his hands, she barreled into the bathroom after him to scrub hers, as if just the thought of being licked by a dog had soiled her.

Enrique found his mother before the mirror in the front room tucking her curls under her hairnet for work. *Don't let Leontina bother you*, she told Enrique in a low voice. *She doesn't like dogs. When she gets used to him, you can bring Boy back inside.*

Mamá, this is our home. Why does she tell us what to do? Enrique asked.

She is Juan's mother. We have to show respect.

I don't respect her, Enrique whispered. *She smokes all the time, she cheats at cards—*

When you show respect for those who haven't yet

earned your respect, you are really showing respect for yourself, his mother said.

But isn't that like lying? Like being fake?

Only when you do it to mock the person.

I don't understand.

You will, she told him. *Someday you will.*

Enrique hated when people said that. It was like they thought his brain wasn't big enough yet.

Before you put him to bed, give Juanito the medicine in the kitchen. Just one half of the dropper, where the line is.

I will.

She kissed Enrique. *If I don't hurry, I will miss the bus.*

After his mother left for work, Enrique decided to take advantage of having the old woman stay with them and to go out for a while with Boy before his brothers woke up. Somehow the apartment seemed hotter and the walls crowded in more closely with Leontina around. For one thing, she sweated a lot. A great cloud of steam seemed to follow her as she lumbered from room to room, filling every pocket of space with damp, dense, and unbreathable heat. While she was washing up in the bathroom, Enrique took the opportunity to retrieve Boy and slam out of the apartment, calling, *I am going out!*

Boy, delighted to be released from the porch, trotted alongside Enrique with his tail curled high, as they headed for Horacio's house.

Again Enrique located his friend outdoors in conference with Stumpy, Chivo, Cobra and Pirata. This time, they were drinking beers. Enrique started to wheel around and head home, but Horacio caught a glimpse of him and waved him over. "Eh, *ese*, come over here!" Enrique crossed the street to join Horacio and the others. "What's up?"

"Eh, *carnal*, you found Boy!"

"Some old lady had him."

Horacio introduced Enrique all around in English. The guy they called Chivo, Enrique remembered, spoke very little Spanish. He was a redheaded, freckle-faced boy with green eyes, whose real name was Brandon Wexler.

Chivo offered Enrique a beer from the six-pack sweating in a bag by the curb. Enrique shook his head. "I'm good." To him, the offer was like an invitation to join the club his stepfather belonged to, an invitation to be stupid and mean. Besides, the smell of beer made Enrique want to gag.

"My friend don't drink, *ese*," Horacio explained a bit awkwardly, "'cause he's driving."

The others laughed, and Enrique gave a weak smile. He wondered how long it would take him to come up with a good excuse to get away.

Pirata rolled an empty can into the gutter and popped open another. Then the pirate scratched his stomach and belched loudly. "I ain't seen you around much," he said to Enrique. "Who you with?"

"Nobody," Enrique said.

"Where do you live?"

"Terrace View Apartments."

The pirate nodded and was silent for a moment before he said, "You're White Fence. Ain't you been initiated yet?"

Stumpy snorted. "He's a kid. Look at him, out for a walk with the little dog."

"It don't matter," Cobra said. He slicked back his hair with a comb. "We got seven-, eight-year-old kids running grass for us in the park. You ain't never too young."

"*Pues,* Stumpy's right. Enrique's just a kid from school. He wants to study French," Horacio said, offering this as evidence of Enrique's unfitness to join the gang.

"You let all these dudes talk for you?" Pirata asked. "You don't got nothing to say for yourself? You looking to be initiated, or what?"

Enrique shook his head, thinking fast. He had heard of one guy who'd been crippled during initiation into White Fence. "Nah, man, don't waste your time. I'm going to be moving soon."

"Oh, yeah," Cobra said. "Where to, man?"

Enrique blurted the first place to come to mind. "Canada."

"*Canada?*" Horacio sounded impressed. No way did Enrique think his friend believed him, but clearly he admired a lie of this size.

"Yeah, I'm moving in a couple of weeks." Enrique shrugged and checked an imaginary watch on his wrist. "Now, I got to go to work."

"Where do you work?" Chivo asked.

"I watch my brothers," Enrique said, dropping his

voice, so maybe they wouldn't hear him, "for my mother."

"A freaking *babysitter*," Pirata said. "You're right, kid. You don't need no initiation. You need Sesame Street, *ese!*"

As Enrique and Boy hurried away, waves of laugher rippled after them. Enrique's whole body burned with shame. *Gallina*, that's what he was to them—a huge chicken in gym shorts, walking a tiny dog. Enrique had always suspected he was *gallina*, and usually, he didn't mind it too much. He knew, for instance, he was more cowardly than others because before Itchy jumped him, he had never been in a fight before. He didn't even count the Itchy incidents as fights because they were mainly attacks in which he only tried to protect himself and squirm away.

Most guys and a lot of girls his age had fights all the time. Even Francisco fought Jorge one time in their garage and bloodied his brother's nose. But Enrique had never punched anyone. He hadn't ever wanted to hit anyone. Of course, he often wished he could flush his stepfather down the toilet, but he never had the urge to strike him. He merely imagined himself transformed into a giant hand that plucked Juan up and dropped him into an enormous toilet bowl and then pressed the handle. No way he would ever try to fight Juan or anyone else.

Sometimes he worried about being a *gallina*. Once he talked to his mother about it, and she told him he was too smart for fighting. Of course, this was the kind of things mothers always said, and he recognized that he probably caught his *gallina*-ism from her in the first place. "*¡Cuidado!*" was her favorite word. It rolled off her tongue at least a dozen times a day.

Enrique and Boy were about a block from the apartment when they passed a man walking a sleek Rottweiler on a short chain. The bigger dog wheezed and snorted, chafing at his choke to get at Boy. The man tried to hold him, but lost his grip. Enrique watched in horror as the Rottweiler lurched at Boy. But Boy simply rolled onto his back, baring his throat and whipping his tail back and forth. Before Enrique could snatch his dog away, the large dog had sniffed Boy's genitals and hefted a mighty back leg to squirt a nearby telephone pole.

"Sorry about that." The man regained his grip on the dog.

"It's okay," Enrique told him. "My dog is fine." On his feet again, Boy shook the dust from his back, ready to continue the walk. Even Boy was *gallina*, Enrique thought, but at least the little dog seemed adjusted to his condition. Unlike Enrique, he accepted it and it didn't bother him.

In the apartment, Leontina was again snoring in front of the television—a stock-car race blared from the set—while the babies whimpered in the bedroom. Enrique figured there was no harm in letting Boy inside while he got the triplets ready to go out. He would give the dog a bonus walk to make up for his exile on the porch. Enrique changed the triplets, fed them, and then called Maricela over to help him manage the walk. The whole time, Leontina never once stirred.

As Maricela pushed the stroller over the cracked and crumbly sidewalk, she was oddly quiet.

"What's wrong?" Enrique asked.

"Nothing."

"Come on, tell me what it is." Enrique stopped and turned to face his friend.

Maricela sighed. "It's nothing. Only, I thought we were friends. And friends tell each other important things, right?"

Enrique nodded.

"They're saying you're going out with that Flor, and you don't even tell me anything. I thought we were friends." Maricela's voice trembled.

"Look, Maricela, I'm sorry. I've been really busy. Juan's mother is at the apartment with us, and she takes up my time. And Juan's drinking again. I've had stuff on my mind."

"You have time for Flor."

"We're just in that project together," Enrique said. "She asked me to the movies 'cause her aunt works there. She said she could get me in for free. She's not my girlfriend or anything."

"That's not what she thinks. She's telling every-one..."

"She's not my girlfriend, and neither are you!"

They didn't speak the rest of the way. Maricela helped him get the babies upstairs without even looking at him once. Holding Hilario and Maclovio in his arms, Enrique stood at Maricela's door. She held Yunior against her shoulder.

"Look, I'm sorry, Mari—"

"You can get Yunior after you put those two in," she said, and then she slammed her door shut.

When Enrique returned for Yunior, Maricela's mother met him at the door and handed him the baby.

Before Leontina woke up, Enrique had to put Boy out on the porch again. Then, he "showed" Leontina how to bathe the babies and how to give Yunior his medicine. He was just "showing" her how to play with the babies to get them worn-out for bed, when Juan stumbled in the front door. This time, his stepfather lugged a double six-pack of beer under one arm.

"*Mamacita!*" he cried, throwing his free arm around Leontina.

This was Enrique's cue to hustle the triplets to bed. While he stuffed them into their pajamas and gave them their last bottles, Juan and his mother popped open beers and smoked their heads off in the front room. They ignored Enrique for the rest of the evening, and he was thankful for that. He made his bed in the kitchen, and in spite of the noise from the television and their yakking, Enrique fell asleep right away on the crackling sheets.

He had no idea what time it was when the shouting woke him. Juan's voice shook the apartment like thunder. All the babies began screaming, and Enrique's mother wept. *No, Juan, no, please, I beg you, no!* she cried. Then Enrique heard a noise that sounded like a slap. Something crashed into the wall. He bolted out of the cot and raced to his mother's room.

Chapter Twenty-One

Enrique yanked open the door. His mother sat on the bed, hugging her shoulders. A thin line of blood trailed from her nose to her chin. The babies howled, standing and holding onto the bars of their cribs like hysterical little prisoners. And Juan was kneeling in the closet, throwing shoes and clothing over his shoulder as if he were digging a burrow for himself. *Where is it, woman? Where did you hide it?* he cried.

Enrique caught his mother's eye and put a finger to his lips, so she wouldn't call out his name. Then he stepped softly on the balls of his feet toward Juan. Enrique felt weirdly calm, like he was watching a movie of himself on a videotape player that he could speed up or slow down as he liked. A slipper flew out of the closet, glanced his thigh. Enrique ignored it.

Where is it, you whore! Juan tore clothes from their hangers. *If I don't find it, I'll kill you!*

Enrique held the closet door. He took a deep breath, and then he pushed it with all his force, shoving Juan into the dark room. He turned the lock.

Juan hollered like a maniac. *Open the door! Open the door!* He beat and kicked at it. But the closet, which used to be a maintenance supply room, held firm, and the lock was a double-bolt.

Enrique's mother leapt from the bed. She pulled open drawers and grabbed out clothes. *Get dressed, son. If we're still here when he gets out, I don't know what he will do.*

Where will we go?

To tía Ceci's house. Go call a taxi.

What about Leontina?

Don't wake her up. Be very quiet.

Enrique tiptoed past the sleeping old woman on the couch to the wall-mounted telephone in the kitchen. He decided to phone his aunt before calling a cab.

Tía Ceci was his favorite person in the world, next to his mother, but he rarely got to see her because Juan hated her so much. Ceci had the habit of saying whatever popped into her head, and sometimes she insulted Juan with her joking remarks. Juan also called her indecent because she was unmarried and had many boyfriends. Because of this, he wouldn't let Enrique's mother call or visit her much.

Enrique dialed his aunt's familiar number, and after a few rings, Ceci picked up the phone. "Hello?"

Tía Ceci, it's me, Enrique.

Enrique, what's happened? Her voice was husky with sleep. *Are you okay? Is the baby sick again?*

No, he's fine. It's Juan. He's acting crazy. I think he hit my mother.

¡Cabrón! Where is he now?

I locked him in the closet.

Did you call the police?

I can't do that. Enrique's mother's citizenship was a complicated matter. *We want to come to your house. I was going to call a cab.*

Don't call a cab. We'll come and get you. Be outside in about fifteen minutes. Until then, you should wait at the neighbors' house. What's the name of that little girl across the way?

Maricela.

Wait at Maricela's place until we get there.

Is someone coming with you?

Yes, you can meet my new boyfriend. We'll be right over. She hung up the phone.

Enrique dressed quickly and threw some underwear, shorts, and t-shirts into a grocery bag. Then he tossed in his copy of *The Little Prince.* He loaded another bag with all the baby food, bottles, and bibs he could round up in the kitchen.

Juan continued pounding and kicking at the closet door, cursing and threatening to kill everyone.

Mamá, Enrique whispered, *tía Ceci is coming for us in a few minutes. I didn't need to call the cab.*

Help me get the babies' things. Hurry. I'm afraid that door won't hold.

Enrique stubbed his toe on the coffee table and dropped the bag full of baby food. Nothing broke, but it made a terrible clunking sound. He shot a glance at Leontina. Still mummified in the sheets, she snored loudly sounding like the pen full of pigs he'd seen at a farm once, grunting at their trough. That Leontina was some kind of sleeper, all right.

His mother had thrown on a pair of jeans and a faded sweatshirt while he was on the phone. She'd wiped the blood from her face and tied back her hair with a rubber band. She looked to Enrique like a teenager. She was so young and pretty that he wondered, as he often did, why she stayed with Juan. He was sure she could get someone much better than his stepfather. But hey, he thought, being alone on a deserted island surrounded by snapping alligators would be better than being with Juan.

Listen, she whispered. *He stopped.*

The closet had gone quiet.

He probably passed out, Enrique said in a low voice. Then a booming sound burst from the closet. A puff of dust and splinters flew from the door. A pause, then another boom shook the room. Juan must have found something with which to batter the door. *I swear I'll kill you when I get out of here!*

Hurry, Mamá. Let's go to Maricela's apartment. I'll grab Maclovio and Hilario. He opened the front door and kicked the bags out into the hall.

Enrique rapped on the neighbors' door.

Maricela's father, wearing only boxer shorts and an undershirt, swung open the door. *What's going on over there? I'm going to call the police.*

Juan's drunk, Enrique explained. *He's says he's going to kill us. Please can we stay with you until my aunt comes for us?*

Pues, come on then before you wake the whole building.

Enrique pushed the bags into his neighbor's arms and dashed back to the apartment to get his brothers and his mother. Then he returned for the diaper bags his mother had filled. Racing through the door, Enrique felt a sudden tightness at his shoulder. His feet flew out ahead of him, but his shoulder was caught, landing him on his bottom in the hall. He dropped the bags and struggled to free his shoulder. The diaper bag strap had caught on the door knob. Enrique breathed deeply in relief.

A face, slathered in what looked like plaster, peered at him from the end of the dark hall. Enrique gasped at the dark eyes staring out from this weird white mask. The creature opened its mouth to speak. "What's going on here? It's the middle of the night, boy."

Enrique recognized his neighbor's voice. It was just Mrs. Santos, wearing some kind of nightly skin treatment and not a monster from hell as he'd thought. "The diaper bag," he said. "It got caught in the door."

"It's the middle of the night," she repeated.

"Yes, I'm sorry," Enrique said.

The face disappeared into the shadows, and a door slammed shut. Then, Enrique heard *tía* Ceci's horn bleating from the street below.

With help from Maricela's father, Enrique and his mother managed to rush the babies and bags downstairs and into Ceci's car before Juan could free himself from the closet. Enrique felt like a daring character in an escape movie as he tossed the bags into his aunt's trunk. With a terse hello to the new boyfriend, Enrique leapt into the backseat with his mother and the babies. As Ceci sped away from the curb, he felt so relieved that he laughed and tickled Maclovio's bare foot.

What happened? Ceci asked.

It's Juan. He's drunk and acting like a fool. Enrique's mother stared out the window, frowning.

He's an idiot, Dora. I don't know how you put up with him. Ceci turned to the silent, bearded man with a ponytail who was sitting beside her. "Hey, I want you to meet my sister and nephews. This is Dora. She doesn't speak much English. And that's her son Enrique and the babies are Maclovio, Hilario, and Yunior. Enrique speaks English pretty well, don't you?"

"I guess so," Enrique said.

Dora, Ceci said to her sister in Spanish, *this is my friend Glen.*

"*¿Es gabacho?*" Enrique's mother asked.

Ceci and Glen laughed. "I don't know much Spanish," he said, "but I do know that word. Yeah, I guess I am a cracker, a honky, or whatever."

"It doesn't mean those things," Ceci protested. "Tell him, Enrique."

"It just means you're a white guy," Enrique said.

"Doesn't it mean I'm a little clue-less? And selfish and stupid too? Doesn't it have a negative meaning?"

"I guess so." Enrique shrugged. There was no real pride associated with being called "gabacho."

"It's like being called 'gringo,'" Ceci said with a laugh. "We won't expect much from you, let's put it that way."

Ceci spoke English very well. She had graduated from college in Mexico, and now she worked as a translator for a book company. She was younger than Enrique's mother and almost as pretty. Ceci changed boyfriends almost as often as she changed into the many dresses stuffed in her closet. It seemed to Enrique, there was a new one for every occasion. That was too bad because this Glen seemed all right. Enrique knew better, though, than to get too attached to any of Ceci's boyfriends.

Tía Ceci was about to cross an intersection with a green light when a spotted dog loped into the middle of the street. She pressed the brakes hard and the car screeched to a stop so as not to hit the stray. "Darn dog," she said.

"Boy!" cried Enrique. "Turn back, *tía*, turn back! I forgot to get Boy!"

Chapter Twenty-Two

Tía Ceci turned the car onto a freeway ramp. "Enrique, we can't go back now," she said. "It's too late. Your mother is upset, and Juan is probably out of that closet by now. It would be too dangerous to go back."

"We have to go back!" Enrique leaned forward as far as he could. "Leontina hates dogs. Juan doesn't like Boy either. They might hurt him."

"You left your dog back there?" Glen asked.

"Yes, we were in a big hurry. I just forgot about him. We have to go back."

"You know I'd do anything for you, Enrique," Ceci said, "but we can't go back there tonight."

"Please, *please!*"

"I have an idea." Glen turned to face Enrique in the backseat. Ceci's new boyfriend had a nose like a beak, but warm, friendly looking eyes. "Let's drop your mother, the little ones, and Ceci at her place, and I'll drive you back to get the dog. Will you let me use your car, Ceci? I've only got the bike at your house."

"You don't get it, Glen. The man is dangerous. I don't want my nephew up in that apartment with him."

"No, no," Enrique's mother said. "Enrique no go back."

"I'll go upstairs and ask for the dog. What can he do to me? He doesn't have a gun, does he?"

"I don't think so." Enrique had never seen one in the apartment, and besides, he was pretty sure he'd have been shot dead long ago if old Juan had a gun.

"I don't know if that's such a good idea, Glen," Ceci said, but Enrique could tell from her voice that she was wavering.

"Come on, Ceci. It's the boy's dog. At least, let me try."

"Please, *tía*, please."

"You promise you won't let Enrique go up there?" Ceci asked Glen.

Glen held up his hand as though he was about to take an oath. "Word of honor."

"I guess you can use the car then." Ceci turned to her sister to explain the plan.

In a short while, they arrived at Ceci's pink stucco duplex and unloaded the babies and bags. Enrique kissed his mother, who made him swear he would not go into the apartment and he would not talk to Juan under any circumstances. Then he and Glen climbed back into the car.

"Ready, Batman?" Glen asked, revving the engine.

"I guess." Enrique wasn't in the mood for kidding around.

They drove in silence most of the way, Enrique hoping his aunt's new boyfriend would be able to persuade Juan to hand over Boy. It didn't seem likely, though. When Juan decided to be mean and stubborn, there wasn't much anyone could do but keep quiet and wait until Juan forgot about whatever it was that bugged him.

"What kind of dog is it?" Glen asked as they approached the apartment building.

"Chihuahua-mix."

"Ah, a little dog. What's its name again?"

"Boy."

"Boy? How old is he?"

"He's about nine years old."

"Holy cow," Glen said. "That's an elderly dog. And you still call him 'Boy'?"

Enrique shrugged. "It's too late to change his name now."

"Isn't that the building?"

"Yes, it's Apartment N, upstairs. Do you want me to go with you?"

"Heck, no! Ceci would skin me alive and bake me in a pie. Wait here for me." Glen jumped out of the car and jogged inside the building, his ponytail bouncing over his collar.

Enrique waited in the darkness. Maybe Juan would be in a "nice" phase by now. He'd noticed that with other adults his stepfather swung from mean to nice a lot. With Enrique, he was mostly mean, but with his mother, Juan went back and forth. This kept her kind of off-balance— confused and anxious about pleasing Juan. But Enrique knew that no one could please him for very long. And no one could tell when he would be nice or mean.

In a few minutes, Glen returned to the car without Boy. "No answer," he said. "I knocked and knocked. I really pounded on that door. Your neighbor threatened to call the police if I didn't stop. I really don't think anyone's there."

"They are there," Enrique said. "Juan is probably passed out, and nothing can wake Leontina."

"Who's that?"

"Juan's mother. She's staying with us."

"I didn't hear a dog in there. Usually dogs get pretty noisy when there's someone at the door, especially in the middle of the night."

He's out on the porch, like a balcony. They made me tie him up out there."

"Where is this porch? Can we see it from here?"

"We have to go to the courtyard," Enrique said. Maybe they could climb the fire escape to reach Boy. "Let's go look."

Glen pulled a flashlight from the glove compartment. Enrique led the way to the courtyard.

"Which one is your apartment?" Glen bounced the light from balcony to balcony.

Enrique caught Glen's wrist and guided the beam. "That one."

"I don't see a dog," Glen said, shining the light between the slats in the railing. "Wait, there's the leash. Oh, God!"

"What?" Enrique said, and then he saw. The leash fell between two slats, and at the end of it, Boy dangled, like a small joint of meat hung in a butcher's shop.

Chapter Twenty-Three

"He must have slipped through the rails." Glen strobed the slats with the flashlight. The night was deep and dark. Shadows in the courtyard shifted like uneasy spirits around the beam of light.

"Or Juan did this." Hot tears of hatred filled Enrique's eyes.

"Shh. Did you hear that?" Glen whispered.

"What?"

"Listen."

Enrique thought he heard a whimpering sound and then a yelp. "Boy?" he called.

The little dog yelped again. Glen shone the light on him. The fake pearls the old woman had draped around Boy's neck had slipped over one of his front paws fashioning a harness around the dog's chest.

"How weird," Glen said. "He's just like suspended up there."

"We got to get him before he hurts himself."

"If you stand on my shoulders, you ought to be able to reach the bottom rung of that fire escape," Glen told Enrique.

Enrique climbed Glen's back and stood shakily on his shoulders. "I can't reach it." He was a good six inches short of the last rung. Boy kept up a steady stream of whimpering and yelping. Enrique worried the dog would twist out of the pearl harness and hang himself.

"Stretch," Glen said. "Stand on your tiptoes and stretch."

"I'll fall." Enrique fought a serious attack of *gallina*-ism.

"You won't fall. But if you do, I'll catch you."

Enrique tiptoed and stretched. He still couldn't reach that last rung.

"Jump for it," Glen told him. "Like you're on a trapeze. Jump!"

If I think about this, I won't do it, he told himself, and Enrique sprung from Glen's shoulders. One hand swung out for the metal bar and caught it, but the other missed, and Enrique swung from his arm like a chimp in a tree. The shadows below rippled like swamp water now, alive with alligators and snakes. Enrique brought his other arm up to grab the rung, steady himself. Then he hoisted up and climbed, quickly but shakily, to the porch.

From there, he carefully reeled Boy's leash up through the railing, and he pulled Boy into his arms. He unbuckled the collar and buried his face in the little dog's coarse fur. Then he kissed Boy's cold nose and ears. Boy yipped and lapped Enrique's face.

"I got him," he whispered down to Glen.

"Can you climb down with him? Or do you want me to catch him?"

"I think I can put him in my shirt and climb down."

The kitchen light flashed on. Enrique stuffed Boy into his t-shirt and knotted it to make a hammock for the tiny dog.

"Hurry!" Glen flicked off the beam.

Enrique swung a leg over the railing and began descending the ladder. The kitchen door yawned open, flooding the narrow porch with light. Leontina's voice rang out: *Who's there?*

How strange, thought Enrique, the woman could probably sleep through a cannon duel in the next room, but whispering, outside on the balcony, wakes her up?

On the last rung, he signaled Glen to catch Boy and chucked the dog into his arms below. Glen set Boy down and reached out to catch Enrique, who closed his eyes before jumping. He didn't open them again until he felt his feet firmly planted on the flagstone walk.

Who is it! Leontina called, as she leaned out into the darkness. *I will call the police.*

Keeping to the shadows in the courtyard, Glen and Enrique, carrying Boy, darted back to the car. They jumped in and coasted—in neutral—away from the building. After half a block, Glen started the ignition. Enrique held Boy close.

"Well done, Rubberman." Glen reached to shake Enrique's hand, and then he pumped Boy's bony paw. "Good job, Wonderdog."

"Thank you, Glen." Enrique forgot for the moment that it was better not to like Ceci's boyfriends too much. "Thanks a lot, and I mean it."

Chapter Twenty-Four

The next morning, Enrique woke on *tía* Ceci's couch with the sun in his face and Boy's muzzle jammed into his ear. The dog's warm, biscuit-y breath rushed in and out like a tuneless accordion. Enrique couldn't remember walking in the door the night before with Glen and Boy. He must have fallen asleep in the car. Had Glen carried him in? He glanced at the clock on the mantel. It was nearly ten o'clock! On a school day!

He kicked off the quilt, startling Boy, who woke the triplets with his yapping.

"I got to get to school," Enrique said aloud. "I got to go to school!"

Ceci had already gone to work in her car. Glen, roused by the crying babies, groggily agreed to take Enrique to school on his "bike," a powerful motorcycle parked behind the duplex.

But Enrique's mother pleaded with him to take the day off. *Stay home with me. What does it matter if you miss one day?*

Enrique was determined to go to school, though he was tired and filthy. He had to see Flor and straighten her out about this boyfriend business and he had to stop the rumors that would spread like wildfire if he wasn't there to douse the first sparks. And, he wanted to know if she still planned to go with him to the movies on Saturday.

Glen lent Enrique his helmet and mounted the huge bike bareheaded. Enrique climbed on behind him, digging his fingers into the leather seat before they roared off. Enrique had noticed that when a woman rode behind a man on a motorcycle, she would lean in and cling to his back. But when men shared motorcycle rides, they never touched one another, as if they feared the other had a horrible contagious disease like leprosy. Amazing how two men on a bike could zoom nearly sideways on a sharp curve and never even come close to brushing each other's jacket. Knowing this, Enrique clutched the sides of the padded saddle, determined not to touch Glen.

The first few blocks, he squeezed his eyes shut and gripped the seat so tightly his fingers went numb and cold. But by the time they climbed the freeway on-ramp, Enrique was holding onto Glen like a monkey to a tree during a hurricane. Glen's ponytail kept lashing his face like a sharp, little whip the whole way. When they arrived at Peralta Middle School, Enrique trembled so that he worried he wouldn't be able to walk.

"Here you go, partner." Glen held the bike still, so Enrique could climb off. "You want me to pick you up?"

Enrique slid off the seat and struggled to remove the helmet. "I get out at three-thirty." He eyed the motorcycle doubtfully. "But I can wait until my aunt Ceci gets off work."

Glen shrugged. "Suit yourself." He slipped on the helmet, revved the engine, and thundered off.

"Thanks!" Enrique called, though he doubted Glen heard him.

He stopped at the attendance office for a late pass

and headed for the auditorium, where his class would be meeting with Mrs. Jaramillo's group.

The whoosh of cool air that greeted him as he pulled open the door reminded Enrique that he hadn't showered and he was wearing the same clothes he'd slept in. But most of the students were absorbed in conversations with their partners, and no one seemed to notice Enrique, except maybe Francisco and, possibly, Flor. He presented the late pass to Ms. Byers.

"I'm glad you could make it," she said.

"Huh?"

"It's good you came."

"Oh, yeah, sure." He searched the rows of huddled heads for Flor's flowing hair. She was near the back with Changa. Though Sandra was smiling and talking, Flor was staring out in silence, gazing straight at Enrique. Her uneven mouth opened in surprise. And a shock stung Enrique, like he'd touched a door knob after rubbing his shoes on a fluffy carpet. He stumbled up the inclined aisle as he made his way toward the girls.

"Hey, what happened to you?" Francisco asked from a seat nearby. He was sitting with German, who shot Enrique the finger with both hands, making a noise like a machine gun. Francisco turned to his partner. "Stop that."

But the wild boy ignored him. "*Rattatattatat*," he chanted.

"You look like Albert Einstein," Francisco told Enrique.

"Albert Einstein, the guy who was a genius?" Enrique asked, pleased.

Francisco shook his head. "Albert Einstein, the guy with messy hair."

"*Rattatattatat.*"

Enrique moved on to the row where Flor sat with Changa.

"Hi." He smiled and waited, as though he expected something nice to happen.

Flor looked away.

No one said anything for a few moments after that until Changa told Enrique to sit down because he was blocking the air-conditioning vent.

He sank into a seat. "Well, I'm here."

"Yeah." Flor licked her finger and rubbed at the scuff marks on her boots.

"What were you talking about?" he asked with a smile.

"Boys," Changa blurted, and then she clapped a hand over her mouth.

Flor blushed, and Changa giggled. Enrique's smile ached. "Um, can we talk about something else?"

"Yeah," Flor said. "Let's talk about how come you're late. We been waiting for you and waiting for you. You're not afraid of us, are you?"

"I had to come on a motorcycle," Enrique began, "from my aunt's house—"

"Yeah, yeah," Flor said, as if she didn't believe him, as if it no longer mattered.

"No, really, my stepfather got all crazy last night, and me and my mother had—"

"What*ever*," Flor said, twirling a long strand of hair.

"Don't say that." Enrique's voice rose. "Don't say that without listening to me."

"What-*ev-er*," Flor repeated.

"Shh." Changa put a finger to her lips. "That's no way for *novios* to talk."

"She's *not* my girlfriend!" Enrique cried. He felt all forty-plus heads swivel to stare at him in the back of the auditorium.

Flor struggled out of her seat, stepped on both of Enrique's feet, pushed her way into the aisle, and clattered on her boot heels out of the auditorium, Changa trailing close behind.

Enrique shrugged, helplessly, at the others staring at him. Ms. Byers frowned, and Francisco shook his head. "*RattatattatattaTAT!*" German aimed his machine gun fingers at Enrique over the back of his folding seat. "*RattatattatatattaTAT!*"

Chapter Twenty-Five

When Changa returned to the auditorium by herself, she informed Enrique that Flor didn't like him anymore.

"What?" Enrique felt like he'd been punched in the stomach.

Changa shrugged. "She don't like you no more."

"Why not?"

"'Cause what you said. She don't like you no more 'cause of that."

Enrique thought for a moment. "I'm sorry I shouted like that. I shouldn't have done that. Is Flor coming back in here?"

"She will stay in the bathroom until the class is over." Changa pulled a folded sheet of paper from her pocket and handed it to Enrique.

"What's this?" Enrique straightened it out. Large numbers that looked like they'd been scrawled by a kindergartner were printed over it.

"The phone number of Flor," Changa told him. "You call her tonight about the movie. You go to the movie with her tomorrow."

"How can I go with her if she doesn't like me anymore."

"She still want to go to the movie." Changa smiled in a mysterious way. "She tell me that."

In the yard during recess, Francisco rushed over to Enrique, saying, "Have you seen him? Have you seen him?"

"Who?" Enrique wondered if he meant Horacio. Enrique hadn't seen Horacio at all that day.

"German. Have you seen German?" Francisco's eyes were wide and shining. "I lost him. Have you seen him anywhere?"

"I don't know where he is," Enrique said. "*Cálmate*, you're not his mother."

Francisco gave him a disgusted look and dashed off into the crowd searching for the wild boy from Mexico. The bell rang and Enrique headed for his next class with Mr. Sanchez. But a line of students stalled outside of his bungalow classroom.

"How come we can't go in?" Enrique asked Marvin, who was holding his grandmother's hand, patting it as though to comfort her.

"*Dios mío*," the old woman muttered.

"There was an accident." Marvin's eyes brimmed, but his voice was steady.

"What happened?"

"Someone died," Marvin said. "I saw him on the roof. He was trying to jump, I think, from one building to another, but he missed. He fell between this building and that one." He pointed to the computer lab next door.

A siren droned in the background, and the cluster of students parted for Mr. Sanchez, who appeared with a key to let them inside. Behind his thick beard, his face looked gray and his eyes dull. His hands shook as he pushed the key into the lock.

"Who was it?" Enrique asked Marvin, though when he spotted Francisco sitting alone, his head in his hands, at a bench near the play area, he thought he already knew.

"That new kid, the strange one, that German," Marvin said.

Mr. Toro jogged across the yard toward them, his megaphone bouncing against his chest. But the stocky man's brown eyes were shadowed with dark circles of weariness, making him look more like a badger than ever—an exhausted badger, ready for a long hibernation. Though there were only about twenty kids in Mr. Sanchez's social studies class that period, Mr. Toro lifted the megaphone to his mouth. "Students in Mr. Sanchez's third period class will report to the bleachers on the P.E. field immediately."

Mr. Sanchez relocked the door and waved everyone away. For once, everyone lined up quickly and marched quietly toward the field. Cake Angie walked in a stiff way that reminded Enrique of a zombie he had seen in a horror movie. Marvin's grandmother produced a glass rosary from her handbag. She fingered the crystalline beads, mumbling as they walked. A few girls sniffled into tissues.

Francisco didn't move from the bench. Enrique wanted to go to him, but he saw Mr. Toro trot over to his friend and hoped the vice principal would comfort him. Mr. Toro put a hand on the big boy's shoulder. A badger with a bear, Enrique thought.

He flashed on the image of German machine-gunning him with his middle fingers in the auditorium earlier. Enrique felt sorry he had never even smiled at the strange kid, let alone tried talking to him. He'd just avoided German. All the kids kept their distance from him, as though his wildness could contaminate them.

Mr. Sanchez had everyone sit on the bleachers while he gave a long, rambling speech about how hard it was growing up. He paced back and forth a lot and scratched below his black beard. He brought up his wife and some of the trouble they had getting their daughter Lupe to follow their rules, and then he talked about how his younger brother died of cancer when he was just a boy. "It's hard for us to lose a life so young," he said. Enrique worried Mr. Sanchez would lose control and weep, but he didn't. He just kept walking back and forth in front of the bleachers, scratching below his beard and talking until the bell rang.

At lunch, kids swooped down on the rumor like greedy pigeons diving for crumbs at the park. Enrique heard people say German had been pushed off the roof by drug dealers, that he jumped believing he could fly, and that he'd killed himself because he didn't have the homework for Mrs. Burwell's class. Everywhere he turned, someone was saying, "Did you hear about the kid that died?"

Enrique felt sickened by this. He didn't even bother to line up at the cafeteria. He knew he wouldn't be able to swallow the food. Instead he searched for Francisco, but he couldn't find his friend anywhere. Toward the end of the period, Monsieur Nassour appeared in the lunch area and waved him over. Enrique was glad to escape the gossiping crowds and follow the old French teacher to his bungalow.

"That was a terrible accident," he said. "How are you feeling?"

Enrique shrugged.

"I have something for you." The old man unlocked the door to the classroom. "I have *two* things for you, *actualment*."

"What?"

Monsieur Nassour pulled a crumpled white bag from his jacket pocket. "You do not have to eat it now."

Enrique lifted a long chocolate-covered pastry from the sack. "A doughnut?"

"*Un éclair*," Monsieur Nassour said with a smile. "It is a French pastry with custard inside. I think you will like it."

"*Merci*, Monsieur Nassour, but do you mind if I save it for later." He placed it back in the bag.

"But of course, save it to eat when you like."

Enrique thought he should explain, so he wouldn't seem ungrateful. "I feel bad about German, the boy who fell from the roof."

"Did you know him well?" Monsieur Nassour asked.

"No, that's what makes me feel bad. I didn't know him. I didn't try to know him. No one did, except my friend Francisco. And now he's dead, they can't stop talking about him."

"I am sorry," Monsieur Nassour said in a quiet voice.

"The worst thing is Francisco had German for a partner in this project we're doing, and I knew he was having problems with him, but I didn't do nothing to help him. You know what I mean?"

"What could you have done?"

"I don't know. Something." Without thinking, Enrique opened the bag and pulled out the éclair. He bit into it. "This is good, Monsieur Nassour. It's way better than a doughnut." His teeth pierced the chocolate-glazed pastry, and he tasted the cool pudding inside. "Thank you."

"It's nothing." Monsieur Nassour shook his head. "You should try *le gaufre* in *Monréal* if you like the sweets. That is even better than this, and it reminds me..." He snapped his fingers and pulled a brochure from another pocket. "I have something else for you." He smoothed the glossy paper and handed it to Enrique.

On it were pictures of old-looking stone buildings and a lot of snow-covered stuff. They reminded Enrique of a glass globe he was given for Christmas one year, a dome filled with water and tiny bits of white confetti that swirled about a gingerbread house when he shook it. "What's this?"

"She is Québec! She is the finest city in North America. I lived there as a boy."

"Looks nice," Enrique said, wondering what he was supposed to do with the brochure.

"I give it to you because we have a club. Nothing fancy, it is just a small club of men and women. We are all old now, but we are all from Québec."

Did Monsieur Nassour expect him to join yet another club? "I don't think I have time for any more meetings—"

"*Non, non, non.*" Monsieur Nassour shook his head. "You will not join this club. It is for old people from

Québec. I tell you this because we had a meeting last night, and I talked about you."

"Me?"

"I told them of your love for French and about you, the kind of boy you are. Well, we have some money saved, and there is an exchange program for students. Do you know what this is?"

Enrique shook his head.

"It's the chance to study French in Québec for one year. Students in the exchange program stay with a French family and go to a French school and in twelve months—*voila!*—they speak French."

"Really?"

"*Oui*, it is perfect. The club would pay your transportation and the expenses. It is a scholarship. Of course, you must apply like everyone else we send, and you must qualify. This is a good opportunity for you, no?"

"Yeah, but…" A year was a long time to Enrique. Who would watch the triplets? Who would help his mother? And who would take care of Boy if he went away?

"I know it is a lot to think about, and of course, you must discuss this with your family. If you like, I will talk to your mother. It is such a great chance for you."

"That's nice of you, Monsieur Nassour, to give me this chance. I need to think about it first, okay?"

"Of course, of course."

The bell sounded, and Enrique popped the last corner of the éclair into his mouth. "*Merci* again, Monsieur, for the egg-clear."

"You are welcome." The old man smiled. "Think about Québec. Think about speaking French like a native in one year."

Chapter Twenty-Six

After school, a familiar horn bleated from the front of the school, and Enrique spotted his *tía* Ceci's compact car in the slow-moving procession formed by parents arriving to pick up their children.

"Hey, 'Rique," Ceci called through the open window. "Get in. I'll take you for an ice cream. It's hotter than an oven today!"

Enrique climbed into the car beside his aunt, wondering if the other kids standing around thought she was his older sister, or maybe even his girlfriend.

"I took the afternoon off to help out your mom," she said. "How was your day? I heard you got a late start." She clicked on the turn signal and pulled out of the line. "So, anything interesting happen?"

Enrique flashed on Flor storming out of the auditorium, German machine-gunning him with his middle fingers and then falling to his death less than an hour later, Mr. Sanchez pacing and talking, the kids gossiping at lunchtime, and Monsieur Nassour offering him an éclair along with a year in Québec. He shrugged. "Nothing, really. Nothing that interesting."

"Well, your mom seems okay at the house, a little sad, but okay." She pulled into the parking lot for the Dairy Queen. "Let's get a quick cone, okay? Your mother's kind of anxious to see you. She really needs you now, and not just to take care of the babies. She really depends on you a lot."

Enrique sighed.

From the telephone in *tía* Ceci's bedroom, Enrique made two phone calls that afternoon.

"Francisco?"

"Yeah?"

"I'm sorry about what happened with German."

"I couldn't help him." Francisco's voice sounded muffled and far away. "I just couldn't help him at all."

Enrique glanced at his own reflection in the mirror part of *tía* Ceci's dresser: he looked like he had a guilty secret. "Nobody could help him."

"I should have watched him better. They told me to watch out for him, and I couldn't do it."

"It wasn't your fault."

"But I was supposed to watch him, and I let him get away—"

"The *teachers* should have watched him, Francisco. That's their job. You are real smart and everything, but they shouldn't ask you to do their job. Everyone knows that German should be in a special school, but they wouldn't put him. Even I know that, and I don't know hardly nothing." Enrique nodded at himself in the mirror.

"I got to go," Francisco said. "My father is taking me to church to pray for the soul of German." A trumpeting sound came through the earpiece as Francisco blew his nose. "I can't talk now, Enrique."

After Francisco hung up, Enrique sat in silence for a few moments on the bed. Then he pulled a comb off the dresser and tried to re-style his hair before dialing the second number.

"Hello, can I talk to Flor?"

"Who is it?" a loud voice demanded.

"Enrique, a friend from school."

Enrique winced at a tumbling, crashing noise that sounded as if someone had not just dropped the phone, but hurled it to the floor. "Flo-o-or! Flo-o-or! It's *lover-boy!*"

"Shut up, shut up, shut up!" someone shouted—maybe Flor?—in the background.

"Yeah, make me," said the loud voice.

Then there was a scuffling sound and a sharp cry. "Ma-a-a-a!"

And finally Flor's voice on the line: "Yeah, what do you want?"

"I, um, just wanted to say, hi, I guess." Enrique couldn't remember why on earth he'd phoned her. Hearing Flor's voice wiped his memory as blank as the blackboards at school right before summer vacation.

"You just want to say, *hi*?" Flor snapped. "You tell everyone you don't even like me and I'm not your girlfriend, and then you call me up to say, *hi!*"

"Oh, right," Enrique said, grateful for the cue. "I'm sorry I shouted like that in the auditorium. I didn't mean it."

"You didn't mean what?"

"I didn't mean to shout like that."

"I *got* to go," she said coolly.

"No, I mean, I didn't mean what I said." The contents of his mind were wiped away once more. Not even a scribble remained. What *had* he said?

"You aren't saying that you didn't mean to say that I'm not your girlfriend?"

"Yeah, I mean, no." Enrique couldn't follow all the twists in that question. "I didn't mean all that."

"What part didn't you mean then?"

"Huh?"

"What did you mean?"

The call-waiting beep sounded in Enrique's ear. Someone else was trying to call through. He'd have ignored it, but this was *tía* Ceci's phone, so he said, "Hold on real quick, will you?"

"*Hold on?*"

Enrique pressed the flash button to hear his stepfather's voice slurring through the phone. *I want to talk to my woman. Put her on the phone.*

Enrique made his voice go as high as it could to make himself sound like a girl. "I am sorry, sir, you have the wrong number."

"Goddamn it, Enrique, put your mother on the phone before I come over there and rip you a new—"

Enrique pushed the flash button again. "Flor? Flor?" The dial tone hummed in his ear. He punched the re-dial button. "Hi, um, Flor, please," he said.

A clattering noise sounded and then, "Flo-o-or! Flo-o-or!"

Enrique held the phone away from his ear.

"It's *lover*-boy again!"

"What do you want now?" Flor said.

"Sorry, I had to get another call. I'm at my aunt's house, and she has call-waiting, so I had to—"

"What did you mean or what didn't you mean," she said, "when you said that I wasn't your girlfriend?"

"All I meant was…"—Enrique examined the few remaining tags of thought left in his brain. He had the idea Flor was holding her breath—"All I meant was… you aren't my girlfriend…*yet.*"

This seemed to satisfy Flor, and she told him where and when to meet her for the movies on Saturday, and then she hung up.

While Enrique helped his mother and Ceci ready the triplets for bed that night, he asked if they were ever going back to the apartment, back to Juan.

"No way!" Ceci said, blowing hair out of her face as she bent to change Hilario's diaper.

Mamá? Enrique asked.

No, my son, I don't know where we will go, but we cannot go back.

You will stay with me, Ceci said. *I have the extra bedroom. This place is small, but it's bigger than that apartment.*

What will happen with your job? Enrique asked.

They already let me go. His mother tugged a t-shirt over Maclovio's head. *When I called to say I couldn't work today, the owner told me I cannot come back.*

Tía Ceci, I want to talk to my mother alone for a minute, Enrique said.

"That's fine." She handed Hilario to Enrique. "I'm done with this stinker. I'll go brew up a big pot of *yerba buena.*" She stepped out of the bedroom and clicked the door shut behind her.

What is it, son? A purple bruise shaded his mother's cheekbone. Worry-lines creased her brow.

Enrique wanted to smooth them with his fingers, but instead, he said, *What if something happened to me, Mamá? How would you get along if I couldn't be with you?*

Don't talk like that. She looked away, busied herself with Yunior's snaps.

But what if I had the chance to go somewhere? To study in another country?

What is it? Has something happened?

No, no, I'm just wondering what would happen if I wasn't here.

You wouldn't go anywhere. You wouldn't leave, she said. *I love you! I wouldn't let you go.*

Is it because you need me to help you with my brothers?

She looked into his eyes. *Listen to me. I said I love you. I would never let you go. Stop these foolish questions. Let's put the babies to bed and have some tea with your aunt.*

One more thing I was wondering about, Mamá.

What is it?

*Why didn't you leave Juan when he hit **me**? All those times, and you never left. Why did you wait until he hit **you**?*

His mother picked up stray baby clothes and folded them as though she was in a hurry, without raising her eyes to meet his. She wouldn't answer his question, and Enrique didn't ask her again.

Chapter Twenty-Seven

According to the bank clock across the street from the Rialto, Flor was seventeen—going on eighteen—minutes late. Enrique wished he hadn't refused Ceci's offer to wait with him until Flor arrived. He would have headed back to the duplex with her by now. Clearly, Flor had stood him up, probably to get even for what he'd shouted in the auditorium yesterday. Or she was still angry that he took the call-waiting call. He couldn't be sure. Understanding Flor was tougher than solving one of Mrs. Burwell's trickiest equations.

He fingered the crumpled five-dollar bill in his pocket. *Tía* Ceci had stuffed it there before he climbed out of the car. He'd told her he didn't need money, that he'd get in for free, but now he was glad to have it. It wasn't enough to get into the theater, but at least he would have bus fare to go back to his aunt's house.

He was about to cross the street for the bus stop when he heard Flor's loud voice from the parking lot at the side of the building. "Hey, Enrique, *hey*, we're over here!"

We? Who's *we*, Enrique wondered, squinting across the street, as Flor clattered her boots toward him. Behind her, Enrique counted one, two, three smaller kids, all wearing the same lime-colored sweats printed with orange dinosaurs.

"I thought you weren't coming," Enrique said, when they were up close.

"I know it's late, huh? The only way I could get to

come is if I brought my brother and sisters with me. Try dressing three little kids in a hurry."

Enrique nodded in sympathy.

"You don't mind, do you?" Flor jutted her chin at the little kids.

Enrique shook his head. Why should he mind? In fact, he felt a bit relieved that he and Flor wouldn't have to sit alone together in the darkened theater. He'd never been on a "date" before, and he'd worried that Flor might expect him to kiss her. Though he'd practiced kissing his reflection a few times in Ceci's dresser mirror, he wasn't sure he felt ready for the real thing.

Enrique couldn't tell from their identical short mops of blue-black hair which two were the girls and which one was the boy. He waved at the kids. "Hi." Then he turned to Flor. "Got a tissue?"

All three of them had thick globs of mucous streaming from their flat noses and crusting on their upper lips.

"*¡Mocosos!*" Flor cried. "I just wiped them in the car. They got head colds. I ain't got no more Kleenex."

As if on cue, one of the three began coughing. Another pulled on Enrique's hand, chanting, "Take me pee-pee, take me pee-pee, take me pee-pee!"

"Well, let's go inside. I can get some tissue in the bathroom. If this one's a boy, I can take him to use the toilet."

"Yeah, that's my brother Sammy."

"The others are girls?"

"That's Yolie," Flor said, pointing, "and that's Nora. I'll find my aunt."

Flor's aunt seemed too young to be working at the theater. She looked Flor's age, maybe even younger. She wore her hair pulled back in a ponytail, and she snapped a wad of gum that was as big as a ping-pong ball. But she wore the bright orange usher's jacket and confidently motioned them into the lobby without charging for tickets.

Enrique led the one Flor said was a boy into the men's room, where he slipped a roll of toilet paper off the holder in one of the stalls. He knew they would need the whole thing the way those kids' noses were dripping. He might even have to come back for a second roll.

The movie had already started when Ernique and Flor burst into the dark theater with the three toddlers. A woman's head, large as a moon, smiled seductively from the screen while Enrique's eyes adjusted.

"I can't see nothing. I can't see nothing. I can't see *nothing!*" Sammy cried.

People shushed him from all directions.

"He always does that," Flor whispered. "He'll be okay once we sit down."

They found three seats together in the very last row and two together in the front row. Enrique wound up sitting with Sammy in the first row and straining his neck as he tipped his head back so he could see the whole screen at once. The movie seemed to consist mostly of close-up shots of a man and a woman talking, smiling, frowning, crying, and then, kissing. They repeated this process several times. The actors' nostrils loomed like pits from the screen.

"What's that?" Sammy asked in a clear, loud voice

throughout the movie. "What's that? Why is he doing that? Why is she kissing him? What's that?"

At first, Enrique tried answering his questions, but then he realized the kid didn't care if he got answers or not. He just enjoyed hearing the sound of his voice in the quiet theater. The people seated nearby kept trying to shush Sammy, and when that didn't work, a few of them cursed him.

Enrique had given Flor most of the bathroom tissue. With his portion, he tried to keep the boy's nose clean.

"Blow," he whispered every now and again, as he held a wad of toilet paper to Sammy's nose. "Blow."

"What's that?" Sammy asked after blowing. "Why is he doing that? What's she doing? What's that?"

When Enrique found Flor in the lobby after the film ended, he saw that her eyes and nose had reddened. Was she getting a cold too? Flor's aunt came by to take the toddlers and buy them candy.

"Wasn't that the best movie you ever saw?" Flor dabbed her eyes with tissue. "Didn't you love it?"

"Hmm, it was okay."

"*Okay*? Are you crazy? It was terrificalistic!"

"I enjoyed it," Enrique said. "Thanks for getting me in."

"Do you want to see it again? It starts up in a little bit. My aunt don't mind."

"Nah, I better go home. I promised to help my mom with some stuff," Enrique said, hoping Flor's feelings wouldn't be hurt.

"Are you going to go now?" she asked. "'Cause they're going to start the movie in another room in a minute or two. I don't want to miss the beginning this time."

"Yeah, I better go."

"If you hurry and leave, I'll walk outside with you."

"You don't have to," Enrique said.

Flor sighed. "I might as well."

Outside, Flor clasped Enrique's hand and held it as they crossed the street to the bus stop, her warm, moist fingers lacing his.

"I guess we're going out together now," Flor observed, in the same tone she might mention that her boots needed polishing.

"Yeah?" Enrique searched the street, trying to spot the bus.

"Yeah."

He shrugged. "Okay."

Flor closed her eyes, pursed her lips, and leaned toward him. When Enrique hesitated, she opened her eyes and said, "You're supposed to kiss me now."

"Oh, okay." Enrique's heart pounded hard against his throat, so hard he worried that Flor would hear it and laugh at him. He bumped her nose with his cheek, but finally managed to land his lips on hers. He kept his eyes open, staring at Flor's closed eyelids which merged together into one double lid over the bridge of her nose. He remembered the actors in the movie and moved his head to imitate them.

"Wow!" Flor said when she pulled back.

"Wow?"

"You're a great kisser, really great." She nodded. "Okay, then, I got to go back and see the movie again.

Remember, you can't have no other girlfriends from now on, except me, okay?"

"Okay." Enrique didn't know if he could handle having one girlfriend, let alone two or three.

"I mean it," Flor said. She released his hand and darted across the street. "No other girlfriends," she called over her shoulder, "or I'll have to kick your butt!"

It was still pretty early when Enrique returned to *tía* Ceci's house. As he rounded the block toward the duplex, he found Ceci in the front yard, yanking dandelions from the grass. She stopped when she noticed Enrique on the walk. "He's in there," she said.

"Who?"

"Juan. He's in there talking to your mother."

Chapter Twenty-Eight

Enrique rushed up the walk.

"Wait, Enrique." *Tía* Ceci grabbed his arm. "Your mother, well, you have to understand, your mother *wants* to talk to him."

"Why? He hit her. He hit me. He's a drunk! Why does she want to talk to him?

Ceci shook her head, rolled her eyes. "She says she still loves him."

"But what about me?" Enrique sank to the concrete step by the door. He buried his head in his hands, too stunned to cry.

Ceci pulled off her garden gloves to stroke his hair.

"What about me?"

Ceci sighed. "I think she's going back with him... probably today."

"She said she wasn't," Enrique murmured. "Last night, remember? She said she wouldn't go back."

"I know what she said, but I think she will go back."

"I won't go back there," Enrique promised. "I won't go back no matter what."

"I know you feel bad, *m'ijo*. I know you must feel terrible."

"I won't go back there," he repeated. "Not me." And Enrique sat on that concrete step until his *nalgas* felt stiff as cement themselves. He didn't move when Ceci went inside to get him a cool drink, which he left untouched. It wept a dark puddle beside him. He didn't shift when Boy scratched the screen door open and leapt into his lap. He didn't even look up when his mother and Juan came out to talk to him.

Son, you must understand, she said, *we belong together, all of us. Our family belongs together. Your brothers need their father.*

What about my father, Enrique wondered, no one ever talked about him, except to say he ought to be glad he was gone.

What I did was wrong, Juan said. *You have to forgive me. Jesus, on the cross, forgives the people who sin. You have to forgive people when they make a mistake.*

Juan droned on and on. Then Enrique's mother had more to say. They both spoke for a very long time. When they started talking, the sun beat down on Enrique's head, but when they were finishing up, the sun had flattened like a dime into the foothills. Enrique felt as though he were disappearing too. His mother's and Juan's words were dissolving him little by little, as they had worn away the sun.

Still, Enrique would not move. He refused to lean out of the way when Juan and his mother brought the bags of diapers, clothes, bottles, and then the babies out of the house to load into a car Juan must have borrowed. He didn't flinch when his mother brushed her lips on his cheek. *I am a statue,* he told himself, *I am a statue made of stone.* And he didn't watch the car pull away from the curb and disappear at the end of the block.

Ceci opened the screened door and leaned out. "You can come inside now if you want. I'm going to fix something to eat."

Enrique remained on the concrete step. Boy had long

ago fallen asleep in his lap, and Enrique didn't want to disturb him. Besides, he had the idea that—if he kept still, if he didn't move—things would stop changing so fast. Everything else might stay still too until he could make some sense of it all. Ceci flipped on the porch light, and warm cooking smells wafted from the kitchen.

Glen's motorcycle sputtered up the drive. Then his shoes scraped on the walk. "I heard what happened. I heard you were sitting out here," he said, lowering himself to sit on the step beside Enrique. "I thought I'd come out here and help."

The two of them sat a long time under the halo of moths attracted by the porch lamp. Across the street, a television set snapped on, and they could hear bursts of applause and laugher spilling through an open window. Cars whooshed past. And somewhere a cat yowled. They sat, and they were quiet until Boy shook himself and yawned. The little dog whimpered to let Enrique know he was hungry.

"Okay, that's it," Enrique said. "I'm ready to go in."

"Yeah, me, too." Glen rose with Enrique and opened the door.

Chapter Twenty-Nine

Sunday passed in a blur. Enrique vaguely remembered he had talked about doing something with Francisco and his family. He thought he should call, but he never got around to doing that. He didn't do much of anything else either.

After breakfast with Ceci and Glen, he scanned the comic section of the newspaper, and then he picked up *The Little Prince*. He read a good bit of that, putting it down at one point to watch Glen take parts off his motorcycle to set them on newspaper in the driveway. Next, Glen dismantled the parts he'd taken off the motorcycle to wipe these smaller pieces with an oiled rag. Enrique had to stop watching, or he thought he might go insane. He returned to his book. The little prince having a conversation with a fox in outer space made more sense than Glen pulling apart bits of his motorcycle just to clean them.

After lunch, he stretched out on the bed in the spare room and closed his eyes for a nap. Minutes later, the phone rang. Ceci answered it and knocked gently on the bedroom door. "It's your mother." She pushed the door open.

But Enrique turned to the wall, kept his eyes shut.

He heard Ceci tell his mother he was sleeping. She talked to Enrique's mother a long time after that. Her muffled voice was barely audible from the front room, as Enrique strained to hear what she said. He couldn't tell much from her end of the conversation, but he did find out that his mother planned to stay with Juan in the apartment and to have Leontina care for the triplets while his mother looked for another job.

When he overheard the bit about Leontina, Enrique nearly jumped out of bed to ask Ceci to put him on the phone. He wanted to tell her what a terrible job Leontina did as a babysitter. But something kept him from interrupting. He wasn't ready to talk to his mother. Not yet. Besides, he told himself, she was pretty smart. She would figure it out and find someone else to watch the babies.

That night, Enrique told Ceci he'd take the city bus to school in the morning and ride it back in the afternoon. He'd use change from the five dollars she'd given him on Saturday. He should have a couple of days of transportation this way. He didn't want to be any trouble to Ceci or to Glen.

"I like having you here, *m'ijo*, but I'm wondering how long you plan to stay. Your mother wants to know too."

"I don't know," Enrique told her. "I'm not sure. Right now, I never want to go back and live in that apartment if Juan is there."

"I don't blame you. You can stay here as long as you want, if it's up to me. And Glen can take you to school in the morning. You don't have to take the bus."

"No, that's okay." Enrique wasn't exactly looking forward to another motorcycle ride. "I like taking the bus. It gives me time to think before school."

The bus only made him a few minutes late, but Ms. Byers insisted he get a late pass (and detention for his

second tardy) from the attendance office. On his way
out of the classroom, he noticed Horacio's desk was
empty again. Since his friend had been out of school for
so many days, Enrique had the habit of saying "*Hay
labio jabón lechuga*" under his breath as he passed
through the breezeway where Horacio usually lounged.
He said it again on his way back to class, and he
wondered where Horacio was all this time. Maybe he'd
take the bus to his friend's house after school instead of
going straight back to the duplex. Ceci wouldn't be
home until early evening. She wouldn't miss him. And
Boy had her small backyard to roam, if he needed
exercise or to relieve himself.

When Enrique returned to the classroom, the door
held fast. It was locked. The class had probably marched
over to the auditorium again to meet with Mrs.
Jaramillo's students. They could have waited. Ms. Byers
knew he'd be returning with his pass. Enrique cut across
campus, taking a shortcut to the auditorium.

He'd nearly made it when he spotted Dean Hardin,
using a paint scraper to pry blackened gobs of gum off
a bench near the lunch area. She glanced at Enrique and
said, "Gum."

"Gum," Enrique repeated, wondering if she remembered his rudeness last week.

"It makes me sick," she said as she stood to speak to
him. "I know it's not my job. I should leave it for
maintenance. But look at it." She waved the scraper at
the gum-splotched benches. "Gum on everything—
these benches, the walkway, even on the walls." She bent
to loosen a black tar-like blob from the backrest.

"Can I help you," Enrique said, hoping the offer would make up for the way he spoke to her about the candy wrapper, and also hoping he would be refused. The hardened disks of old gum disgusted him.

Dean Hardin stood again and pushed her bangs to one side. She glanced at the tardy slip in his hand. "No, you better get to class."

Enrique hesitated before heading for the auditorium. "I think it's a good school."

Dean Hardin smiled. "It's not a good school, but it's not that bad either. I suppose it could be a lot worse."

Enrique nodded.

"Are you doing better?" Dean Harding gave him a sharp look. "You were upset the last time we spoke."

"Oh, about taking French."

"No, Enrique, not then. I mean when I asked you to pick up some trash. Something was bothering you. Are you okay now?"

"Well," Enrique said. "I think so, and… I'm sorry what I said."

Dean Hardin waved his apology away. She bent to continue scraping the gum. "I think you have a chance," she said. "I think you can be one of the ones who gets away from here."

"Huh?"

She pointed the scraper at him. "You should listen to Armand."

"Armand?"

"Monsieur Nassour. He's giving you a wonderful opportunity. Don't pass it up." She returned to scraping. "You better get back to class now."

As he pulled open the auditorium door, Enrique had the strong feeling of doing exactly this before. Again, he stumbled toward Ms. Byers with a late pass. Again, he searched the huddled heads for Flor's long brown hair. The feeling was so strong, he could almost tell what would happen next, but before he could sense exactly what that would be, the feeling passed. And he couldn't find Flor. He spied Changa though, paired with Francisco this time. He made his way up the aisle toward them.

"Francisco's my new partner," Changa informed him when he sat beside her.

"Where's Horacio?" Enrique asked. "Does anyone know?"

"He just stopped coming to school," Francisco said. "They put me with Sandra because German—"

"Don't talk German." Changa placed two fingers over Francisco's lips. "My mother say it is bad luck."

"Where's Flor?" Enrique searched the hall.

"Oh, I forget!" Changa reached into her notebook and pulled out a scrap of paper. "She come in the morning and give this for you."

"What is it?"

"A note for you."

Enrique unfurled the scrap and read the sprawling print: *Letus seezon. I luv U 4ever Flor.*

"She love you," Changa explained. "She check out of school this morning. She move with the family. Pick *lechuga*, how you say?"

"Lettuce," Francisco said.

"They pick lettuce up north. No more Flor. She say to say goodbye."

Chapter Thirty

Enrique decided to walk to Horacio's house after school. Since *tía* Ceci wouldn't be home from work until nearly dark, there would be plenty of time to find out why his friend hadn't been coming to school. He also wanted to talk to Horacio about Flor—going out with her, then losing her. It was the kind of thing that Francisco, for all his brains and ideas, just wouldn't be able to understand as well as Horacio, who claimed to have won and lost many girlfriends.

As Enrique strode through the familiar neighborhood to Horacio's, Enrique wondered if he'd really be able to stay away from the apartment permanently. *Tía* Ceci might get tired of having him around day after day. And it wasn't all that comfortable pulling his toothbrush and clothes out of a grocery bag all the time. Plus, if he lived at her house, he'd have to change schools. That meant he'd rarely see his friends, and some of the teachers at Peralta weren't that bad—he'd miss them too. But most of all, he'd miss his brothers and his mother. He already wanted to see them, and he hadn't even been separated from them a week yet. Though he wasn't exactly ready at this moment, Enrique figured he'd probably end up going home sometime.

Enrique found Horacio outside, leaning against a car parked in front of his house. Horacio was wearing a leather jacket and brand new blue and white gym shoes that Enrique had seen advertised on television by a famous basketball player.

"Eh, homeboy," Enrique called. "You got the chicken pox? How come you don't come to school no more?"

"I don't do school, *ese*," Horacio said in the same way he might reveal that he'd given up playing with plastic soldiers. "I got me a job, real *trabajo*."

"Oh, yeah?"

Yes, I'm working now. Horacio slipped into Spanish. *And I'm making loads of money. I'm going to buy a car for my mother.*

What work are you doing?

I'm selling stuff.

You work in a store?

Horacio didn't answer. He just leaned back, laced his fingers behind his head, and laughed. When he'd raised his arms, Enrique spotted a new tattoo, freshly scabbing on his friend's forearm.

Whatever happened with Itchy and all that? Enrique asked.

No problem. We worked everything out.

I thought he was locked up.

"It don't matter," Horacio said, switching to English when his mother stepped out the front door to water some puny plants on the front porch. "See, my cousin knows these guys, and he set it up so I could talk to Itchy's people. We worked things out good. I mean real good. We're *compadres* now, *ese*."

"What do you mean?"

"Me and Itchy is in business, man."

Before Enrique could ask another question, a big car sailed around the corner, fat tires screeching as it braked alongside the curb. The car door swung open.

Enrique actually saw a puff of smoke before he heard the explosions. The windows of the car Horacio leaned against popped like glass bubbles. Horacio slumped to his knees on the sidewalk, holding his stomach as dark streams of blood trickled through his fingers. He tumbled face down as though he'd been clubbed in the back. Enrique's ears buzzed from the blasts and smoke stung his eyes. The street spun crazily, dizzying him as he sank to Horacio's side. People in the street shouted and ran, disappearing into the houses.

I'm hit, Horacio whispered. *They hit me.*

Horacio's mother appeared. She fell to her knees, pushing Enrique out of the way to cradle her son's head in her lap. She screamed, yelling for Jesus, for God, for anyone to help. *My God help us! Help us! My son, my son! Please somebody help us!*

Don't let them kill me. Horacio's face paled and his eyes went dull.

"Somebody call 9-1-1!" Enrique shouted. "Somebody call an ambulance!"

Horacio's mother beat her chest with a brown-speckled fist. She was raving, threatening God and the saints. Enrique thought she'd lost her mind. Some neighbor women emerged from their houses to comfort her as she held her son's head in her lap. After what seemed a long time, police cars and an ambulance finally wailed in the distance.

The paramedics loaded Horacio onto a gurney and wheeled him to the ambulance, his mother trailing close behind.

"Is he going to be okay?" Enrique asked.

"Don't know yet," an attendant told him.

"Were you hit too?" a policeman asked, pointing to the blood on Enrique's clothing.

"No, I don't think so." Enrique patted himself to be sure. "I'm okay."

As soon as they saw Enrique was unharmed, the police began asking him questions: Did he recognize the car? Did he see the shooter? How many people in the car? What was the make and model? Did he get a license number?

Enrique just shook his head, saying over and over that he didn't know anything, he didn't see anything. He only wanted to get to Ceci's house and wash off the blood. He trembled so much that his teeth rattled. "I didn't see nothing," he said for the hundredth time it seemed. He was beginning to believe if he said this enough times, it might become true. Before the puffs of smoke, before the blasts and the glass cascading from the car window at Horacio's back, Enrique had peered into the car. He had seen the driver, and he recognized him at once. He didn't know who the shooter was, but he knew the driver, and the driver knew him too.

There was a full moment before the gun exploded when the driver turned to face him, and Enrique caught sight of the eye patch and he knew. In that moment, Pirata nodded and pointed at Enrique, as if to say, *okay, so you're next.* Then the shots rang out, but the shooter missed Enrique when he stooped to catch Horacio.

"I didn't see nothing," Enrique told the police one last time. "I swear it."

Chapter Thirty-One

The next day, the entire school buzzed with the news that Horacio had been shot. Almost everyone had a story to tell about what happened, and every story was different. Weird, thought Enrique. He hadn't noticed any of these kids there on the street when Horacio was shot. And no one seemed to know that Enrique *had* been there.

"Did you hear Horacio got shot?" Cake Angie's eyes glittered. She carried a plastic shoebox filled with coconut-iced cupcakes, a project she'd done with her Beginning ESL partner. "They got him yesterday. Some Colombians kidnapped him and blew his brains out." She seemed thrilled, in a sick way, to be the one to tell him his friend was dead. "They took him over by the river and tortured him first."

"Get away from me." Enrique pushed past her to his locker.

"Serves him right!" she called after him.

"Shut up!"

"Don't think you're getting any of my cupcakes either!"

Enrique was sure he'd vomit if he tasted one. He rushed away, looking for Maricela, whose mother was somehow related to Horacio's mother. He couldn't remember if they were cousins or sisters or what. He just knew there was some family connection. He found Maricela on a bench in the lunch area, reading over her homework and waiting for the first period bell.

"Maricela," he called. "Are you still mad at me?"

She looked up from her notebook. Her glasses glinted in the sun, and she smiled. "You know I can't stay mad at you very long. Where have you been?"

"I'm staying with my *tía* Ceci."

"My father told me that you and your mother took the babies that night and left, but then I saw your mother with the babies, so I figured you'd be coming back too."

"I can't go back. I can't live in that place with Juan no more."

Maricela nodded. She didn't have to have things explained to her too much. She understood a lot right away. She was a good friend for that reason.

"How's Horacio?" Enrique asked.

"You know he was shot?"

"I was there when it happened. Don't tell no one, okay?"

"I won't."

"I saw who shot him."

"Oh, no!" As studious and house-bound as Maricela was, she knew in an instant what Enrique had been trying not to admit to himself. "You can't stay here. They'll find you. Where will you go?"

"I'm not going to say anything. I'm not going to tell."

Maricela shook her head. "They won't believe you. You've got to get away."

"Horacio probably knows who it was too, I think. What about him?" Enrique asked.

"They'll probably be after him when he gets out of the hospital."

"How is he? Did your mother talk to his mother?"

"We went to the hospital last night. They wouldn't let me go in to see him, but my mother says he's going to make it."

Enrique sighed. "That's the best thing I've heard all day."

"Well, he's not going to die, thank God. He had an operation to take out the bullet, and he came through that, but the doctors said, well, they told his mother he had been shot in the spine." Maricela chewed her lip, hesitating. "Enrique, Horacio can't walk anymore."

"What?"

"He won't be able to walk when he gets out of the hospital," she said. "His legs are paralyzed."

"But how will he get to school? How will he do anything?" Enrique flashed on an image of Horacio lounging in the breezeway. *Hay labio jabón lechuga.*

"He has to have a wheelchair," Maricela told him.

Horacio in a wheelchair?

The bell rang, and Maricela ducked into the classroom. It would be a few minutes before the tardy bell rang. Enrique knew she'd rushed in so he wouldn't see her tears. He jogged across campus to the bungalows for his first class. He didn't want to be late again to Ms. Byers' class. He didn't trust his voice to come out right, if she asked him why he was late.

He took his seat beside Cake Angie without looking at her. He'd seen a science fiction movie once in which humans, invaded by an alien virus, transformed into dense, dark, foggy-looking shapes. He pretended Cake Angie was one of those dim, blurry things. He acted like he would become infected if he looked in her direction. Enrique knew it was stupid, but the fantasy kept his mind off Horacio lounging in a wheelchair. *Hay labio jabón lechuga.* Would girls stop and talk to a boy in a wheelchair?

"Francisco!" He leaned toward Francisco, who was lining up his pencils and trying to decide which to sharpen before class. Enrique wasn't sure what he'd say when he caught his friend's attention.

"So, you decided to come on time today," Francisco said, without turning to face Enrique.

"What's your problem?" Enrique asked.

"Nothing," Francisco said coolly. "Nothing, really. I guess you were too busy to call us on Sunday. We waited for you to go hiking. My whole family waited so long that, when we got to the foothills, it started to rain and we had to drive all the way back. No problem at all."

Enrique wanted to point out that if they'd left any earlier, they would have gotten caught in the rain, but he resisted this, saying, "Look, Francisco, you don't know what's been going on with me, with my family. I'm sorry you waited. I'm sorry it rained. I'm sorry about all that—"

Cake Angie snorted.

"—but it's not my fault," Enrique said.

Francisco snapped his fingers. "I think I'm going to invent a t-shirt next. I'm going to invent a t-shirt for people like you, Enrique, a t-shirt that says, in big letters: *Hey, it's not my fault!* I think I'll sell a million of them in one week."

As Ms. Byers stepped into the bungalow, Enrique

imagined Francisco as another dark, furry fog. He pulled out the stenographer's tablet *tia* Ceci had given him that morning and wrote heavily on the green lines: *I want to go to Canada. I think the French have a word for everything I want to say.* He counted his sentences and added: *I will never come back! Never! Ever! Ever!*

After she collected the journals, Ms. Byers faced the class and said, "I'm sure you all know that one of our classmates was injured in a drive-by shooting."

Cake Angie looked disappointed to hear the word "injured."

"Horacio Díaz was shot yesterday afternoon. His mother tells me he may never walk again.

"I had a lesson plan. I had arranged for us to work on vocabulary and practice the past perfect tense. But after I heard the news last night, I could only think about what happened to Horacio." For the first time, Ms. Byers looked very young to Enrique. She reminded him of a shivering white rabbit he'd held in his arms once in a pet store. Its moist pink eyes blinked at him fearfully.

"I imagine you are also thinking of Horacio, and of German, and wondering, like I am, how things like this can happen."

For once, the paper rustling, the whispering, the coughing, the desk groaning, the foot shifting ceased, and the classroom fell completely silent. After a few moments, Enrique's stomach rumbled, or maybe it was Cake Angie's. No one spoke and, as far as Enrique could tell, no one even breathed.

Then a chair scraped. There was a scratchy sound like sandpaper rubbing against itself. Enrique glanced up to see Marvin Alfaro's grandmother making her way, starched skirt rustling, to the front of the classroom. In the uneven light slanting from the Venetian blinds, Enrique thought he saw Marvin's *abuela* pouring diamond teardrops from one vein-roped hand to the other. Then, the old woman pressed the prism-like beads, her rosary, into Ms. Byer's hands.

Marvin's hand shot up. "My grandmother is very religious," he blurted. "She thinks we should trust in God. The more you don't know, she says, the more proof there is of God's greatness." Marvin smiled at his grandmother and waved her back to her seat. "But I don't believe there is a God, do you?"

"Why, I don't know." Ms. Byers seemed stunned.

"Of course," Francisco said. "Of course, there is God. Everyone knows that."

Marvin shook his head. "I don't know it. How would I know it?"

"You're stupid," Cake Angie muttered. "How would you know anything?"

"I thought we could talk about Horacio," Ms. Byers said. "I thought we could talk about our feelings."

"I think he deserved it," Cake Angie said in a loud voice. "They said he was dealing drugs. He's a dealer. They're always getting shot or thrown in jail. He should have known better."

"What do you think, Francisco?" Ms. Byers asked. Enrique noticed this was a favorite tactic of many teachers at Peralta—to rely on Francisco to dispute an ignorant statement.

"I think what happened was a terrible thing. I'm glad

Horacio wasn't killed. I don't know if he was dealing drugs. I have known him a long time, and I don't think he would have done anything that would get him shot."

Ms. Byers turned to Enrique. "Enrique, what do you think?"

"I don't want to talk." Enrique hated the way the others sounded like they were being interviewed on television, as though they were experts called on to make sense of what happened to Horacio. Nothing could make sense of that. "I feel sick."

"Do you want to see the nurse?"

"No, I just don't want to talk." He folded his arms and nested his head on the desk, closing his eyes.

"Marvin?"

Marvin cleared his throat, and he stood up. He began talking about the people he had known who were shot in his native country. Then, he discussed what Sue had told him about Viet Nam and the Hmong people. Next, he brought up the Korean War, and then World War Two and his observations on Germany and the treatment of the Jews. Marvin seemed to be working his way backwards through history, naming the atrocities that came to mind for him. What did any of it have to do with Horacio?

Enrique opened one eye to peek at Ms. Byers. Her face was drawn and tense. She looked like she regretted introducing the topic for class discussion. When Marvin took a breath between the Civil War and the Revolutionary War, Ms. Byers interrupted, saying, "That's all very interesting, Marvin, but maybe we ought to take a quick look at the past perfect tense for the test Friday."

Enrique closed his eye and burrowed his head more deeply in his arms.

Chapter Thirty-Two

During the nutrition break, Enrique waited in the long line that had formed for the only pay phone on campus. He stood behind a girl whose large body and teased dark hair completely blocked his view of the front. He couldn't see when people got on or off the phone. He couldn't tell if anyone was taking cuts. This gave him the odd sense of having no future. He only knew the line moved when the heavy girl grunted and shifted forward slightly. Enrique stared at the folds of fat and a hairy mole at the back of her neck. He imagined her skin as the sea and the mole an island with a few palms on it. Then he wondered who was waiting for a call from this girl with a thick neck.

When she finally slumped to the booth, Enrique listened in.

She clanged in her coins and punched a series of buttons. "Ho," she said after a pause. "Ho, who do you think you *are* beeping me and putting 'ho' on my beeper? I know you done it. Get over it! He loves me now!" She slammed down the receiver and stomped off. Enrique stared for a moment, puzzled, until the person behind him nudged him toward the booth.

Enrique inserted a few coins, dialed, and listened to the phone buzz a few times before he heard his mother's voice: "*Alo?*"

Mamá, it's me Enrique. How are you? How are my brothers?

Fine, we are all fine. When will you come home, son?
Are you coming home today?

Mamá, no, I can't come home. Listen to me, they
shot Horacio, and I saw it, Mamá. I saw the ones who
shot Horacio.

My God!

They saw me too.

No!

I can't come home, Mamá. Do you hear me? I can't
come home now.

No! It isn't true. You can come home.

I wish it wasn't true.

A thick, pale finger plunged the receiver cradle
down. "Been looking for you, Enrique. Been all over
school, looking for you," Brandon Wexler said. A smile
flickered on his thin lips.

Enrique stepped away from the phone. The people
standing behind him had disappeared. He searched the
yard for any sign of a teacher, a janitor, anyone. But the
bell must have rung while he was talking to his mother.
The campus was deserted.

"Yeah," he said, determined to be calm. "I'm right
here. What do you want?"

"The Pirate says you have a secret. He thinks you
can't keep a secret. I says to him, hell, maybe he can
keep a secret. But I don't know. Can you?"

"Yeah, I keep secrets real good."

"Now, you see, that's what I thought. But the Pirate,
he don't want to believe me. He wants you to tell him
for yourself. Come on, Enrique—that your name?
Enrique? I got my car just over there on the side of the

school. Let's go see the Pirate. He's waiting there, and you can tell him yourself how good you keep secrets."

Enrique shook his head. "I can't. I, um, I got class. I can't go over there. But I keep secrets good. I swear it."

Brandon had his hands in the pockets of his jacket. Something poked from one pocket, and Enrique heard a faint clicking sound. "Now, you ain't listening too good. You got to come with me. No more bullshit."

"Wexler! Brandon Wexler!" a harsh, but familiar voice called from behind Enrique. "Fifth period, last term. I never forget! At last, you've returned to take that final exam, so I can clear up your incomplete. I hate an incomplete." Mrs. Burwell marched past Enrique to clutch Brandon's elbow in her yellowed, claw-like hand. "You were bad at addition and bad at multiplication, Mr. Wexler, but you could always divide and subtract— very odd."

Brandon wrenched away from the math teacher and clicked his pocket again. Mr. Toro, the reliable badger, jogged from the counseling office toward the trio. "Trouble, Mrs. Burwell?" he asked.

"No, no trouble," she said. "Brandon Wexler is back to take his final at long last, so I can give him a grade. Perhaps you could show him to study hall, so the librarian can proctor the test. I'll send a copy of the final over directly."

"I think I'll proctor this one myself," Mr. Toro said.

"Fine. I'll collect the test after school, and you can have your grade in the morning. And I sincerely hope that's not a calculator clicking in your pocket."

(Enrique sincerely hoped it was.)

Brandon's mouth fell open, his cheeks burned red, and he hung his head, suggesting to Enrique that whatever it was clicking in his pocket, it wasn't anything especially dangerous.

"I'll have him take off the jacket for the test, Mrs. Burwell."

"Thank you, Mr. Toro. I'd appreciate that."

"And this young man?" Mr. Toro turned to Enrique. "Is he making up a test too?"

"Oh, no," Mrs. Burwell said. "He's coming with me."

Mr. Toro led Brandon to the library, and Enrique, not sure where she was headed, trailed after Mrs. Burwell. He followed her to the teachers' lounge, it turned out, where he hesitated at the threshold until she called out to him from inside. "Enrique, do you like root beer or cola?"

"Um, root beer." He stepped into the dimly lit teachers' retreat.

Mrs. Burwell pointed at the vinyl chairs around a dinette table at the center of the room. "Have a seat." She popped open a soft drink can and set it on the table, and then she lit a cigarette for herself. "I hope you don't mind diet. Like the least common denominator, I'm forever trying to reduce." She smiled.

"I think you look fine." Enrique gulped his diet soft drink.

"How is that?"

"Well, you look exactly the way you should look. Any different and you wouldn't be Mrs. Burwell," Enrique tried to explain.

She exhaled two spumes of bluish smoke from her nostrils. "You should be in remedial math."

Enrique nodded.

Mrs. Burwell wolfed down another lungful of smoke and dialed a number on the phone on the wall near a compact refrigerator. "Armand, I've got one of yours here in the lounge," she said into the mouthpiece. "Enrique Suarez... No, he doesn't need to be in class. When is your planning period? Good, I'll have him wait here." She hung up the phone. "Monsieur Nassour will be here in a few minutes."

"I think I got to go to class. I have Social Studies."

"Who's your teacher?"

"Mr. Sanchez."

"I'll send him a note."

"I don't want to get another detention," Enrique said.

"Mr. Suarez," Mrs. Burwell said as she scribbled on a pad she'd produced from her handbag, "if I'm not mistaken, you have bigger problems than detention right now. I should think you'd be more worried about Wexler and his bunch. This is a big school—too many kids, too little staff. If they want you, they will find you, even here, and there's not a lot we can do to prevent that from happening."

"What do you mean?" Enrique wondered what Mrs. Burwell knew about all this.

"I think you know what this is about and why Wexler is after you. I'm sure I don't want to know the details." She crushed out her cigarette and lit another. "Of course, you're free to go to your classes if you think there's no problem." Mrs. Burwell shrugged, as if to suggest it made no difference to her what Enrique did. "Go on, if you want."

"I'll wait for Monsieur Nassour," Enrique said. He sipped his drink.

Mrs. Burwell handed him the note. "Did you know the boy who was shot yesterday?"

"Yeah, he was my friend."

"I'm sorry that happened." She gathered up her cigarettes, keys, and notepad and shoved them into her purse. "I've got to make copies for the next class and get that test over to the library." Mrs. Burwell stuck out her hand suddenly, startling Enrique before he realized she expected a handshake. He offered his hand to her crushing grip. "Keep safe," she said, and she turned to leave.

"Thank you, Mrs. Burwell. Thank you for the root beer and for everything," Enrique called after her, shaking his hand to release the pain.

He didn't have to wait long for Monsieur Nassour, but while he waited, Enrique pulled open the small refrigerator's door. He was curious about what the teachers ate. The shelves nearly buckled under cans of soft drinks, stacks of chocolate bars, boxes of donuts, and bags from fast-food takeouts. On one shelf, Enrique spied a white carton that looked like it came from a Chinese restaurant, but the word scribbled atop it read: *bait.*

"They eat such terrible things," Monsieur Nassour said at his back.

"Oh, Monsieur Nassour, I wasn't going to eat

anything. I just wanted to look." He shut the door in a hurry.

"Who can eat that, that, that so-called food?" Monsieur Nassour asked with a shudder. "I would not serve it to a dog."

Enrique pictured Boy, muzzle-deep in the carton of bait, and he shuddered too.

"In Québec," Monsieur Nassour continued, "in Québec, you will have real food. The lady of the family we have chosen is *magnifique* in the kitchen. I have eaten in this house, and I can tell you for certain you will turn your back on the hamburgers after tasting her cooking. It is perfect!" Monsieur Nassour kissed a pinch of air. "Now, tell me, Henri, have you spoken to your mother about this opportunity?"

"I tried."

"And?"

"She says she doesn't want me to go away."

The wrinkles in Monsieur Nassour's face deepened. "She said no?"

"I didn't exactly ask her about Québec. I just said what if I had a chance to go away for a while. She didn't like the idea too much. But a lot of stuff happened since then, and I think she might change her mind. She might even want me to go now," Enrique said.

"What has happened?" Monsieur Nassour drew out a dinette chair and sank into it. He leaned toward Enrique to listen.

It took almost the entire period, but Enrique described most everything to Monsieur Nassour, starting with running away from Juan to Horacio's shooting and ending with Brandon Wexler threatening him at the payphone.

"Ah!" Monsieur Nassour tapped his forehead with his fingers. "But that is too much for one boy!"

Enrique nodded, swallowing a fist-sized knot in his throat. The old French teacher's words churned up a flood of unspent tears. Enrique blinked them back, as Monsieur Nassour cupped his shoulder with a warm hand. "Monsieur Nassour," he said, forcing his lips not to quirk. "Do you really think they'll want me in Québec?"

"*Oui, oui, Henri.*" The old man nodded. "They will be very lucky to have you there."

"Do you speak any Spanish, Monsieur?"

"*Sí, hablo español muy bien.*"

"Maybe you can talk to my mother about this. I think she will listen to you."

"I will talk to her after school today, *Henri*. I will drive you home after the Drama Club meeting. Don't forget about the Drama Club! After that, I will take you and talk to your mother."

"I don't think I can go to the meeting. I have detention today."

Monsieur Nassour wagged a finger at Enrique. "The Drama Club comes first. I will tell Dean Hardin you are serving detention with me. This reminds me. I have your copy of the play we are rehearsing today. Remember I told you about the play?"

"Yeah, I'm the telephone."

"You are also the understudy, remember? Read the play, and study the part of Bennie. Our Bennie is absent today, so you will replace Bennie in the rehearsal, okay?" Monsieur Nassour handed Enrique a folded sheaf of papers from the inner pocket of his blazer.

"What's the play called?" Enrique smoothed out the pages.

"She is *A Raisin in the Sun*, a short version," Monsieur Nassour said. "Look to the lines for Bennie."

"Is this Bennie a good guy or a bad guy?"

"A good character, definitely a good character," he said. "I think you will like Bennie. Now, I must go. Read the play. I will send you a lunch from the cafeteria." Monsieur Nassour tipped his beret and hurried out of the teachers' lounge.

Enrique settled on the vinyl divan, which looked more comfortable than the dinette chair, and began reading the play. After a few lines, he read: *Bennie is Walter's sister. She wants to be a doctor.* Enrique skimmed further. "Oh, no, I don't want to do this! I'm supposed to be a *black girl!*"

"So what?" piped a voice at the door. "So am I." Enrique glanced up from the play to find Karis, balancing a tray of food as she stepped into the lounge. She narrowed her eyes at Enrique. "What's wrong with being a black girl?" she said. "Here I am bringing you food, and here you are complaining about being a black girl. You ain't even a black girl. I am. But do you hear me complaining? I got a mind to take this food, nasty as it is, back to the cafeteria. What you got against being a black girl anyway?"

"Nothing," Enrique said. "There's nothing wrong with being a black girl." He rose to take the tray from her before she decided to take it back. The warm smell of grilled cheese, fries, and vinegary pickles filled the room. His stomach growled. "Thanks for bringing me stuff to eat."

Karis wouldn't let go of the tray. "Why were you complaining, then, about being a black girl?"

"It's the play," Enrique explained. He gripped the tray firmly. "Monsieur Nassour wants me to be a girl in the play."

Karis clutched the tray, held it to her chest. "Well, what's wrong with that?"

"Nothing," Enrique said, "if you're a girl. I'm not a girl, and I don't want to be one in the play."

"Think you're too good to be a girl? Is that it?"

"No, it's just that girls make better girls than guys do."

Karis snorted and released the tray. Enrique nearly stumbled backwards, taking it. Luckily, nothing spilled. He placed it on the table and sat down to eat. "You want some?" he asked her.

Karis took a seat across from him. "You going to eat those pickles?"

"Have them," he said. "Have some fries too." He was mainly interested in the sandwich.

Karis gazed around the room. "So this is where the teachers hide out."

"Yeah, but I don't know where they are now. It's lunchtime, no?"

"Oh, they got some PTA luncheon for the teachers today." Karis plucked another dill slice from Enrique's tray. "My mamá made me bring in a tub of potato salad bigger than that trashcan over there. Felt like a drummer in the band carrying that thing on the bus." She scooped up a few fries.

"You got nice nails," Enrique said.

"You like them?" Her dimples deepened. "At first, I wasn't sure I wanted blue, but with the Playboy bunny studs, it looks pretty nice, huh?"

"Real nice."

"Shh." Karis put a finger to her lips. "Hear that?"

Static crackled from the public address speaker mounted over the door. Enrique climbed on the counter, reaching for the speaker's dials to adjust the sound. He twisted the volume knob and heard the attendance clerk's voice: *Enrique Suarez, report to the main office. Enrique Suarez, report to the main office immediately.*

Karis smiled. "Ooh, you in big trouble, I bet."

Chapter Thirty-Three

The lunch bell rang, scattering the crowds under the shelter. Groups of students milled toward the bungalows while Enrique hurried out of the teachers' lounge, hoping to blend in with the bunch headed toward the front of the school. He felt pretty sure Pirata wasn't the kind of person to sit patiently in his car while Brandon took his final exam.

The crowd Enrique joined vanished into the tech lab, filling him with the feeling he had when he dreamed about coming to school without pants—exposed and horrified. He longed to race for the office, but that would attract even more attention. Enrique forced himself to walk in a calm way, even though his heart pounded his lungs with such force he could barely breathe.

A heavy hand clasped his shoulder. His knees wobbled, and he nearly collapsed. But he steadied himself and slowly turned around. "Francisco!"

"Hey, where have you been? You just disappeared. I thought you got sick."

"I'm not sick." Enrique picked up his pace to the office.

Francisco kept up with him. "How come you're walking like that?"

"Like what?"

"Like a puppet. You look all stiff and jerky like Pinocchio."

"Look, Francisco, I'm in a big hurry. Didn't you hear

them call my name on the speaker? I got to go to the office."

"Yeah, I heard that. It's like everyone's looking for you. Even that one-eyed guy who never comes to school, he was here asking for you during lunch."

Enrique searched the schoolyard. "Where is he now?"

Francisco shrugged. "I don't know. I saw him a little while ago. He could be anywhere."

Enrique didn't want his friend with him when Pirata appeared. What if he pulled a gun? "Didn't you hear the bell ring? Don't you have to go to class?"

"I rather walk with you a bit. I've never been late to a class before, you know. What can they do to me the first time? Shoot me?" Francisco laughed.

"Look, you don't have to walk with me." Enrique quickened his pace.

Francisco kept up. "I know I don't, but I want to talk to you. I've been acting like a jerk, and I want to tell you I'm sorry."

"Okay, thanks. You better go back to class." He slipped into his "power" stride, legs churning and arms swinging.

"No, wait. I said some terrible things to you," Francisco persisted. "I didn't mean what I said. I've been feeling bad since German died, and I guess I was taking it out on you."

"That's okay. You better go now."

Francisco caught Enrique's arm and stopped him. "What's the matter with you? Are you mad at me?"

"No, I swear it." Eyes darting this way and that,

Enrique took a moment to explain. "There's something going on right now that's serious, Francisco. I can't talk about it now, but I'll tell you later. All I can say is that it's better if you go to class right now."

"But if you have a problem, maybe I can—"

"No," Enrique said, using up his last bit of patience. "Not this time."

Francisco's dark eyes bored into his. "Are you sure?"

"I'm sure."

"Okay, then." Francisco turned to head for class. "Call me later."

"I will." Enrique said.

"Hey, wait," Francisco called, over his shoulder. "I almost forgot." He pivoted and hurried back to Enrique. Then he dug into his backpack and pulled out a paperback book. "Here."

Enrique reached to take it. "What's this?"

"The French-English dictionary—I ordered it for you. It just came today. Happy Tuesday!" Francisco grinned.

Enrique quickly flipped through the book. "Thanks, I really wanted this."

"That's why I got it for you."

Enrique tucked the book into the waistband of his shorts. "I'll call you later."

As he jogged toward the administration building, Enrique caught sight of Pirata, several yards away and bounding across the quad to the front of the school. Enrique yanked open the door to the main office building as though it were an escape hatch in a disaster movie. He slammed it hard behind him and twisted the bolt above the door knob.

"Young man," the blue-haired receptionist said in a dry voice, "you've locked the front entrance to this building."

"I know." Enrique nodded, trying to catch his breath. "The wind—it's windy out there. Got to keep out the wind."

The receptionist glanced at the oversized thermometer on the wall—the mercury reached the eighty-five degree mark—and out the window at a cluster of trees whose leaves were as still and unruffled as those in a painting. She shook her head and continued typing, as though Enrique was not the first lunatic to come barreling through the door, not by a long shot.

"They called me," Enrique said as he approached the counter separating her desk from the waiting area. "They called me on the speaker a few minutes ago."

She stopped typing to peer at him over the top of her glasses. "Are you the Suarez boy?"

"Yeah."

"Mr. Toro's office," she said. "Second door on the right."

Enrique pointed. "That one?"

"Yes, and unlock the main entrance, please."

Enrique made a show of jiggling the knob and sliding the bolt a little, but he didn't unlock the door before heading to Mr. Toro's office. He knocked on the door.

"Come in!" Mr. Toro called from within.

Enrique opened the door to find his mother, with

the triplets napping in their stroller, talking quietly with the vice principal in Spanish.

¡Mamá! He rushed into her arms and held her tightly. Until that moment, he had not known how much he'd missed her. *¡Mamá!*

Enrique, what is happening? Tell me. She kissed his cheek and stroked his hair.

Mr. Toro, the circles under his eyes darker than ever, stood and gathered a few files together. "Enrique, I think you probably want to talk to your mother alone. Remember, as an administrator and an officer on this campus, I am required to report any information related to the commission of a crime to the police."

"Are you going to call the police?" Enrique asked.

"Your mother tells me you witnessed a serious crime, an attempted homicide. I have to alert the authorities," he said.

"But I already talked to the police. I already answered their questions. I can't tell them anything else. I swear it."

"When is it going to stop, son?" Mr. Toro leaned to peer into Enrique's face. "When is it going to stop, if people like you don't step up and take responsibility? You've got to be a man, son. Tell what you saw, who you saw. Take responsibility."

Enrique clenched his jaw. Mr. Toro's little speech might work with a younger kid or a dumber kid, but he wasn't buying it. Finking to the police wasn't going to make him a man. That would only make him a corpse. He called to mind yet another Angie, Vanished Angie who had witnessed one of the Paiute Street Regulars dumping a body in the duck pond at the park. When word got around that she'd seen this, her entire family had to go into hiding. Some said they disappeared themselves all the way down to South America, where they were tracked down and slaughtered. But those were only rumors. Enrique hoped they'd gotten away.

"Think about what I've said, Enrique. I'll step outside, so you can talk to your mother privately." Mr. Toro scuttled out of the room, shutting the door gently behind him.

His mother's shoulders quaked and tears dripped from her nose. *Did they see you? The boys who shot Horacio? Are you sure they saw you?*

Yes, Mamá. They came to school today to get me. One of them is just outside, right now.

We must call the police.

If we call the police, they will make me tell what I saw. And then, there will be more, Mamá, more and more of these people to get me, and maybe they will try to hurt you and my brothers too.

What are we going to do? My God, what can we do? Her face paled and her eyes grew wide.

I have to go away. They will get me for certain if I stay.

We will move. I will borrow money from Ceci, and maybe from that Glen too, and we will move back to Mexico.

I don't want to move to Mexico. And Juan hates Mexico. Enrique knew well that his stepfather had grudges against most of his relatives living in Mexico.

He'd turned his back on his native country years ago, vowing never to return.

We will go without him, his mother said.

Do you really want to leave Juan? Enrique asked, doubting this.

What will we do? What will we do?

The babies stirred and began howling too. Enrique unstrapped Maclovio from the stroller seat and handed him to his mother. He was just lifting out Hilario when the door swung open.

Monsieur Nassour stood in the threshold, a soft look on his face as he gazed in at Enrique and his family. When he stepped into Mr. Toro's office, Monsieur Nassour reached to take Hilario from Enrique, so the boy could heft Yunior out of the stroller. They all sat around Mr. Toro's broad desk, each of them holding a fussy baby. Enrique's mother produced bottles of apple juice from a diaper bag. Gradually, the babies quieted to drink their juice.

Enrique has the chance to study French in Canada, Monsieur Nassour began in his oddly accented Spanish.

Chapter Thirty-Four

While Monsieur Nassour explained Enrique's opportunity to be an exchange student in Québec, Enrique's mother just stared at the baby in her lap and shook her head, as though she didn't want to hear him. Her black curls swayed from one side to the other until Maclovio reached out to catch one in his plump fist. She stopped shaking her head, then, to peel his fingers from her hair. Afterwards, she just listened, and finally she said, *When will he come back?*

One year, Monsieur Nassour told her. *He will return in one year when all this trouble is over.*

In a year, Mamá, those guys will forget about me. And, if not, at least they will know that I didn't go to the police. I think they will leave me alone.

Enrique's mother turned to Monsieur Nassour. *I will have to speak to my husband about this tonight.*

There's no time, Señora, he said. *If I can make all the arrangements, Enrique should leave today, this afternoon.*

You already know what Juan will say, Mamá. He will be glad for me to go.

I can't do this, his mother said. *No, I cannot be without my son. He belongs with me. We are a family. We have always been together.*

But I'm not with you now, Enrique pointed out.

This is a chance for Enrique, Señora, Monsieur Nassour told her. *This is a chance for him to learn a language he loves and to experience a new life away from danger, away from fear. Every parent wants this for his or her child. You want this for your son. You want him to live free from fear, and you want him to learn.*

They will try to kill me, Mamá. They will try to hurt us if I stay.

Mothers who do not love their sons are those who send them away, Enrique's mother insisted.

That's not the truth, Monsieur Nassour said. *Mothers who love their sons give them the chance to live and learn, even if they must be separated for a short time.*

She turned to Enrique. *Do you believe this?*

He stared deeply into her welling eyes, and he nodded.

Will you know that I love you even if you are far away from me?

Enrique swallowed hard and clasped his mother's hand. He raised it to his cheek and rubbed his face against her cool, smooth skin the way he used to do when he was a small boy. *I will know that you love me because you let me go.*

His mother sighed. Tears streaming from her eyes, she turned to Monsieur Nassour to ask questions about the family Enrique would live with, the school he would attend. And after a bit more discussion, it was settled: Enrique would go to Québec to study French.

He had, it turned out, a passport that his mother kept in a locked box in their apartment. *You mean I was born here? In the United States?*

When I saw the trouble tía Ceci had getting naturalized

to live and work over here, I stayed with her until you were born, and went back to Mexico afterwards.

I can't believe it. How come we went back to Mexico?

That is where my mother and father lived. When your father left before you were born, I had no one but my family. After my parents died, we came north to be with Ceci.

Why didn't you ever tell me this?

I don't like to think about the past. Those were terrible times. I prefer to forget.

Monsieur Nassour persuaded Mr. Toro to find someone to drive Enrique's mother to the apartment with the triplets to get Enrique's passport and grab a suitcase for him. They would stop at Ceci's to get Enrique's belongings from her place. Monsieur Nassour, then, helped her withdraw Enrique from school and collect his transcripts and immunization records to forward to the school he would attend in Québec. Finally, he pulled out a credit card and made a series of calls from the phone on Mr. Toro's desk.

Monsieur Nassour was so successful at getting everyone—from the middle school staff to his club of cronies and the family in Québec—to be flexible and cooperative about this sudden departure that Enrique was certain the old French teacher would have no problem releasing him from rehearsal for the play that afternoon.

"That I cannot do," Monsieur Nassour said when Enrique asked him about it. "It is your responsibility. I have made the airline reservation for early evening so that you can participate in the rehearsal."

"But I'm not going to be here for the play. I don't see why I have to rehearse."

"It is a very important dress rehearsal, Enrique. Everything depends upon this. You must be there." The old man would not be moved.

"I haven't had a chance to learn the lines," Enrique said. "I only got the play a little while ago."

"You can read from your script for this rehearsal."

"Will I have to wear a dress?"

"*Non, non,* not a dress."

"Whew!"

"You will wear a skirt—pleated, black, very becoming."

Enrique spent the remainder of the school day reading the play on the bench outside of Mr. Toro's office. It wasn't a bad play, he decided. In fact, it was pretty good. Only why couldn't he have been given the part of Walter or even Travis, the little boy? He would have been happy to play one of Walter's no-good friends or even that mean Mr. Linder.

"I'm not kissing anyone," he mumbled, reading about Bennie and her boyfriends. Apart from this, he had to admit that he liked the character he was to play. She was smart and said funny things. But *why* did she have to be a girl? When he finished reading the play, he peered in Mr. Toro's office at Monsieur Nassour, who was between phone calls. "This is a real long play. We might not have time to—"

"It is a shortened version, only a few scenes. We

have done this many times. It does not take long." The French teacher glanced at his watch. *"C'est bon!* I have made all the plans. Do you feel ready to go to Québec for one year?"

For the first time, Enrique thought about this, really thought about this, and he panicked. He would be gone for a whole year! What would happen in a year to his mother and Juan? His brothers? They would be walking, maybe even talking when he returned. Would they know him? What about Horacio and Francisco? Would they remember him when he got back? What about Boy?

Again, he had forgotten all about his little dog. Who would take care of him? Who would make sure that he got enough food and water and exercise? Boy was already pretty old. What if he should die while Enrique was away? He had heard about dogs who grew so depressed when their masters left them that they stopped eating…

Enrique longed to shout, *"Stop!"* He wanted to tell Monsieur Nassour that this was all a mistake. That he couldn't go after all. That he had to be here for his brothers, for his mother. That he couldn't leave his friends—they'd forget him. That he shouldn't leave his dog.

Then Enrique remembered Horacio, flying forward with the gun blasts, his blood welling on the pavement, and now lying in a hospital bed. Pirata, Chivo, and the others would do the same to him, or worse.

"Well, you are thinking about this a long time," Monsieur Nassour said. "Are you having what they call second thoughts? Is your mind changing?"

"I guess I'm scared, Monsieur," Enrique admitted. "But I know I have to go. I can't change my mind."

Monsieur Nassour brought Enrique his costume— the skirt, a blouse, some high-heeled shoes and a wig to change into before they headed to the auditorium for the rehearsal. Enrique slipped the blouse over his t-shirt and pulled the skirt over his shorts. The black pleats felt soft on his knees and twirled gracefully when he pirouetted before the mirror in the faculty restroom where he changed. As he was spinning, the receptionist opened the door.

"Very nice, dearie," she said. "Let me help you with that wig." Her flat tone suggested that helping boys dress up as girls in the faculty restroom was just another part of her regular duties, like collecting attendance cards. "There, you go." She tugged at the wig to center it and then fluffed it out with a pick. "You make a very pretty girl. Lipstick?"

"No!"

But she produced a tube and applied two deft strokes before he could squirm away. "Very nice," she murmured. "*Very* nice."

"Are you ready, Benny?" Monsieur Nassour asked.

"I guess so." Enrique rubbed most of the lipstick off with the back of his hand.

"Let's go then." The French teacher opened the main door, which someone must have unlocked earlier, and they stepped out into the schoolyard.

Enrique spied Pirata and Brandon Wexler huddled together near the bus kiosk a few yards away, and he froze.

Chapter Thirty-Five

Though Pirata and Chivo stood watching the entrance to the main office, they didn't recognize Enrique under the wig and in the black skirt. Pirata even looked straight at Enrique and then back at Chivo to laugh at something he had said.

"Keep walking," Monsieur Nassour said. "Don't stare. Keep walking, with your hips, like a girl."

Enrique took smallish steps and fastened his eyes on the walk. Dean Hardin must not have gotten this far with her scraper, he thought. Smudges of gum splotched the pavement everywhere he looked. He'd never noticed before what a long way it was to the auditorium. Perspiration tickled his underarms and he could feel the curious stares of people they passed, but he didn't dare look up.

"We're here." Monsieur Nassour pulled open the heavy doors, and they slipped into air-conditioned darkness. Monsieur Nassour flipped on a switch and the snaky fluorescent tubes overhead hummed, pulsing with light.

"Monsieur Nassour, did you make me put on that dress and the wig so those guys wouldn't recognize me?" As soon as he'd said it, Enrique felt it was a foolish question.

"What do you think, Enrique," Monsieur Nassour asked as they strode down the aisle to the stage.

"I don't know. Maybe you planned everything.

Maybe you made me be a girl in the play to give me a disguise to get out of the office."

Monsieur Nassour turned to Enrique. "What do you think I am? A spy? A secret agent? *Mon Dieu!* You give me too much credit." He laughed. "Now help me decide which stage lights to use for the rehearsal."

When the other club members arrived and got into costume, Enrique was relieved to find he wasn't the only boy with a female part. In fact, there was a competition among the boys to play the part of Mama, Bennie's mother. Despite the fact that Dantonio won the role, he still wanted the club to perform *Westside Story*. He kept singing snatches from the musical to tempt the others as he pulled on a gingham dress and tied an apron over it.

"Listen to him," Rico said. "He don't deserve to be Mama."

Karis shook her head. "He can't even sing good."

"No," Howard said in his deep, rumbling voice.

"I could have been Mama," said a small boy named Sidney. "I'd make a good Mama."

"You're too skinny," Karis told him.

"When you're a Jet, you're a Jet—" Dantonio sang, "from your first cigarette—"

Monsieur Nassour clapped his hands. "Okay, okay, let's start at the beginning."

The play opened on a sleepy morning in the Younger household. Howard played Walter, and Karis was his wife, Ruth. Watching them read their lines, Enrique was amazed that Howard was such a powerful actor that he made everyone forget for a while that they were just a bunch of middle-school kids dressed in secondhand clothes practicing a shortened version of a play. The lanky boy seethed and snapped dangerously in his role, inspiring the others to slip into their parts easily, even naturally.

By the time Enrique came onstage to read his lines, he almost felt he was Bennie. He spited Walter and sassed Mama, and then flirted with George Murchison and Asagai. As he played the part of Bennie, he felt strangely happy and free.

"Good job, Howard," Monsieur Nassour said when the rehearsal had ended. "Someday you will be a great actor."

"Yeah," Howard said, returning to his single-word speech.

"I think Enrique was pretty good, too," Karis said. "He's way better than what's-her-name, the girl who usually does Bennie. We ought to keep him and cancel her. She's absent even more than me."

"You were *tres bien*, Enrique," Monsieur Nassour said.

"*Merci*," Enrique said, starting to unbutton the skirt.

But Monsieur Nassour shook his head, and Enrique left it on.

"Hurry," he said to the other club members. "Hurry, so you don't miss the activities bus. I am not driving anyone home tonight."

After the last club member raced for the bus, Monsieur Nassour and Enrique began their long walk back to the office. Though Enrique didn't see the two boys who were after him this time, he felt they were nearby, watching and waiting. But they didn't know him in the costume.

Even his mother, waiting in the office, didn't recognize him at first.

Mamá, it's me.

Enrique?

Yes, it's me.

Why are you wearing that?

For the play practice, Mamá, and so I can leave the school without those guys seeing me. Where are the babies? Where are my brothers?

I left them at the apartment with Leontina. It would be too much to manage them at the airport.

But I won't get to see them again. I won't get to say goodbye.

I am sorry, but it was too much.

I wanted to kiss them. I wanted to tell them I would be back.

His mother touched his cheek. *I will tell them. I will kiss them for you. I did bring a surprise for you. Look in my bag.* She pulled open the drawstring of her oversized tote bag, and Boy wiggled his way out.

"Boy!"

Chapter Thirty-Six

Enrique held Boy in his lap in the backseat while his mother sat up front with Monsieur Nassour. As the French teacher's old car rumbled out of the teachers' parking lot, Enrique caught a glimpse of Mrs. Burwell loading a heavy box of papers into the trunk of her car. A cigarette dangled from her lips, smoke spumes blending with her snowy cap of hair. She set the box in the trunk. He waved at her, smiling to think that his work wouldn't be among those papers to be savaged by her red pen that night.

"Monsieur Nassour, do we have time to make one stop?" Enrique asked. "It's close to here."

"Are you hungry? There will be food at the airport."

"No, it's not that. I have to see one person. It will only take a minute. She lives up this street."

"I suppose we have a little time." Monsieur Nassour followed Enrique's directions to the neat yellow house.

"*¿Es un amigo?*" his mother asked when they stopped.

"*Sí,*" Enrique told her. He clutched Boy to his chest as he climbed out of the car. "I'll be right back."

He opened the gate and jogged up the path to the front door. He rang the doorbell and listened to the approach of shuffling footsteps from within.

"Who's there?"

He held Boy up to the peephole. "It's Simon," Enrique said. "I brought Simon back."

The door whooshed open. "Simon! Simon!" Mrs. Dablowski cried, reaching for Boy. "I've missed you and missed you." She took Boy into her arms and kissed him. He lapped her face, his tail whipping wildly. "Thank you for bringing my little dog back."

Enrique ruffled Boy's ears. "He likes walks," he told the old woman.

"I will walk him every day."

"He's a little bit of a chicken."

"The smartest ones are always chicken." Mrs. Dablowski kissed Boy's head as though she was proud of him for being afraid of just about everything. "There's nothing wrong with being a chicken. If you leave them alone, chickens will live forty years or more. That's almost three times as long as the wolf. Why, chickens..."

"Well, goodbye, Boy," Enrique said, not wanting to be delayed talking about chickens with the lonely old woman, and maybe even trapped into coming inside to look at pictures of them. "Be good."

"Wait a minute," she said.

Enrique glanced at his imaginary watch. "I'm in a hurry."

"I suppose you want your reward."

Enrique shook his head. He just wanted to get back to the car.

"I don't want you telling people I didn't give you your reward." She fished in the pocket of her housecoat and produced a quarter. "Take it, young lady. Go on. You deserve it."

Enrique snatched the quarter and raced back to the car. He gave his mother a look when she turned to him, so she would let him sit in silence the rest of the way to the airport. As soon as they sped up the on-ramp to the freeway, Enrique tore off the wig and wriggled out of the costume.

Chapter Thirty-Seven

At the airport, the many sights and sounds crowded Enrique's senses giving him a numb feeling. He held his mother's hand and carried his own bag while Monsieur Nassour navigated through the terminal. There had been traffic and such a long line to check in that Enrique had only a few minutes with his mother before he had to get through security to board the plane. Monsieur Nassour went to find Enrique a snack to eat on the plane.

Son, you can still change your mind. You can stay.

Enrique shook his head. *I have to go.*

Except for the time you stayed with Ceci, you have never been away from me.

I know.

I don't know how it will be without you.

I guess it will be different for both of us.

I cannot be the same without you. I will be changed.

I will be changed too, Mamá.

Enrique's mother wiped her eyes with the hand-kerchief Monsieur Nassour had given her earlier. *You won't forget that I love you. I love you, and that's why I have to let you go.*

She held him close.

A rush of people swept past, and Enrique worried he wouldn't have time to find his plane. He pulled away, hefting his bag. *Tell Monsieur Nassour I'm sorry I didn't get to see him to say goodbye.*

There he is. You can tell him goodbye.

The old man appeared with two small bags. "Do you like biscotti? It was the only thing that I could find fit to eat." He breathed heavily, as though he'd been running. "I got you something to read on the airplane and some paper so you can write letters to your family and your friends."

Enrique remembered the dictionary Francisco gave him. He could still feel its weight against his waistband. He wouldn't be able to keep his promise and call his friend, but he would write to him.

"This is a good book." Monsieur Nassour handed him a copy of *Le Petit Prince* from one of the bags. "It is in French and English, Enrique. I think you will like the story." He stuffed it into a pocket of Enrique's suitcase.

"*Merci,* Monsieur Nassour*, merci*, and, really, I mean it, for everything." Enrique shook the old French teacher's hand.

Monsieur Nassour pulled him close for quick kisses on both cheeks. "*Au revoir, Henri.*"

Enrique embraced his mother one last time. *Don't forget to tell my brothers about me. Tell them I will be home in a year.*

Oh, Enrique... His mother covered her face. She could say no more.

Enrique lugged his bag to the first security checkpoint and then into the line where his luggage would be examined. Enrique turned once to wave, and then he didn't look back. He rushed through the terminal to find his gate. He was winded, but he made it on time and handed the attendant his ticket. As he walked through the steamy tunnel to board the plane, he forced himself to think about the future. He would write some letters on the plane. He'd write one to Maricela and send her a letter to give Horacio. *Querido Horacio...* Or maybe he should write in English. Horacio could use the practice. He'd sure be surprised to find out that Enrique had gone to Canada. Enrique imagined his friend reading his letter with astonishment in his hospital bed, and maybe a nurse would walk in, and Horacio would put down the letter to smile at her. *Hay labio jabón lechuga.*

He would write Francisco after he got to Canada, and he'd tell him about Québec. Enrique wondered what it would be like to live there. He was curious about the family whose home he'd share. What would the school be like? He was pretty sure there was no one like Monsieur Nassour, anywhere, but maybe he'd have a teacher like Ms. Byers who would make him write journals in French. He imagined himself writing in his journal on that first day:

Je m'appele Enrique.

LORRAINE M. LÓPEZ has a doctoral degree in English through the Creative Writing Program at the University of Georgia. Her first book, *Soy La Avon Lady and Other Stories*, was selected by Sandra Cisneros to win the inaugural Mármol Prize for Fiction. It also received the Independent Publishers Book Award for Multicultural Fiction and the Latino Book Award for Short Stories, awarded by the Latino Literary Hall of Fame. She has just finished co-editing a collection of critical articles on the work of Judith Ortiz Cofer. López was born and raised in Los Angeles, California. She currently resides in Nashville, Tennessee, where she is an Assistant Professor of English at Vanderbilt University.

CURBSTONE PRESS, INC.

is a nonprofit publishing house dedicated to literature that reflects a commitment to social change, with an emphasis on contemporary writing from Latino, Latin American and Vietnamese cultures. Curbstone presents writers who give voice to the unheard in a language that goes beyond denunciation to celebrate, honor and teach. Curbstone builds bridges between its writers and the public – from inner-city to rural areas, colleges to community centers, children to adults. Curbstone seeks out the highest aesthetic expression of the dedication to human rights and intercultural understanding: poetry, testimonies, novels, stories, and children's books.

This mission requires more than just producing books. It requires ensuring that as many people as possible learn about these books and read them. To achieve this, a large portion of Curbstone's schedule is dedicated to arranging tours and programs for its authors, working with public school and university teachers to enrich curricula, reaching out to underserved audiences by donating books and conducting readings and community programs, and promoting discussion in the media. It is only through these combined efforts that literature can truly make a difference.

Curbstone Press, like all nonprofit presses, depends on the support of individuals, foundations, and government agencies to bring you, the reader, works of literary merit and social significance which might not find a place in profit-driven publishing channels, and to bring the authors and their books into communities across the country. Our sincere thanks to the many individuals, foundations, and government agencies who have recently supported this endeavor: Community Foundation of Northeast Connecticut, Connecticut Commission on Culture & Tourism, Connecticut Humanities Council, Greater Hartford Arts Council, Hartford Courant Foundation, Lannan Foundation, National Endowment for the Arts, and the United Way of the Capital Area.

Please help to support Curbstone's efforts to present the diverse voices and views that make our culture richer. Tax-deductible donations can be made by check or credit card to:
Curbstone Press, 321 Jackson Street, Willimantic, CT 06226
phone: (860) 423-5110   fax: (860) 423-9242
www.curbstone.org

CAKE

Also by Joyce Magnin

Harriet Beamer Takes the Bus

Carrying Mason

The Prayers of Agnes Sparrow

Charlotte Figg Takes Over Paradise

Griselda Takes Flight

Blame It on the Mistletoe

Joyce Magnin

ZONDERVAN.com/
AUTHORTRACKER
follow your favorite authors

ZONDERKIDZ

Cake
Copyright © 2012 by Joyce Magnin Moccero

Illustrations copyright © Olga & Aleksey Ivanov

This title is also available as a Zondervan ebook.
Visit www.zondervan.com/ebooks.

Requests for information should be addressed to:
Zonderkidz, 5300 Patterson Ave., SE Grand Rapids, Michigan 49530

Library of Congress Cataloging-in-Publication Data

Moccero, Joyce Magnin.
    Cake : love, chickens, and a taste of peculiar / Joyce Magnin.
      p. cm.
    Summary: Wilma Sue is wary of the eccentric sisters, Ruth and Naomi, at her
new foster home, but wonders if she might have a true home with them, baking and
delivering cakes and tending their chickens, until she is implicated in a series of
neighborhood crimes.
    ISBN 978-0-310-73333-1 (hardcover : alk. paper)
    1. Foster home care—Fiction. 2. Conduct of life—Fiction. 3. Eccentrics and
eccentricities—Fiction. 4. Bakers and bakeries—Fiction. 5. Neighbors—Fiction.
6. Chickens—Fiction. 7. Sisters—Fiction. I. Title.
PZ7.M71277Cak 2013
[Fic]—dc23   2012037297

All Scripture quotations, unless otherwise indicated, are taken from the Holy Bible, *King James Version, KJV.*

Art direction: Cindy Davis
Cover illustration: Gayle Raymer
Interior Illustrations: Olga & Aleksey Ivanov
Interior design: Greg Johnson/Textbook Perfect

Printed in the United States of America

12 13 14 15 16 17 18 /DCI/ 21 20 19 18 17 16 15 14 13 12 11 10 9 8 7 6 5 4 3 2 1

For my son, Adam

Chapter

1

Hope is the thing with feathers . . .
— *Emily Dickinson*

Birds have hollow bones. That's how they can fly.
Sometimes I wish I had hollow bones so I could fly. I would
fly so far away no one would ever find me. I would fly to the
highest mountain on the furthest continent. I would perch there
and wait for just the right air current to come my way, and then
I'd fly some more. I'd fly over oceans and farms fat with corn
and wheat and cows. I'd rise with the air and fall with my wings
outstretched so wide you'd think they might snap . . . but they
won't. My wings are strong.

⸻

That night I stayed awake. I didn't want to sleep. I knew if I
did the morning would come too fast. So I kept myself awake,
awake dreaming about flying over the ocean and watching the
waves build and roll and crash on the shore. Awake dreaming

that I could fly over the Great Redwood Forest. That I could fly above the green tree canopy where salamanders live on the branches of the world's tallest trees.

I flap my wings but only a few times so I won't get tired. Mostly I rest on the air currents like dandelion seeds. Mostly I fly with only the wind under my wings.

Miss Tate arrived the next morning. She's my social worker from Miss Daylily's Home for Children, or Miss Daylily's Home for Unwanted and Misunderstood Children. That's what I call it. I lived there before I went to live with the Crums. Actually, I've lived at Miss Daylily's Home off and on since I was a baby, but I'll tell you more about that later.

The Crums don't want me anymore. So Miss Tate—tall, dark, and skinny like a Slim Jim—is taking me to a new foster home.

Lester and Mauveleen Crum have had me long enough, they said. Time for someone else to take over. Reason one: Lester won a boatload of money in the lottery, and now he wants to take Mauveleen on a trip around the world. They don't have room for me to go along, even though I am small, like a wren. They only have room for their three real children. Mauveleen said I'd just be in the way.

Reason two: I put shaving cream inside Lola's pillowcase. She's the oldest Crum child. I put honey on one of the kitchen chairs, and Lester sat in it. And I rigged a small bucket of water over a doorjamb, and it rained down on Lola.

So I had kind of a record with them. Mauveleen said they couldn't have a prankster along on the trip, and they were sending me back. Fortunately, Miss Tate told me she had some people who were interested in taking me right away, so I wouldn't need to go back to the home. No siree, Bob! I was going straight from the Crum house to my new foster family.

"Come on, Wilma Sue," Miss Tate called from downstairs. "It's time to go."

I had one suitcase. The same one I carried into the Crum house three years ago. It's brown with wrinkled leather that reminds me of cracked sidewalks and trees and maps of places I'd like to see. I crammed my book *Emily of New Moon* inside, along with my most secret possessions: a spiral-bound journal where I write my deepest thoughts, and the dictionary I won in a fourth-grade spelling bee. Ever since then, words have become my hobby. I'm always looking up new ones and figuring out a way to use them during the day. I also crammed my walk-around notebook into my back pocket because I never know when "the flash" will strike. That's what Emily, in *Emily of New Moon*, called that sudden urge to express what's in your deepest heart. Sometimes it's like a lightning bolt; sometimes it comes on slow, like Christmas.

Next, I stuffed a brown bear that I've had forever inside my suitcase and zipped it closed. I think I got the bear when I was a baby, but I can't be sure. I don't remember too much about those baby days. I just remember sounds. Loud sounds like crying or muffled sounds like water running.

"I'm coming!" I called. I took one more look around the little bedroom that had been my nest—at least a small part of it. I'd shared the room with Lola.

I lugged my suitcase down the steps. Lester Crum was out getting a haircut. Mauveleen stood near the front door with Miss Tate. Mauveleen wore her brand-new dress, hot pink with black buttons. She had her hair all done up like a princess, complete with a diamond tiara. I knew she couldn't wait for me to go so she could climb into her brand-new red Porsche and drive away.

"You take care, Wilma Sue," she said. "It was good having you."

I smiled at her. For a second I thought I should hug her, but she was closed that morning, the way she was closed most every day. Mauveleen Crum rarely looked me square in the eye, unless it was to holler at me about some such thing that I might or might not have had a hand in. And she always seemed to stand with her arms crossed against her chest, the best way of all to say, "No hugs allowed." I had written in my notebook a few months back, *I will always look people in the eye and always be ready to give out hugs.*

I looked at Miss Tate. Her face reminded me of a walnut, warm but wrinkly.

"Can I help with your suitcase?" Miss Tate asked.

"No, thank you. It's not heavy," I said. I smiled just so she'd believe me. I figured a girl's got to carry her own bag through life.

We drove in Miss Tate's van. It was black like midnight and had the words

Miss Daylily's Home for Children

emblazoned on the side in big yellow letters. The van was large enough to carry nine unwanted children. I was certain that everybody we passed knew the kid in the backseat was Unwanted and probably Misunderstood.

Miss Daylily's Home sat like a great stone factory with billowing smokestacks and chain-link fences in Philadelphia, all the way down near the waterfront. I had lived there off and on my entire life. Miss Tate said I arrived one cold winter day as a baby. She found me on the front steps with a small note pinned to my yellow blanket. The note said my name was Wilma Sue. She and Miss Daylily took care of me until I went to live with the McAllisters. I'd been two years old when I went there, and the thought of Mrs. McAllister gave me a slight pain in my chest. It was probably just heartburn, which I had pretty much all the time when I lived at the Crum house. But after the McAllisters, I lived at Miss Daylily's again for a whole year—almost to the day—from the time I was eight until nine. And then I went to live with the Crums.

Before Miss Tate took me to the Crum house, for a while I was the oldest kid at Miss Daylily's, and Miss Daylily and Miss Tate expected me to do a whole lot to "earn my keep," like change little Earl's diaper. And when Miss Daylily told me to do something, you betcha I jumped, cause otherwise she'd have me writing an entire essay on the origin of diapers or something.

Even so, I liked Miss Daylily. She was big and fat and wore long skirts down to her ankles. She wore her hair in a large gray bun that she secured to her head with two chopsticks, and most of the time she smelled like cherry cola. She made the best applesauce on the planet. And every once in a while, she would hold me in her lap and read me a book.

As Miss Tate and I drove, we passed block after block of row homes, some in better shape than others, with flower gardens and wrought-iron fences and lawn gnomes. Some of the houses we passed looked like ruins, with broken or missing windows and doors hanging off their hinges like dislocated shoulders. One house had yellow police tape stretched across the front door.

We drove through the large shopping district they called simply Forty-fifth Street, where I saw people on foot pushing shopping carts or carrying tote bags. We finally made it out of the city and into the suburbs. I knew this because I could see the summer sky again, blue and cloudless.

Miss Tate didn't have much to say the whole way. Me neither. She did tell me three times that the weather was nice for early summer, but she'd heard rain was moving in later in the day. She also looked at me in the rearview mirror, and I saw her eyes were a little stern and thin. She said, "Do your best to get along in the new house, Wilma Sue. The most important thing is to do your best to get along with everyone."

This is exactly what she told me when she took me to the Crums'. It was probably what she told me when she took me to the McAllisters', too. And now she said it again.

Millie and Meg McAllister were very nice people. Millie was the mother. My mother for all of six years.

Her husband, Mervin, died about two years before I got there. They had one other daughter, Meg, and she was a lot older than me. But that was okay. Meg treated me real nice. But when Meg went away to college, Millie sent me back to Miss Daylily's Home. I was so sad that day; I thought my heart would break into a gazillion pieces.

Do you ever feel that way? So sad that you can't even stand it another second and think for sure that your heart is breaking into a gazillion tiny pieces never to be put together again—ever? That's how sad I felt when I left the McAllisters' house. It was the first time I wished I had hollow bones.

"Did you hear me, Wilma Sue?" Miss Tate asked. "I said for you to get along in the new house." She pointed her index finger into the mirror. "And no more pranks! I mean it, Wilma Sue. This is a trial run. Just one infraction and back you go to the orphanage. That's the rule."

"Yes, ma'am," I said as I watched out the van window as neighborhoods of large houses whizzed past. Giant trees lined most of the streets. "No more pranks."

Then we turned onto a street called Bloomingdale Avenue. I liked the name but decided it was too soon to say it out loud. There were fewer cars on Bloomingdale Avenue and most were parked in driveways. We drove more slowly, and I noticed the houses grew further and further apart. They had larger and larger yards and longer fences. I thought maybe the longer the fence, the richer the people who lived on the other side.

"Here we are," Miss Tate said as she pulled up in front of a big stone house. It looked creepy, like a haunted house, with many roofs and porches and funny round windows like the kind you'd see on a ship. It sat on the corner of the street all by itself.

"This is the parsonage," Miss Tate said. "Your new home."

"Parsonage." I knew that word from all the time I spent reading. It's where the pastor of a church lived. "Am I going to live with a pastor?"

Miss Tate laughed a little. "No. Not a pastor. Missionaries. The church is letting them live in the house."

"Oh."

"Their names are Ruth and Naomi Beedlemeyer. They're sisters. Never married. They lived in Africa until last year."

"Africa?" That part sounded extravagant. Imagine that, Africa. I would like to fly to Africa. "Are they black?"

Miss Tate looked at me in the rearview mirror. "No. They're ... they're like you. They worked as missionaries in Africa."

I didn't know much about Africa, only what I learned in school. While Miss Tate snagged some papers from her briefcase, I imagined flying over Africa like a pink flamingo, sleek and fast, eyeing the continent for a lake.

I lugged my suitcase up the long cement path to the steps that led to the front door. The whole house was made from stone that looked like mica schist, great huge rocks with flecks of silver and gray that twinkled suddenly in the afternoon sun. The house had many slanty roofs and windows and two crooked chimneys. Even the roofs were covered with slate rock. I would call it Gray House.

The Crums' house was Black House. The house itself was white with shutters the most awful shade of dark purple you'd ever seen. It was like the color of plums left in the refrigerator too long. And when I walked inside, it was like walking into a black, dark cave. At least that was how it felt. Somebody was always fighting with somebody.

My favorite house so far was the McAllisters' — Yellow House. It was sunshine yellow with black shutters, and walking inside it was like walking into a field of Black-eyed Susans.

Gray House had several wind chimes that dangled from the porch roof. But they were silent. There was no wind that day. But I figured that if Miss Tate was right about the rain, then I'd probably get to hear the wind chimes tonight. I liked them. They were birds suspended from long chains. Miss Tate was just about to push the doorbell when the door flung open with gusto.

"Well, hello there! Come in. Come in." The woman, tall, old, and smelling of buttercream frosting, stepped aside and waved her arm with a flourish. She was barefoot. "Welcome home, Wilma Sue."

And then I saw a long cardboard sign made up of individual letters hung on a piece of string draped across the mantel:

Each letter was gold. Only the C was crooked and hung by a single strand of string.

I looked at Miss Tate.

"Go on, Wilma Sue, say hello."

"Hello."

"Here we are," Miss Tate said when she pulled up out front of a big stone house. It looked creepy, like a haunted house, with many roofs and porches and funny round windows like you'd see on a ship.

That was when the other woman appeared. She was fatter around the middle but with skinny ankles like a sparrow. "Oh my goodness gracious! Aren't you just the sweetest little thing to ever walk the earth? Come on over and sit down on the sofa." She sat first and patted the seat next to her. She talked to me like I was five.

I looked at Miss Tate. She moved her eyes in a way that told me I should sit.

"Isn't she darling, Naomi?" the woman on the sofa said.

I felt like a Christmas present.

"Yes, yes she is," the other woman said. "Darling. Darling. Darling."

I felt my eyes roll, even if I didn't show it.

"And you must be Ruth," Miss Tate said to the woman on the sofa.

"Yes. That's right. I'm Ruth, and this, of course, is my sister Naomi." She giggled with three fingers to her mouth. "But I just told you that, now didn't I? I must be nervous."

Miss Tate smiled with tight lips.

"Are you thirsty, Wilma Sue?" Naomi asked. "We have lemonade."

A minute later she returned with a tall, sweaty glass of lemonade. I sipped it as they all stared at me like I was the royal food tester checking for poison. "It's good. Thank you."

They all let go of their collective breath. "Oh, and such nice manners," Naomi said.

"Good, good," Ruth said.

I tried to listen to what Miss Tate was telling Ruth and Naomi, but after a while I stopped. The sisters' house was kind of weird. The sofa smelled like bread dough, and it was thin and lumpy, like they had mice tucked away underneath the cushions.

Strange and colorful blankets hung on the walls. One of the blankets had a picture—a sunset had been woven into it with a silhouette of two giraffes in the foreground. It was pretty and colorful, orange, red, purple, and yellow. I thought about the person who might have made it and imagined that her hands were thin and callused.

On the table next to me stood a lifelike wooden carving of a tall, skinny black woman with a long face holding a naked baby to her breast. The woman wore a long skirt, and even though it was carved in wood, it flowed like ocean waves, like the woman and her baby were standing on a mountaintop letting a warm summer breeze swirl about them.

Ruth and Naomi had shelves and shelves of old books crammed together with pottery bowls and cups and animal statues tucked in places haphazardly, like the sisters never gave a single thought to it. Like the tiny wooden animals chose their own places. A tingle of excitement sparked in my belly at the thought of all those books, but I quickly extinguished it. I doubted I'd be here long enough to read many of them.

The Crum house had been bookless, except for the ones I brought from the public library.

"Would you like a slice of cake?" Ruth asked. She patted my knee again. I decided she was a knee-tapper. I'd have to live with it if I wanted to get along. Getting along, said Miss Tate, was important wherever I went. Getting along.

I popped back into the discussion. "No, thank you." I lied. I did want cake but I didn't want to sound eager.

"Are you certain?" Ruth asked. "Are you quite certain? Because it's no trouble. No trouble at all. Is it, Naomi?" She looked at Naomi, who was whispering to Miss Tate.

"What? Oh, certainly not, my dear. Cake is never a problem."

"No. I'm not hungry."

"Just as well," Ruth said. "It will be suppertime soon." She put one of her long, thin hands on my knee again. "You do eat supper, don't you?" She laughed and laughed.

We were all silent. I held my lemonade in both hands and let the dewy condensation drip down my wrists. It felt cool. The house was warm. I could feel my eyes darting around like lizard eyes. I couldn't help it; there was so much to see. I avoided looking into Naomi's eyes or Ruth's eyes. But I could not avoid Miss Tate's eyes.

She stood and smoothed her skirt.

"Well then," Miss Tate said. "I should be going."

Ruth and Naomi stood.

I stood, still holding my glass.

"Thank you," Ruth and Naomi said together.

Miss Tate nodded.

She looked at me. "I'll call in a few days, Wilma Sue. See how you're getting along."

I nodded and held my glass tighter, wishing my bones were hollow.

We all walked her to the door. We watched Miss Tate climb into the van and pull away. My stomach wobbled and a burp formed in my throat. I held it in for as long as I could. Until Miss Tate was out of sight.

Just then, I looked down at my lemonade and saw a goldfish swimming around inside the glass. And not just a little one, but the kind with big, bugged-out eyes. The fish seemed to say, "Glub, glub." It startled me so much that I let go of another giant burp and dropped the glass. The fish flopped around on the blue shag carpet.

"There's a . . . a goldfish in my lemonade," I said.

"Most interesting," Ruth said.

Naomi picked up my glass and scooped up the fish. "I'll take these to the kitchen."

I wanted to scream for Miss Tate. But I didn't.

I swallowed and walked back to the sofa on jelly legs.

Chapter
2

Ruth served supper at exactly five o'clock, which was about an hour after Miss Tate left. I'd spent that sixty minutes sitting in the library near the welcome sign. Just sitting.

"Come, come," Ruth called with a kind of lilting voice. The dining room table was set with colorful, mismatched dishes on a pure white tablecloth. I noticed cloth napkins, blue with tiny peacocks all over them. The Crums never had cloth napkins, but sometimes Lola folded paper towels into triangles. That was about as fancy as any Crum ever got.

I shrugged and looked at the serving dishes. The fried chicken looked okay, but next to that was a big yellow bowl filled with something green and slimy looking. I didn't say anything bad, since I knew that wasn't mannerly. Instead I commented on a green bowl filled with large white scoops of mashed potatoes.

"I love mashed potatoes," I said.

Ruth, who was sitting at the head of the table, laughed.

"That's *nsima*," Naomi said.

I swallowed. "What's that?"

"It's a staple in Malawi, where we lived. It is made from corn and water. Here look, this is how you eat it."

I watched Naomi scoop some in her hand and eat it.

"Or you can mix it with your greens," Ruth said.

"Or you can take a bite of chicken and then a scoop of nsima and ..." She looked at me. "Go on, try it. I promise you'll like it. The children in the village love it. They even grind the corn for their mothers."

"But wait, wait," Ruth said. "We got so excited, we forgot to ask the blessing."

"The blessing?" I said it out loud on account of how surprised I was. No Crum ever asked for a single blessing. That was a McAllister thing. The McAllisters were always asking God's blessing and praying over pretty much everything. I used to like them doing that, and I missed it when I left. But that had been a long time ago.

I folded my hands and closed my eyes, and Ruth said the prayer—at least I think it was a prayer. I didn't understand a single word. She must have spoken it in ... in whatever language they speak in Malawi.

"Go on, try it," Naomi said. "Try the nsima."

I tasted a teeny-tiny bit. It wasn't awful. It wasn't good. It wasn't really anything. Kind of like the worst Cream of Wheat you'd ever want to eat. Thick and pasty.

"That's why you mix it with your other food," Ruth said.

"Don't rush her," Naomi said. "It's an acquired taste if you haven't grown up with it."

She got that right.

After supper the sisters showed me my new room.

We climbed the skinniest and most crooked stairs I'd ever

seen, all the way to the third floor. Ruth needed to turn a trifle sideways to fit through.

"We gave you a room at the back of the house on the third floor," Ruth said. "You can see the birds in the trees and the church just down the path. And of course you have a lovely view of the chicken coop."

Chicken coop? Miss Tate didn't mention chickens. This would take more scrutiny. *Scrutiny* was my new word.

"And," Naomi said, "you can also see the moon and the stars when the sky is clear. And it's the best view for thunderstorms and lightning."

Ruth pushed open the bedroom door and stood aside. "Go on, take a look. We decorated it ourselves."

"I forgot my suitcase," I said, suddenly feeling very high up and a little dizzy, almost birdlike.

"Oh, you can get that in a minute," Naomi said. "Take a look around."

I stepped over the threshold. The room smelled like bread dough—same as downstairs. The bed was situated under a thin, white tent.

"We hope you like the canopy," Ruth said. "In Africa it's necessary to have a canopy and mosquito nets."

I went right to the window and looked out. I could see the trees and the church and the chicken coop. I could even see some chickens running around and worried for a second that the sisters had made me their foster child for the express purpose of working like a farmhand, and I didn't know the first thing about farms. I read a book once about a boy who was adopted just so he could help a really mean man on the farm.

I moved from the window and noticed a lamp on a small table next to the bed.

Across from the bed was a tall orange dresser with six drawers. A delicate lace doily was on top, and on top of the doily was another statue of a tall black woman, also with a long face. Next to her was a large pecan-colored elephant. A round rug made from rag braids near the bed was the only carpet. The rest of the floor was wood—gold and hard with black dots of nail heads in crooked lines.

"Now there isn't too much, yet," Naomi said. "We thought you'd like to ... make it your own."

I looked at her and swallowed. "It's very pretty," I said. "Can I go get my suitcase now?"

"You go right ahead." Ruth sniffled into a hanky she took from her sleeve. "I think it's still by the door." Then she giggled and said, "Oh Naomi, I think I might cry, I'm so happy."

That night it rained just like Miss Tate said it might. I stayed in my room with the windows open. The curtains puffed out like pregnant bellies when the breeze blew. But soon I had to close them because it started to rain inside. There was a chair—old and fat and comfortable—by the windows. I sat in it and watched the rain and thought about the birds, wondering where they went with their hollow bones in the rain, and if hollow bones made them extra cold.

My bed was nice. It didn't smell like bread dough, and it was smooth and soft. I didn't think mice lived underneath the mattress, like the couch downstairs. The sheets were striped—blue and white. It was warm, like in a terrarium. I slept in my shorts and top because I wasn't ready to undress in a house I'd never been to before.

I wrote in my secret notebook:

Tonight is my first night at Gray House. So far it smells like bread dough. I live with two sisters from Africa. They are nice. I tried nsima. It was okay. The house is quiet, not like the Crum house.

Cake

I slept. I was too tired to stay awake, and the soft sound of the rain splattering against the roof was like a lullaby. But when morning came and I opened my eyes, I didn't remember where I was. I only saw that I wasn't in the Crum house anymore.

"Wilma Sue, are you coming down, dear?" It was Ruth. Her voice was more springy than Naomi's, and it seemed to linger in the air like dust particles.

I got out of bed and found the bathroom on the second floor. It was a large, funny room with a tub that stood on claws like an eagle's. A bright yellow curtain wrapped all the way around. The sink was big and white with rust stains that looked like sunsets. It had spigots—one hot, one cold. The toilet was white, and the flusher was on a chain, and it made such a noise when it flushed that I figured Miss Tate could hear it—wherever she was. The wallpaper, a field of pink roses and green wiggly vines, was hung crooked and made me dizzy.

The sisters were in the kitchen sitting at a table with green picnic benches for seats.

"*Mwauka bwanji*," Naomi said.

"What?" I looked at her.

"It's Tumbuka," Ruth said. "The language they speak in Zowe. Our village."

"That's how we say 'good morning,'" Naomi said. "Now you say, '*Ndadzuka bwino.*'"

I didn't even try to pronounce it. "Good morning."

"Hope you like eggs and bacon." Naomi pushed scrambled eggs from a pan onto a plate. My stomach growled.

"Yes, please."

I sat at the table. Ruth smiled directly into my eyes. I smiled back and said, "Thank you."

"You're welcome," Ruth replied. "We hope you'll like breakfast better than supper."

"No, that's not what I meant, although thank you for breakfast," I said. "I meant, thank you for taking me." I looked at the floor thinking I was doing a good job of getting along so far. Then I looked at the ceiling, which I noticed was made of metal and had a design of flowers embossed in it. And then I thought of Yellow House, and Millie's garden with all of the flowers, and how hundreds of butterflies would visit the garden in the summer. The thought made me smile.

Ruth patted my hand. "We should be thanking you."

I swallowed. Me? Why would they need to thank me? Unless ... unless they really did take me so I could help with farm stuff, like the chickens. Maybe they had a cow that needed milking or a garden that needed weeding and corn to shuck, and maybe someone had to clean the chimneys. But I didn't let on that I was suspicious at all. I smiled and kept on eating my breakfast. I figured a girl needs to keep up her strength and keep her thoughts to herself. Until the right time. Timing is everything.

After breakfast we all went into the library. I asked Ruth and Naomi about the statues of animals and the black women in the long skirts.

"We got them in Africa," Ruth said. "I'm sure Miss Tate told you we were missionaries in Malawi for ... for a very long time."

"That's right," Naomi said. "I delivered the mamas' babies and helped in the clinic."

"Are you a doctor?" I asked, thinking that being a doctor must be the hardest job in the world.

She nodded.

"And I taught the children how to read and do math, and I also taught them about Jesus," added Ruth.

Cake

"Jesus?" I said out loud. "You know about Jesus?"

Naomi and Ruth smiled wider than ever. Wider, I think, than all outdoors, and their eyes twinkled like stardust. It was like I had opened the door and invited their best friend to come in and sit with us.

"Yes," Ruth said. "We have known Jesus for many, many years."

I took a deep breath. The only other person I knew who knew about Jesus was Millie. She talked and sang about him all the time, and I learned Bible verses about Jesus in Sunday school. My stomach roiled a little on account of how I didn't want to say too much. On account of how just when I thought I was getting to understand about Jesus, I was snatched from the McAllisters' like a fly on the curtains. There was no talk of Jesus at Miss Daylily's Home—and especially not at the Crums'. No Crum ever talked of Jesus.

"That reminds me," Naomi said, "do you have a dress for Sunday?"

I swallowed. A dress? I never wore them. Especially in the summer.

"No, I don't," I said, waiting for Naomi's smile to turn into a frown or even a sneer. But instead her lips puckered for a second, and then she tapped her knee and said, "I'll take you down to the mall then. You could use some new clothes."

"And shoes," Ruth added. "Sunday shoes."

Sunday shoes. My mind jumped back to a time when I'd slipped my feet into a pair of Meg's shoes. They were too big and my feet swam like two fish inside of them, but I'd insisted on wearing them to church one Sunday. Millie laughed. Meg laughed. But off I went in wobbly shoes feeling like Meg's little sister, even though I really wasn't.

Ruth stood and picked up one of the giraffes that sat looking out the library window. "But our missionary days are done now," she said softly, and her thoughts seemed far away, like she wished she could climb on the back of that giraffe and ride clear to Malawi. "We want to be your mamas now."

I chewed my pinkie nail. Mamas. So now I had two new fake mamas, just like Mrs. McAllister had been my fake mama. I'd had one real mother for seventeen whole days, until she put me up for adoption at Miss Daylily's Home for Unwanted and Misunderstood Children. She decided she didn't want me anymore.

I shook my head, not wanting to think about my real mother because it made me angry and sad, a mixture of feelings that could be hard to tame. Sometimes the thoughts made me cry, and I didn't want to cry about a mother who held me in her arms for a little more than two weeks before she didn't want to do it anymore.

"Do you like cake?" Naomi asked, almost like she'd sensed I needed a change of subject.

"Yes. I like cake. But I'm full from breakfast."

"Later," Ruth said with a laugh "Later." She turned from the window and looked at Naomi. "I'd best be off to the Life Center."

"Fine," Naomi said. "Wilma Sue and I will have a lovely day."

"Life Center?"

"That's the homeless shelter where Ruth volunteers. She serves meals and tutors the children—and a couple of adults."

"Homeless shelter? Around here?"

"Yes, yes, my yes," said Ruth. "Even places that look rich or affluent have their fair share of folks who, for one reason or another, are homeless and need our help."

I wasn't sure if being a foster kid was the same as being homeless, and just when I was about to ask, Naomi said, "You can go play now. Maybe go talk to the chickens."

Ah, the chicken coop. Now was a good time to do a little investigating, but not too much. I didn't want to arouse suspicions before I figured out for sure whether they took me in so I could be their Cinderella. "Why is there a chicken coop in your backyard?"

"We like chickens," Ruth said.

"Reminds us a little bit of Africa," Naomi said. "There were lots of chickens in the village."

I squared them both in my sight for a few seconds. I didn't see any meanness, but still — I wanted to be cautious. "What do you mean, *talk to the chickens*?"

"Visit a while," Ruth said. "You'll be talking to them in no time. Get to know them. Chickens are very smart. They'll learn to recognize you."

"It's a great idea to get to know the chickens," Naomi said.

I knew it. They were sizing me up for chicken duty.

As I made my way to the chicken coop, I noticed there were many trees on the parsonage property. A large silver maple stood on the side of the house next to my room. Its branches reached above my window, large and full, with bright healthy leaves. She was beautiful. I named her Sweet Silver Maple.

There was also a cemetery behind the church. It was inside a tall, black wrought-iron fence. Cemeteries didn't scare me the way they did some people. There was a cemetery on the way to school from the Crum house. Some days I cut through it and read the engravings on the stones and markers and wondered about the people. Mostly I cut through it because no Crum ever went inside the graveyard. They were too chicken. But I thought the walk home through the cemetery was peaceful.

I was glad it was summer. School was out. Lester and Mauveleen had waited until school was over to tell me they

I stood outside the wire fence and counted five birds. They scratched at the hay-covered ground and made a lot of noise.

didn't want me anymore and to take their trip around the world. It was hard to imagine what it would be like to take a trip around the entire world. Even if I were a bird and had hollow bones.

The coop stood inside a fenced-off area on the side of the house. It was small and painted green, and it was more of a shack with a slanty roof. A small door on the side had a ramp that the chickens used to go in and out. There was also a door that was large enough for a person to fit through. I stood outside the wire fence and counted five birds. They scratched at the hay-covered ground and made a lot of noise.

I wasn't too keen on venturing inside the little yard right away. I mean, the way they pecked at the ground and at each other gave me cause for worry. I did *not* want to be pecked.

But the longer I stood there, the braver I grew, until I finally opened the gate and stepped inside. The cluckers scrambled like I was a fairy-tale giant come to eat them.

"Hey," I said. "Don't run. I'm here to visit."

I saw three galvanized buckets. One was filled with cracked corn, one with small pellets, and the third I wasn't sure about. But when I scooped some out with my hand, it felt like shattered seashells.

I figured the corn was for eating and the pellets probably were too. I tossed some corn on the ground, and the chickens hurried near, pecking and clucking like they were crazy or something. And that was when the rooster came out of the coop—big, white, and fat with a bright red comb on his head.

I thought for sure he was going to muscle his way in to the corn and scare the girls away. But no, he was a gentleman, inviting the hens to eat first. Three more hens ran from the coop. I tossed more corn and some of the pellets.

I must have stayed with the chickens for ten minutes. I even ventured inside the coop. It wasn't too smelly, not like you'd think. But there sure was a lot of poop to sidestep. I saw two rows of boxes nailed to the wall. Each one had hay inside of it, like a nest, but only one nest had any eggs. Two of them.

I didn't know if chickens had hollow bones. Maybe that's why they don't fly so well.

After a few minutes I decided I'd had enough of corn and pellets and squawking. If the sisters thought I was going to be their farmhand, then they had another think coming. I mean, the chickens were fun to watch. I liked the way they strutted around, bobbing and weaving like tiny boxers in a ring. But really, what does an orphaned city girl know about chickens?

Chapter

3

So I went for a walk down the street toward the other house on Bloomingdale Avenue. It wasn't gray and slanty like the sisters'. It was pink like a flamingo and all one floor. I saw a girl with one long blonde braid hanging down her back like a ladder, sitting cross-legged in the front yard. From the looks of it she had feet as big as canoes.

First I walked straight past her like I had somewhere to go, pretending not to pay her any never mind. Then I turned back and walked past her again.

"Hey," she hollered.

I turned around.

"Hey," she hollered again.

So I moved closer. Her yard didn't have a fence around it. Just some hedges. She sat on the grass with two Barbie dolls. I'd never had a Barbie, and I didn't want one.

"I just moved here," I said, walking up to the hedges.

"I know. You're that girl who has no parents. I heard Mrs. Agabeedies telling my mother. She said the spinster sisters were taking in an orphan. You must be the orphan from Miss

Daylily's Home. I've heard wretched things about that place. My mother has told me stories."

I only nodded because I didn't want to talk about the home, and I wasn't sure I wanted to know who Mrs. Agabeedies was. And even though I knew this girl was talking about Naomi and Ruth, I didn't understand what she meant by *spinster sisters*. Plus, I did *not* like being called an orphan. That girl could sure pack a lot into one annoying sentence.

"Want to play with dolls?" she asked.

Not really. But I didn't say that.

"Okay." I walked to the other side of the hedge. "My name is Wilma Sue."

The girl never looked at me. "Penny. My full name is Penelope Pigsworthy. But I think *Penny* is so much nicer, don't you? I'm twelve years old."

I sat cross-legged across from her on the lawn. The grass itched my knees.

"How come you got no parents?"

I shrugged. "Dead." It was easier for me to lie. I didn't know my father, and as far as I knew, my mother—my actual birth mother—was still alive.

"Oh." She tugged a skirt onto one of the dolls. "You can be Hiawatha Barbie." She pushed the doll in my face.

"She doesn't look like an Indian."

"But she is. You don't have to look like an Indian to be an Indian."

"Yes you do."

"No. You. Don't!"

"Yes. You. Do!"

That was when she bopped me over the head with her Barbie. "Do not."

"Dang blame it! Why'd you do that?" I rubbed my head.

"Because."

Cake

Her answer made me so mad, I bopped her right back with Hiawatha Barbie. Hiawatha Barbie's shoe flew off into the grass. "How'd you like it?" I asked.

She looked at me with the funniest expression on her face. It was like what I'd done was so unexpected that she didn't know what to do — like this had been the first time anyone had bopped her back.

Her eyes watered. "Now look what you did. You lost one of her shoes. Those are her best red pumps."

"You hit me first. And Indians do not wear pumps."

"You lost her shoe!" She burst into all-out sobs.

"Sheesh," I said. "I'm goin' home." I didn't like crybabies, and she sure acted like she was younger than twelve.

"I hope the spinster sisters don't cook you for dinner tonight," she said.

"You're crazy," I said, and then I turned for home. *Why would they cook me for dinner?*

When I got back to the house, Naomi was making a cake. She wore a long, colorful dress with a mosaic design like mixed-up finger paints, with red, yellow, blue, gold, purple, and green. I thought it was the prettiest dress I had ever seen. She was barefoot like yesterday. *Did she ever wear shoes?*

"Just in time," Naomi said. "You can help me bake."

I looked into Naomi's bright, round eyes. They twinkled like stars. "I cooked a lot at the Crums', but we never baked cakes. Ever."

"Now's your chance to learn. We bake a lot of cakes."

I should've known. They took me as their foster kid so I could do chores. Chicken chores, cake chores, cleaning chores, and who knows what else they had in store for me? The truth was I didn't mind cooking so much, but chickens?

I cooked a lot at the Crum house, mostly pancakes and hamburgers, hot dogs that only needed boiling, and once I made a green bean casserole with a Doritos crumble, pecans, cranberries, and then I topped it off with a peanut butter spread. It tasted better than it sounds. But I hadn't made many cakes. Cakes were for celebrating, and there weren't many celebrations in my life. It seemed the sisters had celebration cake every day.

"First things first," Naomi gave a hearty laugh. "Wash your hands and then crack those eggs into that bowl. But be careful. No shells."

"Oh yeah," I said. "What's the stuff in the third can, the one next to the corn and pellets?"

Naomi rinsed her fingers under the tap. "That's ground up oyster shells. It helps the chickens make healthy, hard eggshells. It provides calcium."

"Yuck. They eat shells?"

Naomi laughed. "Yep. Now go on, crack those eggs. You're sure you know how?"

I looked at the three eggs sitting in a bowl on the counter. "Anyone can crack eggs," I said, like she should have known.

The sisters' kitchen was big. Way bigger than the Crums'. It had plenty of counter space and three walls full of cabinets.

"Are these eggs spoiled?" I asked, holding one up. "They're brown."

Naomi laughed. "They're perfectly okay. Eggs come in many colors, even green and blue. Now go on. After you crack them, whisk them up and then I'll fold them into my batter." She worked the batter, adding ingredients one after the other. And the whole time she sang this song that sounded familiar, but I couldn't quite place it:

What a fellowship, what a joy divine,
Leaning on the everlasting arms;

Cake

Naomi continued blending ingredients in the bowl of her big stand mixer. It was bigger than any I'd ever seen. And it was orange with pretty flowers painted on it. She used a huge spatula to scrape the sides of the bowl as it spun.

> *What a blessedness, what a peace is mine,*
> *Leaning on the everlasting arms.*

I tapped the first egg on the side of the bowl. Too hard. It burst and all the insides ran out onto the floor.

"I'm sorry," I said. I pushed back some surprise tears. Tears could be like that. You never knew when your eyes would puddle up. I thought of Penny crying over her Barbie, and my stomach gave a little lurch. Then I thought of Miss Tate and how I'd fallen on the playground at the orphanage once. I was crying and crying over a little scratch on my knee, and she'd looked at me while she covered my cut with a Band-Aid. She told me my eyes glistened like blue crystal when they were filled with tears.

Naomi smiled and handed me a paper towel. "Wipe it up. We have plenty of eggs. You might be nervous. Stage fright, as it were."

Naomi continued blending ingredients in the bowl of her big stand mixer. It was bigger than any I'd ever seen. And it was orange with pretty flowers painted on it. She used a huge spatula to scrape the sides of the bowl as it spun.

While she worked, she kept singing that song:

Leaning, leaning, safe and secure from all alarms;
Leaning, leaning, leaning on the everlasting arms.

I thought about an organ playing and a thick, sweet smell, like oranges and honey. And then it hit me: a memory of sitting in a church pew between Millie and Meg, my legs so short that my feet dangled and swung. I doodled stick figures on a church bulletin as Millie patted my knee.

I finished cracking the eggs. This time I got all of them into the glass bowl, no shells. I showed Naomi the mass of thick goo with three of the yellowest yolks I had ever seen, more yellow than a sunflower. "Did these eggs come out of your chickens?"

"Yes. Nice and fresh. Ruth got them this morning. You can gather them tomorrow."

I knew it. It's official. I am their maid, a … scullery maid. I knew that word from reading pirate books. My stomach went a little wobbly, but there was nothing I could do. Orphans pretty much had to go with the flow if they wanted to get along the way Miss Tate always said.

"We make many cakes here and that takes a lot of eggs," Naomi said. "We keep most of the eggs we gather, but we give some to the Life Center, when there are extras. You can never tell how many eggs you'll get with your own chickens, so sometimes … " she leaned closer to me and whispered, "we buy them."

I smiled like I had been made privy to a wonderful secret.

"Ruth mainly cares for the chickens," Naomi went on. She dropped another ingredient into the batter. "She's raised our chickens since they were chicks, but she's very involved with her volunteer work, and your help with the chickens would be a downright blessing."

A blessing. The last person to say I was a blessing was Millie, and then only the one time that I remember. Although, she did always make me *feel* like I was a blessing to her—nearly all of the time. But then when Meg went off to college and Millie got too sick to care for me anymore, I stopped being a blessing.

"Right now we have seven hens and one rooster. They're all egg-layers, except for the rooster of course." Naomi rinsed her fingers under the tap and dried them on a small red towel. "Of course we eat only the eggs, not the chickens, like some back-yard chicken enthusiasts do."

"You mean, some people kill and eat their own chickens?" I asked, a bit interested and a bit nauseated at the same time as I thought about the fried chicken we ate for supper last night.

"In Zowe the children were sometimes responsible for catching and killing the evening meal."

I swallowed. "Really? Kids. Little kids killed chickens?"

"Yep. But the mama of the family did the plucking and the cleaning and the cooking."

I swallowed again. I wanted to get rid of the entire thought of children killing chickens, but at the same time I wanted to know more. "How'd they do it? With a big machete or something?"

Naomi chuckled. "No, no, a small knife. Chicken necks are scrawny. The child would catch the bird, step on its wing to keep it from running or flying off, and then—" She drew her finger across her neck.

And at that moment I was never so thankful that God did not make me a child in Zowe.

She scraped down the sides of the bowl as it twirled beneath the beaters. "Go ahead and dump in the eggs, and then I'll add the lemon zest and lemon juice."

"Lemon? In a cake? I like lemon."

"So does Mrs. Snipplesmith."

"Who?" I asked, tasting the batter after she'd mixed in the eggs. I swallowed and tasted a hint of lemon, like a bright ray of sunshine, warm and tingly on my tongue.

"Margaret Snipplesmith. She lives down the road a piece. We've known her for years, from before our time in Africa. We saw her married to Mr. Snipplesmith. What a lovely day that was." Naomi tapped her spatula on the side of the mixing bowl and then sat at the table. "I'll never forget it. I was Margaret's . . . Mrs. Snipplesmith's maid of honor. We were both just twenty-three years old. I was in medical school, neck-high in my studies, and Margaret . . . well Margaret only had eyes for John, that would be Mr. Snipplesmith, and becoming a wife and mother."

"Did she become a mother while you were becoming a doctor?" I snagged some more of the batter and then sat on a stool next to the counter.

Naomi pushed her glasses up on her nose, leaving streaks of batter the color of straw through her black hair. "Eventually, the good Lord saw fit to bless them with one child, and then not until their later years."

"Like Sarah in the Bible," I said, suddenly remembering a Bible story Millie had read to me.

Naomi smiled into my eyes. "That's right. Like Sarah. Only, Margaret was not quite so old."

"So why are you baking her a cake? A lemon cake?"

"She has been feeling sad lately, missing her child—Sadie. So we'll bring her this cake and see if it doesn't lift her spirits."

"Why doesn't she go and visit Sadie?"

Naomi took my hands in hers. "Sadie died several years ago."

"What?" The whole idea of a child dying made me mad. I jumped off the stool. "Why? Why did a child die?"

"She wasn't exactly a child," Naomi said. "She was a young woman, almost thirty, when she was in an car accident."

I swallowed again. "I don't get it. Why did God let that happen?"

Naomi shrugged. "I don't have answers for that. No one does."

I sat back down on the stool. "At least she had Mr. Snipplesmith."

Naomi shook her head. "Not really. John passed away only two months after Sadie died. They say he couldn't live with such a shattered heart."

"Do you believe that? Because I don't. I believe folks can live with broken hearts."

"Of course they can. And as a doctor, I can tell you why John died. And even why Sadie died. What I can't explain is the timing."

I didn't say it, but I thought it. *Timing is everything, even if we don't understand.*

I watched Naomi use her fingers to spread Crisco on the bottoms of three pans, and then she rubbed the rest into her hands and elbows. I swallowed a lump of nausea.

"Crisco," she said with a grin. "It keeps my hands soft and smooth."

Next she wiped her hands on a fresh terry towel. I was surprised she didn't wipe Crisco on her feet. "Okay, would you like to dump the batter into the pans?"

I nodded. The metal bowl was large. It would take four hands to pour the batter, but I didn't want Naomi to know I needed help. Fortunately, the bowl had a handle that made it easier to grip. Maybe if I dumped it on the floor, she'd think I was the worst scullery maid in the world, and then I'd never have to help in the kitchen again.

Nah, then I'd have a big mess to clean up, and I could almost hear Naomi sweetly say, *"That's all right, dear, let's clean it up. We can always make more batter."*

So I carefully divided the bright yellow contents of the mixing bowl across three cake pans. Naomi helped a little, and then she let me lick the spatula.

"I think Mrs. Snipplesmith will love it," Naomi said.

Naomi washed the mixing bowl and then swiped it dry with a red terry towel. She replaced the bowl onto the mixer.

"Let's see," she said, glancing around the room. "I think just a plain buttercream frosting will do for lemon cake. The first thing we need to do is put those sticks of butter into the mixing bowl. I prefer to use unsalted butter."

I peeled the paper off of two sticks of butter and plopped them into the bowl.

"Excellent. Now let me just switch out the beaters. I like to use the paddle attachment when I make frosting. It makes it so much smoother, kind of like ice cream."

"I like ice cream."

"We can make that also. I don't think there is anything more scrumptious than fresh peach ice cream made from our own peaches."

"You have peach trees?" I didn't remember seeing any.

"Yes we do—on the other side of the church. And they're just starting to bloom. We'll be picking peaches by Labor Day."

Aha! Another chore for me to do: fruit picking. Except I did kind of like the idea of growing our own fruit. It would have taken more than a miracle for anything to grow in Lester and Mauveleen's yard, it was so small and overrun with weeds and Crums.

I watched as Naomi let the butter get soft and creamy.

"Now dump in all of the sugar. I use Ten-X."

"Ten-X?"

"Confectioner's sugar. It's soft and powdery." She wiped the back of her arm across her forehead, leaving a strip of white powder. "Oh dear, I have yet to bake a cake or make frosting when I didn't get half of it on me."

I smiled. I was the same way. I am not a neat cook.

"Always make sure you turn the mixer to a lower speed first, or you'll have powdered sugar blowing everywhere."

"Like a blizzard."

"Yep."

I dumped the sugar into the metal mixing bowl and watched it swirl together with the butter. A little sugar dust flew up. A small blizzard. I got out my small walk-around notebook and wrote:

Ten-X sugar is the softest ingredient I've ever felt.

Then I shoved the book back into my hip pocket. I didn't think Naomi noticed me writing. That was something I liked to keep private. I figured a girl has to have *some* private things in life.

"Okay," Naomi said as she tapped the spatula on the still-spinning bowl. "What's buttercream without the cream?"

I shrugged and smiled at Naomi. She had white Ten-X powdered sugar in her hair and on her nose, and there were specks of it on her glasses too.

"I start with three tablespoons and then we'll see."

I waited.

"Go on, measure out one tablespoon of the cream."

I poured a small amount of cream onto a spoon and dumped it into the bowl.

"Now two more times. And then a tablespoon — a full, almost overflowing tablespoon — of vanilla."

And voilà! That was it. Buttercream frosting.

"It's delicious," I said while licking the spatula.

"Of course we'll have to wait for the cakes to cool before we frost them."

"When will they be baked?" I asked.

"In a few minutes. I'll know."

I sat on one of the green picnic benches next to the table. "How?"

"I always know when the cakes are ready. It's a sense I learned while living in Africa. I learned to bake using a brick oven, outside."

"Really? You can do that?" *How in the world?* I wondered.

"Yes," Naomi said. She washed the sugar off her face and dried her hands on her dress. "It wasn't easy. Cakes are hard to bake that way, but I managed to make scones and biscuits."

"Did you always like to bake?"

"In Africa?"

I nodded.

"Not at first. But then it got interesting. Maybe it's the scientist in me. I enjoyed figuring out how to make the brick ovens work and how to use exactly the right ingredients. I followed my instincts a lot."

I could smell lemon in the air. It seemed to wrap around the kitchen; and when I closed my eyes, I could see it swirling, a thin yellow trail.

"What do you like to do?" Naomi asked.

I stared at the ceiling. "I don't know. Nothing."

"Nothing? Well there must be something."

"I like to read."

"Reading is good," Naomi said.

I looked around the kitchen.

"Why do you live here?"

"Here in the United States? Or here in this house?"

"In this house."

"Well, when we got home from Africa, we retired. So we needed a place to live that wasn't too expensive, and the pastor said we could stay here rent-free."

"Rent-free?"

She laughed. "God has a way of working things out."

I didn't say anything because I didn't believe for one second that this house or anything else was free. Somebody always gets paid—in one way or another.

We sat quietly. I looked at the ceiling again. "Are you gonna cook me?"

Naomi laughed with such force that the whole table shook. "Cook you? Now where in the world did you get that notion?"

"Some girl."

"Making friends already?"

"I guess. She said you would cook me for dinner."

Naomi held my hand. "Ignorance is a dangerous thing, my dear. Some people think that because we lived in Africa, we do things like cook children."

"Do you?"

"No."

I thought about the goldfish in the lemonade.

Chapter 4

Ten minutes later, Naomi and I were still sitting at the table. She fidgeted with a saltshaker.

"Not much longer," she said. "I'm beginning to smell the lemon. That means the cake is nearly baked."

"It does?"

"Yep. Usually when the aroma reaches the library, I know the cakes are done."

"That's weird," I said.

"It's how I learned when the scones and biscuits were baked in Africa. By the smell. It was hard to bake cakes in a brick oven. They always came out so dry, like the ground in the summer. By the way, when it's summer in Africa, it's winter here."

I felt my eyebrows crumple.

"Malawi is on the other side of the equator. The seasons are the opposite of ours," Naomi said.

"So right now it's cold in Zowe?"

"Yep. It's freezing at night."

I looked at Naomi for a long second. The word *spinster* popped into my mind. Did she look like a spinster? I wasn't sure.

"Say," I said. "I can run to the library and see if I can smell the lemon cakes."

"Good idea," Naomi said.

Off I went. I didn't want to tell her that I was actually going to look up the word *spinster*, but that's what I did. I found their dictionary. It was a big red book. A Merriam-Webster edition. And then I found the word:

Spinster: an unmarried woman, typically an older woman beyond the usual age for marriage.

I closed the dictionary and set it back on the shelf. *Beyond the usual age for marriage.* I wondered what that meant. But I wrote the word in my notebook anyway.

The lemony smell had definitely reached the library. So I dashed back to the kitchen. "I think they're done," I said. "The library smells like lemons."

"Already?" Naomi said. "They baked fast." She pulled open the oven door. I watched her lightly tap both cakes in the center.

"I guess they are done. We must have been talking longer than I thought."

She grabbed potholders, blue ones with black stripes, and removed the cakes from the oven. She set the pans on a cooling rack on the counter. The lemon smell grew stronger, and that was when I asked a question I didn't know if I had the right to ask. But it was on my mind—especially now.

"How come you're a spinster?"

Naomi laughed, only with not so much heart. "Never had the time. Not that I wasn't asked, mind you. But I wouldn't trade my days in Malawi for anything. Ruth decided not to marry so she could concentrate on her missionary work. It all worked out exactly the way God intended."

I supposed Miss Tate was a spinster too. It was okay with

me. Still, I wondered if maybe the sisters had been Unwanted or Misunderstood and that's why they never got married.

Naomi and I sat still and quiet for what felt like ages waiting for the cakes to cool so she could frost them. And that was fine with me. I liked being next to her. Mauveleen Crum used to shoo me away all the time like I was a mosquito. But Naomi didn't seem to mind having me around.

"The cakes will be cool enough to frost soon. Ruth should be back from the shelter anytime now, and then we can take the cake over to Mrs. Snipplesmith."

"You mean me? Go with you?"

"Of course," Naomi said. "I think you will enjoy meeting Mrs. Snipplesmith."

Even though she misses her daughter? I hoped I wouldn't be in the way. I hoped Mrs. Snipplesmith wouldn't think I was an imposition or a distraction or any number of other words I could come up with that defined a person who was in the way and not welcome.

I stared out the kitchen window toward the chicken coop. I couldn't see it, but I knew it was in that direction. "I like the chickens, Naomi."

"That's good, dear, because guess what?"

"What?"

"Ruth and I talked last night, and we decided it would be good for you to take over the care of the chickens, at least somewhat. Ruth will still be in charge; she'll be the one you talk to about the birds and what they might need. That means feeding them, gathering the eggs every morning, and making sure there is fresh hay every now and again."

Ewww. Chicken poop. I knew it! I was right. I was to be the new chicken keeper. "But . . . but I don't know how to get the eggs or sweep up poop and feathers and—"

Naomi patted my knee. "Now, now, Wilma Sue, you'll learn.

They might peck at first. Especially the really big one. She's kind
of the leader of the pack." Naomi laughed again. "And besides,
they usually leave their nests after they deposit their eggs, which
makes gathering the eggs as simple as baking a cake. I know we
have some books about chickens in the library. You might want
to look through one or two to get some ideas."

Just past noon, we finished putting the last of the frosting on
the lemon cake. "Why don't you go feed the chickens lunch
while I clean up the kitchen?" Naomi said. "But just give them
the cracked corn for now. Ruth will tell you when to give them
other stuff."

It seemed the sisters were leaving a lot up to me. Did
that mean they trusted me? Or was I going to be their little
Cinderella?

The chickens came running and cackling the minute they
saw me. It was like they knew me already.

"Do you guys have names?"

I always thought chickens were white. But not these chickens. They were different from anything I'd ever seen. Two
were kind of gold and brownish with tinges of yellow. There
were three dark ones with black feathers—but not quite black,
maybe dark, dark blue or purple. They all had big chicken eyes,
perfectly round. The dark chickens had bright red heads with
baggy red wattles and yellowish feet, and the golden ones had
feathers on their feet. I had no trouble choosing names for the
ones that came out of the chicken house.

Florence was skinny and seemed light on her feet. Slowpoke
was slow and pecked at the seed like it was the last thing in
the world she wanted to eat. Starlight had bright eyes and even
brighter yellow feet. Eggberry was the prettiest—with the
brightest red comb. And last was Dottie, the biggest. The leader

of the whole pack. Or was it flock? She was fat and proud and had the largest eyes. I figured the other chickens that stayed inside the coop were standoffish. I'd name them later, and I'd probably call one of them Penny.

The rooster was always outside when I visited. He strutted around, bobbing his head and moving like he was Sonny Liston, a boxer from the 1950s I saw on a TV documentary once. The rooster was tall and white with a red comb. And while I was standing there inside the fence, he let go a *cock-a-doodle-doo!* that just about scared the bejeebers out of me. It was the first time I'd heard it. He did it three times, and then he flew—the best he could, I figured—up to a perch that was actually a tree branch wired into the fence. I named him Sonny.

I tossed some feed on the dusty ground, and all of the chickens cackled and fought over it. Except Slowpoke. She took her time. She cackled once and ate the corn that got tossed out of the rumble. Maybe she was the smartest. She might be my favorite.

The coop was big enough for me to go inside. Each bird had her own little nesting box filled with hay and straw and scraps of material and newspaper. I saw two small eggs sitting in one of the boxes. I left them there because Naomi didn't tell me to get them.

When I crawled out of the coop, I saw Penny. She had the two Barbies with her.

"Hey," she said. "Want to play?"

I shook my head. "Not dolls." After what happened the last time, I thought it might be better to stay inside the fence. I did not want to get bopped on the head by Hiawatha Barbie again.

Penny kicked at the ground. She looked me square in the eyes for a second and then looked away, like she'd heard her mother calling for her. "I'm sorry I hit you."

She said it quickly and so low that I hardly heard her. But I stepped outside of the fence.

"You are?" I said.

She nodded. "I was just in one of my moods. That's what my mother calls it."

"I guess it's okay. Come on, let's go find something to do."

Penny and I walked back to Gray House and sat on the porch steps.

"How come they have chickens?" she asked.

I shrugged. "They like the eggs."

"That's stupid. You can get eggs at the store."

"Not brown ones."

"Can too. I've seen them."

"The sisters like their own backyard eggs."

Just then Ruth came home. She pulled into the driveway in a long turquoise-colored station wagon. The engine was loud, and steam poured out from under the hood.

She got out of the car and slammed the door. Then she walked around to the front and practically threw open the hood with a great clanging sound. "Jumpin' blue lizards!" she said. "This infernal radiator will be the death of me yet."

I watched her go back and grab a blue cloth from the passenger side. She used it as kind of a potholder and screwed the lid off the radiator. "Now you just cool down," she said, as more steam rose to the sky.

"Is it broken?" I called from the steps.

Ruth turned with a start. "Oh, Wilma Sue! I didn't know you were there. 'Course it's broken. Been broken for weeks. Keeps overheating. The car needs a new radiator."

"Come on, Penny," I said. "Let's go see."

"I really don't want to go see some dumb old car," she said. But she followed me anyway.

"I'll let her rest a while," Ruth said. "And then I'll fill her with H-2-O. In the meantime, help me with these bags, please."

"Okay," I said.

Penny just stood there.

Ruth and I carried five shopping bags onto the covered porch.

"Thank you, Wilma Sue," Ruth said. "You're a big help."

"This is a lot of stuff," I said.

"Not really. Yarn for knitting. Sewing supplies and a few groceries."

Penny was still standing near the car. Not moving a muscle.

"How come you aren't helping?" I asked.

Penny looked at me funny. "They're *your* groceries."

There she goes again. Another one of her moods?

"Doesn't matter," I said. "Help is help." I learned that while living at the McAllisters' and at the home and especially at the Crums'. Help is help no matter whose junk it is. Millie was always saying things like, "Many hands make light work."

After the car was unloaded, Penny said, "Let's play dolls." She shoved Hiawatha Barbie at me.

Oh no. But I didn't protest. "Is she still an Indian?"

"Yep."

"I want her to be a pirate."

"She doesn't look like a pirate."

"She doesn't look like an Indian either."

Penny's eyes grew wide and her face turned red like a tomato. She bopped me in the teeth that time. Then she grabbed Hiawatha Barbie from my hand. I couldn't help but cry. My whole mouth hurt. First my head and now my mouth.

I was bleeding all over the ground. Penny hit me so hard that I bit right into my lower lip.

It was a good thing that Naomi was a doctor.

All I did for about fifty seconds was stand there looking at Penny. Penny stood there looking back at me. I wanted to speak but I couldn't. Sometimes all a girl can do is stand there and not say a word because she knows that if she says anything, it will be the vilest stuff ever said. So I didn't say a word.

I was about to head up the porch steps with my bloody lip, when I spied a strange-looking woman walking down the path from the church. As she got closer, I saw she was short with fuzzy blonde hair and a large purple headband with a bow on top. She wore a dress covered with pictures of purple grapes, and her funny purple socks were rolled down at the ankles. Her very large feet were stuffed into very small shoes. She walked straight for me, and I could hear her clodhoppers on the pavement. I held my arm up to hide the blood on my mouth, and I wished I had hollow bones.

Chapter 5

Before she reached me, the woman started talking quickly and in a way that reminded me of the chickens.

"You must be the orphan girl that Ruth and Naomi are sheltering."

I nodded.

"Well aren't you?" she said.

I nodded again.

"What's wrong?" she said. "Cat got your tongue?"

I shook my head and tried to turn around so I could get into the house and hide my bloody mouth.

But she grabbed my arm and pulled it away from my face. "What in the world?"

"Mrs. Agabeedies," Penny said. "She was so mean to me!" Then Penny started to fake cry.

So this was Mrs. Agabeedies. I took a step back. She looked at me with squinty, beady eyes. "Did you hurt Penny?" she asked.

"Me hurt Penny?" I said the words, but they were muffled behind my hand. "I'm the one who's bleeding."

Cake

"Don't take that tone with me, young lady," Mrs. Agabeedies said. "The impertinence! The ... the ... " She stopped talking as though she'd thought better of what she'd been about to say. Since she'd called Ruth and Naomi "spinsters," I could only imagine what she'd call me. "Orphan girl" was bad enough.

"I am Mrs. Agabeedies, the church secretary. And as such, I am also concerned with the goings on here at the parsonage. It is my right to know."

Oh boy, she must be the Miss Daylily of Bloomingdale Avenue Church of Faith and Parsonage.

I shoved the hem of my shirt into my mouth and sucked on it to stop the bleeding.

"Ruth! Naomi!" Mrs. Agabeedies called as she pushed past me. "You must come out here! Your little ... *charge* has started a fight with our darling Penny Pigsworthy, and she's bleeding all over my shoe!"

Charge? I didn't like the sound of that. I tried not to swallow the blood.

Naomi came out onto the porch and looked first at Mrs. Agabeedies and then at me. She didn't say anything to Mrs. Agabeedies but came straight to me. "Oh dear, Wilma Sue, what happened? Let me see that mouth."

"It's Penny you should be looking over!" Mrs. Agabeedies said. "What kind of a doctor are you? The kind that takes care of other children before our own, that's what kind."

Naomi glanced at Penny and said, "Penny looks okay to me." And at that Penny really turned on the waterworks. But Naomi kept right on ignoring her.

"You, on the other hand, Wilma Sue, got a pretty good cut. Let's take a look." She put her arm around my shoulders and led me into the house and on through to the kitchen. We left Mrs. Agabeedies and Penny with her crocodile tears pouring down her face like creeks.

53

I rinsed my mouth six times. Naomi took a doctorly look. "The good thing about lips is that they heal fast. The bad thing is that they bleed so much."

She gave me a towel with an ice pack wrapped inside. "Now you just sit here a few minutes with that ice on your mouth. It'll keep the swelling down and help with the pain."

I shook my head. "It doesn't hurt much," I said through the towel.

If this were the Crum house I'd be in the bathroom taking care of my own fat lip while the Crum kids laughed.

I sat at the table holding the towel to my mouth. The lemon cake was sitting there—three layers high with white butter-cream frosting. It was slightly crooked, but it still looked good.

"Are you going to take the cake to Mrs. Snipplesmith?"

"Yes. Just as soon as you're ready."

I thought maybe my bloody mouth would mean I didn't have to go. "I guess I'm ready."

"Good, we can walk down the road. No need to drive."

That was a good thing on account of the car overheating. Which reminded me. "Where's Ruth?"

"Oh, she's probably out with the chickens or upstairs putting away her new yarn. That woman loves yarn. Or 'fibers,' as she calls it. She has about a million different types and colors. Ruth says one of these days she's going to get her own sheep so she can spin her own yarn." Naomi slapped her knee. "That Ruth. She cracks me up."

Naomi took the towel from me. "That doesn't look too bad. It'll be good as new by morning." She dropped the towel and ice pack into the sink. "Shall we go? Margaret is expecting us."

"Do you put it in a box like they do at the bakery?" I thought it would look strange for Naomi and me to be carrying a cake down the street all exposed.

"No, no, I'll just carry it. It's not far, and the sun isn't too hot so the frosting won't melt." She dabbed a stray glob of frosting from the cake plate. "Goodness gracious. One time we carried a cake down the road on a hot day, and it was nothing but a puddle by the time we got there."

I imagined a melted cake on the ground and laughed.

Naomi, still barefoot, picked up the cake. It wobbled a little but she corrected it. "Phew. Wouldn't want to lose this one."

I opened the front door for her. "Did you ever?"

"Ever what?"

"Lose one."

"Oh goodness yes. But we just made a new one. Sometimes things get lost or broken for a reason. It's best not to dwell on it and then start over."

I walked next to her as she carried the cake out in front of her, almost like it was a wedge of stinky cheese. She walked a bit fast, but I figured she knew what she was doing. I had never delivered a cake before.

We walked a couple of blocks in the opposite direction of Penny's house, which I was very glad for, considering our last meeting and my still fat lip.

"That's her house, right there. The one with the plastic tulips in the garden."

"Plastic tulips?"

"She says it's easier to care for plastic flowers than real ones."

I couldn't argue. Naomi instructed me to go ahead of her and ring the doorbell. "Now ring it long. Mrs. Snipplesmith is a touch hard of hearing."

I pushed the little button and we waited. Mrs. Snipplesmith's house was large and old and very blue with purple shutters. It had a long, wraparound porch with about a thousand spindles beneath the railing. After a minute I heard a dog bark.

"Oh good, that's Missy. Her dachshund. Margaret will be along momentarily." With that the cake wobbled, and Naomi had to play a balancing act, moving the plate from side to side and up and down, trying to keep the cake from smashing to the porch floor. I tried to help, but then the door swung open and there stood Mrs. Snipplesmith, I presumed. She was tall and skinny like a pool cue, with gray hair piled to a point on her head. She wore perfectly round glasses, and her nose was long. When she turned to the side to look at me, I noticed her head was shaped like a hatchet.

"Hello, Naomi," she said in a high but very soft voice.

"I thought you could use some lemon cake today," Naomi said. "And I wanted you to meet Wilma Sue."

Mrs. Snipplesmith held her folded hands under her chin. "So this is the sad little orphan girl we've heard so much about. It's nice to meet you, Wilma Sue." Then she let go such a great, long, sad sigh that if a person could see a sigh, this one would look like the darkest cloud in the sky.

"Thank you," I said, "but I'm not sad." I *was* worried about the cake falling to the ground though.

Naomi went inside as Mrs. Snipplesmith held open the large wooden door. I followed. Naomi set the cake on the kitchen table, and I was glad for that. "Phew!" Naomi said. "It was heavier than I thought. Shall we have a piece?"

Mrs. Snipplesmith let go another sigh, and this time it smelled like dust. "If you insist, Naomi."

"I do," Naomi said.

So Naomi sliced into the cake with a long knife, and immediately the room filled with the scent of fresh lemons. The whole kitchen seemed to grow brighter with each cut she made. And I could have sworn that a wilted potted plant sitting on the windowsill perked up. It even bloomed. Or at least I think it did.

Naomi placed a slice of cake onto three plates. Mrs. Snipplesmith, who hadn't smiled yet, finally did as she inhaled the aroma. I took a big bite. The flavors danced in my mouth,

Cake

The door swung open and there stood Mrs. Snipplesmith, I presumed. She was tall and skinny like a pool cue, with gray hair piled to a point on her head. She wore perfectly round glasses, and her nose was long.

and the lemon made my sore lip sting. I winced, but only for a fraction of a second because all of a sudden Miss Snipplesmith began to laugh. "This cake is so light and delicious," she said. "I feel as though I could ... I could ..."

And then for just a moment, I'm pretty sure I saw her chair, with her still in it, lift off the floor an inch. But before I could say anything, it was back on the floor like normal. Missy barked and ran in circles until Naomi gave her a small slice of her own. Next I saw Missy and Mrs. Snipplesmith lift off the floor, but no one else seemed to notice—including Mrs. Snipplesmith. But I'm pretty certain I saw Missy swimming in the air for a few seconds.

Finally Mrs. Snipplesmith finished her slice. She pushed the plate away, stood up, and smiled. Her small blue eyes shone like crystals. "I feel a trifle better," she said.

"Good, good." Naomi nodded. "Now I recommend that you eat one small slice three times a day until the cake is all gone. But be careful, lemon cake is mighty strong stuff."

"I'll say," I said.

"What's that, dear?" Naomi asked.

I shook my head and didn't say a word about what I thought I saw. Maybe Penny had bopped me harder than I thought.

Naomi hugged Mrs. Snipplesmith. In fact, she almost smothered her. "Don't forget," Naomi said. "Eat the whole cake."

Chapter

6

During dinner Naomi asked me why Penny had slugged me in the mouth.

I swallowed my bite of meatball and said, "Penny socked me in the mouth because I wanted Hiawatha Barbie to be Pirate Barbie."

Ruth and Naomi glanced at each other, then at me, and then they burst into laughter.

"Well now, matey," Ruth said in the worst pirate voice I'd ever heard. "That be a curious reason ta be gettin' bopped in the kisser."

"Aye," Naomi said.

I couldn't help but laugh along with them. My lip still felt funny.

"I think I'll be needin' ta speak with young Penny's mother," Naomi said.

I dropped my fork onto my plate. "No. Please. Don't. It's okay. I . . . I should have let her be an Indian even though she didn't look like an Indian."

"Did she look like a pirate?" Ruth asked.

"No," I said. "That was my point, and Penny didn't like it."

The sisters laughed at that. But Naomi remained adamant. "Sorry, Wilma Sue, but this is not a matter to be swept under the carpet."

Then Ruth changed the subject and asked about Mrs. Snipplesmith.

"She was feeling much . . . lighter when we left," Naomi said.

I didn't say a word. Not a single word.

<hr />

After dinner Ruth put on some music. She said it was recorded in the village where she and Naomi had worked and lived. It sounded mostly like drums and voices. "The Malawi children love to sing," Ruth said.

"And dance," added Naomi. "Sometimes they would start dancing for no reason at all, just because."

Ruth took me by the hand. "Like this," she said as she started moving and clapping her hands in rhythm with the drums. The voices sounded like instruments. Ruth's long dress was red and orange and yellow and black with geometric patterns and lines all over it. As she moved her dress swirled around her. It swirled around me.

Naomi laughed and clapped too. "Come on, Wilma Sue, dance!"

I didn't want to at first, but I stood in the middle of the living room. I let the music tug at my arms and legs until finally I was moving. I don't think I danced very well, but that didn't matter to Ruth and Naomi. I felt a little embarrassed. I had never danced before. No Crum ever danced—except when Lester won the lottery, of course, but I wasn't included. Now, for a fraction of a second, I knew I would rather be dancing in Gray House than traveling around the world with a bunch of Crums.

Cake

The three of us laughed and held hands until we were out of breath and panting a little. Ruth flopped onto the lumpy sofa. "Phew! That wore me out. You're a good dancer, Wilma Sue."

I felt my face grow warm. I looked at Naomi sitting in the big overstuffed chair in the corner of the room. She smiled at me. No one had ever told me I was good—at anything. I almost felt like I could fly.

"How about some cake?" Naomi asked.

"Sure," Ruth said. "How about you, Wilma Sue?"

I smiled. "You're a poet and you don't know it." That was something Miss Tate would say whenever I said a rhyming sentence.

Ruth smiled at Naomi. "And quite by accident. Naomi was always the scientist and not interested in things like poetry or literature."

Naomi took a breath. "That's right. And Ruth always had her nose in a book. *Beowulf* and such."

"Beowulf?" I said.

"Oh yes," Ruth said. "I'll give you my copy. It's an epic adventure with dragons."

I liked the sound of *Beowulf.*

"Anyhoo," Naomi said. "How about some dessert? Cake?"

"Yeah, cake sounds good," I said. "But you gave it to Mrs. Snipplesmith."

"We always have a cake or two lying around," Ruth said.

I shook my head. There was definitely something strange going on in the Beedlemeyer house. I would write about it in my secret notebook that night.

We walked into the kitchen, and Naomi pulled three plates—a yellow one, a blue one, and a red one—from the kitchen cabinet. "Will you get us three forks—the ones in the dish drainer will do. And then carry these plates and the forks into the living room. I'll carry the cake."

I watched as she uncovered a three-layer work of art from beneath a large plastic cake carrier on the counter. I hadn't noticed it earlier, but that didn't mean it wasn't there. The cake was covered with chocolate frosting, and there were raspberries all over the top. I'd never seen a cake that pretty. Mauveleen Crum never made cake. Hers were store-bought and purchased only to celebrate one of her real children's birthdays. There were three of them. Lola, the oldest, always smelled like the zit cream she smeared on her face. She was sixteen and just learning how to drive when I left. Lester, with his newfound millionaire status, had promised her a car—any car. I hoped he'd throw in an endless supply of zit cream since Lola had a problem in that area.

Then there was Martin, the middle boy. He was tall and big and had a notion he'd like to play professional football, which was evidenced by his constant desire to tackle anyone and anything in his way. Martin infuriated me most days because I never understood how anyone could be so big and so lazy except when it came to playing football. Martin always made Zachary, the youngest Crum, do his chores upon threat of death—or worse. I sort of almost liked Zachary. He was bookish and a little bit harebrained, but I figured that was on account of getting tackled by Martin the Destroyer on a daily basis. You could often find Zachary sitting in the closet of his bedroom, which he shared with Martin, reading a book by flashlight.

The Crums were five people who I thought never really liked each other or me—especially me.

"Here we are," Naomi said. She walked into the living room carrying the cake and a large knife that might have been a machete. "It's cake time."

"Ready?" Ruth asked. She took a deep breath.

Naomi took a deep breath as well. "Ready."

I also took a deep breath but only because the sisters did.

Cake

Naomi cut into the cake with the machete, and as she did a small blackbird about the size of a quarter flew out. Then another. And another.

My knees wobbled.

"Well, Naomi," Ruth said, "you outdid yourself this time."

We watched the birds flitter around us.

"But ... but how ... ?" I couldn't talk anymore.

"According to the rhyme, it's 'four and twenty blackbirds baked in a pie,'" Ruth said. "But Naomi prefers cake."

"Maybe you should open the front door, Wilma Sue," Naomi said. "Let the birds out." Then she laughed. "More birds, Ruth. More birds."

I swallowed and said, "Okay," like it was the most ordinary thing in the world to do.

Naomi cut three slices of cake.

"Enjoy!" she said.

I swallowed a bite of cake. It was delicious. The raspberry taste lingered in my mouth for a few seconds after the chocolate taste was gone. It was tart but not sour, with a hint of sweet that reminded me of Meg McAllister. But I shook the memory from my mind. Sometimes I didn't want to think about the people I missed the most. I could only count on the things and people that were with me right now.

"How come there are birds inside this cake? How did you get them in there?" I asked.

Naomi pulled her fork through her large slice and raised it to her mouth. A bit of frosting hung from the fork in a curlicue. "Well, that's a funny question because you never know what's on the inside of anything, now do you?"

The question confused me, but I supposed she was correct.

"Can't judge a book by its cover," Ruth said.

"Or a rock," Naomi said.

"A rock?" I asked.

Ruth reached behind her and pulled a round, lumpy rock that was about as big as a coconut from the bookshelf. A wide swath of black electrical tape was wrapped around it.

"Now this," she said, "is an ugly rock. Here, take it."

I put my fork and plate on the table.

"Go on. Pull off the tape."

I did as she said, and the rock opened into two pieces. Inside, the rock was filled with purple and blue glittering crystals. It was a whole other world inside that ugly gray rock. It took my breath away for a second—just like the blackbirds did.

"What kind of rock is this? Did it come from Africa?" I asked.

"Yes," Naomi said. "It's called a *geode*."

I moved it around in the light and watched the crystals shimmer like crown jewels. How could anything so ugly on the outside be so beautiful on the inside?

"It's so pretty inside," I said. "Like a whole other world."

"Sure is," Naomi said. "So you see, you really can't jump to conclusions about anything."

"Or anyone," Ruth said.

I thought of Penny and Mrs. Agabeedies.

I rewrapped the tape around the rock and set it back on the bookshelf. I wanted to ask the sisters about the little blackbirds again, but for some reason I couldn't. I felt like the birds were something I was supposed to accept. Like the way I had to accept being an orphan, or how pretty jewels are sometimes buried inside an ugly rock.

After we finished our cake, Ruth said, "Wilma Sue, dear, take the leftover spaghetti and meatballs out to the chickens. They'd love an evening snack."

I looked at her like she was nuts. "You mean they eat spaghetti and meatballs?"

"Oh, dear me, yes," Ruth said. "Chickens will eat just about anything."

"Why do you think our eggs are so special?" Naomi said.

I carried the bowl of leftovers out to the chicken yard. They saw me coming and started cackling and scratching. Now how in the world was I supposed to feed spaghetti and meatballs to chickens? It wasn't like I could toss it on the ground like I did the regular chicken feed. So I dumped it in a heap—a small hill of pasta with meatball rocks.

The chickens, especially Dottie, went wild. Even the chickens that normally stayed in the coop most of the time came out for spaghetti and meatballs. They pecked and slurped up the spaghetti strands so fast that Eggberry kicked a meatball, and it rolled toward Slowpoke, who just took her time and casually pecked at it.

Then Dottie and Florence each got an end of the same spaghetti strand and started a game of tug-of-war with it. They looked kind of fierce with their eyes all big, staring each other down and pulling on the pasta until it finally broke. The longer part went to Dottie, so Florence wasn't very happy. She dropped her piece, which was all of an inch long, and went chasing Dottie all over the pen. The other chickens ignored the two as though chases like this happened every day, and they kept pecking and slurping away at their special supper.

"Okay, you ... you chickens. Enjoy your supper."

I stepped outside the pen and watched them a little longer. Chickens certainly were interesting creatures. In some ways they were like Crums—always pecking at each other. And in other ways they were the perfect family, taking care of each other.

Back inside the house, the sisters were busy cleaning up the dinner dishes.

"I'll help," I said.

"No," Ruth said. "Go find a good book to read. There are plenty of good books in the library."

"Television?" I asked.

They giggled—sounding a little like the chickens. "We don't own a television machine, dear," Naomi said.

"No TV?" I tried to keep my voice calm despite the panic I felt rising inside of me. TV was all we had at the Crum house. It was on from morning 'til night, seven days a week, and most of the time you'd find Mauveleen stretched out on the sofa watching it.

"Never saw the need," Ruth said.

No TV. I didn't like the sound of that, no siree, Bob!

With no other choice, I settled into the big chair with a copy of *Beowulf,* which I just happened to find on the coffee table like it had been placed there especially for me. It hadn't been sitting there when we were eating cake. I'd just opened to chapter one and read, *Now Beowulf bode in the burg of the Scyldings . . .* when I heard a knock on the front door.

Naomi came running past. "Oh, my, my, visitors! We so seldom get visitors."

She pulled open the front door. Penny was standing on the porch holding one of her stupid dolls. A tall, skinny woman with red hair and long arms stood next to her. She resembled

Penny in that they both had a puckered, snooty look on their faces, like they owned the whole world or something. The woman wore black pants and a pink blouse and pink shoes with open toes. I saw one bright red toenail in each opening.

"I believe you owe my daughter a new pair of Barbie shoes."

"I do?" Naomi said.

"No," Penny said. "She does." And she pointed straight at me. My knees turned to jelly, and I tasted spaghetti in my mouth.

Naomi looked back at me and winked. "Come in, please. I was going to call you myself in a little while, so it's quite prudent that you happened to visit us."

Penny and her mother took two steps inside the house and stopped.

"I am Portia Pigsworthy," the woman said in my direction. "And this is my daughter Penelope."

Naomi looked at me a second time—this time with raised eyebrows.

"As I said," Portia Pigsworthy continued, "your orphan owes my Penelope a pair of shoes."

"Is that right?" Naomi said. "Well, your daughter owes Wilma Sue an apology."

"Whaaaaat?" Portia asked. She sounded like a large bird. A large pink-and-black bird.

"That's right," I said, jumping up from the chair. "Penny slugged me in the mouth and gave me this fat lip." I pulled my lip down so both of them could get a good gander at what was left of my fat lip with an incisor hole in it.

Portia gasped. "My Penelope would . . . would *never* resort to violence." She clutched her chest. "*Never*, I tell you. It was that . . . that orphan."

I watched Penny slink behind her mother like she was embarrassed. We locked eyes for just a second, and I made a note in my mind to ask Penny about it later. To ask her why she looked sort of sad when her mother spoke.

"Nevertheless," Naomi said, "as you can plainly see, Wilma Sue does have a rather obese lip."

Portia stuttered over some words and finally said, "Why, she could have done that herself, banged into something or other. And that does not discount the fact that she still owes Penny a new pair of Barbie shoes."

"That's only because she bopped me over the head with her stupid Hiawatha Barbie—who isn't even an Indian—and her stupid shoe went flying off." I wanted to cry but I didn't.

Ruth joined us now, drying her hands on her apron. "What seems to be the trouble?"

No one said a word for a really long time. I think it's called *reaching an impasse.*

Naomi picked up her purse, which was hanging on the coatrack near the door. She pulled out her small change purse, opened it, removed a five-dollar bill, and presented it to Portia. "This should cover the cost of replacing the shoes."

"Thank you," Portia said.

"No problem," Naomi said. "And I will send my doctoring bill to you." Then she ushered Penny and Portia out the door.

"That'll teach them," Naomi said.

"Too bad, really," Ruth said. "I would have liked to invite them in for cake."

Naomi clicked her tongue. "No, no. I don't think they're ready."

"Quite correct," Ruth said. "Portia still needs more time."

My eyebrows wrinkled. "Time? What does she need time for?"

Naomi set her purse on the coffee table. "You see, dear, it's not her fault. Not entirely. Portia was an orphan."

I swallowed. "Like me?"

"Not exactly like you. No one is exactly like another person," Ruth said.

"But she did live at the home," Naomi said. "It was called something different back then. This was before Miss Daylily took it over. Portia never got adopted, although she did have several trial runs."

I was suddenly reminded that I was on a trial run with the sisters.

Ruth coughed. "And each time she was sent back. No one knows why."

"The only thing anyone knows for certain," Naomi said, "is that the home was run by a despicable man named Thursday. As a matter of fact, I remember now. That was the name of the place: The Thursday Home for Children."

I was all of a sudden very glad for Miss Daylily and Miss Tate and the sisters. I felt a twinge for Penny in my chest as Naomi and Ruth talked about Portia Pigsworthy. Maybe Penny wished for hollow bones also.

Chapter
7

Sunday. It had been a long time since Sunday was set apart from all the other days of the week — not since the McAllisters. But now it was again. I woke a little early, not sure why; it might have been the mockingbird sitting in Sweet Silver Maple. He was making a huge ruckus. Or I might have woken up because I was nervous. Nervous about going to church for the first time with the sisters. I mean, a girl should know what to expect. But all I knew about the church was that Mrs. Agabeedies was the secretary, and she made me nervous.

I got dressed in a pair of shorts and a top. Ruth had said something about my needing a dress for Sunday, but I figured God was okay with me in shorts — especially during the summer.

The sisters were already in the kitchen when I got downstairs. They weren't dressed for church either. Naomi was in her bathrobe, a long purple terrycloth thing that looked like it had traveled the world a gazillion times. Her hair was all twisted up on her head in knots and snarls. Ruth was also in a bathrobe, only she had long jammie bottoms sticking out from under it. I think it must have been way too early because they were surprised to see me.

"Wilma Sue," Ruth said. "My, my, but it's early for you to be getting out of bed." Then she smiled.

"I'll say," Naomi said. "But come on now, sit at the table and I'll make you breakfast. That is, if you're hungry."

I touched my stomach. "No, not really." I felt more nervous than hungry, but I didn't want to tell them that.

"Are you sure?" Naomi asked. "How about one egg and toast?"

"Okay. But maybe just toast."

Naomi got up and took two slices of bread from the bag.

"And bacon, if it's okay," I said.

"Certainly," Ruth said. She stood and pulled the bacon from the refrigerator.

I watched Naomi and Ruth cook, and it gave me a nice feeling. They were as different as night and day in some ways, but that morning it was like they were one person, working together for no other reason than the fact that they wanted to. They weren't in each other's way; they moved around each other like a dance.

Naomi set a plate in front of me with two slices of toast, perfectly brown and crispy, and four strips of bacon, also crispy but not burnt.

"I'll go feed the chickens after I eat," I said.

"This is a big day," Naomi said.

"It is?" I broke a strip of bacon in half.

"Yep," Ruth said. "It's your first Sunday at church."

"I know," was all I said. The two looked like proud mama peacocks standing there in the kitchen with the sun gleaming through the window behind them. They were like two stained-glass windows bursting with stories to tell.

"You'll like the church," Naomi said. "Pastor Shoemaker is the sweetest, kindest man."

"And a great teacher," Ruth added. "I could sit and listen to him talk for days. He brings the Scriptures alive."

I thought about Meg McAllister and how we sometimes laid on our backs and looked up at the fluffy clouds in the sky. I used to think Jesus wore a sky-blue robe and the clouds were the folds and wrinkles as he stood over the world, keeping watch.

"Now you go on and eat," Ruth said, "while Naomi and I get ready for the service."

I finished eating and then headed out to the coop. The chickens were busy already, pecking and scrambling around. I tossed feed and some of the oyster shells on the ground. Then I checked the nests. Three eggs. I took them and backed out of the coop. The chickens were all busy eating and pecking and squabbling amongst themselves, so I didn't stick around.

"See you all later," I said as I closed the gate. "I'm going to church." I kind of liked the idea. I'd missed going to church. And even though I was a little worried about what kind of people would be at the new church, I liked knowing that I was going someplace where they talked about God.

On my way back to Gray House, I wondered if Penny and her mother would be there. Naomi and Ruth had never said if the Pigsworthys went to church, and Penny had certainly never told me.

As I passed Sweet Silver Maple, I saw a garter snake skitter over a rock. She was just a small one, a baby. It took a little trying, but I finally grabbed her in some tall grass. She was cute and wiggly but small enough that I figured she'd be okay in my pocket for a while. Garter snakes don't bite, and they aren't poisonous like some snakes. A girl can never tell when an itty-bitty garter snake might come in handy.

Back at the house I placed the eggs in the bowl on the counter, and then I went to the library. The snake wiggled a bit but not much. She was probably a little scared, and this wasn't the first time I'd carried a small snake or worm around in my pocket.

I checked the clock on the table. It was barely nine o'clock. I thought about reading more *Beowulf* even though it isn't the easiest story to read. Sometimes I had to read the lines of the story three or four times before I understood it. But as I scanned the shelves, my eyes fell on a book entitled *Storey's Guide to Raising Chickens*.

I sat in the big overstuffed chair and opened the book to any old page. This is what I read:

> *A chicken has a right-eye system and a left-eye system each with different and complementary capabilities. The right-eye system works best for activities requiring recognition, such as identifying items of food. The left-eye system works best for activities involving depth perception, which is why a chicken watching an approaching hawk is likely to peer warily at the raptor out of its left eye.*

Now that was something I didn't know about chickens. It explained why they're always looking around with one eye and then the other. I kept reading about chickens until I heard Ruth at the doorway.

"Ready?" she asked as she walked into the library.

I closed the chicken book. "Yes. I'm ready." I stuck my hand into my pocket and felt for the snake. Still there. Still squirming.

"You look fine," Ruth said. "But I do think we'll take you shopping for some Sunday clothes."

Then Naomi appeared wearing a green dress with a paisley print and black shoes. The shoes kind of surprised me, since she hardly ever wore them. And she walked kind of funny like the shoes didn't fit right or she wasn't used to them. Ruth was wearing a blue dress with a white ruffled collar and a small, white, veiled hat that was tilted a little to the right.

Off we went down the path. Cars pulled into the lot and parked. My stomach got more and more jumpy the closer we got. But I kept my hand on the little garter snake all the way to the front doors.

Inside, the church smelled like dust and mold and fruity perfumes. A few people stood around gabbing, while others made their way into the sanctuary. I kept my left eye peeled for Penny and Mrs. Agabeedies.

I spied Mrs. Agabeedies the instant we stepped into the sanctuary. She was sitting toward the front on the aisle. Naomi and Ruth went straight to the fourth pew from the front. I sat on the end, which meant Mrs. Agabeedies was sitting right across from me on the other side of the center aisle. I smiled at her. She sort of smiled back but not really.

I tugged Naomi's sleeve. "How come Mrs. Agabeedies doesn't like me?" I whispered.

Naomi leaned down and whispered into my ear, "Mrs. Agabeedies doesn't like Ruth and me. So I guess she doesn't like you by association, you might say."

Ruth leaned across Naomi and said, "She's a bigot."

"Ruth," Naomi said in a voice louder than a whisper. "Not in church."

"It's true," Ruth said. "She thinks we shouldn't have gone to Africa."

I swallowed and looked at Mrs. Agabeedies out of my left eye. She wore a black-and-white striped dress and a big white hat with a black veil. Her shoes were shiny black and pointy, and in that instant she looked like the meanest woman on the planet.

"Maybe she needs a cake," I said to Naomi.

Ruth cleared her throat and clicked her tongue.

Naomi patted my hand. "All in due time. All in due time."

Then a woman wearing a flowery, purple dress sat down at the organ and smashed the keys with such a fervor, I thought the organ would catch fire. The music lifted and swirled around the room and filled my chest with such a surprising, peaceful feeling that I didn't think about Mrs. Agabeedies again. Besides, that was when Penny and her mother sat down right in front of us. Penny looked straight at me before she sat down, but her mother never made eye contact.

I reached into my pocket and felt the snake. The music grew louder and then softer until it finally stopped and the room grew quiet. I kept my hand on the little snake during some announcements by Pastor Shoemaker and all the way to the taking of the offering before the snake started to get a little too squirmy and wanted to be on her way. So after the collection plate was passed to me and I handed it off to Naomi and she handed it to Ruth who passed it to the man sitting next to her, I took the snake from my pocket. My plan was to ask to go to the bathroom and let the little snake out the back door. But that didn't happen.

Naomi leaned down and asked, "Is that a snake?"

I guess she must have startled me because I dropped it. The snake scooted onto my lap, then my knee, and then down onto the floor where, for some reason—maybe because she didn't know where she was and the linoleum floor was weird to a snake's touch—she slithered slowly under Penny's pew. I swallowed and waited. Just as the pastor stood up to speak, Penny let go a scream of such proportions that I figured she'd pretty much woken up anyone in town who wasn't attending church services and scared the bats right out of the church bell tower.

This, in turn, made Mrs. Pigsworthy scream, and then some other woman I didn't know hollered, "SNAKE!"

Penny jumped up onto the pew. "A snake!" she screamed. "There was a snake!"

Naomi grabbed my hand. If ever I'd wished for hollow bones, it was this day for sure.

Penny turned around and pointed her long index finger at me. "She did it!" Penny yelled. "That orphan. Wilma Sue. She brought a snake to church!"

I figured I'd be packing my bags for the home that afternoon, even though I didn't mean to scare Penny or half the congregation of the Bloomingdale Avenue Church of Faith. I believe the little snake made it all the way up to the organist, who then also screamed, before Pastor Shoemaker nabbed the snake and handed her off to another man who then took her out a side door.

While I was watching all of that, Mrs. Agabeedies stood up and said, "I knew it. I *knew* that child was nothing but trouble. Trouble with a capital T."

Next, Mrs. Pigsworthy stood up and hollered. Only she hollered at Naomi and Ruth. By then the pastor was standing right next to me. He raised his arms and the room quieted down. I swallowed as the pastor stared into my eyes for only a second, but it was long enough to know that he was not pleased with me. Then he looked at Naomi.

"I don't want to interrupt the service any longer, Naomi," he said. "Let's all settle down. I trust you can handle it."

Naomi nodded. Ruth had her hand to her mouth, and I thought she might be keeping a chuckle or two inside.

Pastor looked at me again but didn't say a word. Not one single word. Then he went back to his place up front.

Blast it! Now I was in hot water for sure. I looked down the line of the pew. I caught the attention of the man sitting next to Ruth, and he was smiling at me with bright eyes. I smiled back.

Everyone calmed down. The pastor went back to his preaching. And finally, after what felt like forever, he called for the final hymn. We all stood and sang. I wanted to bolt out the back door. But that wasn't going to happen either.

Naomi took my hand. "Slow down, Wilma Sue, let the others go first."

Penny and Portia Pigsworthy did not utter a single syllable. Not at me. Not at Naomi and not at Ruth. Instead, they teamed up with Mrs. Agabeedies and slipped by us, clucking like a trio of chickens. I swallowed when I caught Penny's eye. I did not like what I saw there. It was about as close to bloodlust as I had ever seen, and that included the looks Martin the Destroyer could muster. One look from Martin and people melted into blithering idiots. If it hadn't been for Naomi's tight grasp of my hand that morning, I might have turned into a puddle.

"C'mon," Naomi said. "Maybe it would be best if we skedaddled."

"But I didn't mean to drop the snake," I said. "She got away. That's all that happened. Honest."

"You shouldn't have brought it to church to begin with," said Ruth, taking my other hand in hers. "What were you thinking?"

I wasn't thinking anything. Except now. Now I was thinking I was in deep, hot H-2-O and nothing could save me. Not even God, I supposed when I saw Pastor Shoemaker at the door shaking hands with members of the congregation. I hoped he had forgotten the snake. But I didn't think pastors forgot much, especially snakes.

That was when I heard a cough from behind me. It was a deep sound that might have shaken the rafters of Gray House. I turned around and found myself looking up at the man who'd been sitting next to Ruth. The man who smiled at me. He was nine feet tall—or at least he seemed that tall. I had never met a person so tall. He was a giant with a big, almost square head, short gray hair, and a long nose. His cheeks were rosy, and the way he stood with his long arms dangling at his sides made me think this was what a grandfather clock would like if it sprang to life.

"Good morning again, Jacob," Naomi said.

"Good morning," he said with his booming voice.

I couldn't take my eyes off him.

"Wilma Sue," Ruth said, "this is Mr. Jacob Woolrich. He is one of our oldest and dearest friends."

When we shook hands, his hand swallowed mine clear up to my elbow. "Hi," I said.

"Pleasure to meet you," he said.

Nobody said much after that. And the next thing I knew, we were standing in front of the pastor.

"Great message," Ruth said.

"Sure was," Naomi said.

Now here was an interesting dilemma. If I said nothing, he might launch into a lecture about the evils of bringing snakes, even itty-bitty garter snakes, into church. But if I complimented his message, he might forget and say thank you instead.

"Excellent sermon, sir," I said. "I particularly liked the part where you quoted Phyllis."

"Phyllis?" he asked with a chuckle. "Oh, you mean Philippians."

"Yes, sir," I said.

"Thank you," he said.

Good. I'd dodged a bullet. The people behind us were getting anxious to have their turn at shaking Pastor's hand, so Ruth pulled me along out the doors and into the fresh air.

Mrs. Agabeedies was now approaching us. I looked up at Naomi. She said, "Run along, Wilma Sue."

I took off toward Gray House, but I still had my left eye peeled for Penny. I pretty much expected another bop in the mouth.

Cake

And then I saw her. Penny and her mother were standing in the cemetery. My heart sank so low it could have been a snake on the ground. Even from where I stood in the shadow of the church steeple, I could tell Mrs. Pigsworthy was wiping away tears.

I looked back at Ruth and Naomi. I could hear Mrs. Agabeedies screeching at them like some huge bird. But they just stood there listening. Polite. They were not screeching back even though I kind of wanted them to. I knew it was better for them to get along with her and be polite. I figured some people are not worth arguing with.

Chapter

8

I didn't see Penny for a few days after the snake incident. I went by her house expecting to see her outside with her Barbies, but she wasn't there. A couple of times I thought I saw her in the church cemetery from my bedroom window. But every time I got down there, she was gone. I kept meaning to ask the sisters if they knew who she visited. I wasn't sure I really wanted to know.

And besides, I was grounded for bringing the snake to church, "and on your first Sunday." So I mostly tended the hens, read about chickens and Beowulf, and did other chores around Gray House. Funny thing is, I didn't mind dusting the shelves full of animal statues or taking the trash to the curb. Maybe it was because they didn't tell Miss Tate about the snake and I didn't move back to the home on account of my infraction.

One day after breakfast, Naomi said, "Today is the day to bake a cake for Dr. Mergenthaler."

Ruth, who was just finishing up her cereal, said, "Poor Dr.

Mergenthaler." But that was all she said since she was on her way to the homeless shelter and didn't want to dawdle.

I finished my cornflakes and dropped my bowl in the sink. Naomi sat at the table with a cup of coffee.

"How do you know?" I asked.

She sipped. "How do I know what?"

"That Dr. Mergenthaler needs a cake?"

She stood and rinsed her cup. "Just about everyone needs a cake now and again. It's his turn."

She didn't really answer my question, but I let it go.

"Strawberry shortcake," Naomi said. "Ever make a strawberry shortcake, Wilma Sue?"

"No," I said. "But I sure like eating them." Another McAllister memory skittered across my mind: Millie used to make strawberry shortcake. I didn't think there was anything better on a hot summer day.

"Let's get started," Naomi said.

We assembled all of the ingredients, including about a gallon of strawberries, which Naomi taught me how to rinse and hull and quarter with a sharp paring knife. "Be sure and save a few nice big ones for decoration."

"Okay." I stood at the sink and prepared the berries slowly while Naomi made shortcake.

"Why is he poor?" I asked.

Naomi was cutting butter into flour with two knives, crisscross. "I think we'll need to make his cake tall. Tall and straight."

I repeated my question. "Why is Dr. Mergenthaler poor?"

Naomi brushed her forehead with the back of her hand and took a deep breath as if cutting-in butter was hard work. She left traces of flour in her hair. "*Poor* is one of those funny words," she said. "It means different things depending on the context of the situation."

"Right," I said. "Poor can mean you have no money." I dropped two halves of a berry into the yellow bowl beside me. Then I wrote in my notebook:

Poor. It means different things.

I watched her transfer the flour mixture, which was kind of lumpy, into a large green bowl. Then she used her fist to make a well in the center of the small dough mountain.

"Is that what Ruth meant about Dr. Mergenthaler? Does he need money?"

"No, she meant poor in the sad way, or when someone is feeling pity toward another person."

"Why should we pity him?"

"You should finish those berries," she said. "And I need to get a lot of shortcake baked. Like I said, tall and straight."

Naomi poured heavy cream into the well. "This is an important step," she said. "I need to mix the cream into the flour-and-butter mixture but not overwork the dough."

"What happens if you overwork the dough?"

"It gets tough and won't hold together very well."

I thought about Dr. Mergenthaler and wondered if she was trying to tell me something about him. I imagined a tall, tough man with rough and callused hands from overwork.

I finished the strawberries and left them sitting in the bowl with a small amount of added sugar. A buttery, soft aroma filled the kitchen as Naomi baked the shortcake layers. When they were done, she sliced each golden one in half with a long serrated knife until there were twenty layers to fill, arranged like checkers on the cooling racks. I looked at my bowl full of strawberries and wondered if there would be enough.

Next, Naomi assembled the cake with alternating layers of berries and whipped cream. And every time I thought she'd run out of berries, there were more.

"Go on, place those whole berries on the top."

I stood on the chair and delicately placed seven large straw-berries into the smooth, white whipped cream as Naomi hummed and sang:

A mighty fortress is our God,
a bulwark never failing;
Our helper He amid the flood
of mortal ills prevailing.

"All finished," I said, stepping down from the chair. "It's amazing." And it was not crooked. Not crooked like Mrs. Snipplesmith's lemon cake but tall and straight, unbending. A mighty fortress.

Naomi smiled at the finished creation. "I say we get this over to Dr. Mergenthaler's immediately."

"How?" I asked. "It's so tall and heavy."

Naomi drummed her fingers on her cheek. Then she snapped her fingers. "I got it."

The next thing I knew, we were hauling the cake down Bloomingdale Avenue in a wagon. A large red wagon with wooden sides. Naomi pulled the wagon while I kept the cake steady. This time we walked past Penny's house. She wasn't outside, although I'm pretty sure I saw her in a window, peeking out from the side of the curtains.

"Not much farther," Naomi said. "Just up a little hill and then down."

"Up a hill?" I asked.

"And down," Naomi said. "We'll need to be extra careful."

We walked on for another block and then turned onto Rosemont Avenue where the hill was. "You still haven't told me why he's poor."

"Arthritis, dear. Dr. Mergenthaler has been stricken with a terrible case of osteoarthritis. It's made him quite debilitated and somewhat crooked with swollen joints."

We reached his house, which was a small one-story home. Naomi pushed the door buzzer and we waited. Then Dr. Mergenthaler appeared. He was not what I'd imagined—a big man with callused hands. He was small and bent like a pretzel with twisted, gnarled fingers that reminded me of tree branches.

"Naomi Beedlemeyer," he said. "What brings you by?"

"Cake," she said. "May we come in?"

Dr. Mergenthaler moved aside slowly, tapping a gnarled and crooked cane on the floor. "Yes, yes, do come in."

I followed Naomi as she carried the cake right into the living room. The room was filled with skeletons. Not human bones but the bones of small animals and odd-shaped skulls. They were mostly in display cases, but a full skeleton of some kind of bird hung from the ceiling on a piece of nearly invisible thread.

"What's that?" I asked, pointing.

"A Great Blue Heron," Dr. Mergenthaler said.

"He is an ornithologist," Naomi said. "That's what he has his doctorate in."

"You study birds?"

He nodded. "Fascinating. Fascinating subject." He sat in a hard-backed rocking chair still holding his cane. "Did you know there are more than ten thousand species of birds in the world?"

I took a deep breath. "No. Wow. Who counted them?"

Dr. Mergenthaler chuckled lightly.

That's when I told him how some days I wished I were a bird and that my bones were hollow.

He smiled and patted my head as I was sitting near him on the couch. "Oh my sweetikins," he said, "that sounds lovely indeed. I used to think I would trade my brittle deformed bones for hollow flying bones in a second. But God is so good to me. Would I have met Naomi and Ruth—and now you—if I were a bird or even a man without crooked bones? Think of what I would have missed."

Dr. Mergenthaler appeared. He was not what I'd imagined—a big man with callused hands. He was small and bent like a pretzel with twisted, gnarled fingers that reminded me of tree branches.

I swallowed and felt tears rush to my eyes. I had never thought like that. Like what if my mother had kept me, how different life would be. I certainly never would have met Naomi and Ruth or even the Crums or Miss Tate, and I . . .

Dr. Mergenthaler picked up a piece of bone that was sitting on the coffee table. "This is a hawk's tibia, a leg bone." He handed it to me.

"It's so light."

"That's because you're right. It's hollow. Did you know a hawk's feathers weigh more than its bones do?"

I took another deep breath and admired the hawk tibia.

"Now then," Naomi said when she returned from the kitchen with a knife and plates and forks. "How about some cake?"

Dr. Mergenthaler leaned back in the chair. "Oh, dear me. I don't know. I haven't been very hungry of late."

"Now, now," Naomi said. "Doctor's orders."

Naomi sliced into the tall and straight strawberry shortcake. She gave the first slice to me and the second one to Dr. Mergenthaler. He took only a small, bird-sized bite at first, but then a second larger bite and a third larger still. And as he did, I was pretty sure his right hand grew just a little straighter and his smile got a little brighter. But I couldn't be one hundred percent certain.

Naomi finished her slice and I finished mine, all with one eye on Dr. Mergenthaler and the other on the bones.

Dr. Mergenthaler was a quiet sort of man. He didn't say much as he ate his cake, and I was having trouble keeping my eyes off all the skeletons.

"Now we must be going," Naomi said. "But remember, start at the top of the cake and eat your way down. It's good for you."

"I will," he said. "But it's hard to think anything can help these bones."

"Now, now, Braxton Mergenthaler, don't stop believing."

He stood, and I think he was standing straighter and an inch taller.

He gave me the hawk bone. "Take it," he said. "Those who wait on the Lord shall renew their strength."

Naomi put her hand on his shoulder. "They shall mount up with wings like eagles, they shall run and not be weary, they shall walk and not faint."

This time on our way back to Gray House, I didn't question Naomi about the cake but decided it was time to do some snooping. There had to be a secret ingredient or two that she used. She put something amazing into the cakes that made them work. She was a doctor, after all, so I was pretty sure she had some amazing prescription.

So I came up with a plan: After the sisters went to bed, I'd sneak into the kitchen and scrutinize the place. I wrote in my secret notebook:

There must be something special — some magical formula that Naomi uses in her cakes. And tonight, I will find it.

Then I closed my notebook and thought of Braxton Mergenthaler and bones, Mrs. Snipplesmith and sadness. I opened my notebook again and wrote:

I think Penny and her mother could use a cake. Dr. Mergenthaler gave me a hawk tibia. It is the best gift I ever received because now I have one hollow bone.

⌢⌢⌢⌢⌢⌢⌢⌢⌢⌢⌢

After dinner Naomi, Ruth, and I sat out on the front porch, like we did most evenings, in the thick, humid air watching fireflies flit about until it was totally dark, and we were totally tired. Ruth knit with long knitting needles and a ball of orange yarn she kept in a bag. I didn't bother catching any fireflies. It was more interesting to listen to Naomi tell stories about the village in Malawi and the night sounds she heard there.

"The birds were noisy all night long, owls mostly; they were like toddlers."

"Were they lost?" I asked.

"Oh no, dear," Ruth said. "Owls prowled all night for mice and shrews. You could hear their wings—the owls' wings, that is—flapping nearby."

I shivered. "It sounds scary."

"Sometimes it was," Naomi said. "But we got used to it. I think the dogs bothered me more. Always yapping."

"And the roosters," Ruth said. "They woke so early. Three o'clock in the morning they'd start."

I looked out at the darkening sky. It was nearly gray, like the color of the pasta pot Mauveleen Crum used for making oatmeal. She never sat with me and talked like the sisters did.

"But we got plenty of sleep," Naomi said.

"Even with all of the creatures making noise?"

Naomi rocked. "Sure. Most nights the sounds were a lullaby. But sometimes it was the villagers who kept us up."

Ruth slapped her knee. "Do you remember Dulani?"

Naomi chuckled. "Yes. He kept us busy."

I leaned forward in my chair. "Who was Dulani?"

"You tell her, Ruth," Naomi said. "You tell it better than I do."

"Okay," Ruth said. "Dulani was one of the teenagers in the village. He never listened to the headman."

"Who?"

"The headman," Naomi said. "He is like a mayor. There is a headman for each clan in the village."

"Yes," Ruth said, "and the headman for Dulani's family was very strict. His name was Onani, and he didn't like the boys to be out after dark. But Dulani liked to sneak out and run. He loved to run in the moonlight." Ruth slapped her knee again. "You never saw anyone so fast as Dulani."

"Could he outrun the headman?"

Naomi nodded. "That was the trouble. He was faster than anyone. He would run past the headman's house and make lots of noise. And then when the headman came out, Dulani would run away while Onani chased him with a stick. But the headman never caught Dulani."

"Until one night when Onani had a surprise waiting for him."

"That's right," Naomi said. "You see, Dulani always ran the same course. He had a dream of running in the Olympics someday."

Ruth tapped my arm. "But on this night, Onani had dug a large hole and filled it with water from the lake. He made a big mud puddle."

I started to laugh. "So Dulani fell into the mud."

Naomi and Ruth laughed. "That's right," Ruth said. "He was covered with mud from head to toe. And not only that, but Onani had the family gather in the village so that when Dulani came back caked with dirt and mud, they all laughed at him."

"They laughed?"

"Yes, yes," Naomi said. "In Zowe it is quite shameful to be laughed at like that. It's sometimes the worst kind of punishment."

I looked up at the stars. I knew what that was like. The entire Crum village had laughed at me sometimes. "Did Dulani stop running at night after that?"

"For a little while. But when Onani learned the reason why Dulani ran so much, he gave him special permission to do it."

"Just as long as he didn't make so much noise when he ran past Onani's house," Ruth added.

"That's good," I said. "I'd hate for Dulani not to make the Olympics on account of not being allowed to run at night."

Ruth and Naomi exchanged a sad look. I knew there was something more to the story they weren't telling me. I asked about it, but Naomi only said, "I'll tell you more about Dulani another day. It's late now and we should be getting off to bed."

I fiddled with the shoelace of my sneaker while thinking about roosters and owls and dogs and trying to imagine what it would be like to run at night under the moon and stars.

"May I go to bed now?"

"Of course," Ruth said. "We'll be up to tuck you in."

"No. That's all right. Not tonight."

"Okay, dear," Naomi said. "Have a good sleep."

I climbed the crooked steps to the third floor and peered into my room. My room. I wondered how long it would be my room, especially if they caught me snooping around downstairs. It would be my second infraction, and they might not be so quick to forgive and forget. But I had to see if I could find the secret ingredient, and I decided to take the chance.

I sat down on the bed with the small light turned on and yawned. Naomi said people could get used to most anything. Getting used to this new bed would not be easy. I lay on top of the covers again with my hands behind my head. But it was hot anyway. Through the mosquito net, I could see the moon outside my window, and a wisp of a cloud passed over it. I closed my eyes and thought about Dulani running in the tall grass in the silver moonlight. I thought about his family laughing at him as he stood near them caked in mud. I thought about family, about the McAllisters and the Crums, and then I thought about my real mother.

In my mind I checked my list of the three things I know about her:

Cake

1. She didn't want me.
2. She was seventeen when I was born.
3. She didn't want me. Maybe I cried too loud.

<center>~~~~~~~~~~~~</center>

I'm not sure how long I lay there in bed watching the moon and thinking about my mother, about the home, about Mrs. Snipplesmith and the sisters and anything else I could think of to keep me from falling asleep. I wrote in my notebook about my plan and about Dr. Mergenthaler, who was now my favorite neighbor. I wrote:

> If I had a grandfather, I would like him to be just like Dr. Mergenthaler. I would even want him to be crooked because I think he could teach me many things. Especially about birds and hollow bones and why it is sometimes optimal to see the good in things even when it is crooked.

When I heard the sisters go to their rooms, I waited a little bit longer and then crept down the steps. I made certain to step over the squeaky places. I flipped on the small light over the kitchen sink and began my search. I started with the spices. Naomi had many, many jars—some marked and some not. I saw nutmeg and thyme, rosemary and cardamom, sage and a small wooden box of orangey-red stuff that looked more like something a bird would use to build a nest than a spice. I thought it could be top-secret because it was in a special box without a label. I figured that if I were going to keep a magic spice, then I wouldn't write anything on the label. But then again, maybe I would write something just to throw someone off the track.

Next I opened the bottle of vanilla. It was a large brown bottle with a very fancy label that said it came from Madagascar. That was one of the places I liked to imagine flying over if I were

91

a Black-crowned Night-Heron. Vanilla was one of those funny things that smelled so good but tasted so bad straight from the bottle. But other than the stuff in the box, I couldn't find anything that twinkled or lit up or looked the least bit amazing or incredible.

I checked the cabinet where she kept the flour and sugar and baking powder. Nothing. I went about searching slowly and quietly. I didn't want to wake the sisters. I thought about the Crisco Naomi had used to grease the cake pans for Mrs. Snipplesmith's lemon cake, and I wondered if that was where the magic came from. She'd rubbed it on her hands; so maybe, just maybe, it made *her* magical. I couldn't be certain.

After searching and searching, I sat at the table and my shoulders slumped. Nothing. I couldn't find even one thing that might be magical except for the stuff in that fancy box. But there was only a tiny bit of it left, and it would seem to me that Naomi would need a huge supply on account of all the cakes she baked.

Chapter

9

The next morning I went straight out to the chickens. On my way outside, I could hear Naomi singing in the kitchen. She sounded a little bit like the chickens. I guess I liked the sisters well enough, but they sort of gave me the willies — especially with this cake business. But it was a little too soon to say whether or not I liked them. The trouble with being an Unwanted and Misunderstood child is that you just never know about people. I thought I'd be with the Crums for a good long time, but look how that turned out. Seems like no one ever wanted me for too long. I'd have to give the sisters more time and scrutiny before I knew for sure if I liked them.

Hanging out with the chickens was getting easier and easier, and it was also becoming one of my favorite things to do. They pecked and clucked and pecked and clucked — mostly they pecked my sneakers. I grabbed the egg basket and took a deep breath. I opened the chain-link door, and three hens exploded like firecrackers, clucking and hollering.

They knew I'd come to feed them. I think chickens would eat

all day long if you let them. Just like every morning, I dumped some cracked corn on the ground and then some pellets. Ruth called the pellets *Chicken Lay*. She said they had all the necessary nutrients to keep the chickens healthy and help them lay healthy eggs. I scattered some of the ground-up oyster shells on the ground too.

I watched them peck and eat a while. Sonny finally ambled his way into the circle and pecked at some corn. Then he scooted back to his place in the corner of the yard and watched. He let go a strong *cock-a-doodle-do*. But the hens ignored him.

Next, I needed to collect the eggs. So while the birds were busy with breakfast, I went inside the coop. I saw only three eggs. Two white and one brown.

I walked back into the yard with the three eggs.

"*Mwauka bwanji,*" called Naomi.

"Good morning," I said. "I've got only three eggs." I held up the basket for her to see.

"That's just dandy, Wilma Sue. Bring them into the house and I'll make us some breakfast."

I swallowed. It was one thing to gather the eggs, but to eat them fresh from the chickens I'd just touched—that was a little sickening.

"No thanks," I said. "I'm not hungry."

"Come on now, dear. How about a bowl of cornflakes?"

Cornflakes. Now *that* sounded like something I could eat.

"Okay."

She draped her arm around my shoulders. "Then we have another cake to bake."

"Can I help?" I hoped I didn't sound too excited, but I thought I would look more closely and see if I could figure out when she put in the secret ingredient.

"Of course. I hope you put everything back in its place last night."

I stopped dead in my tracks. "But how did you—"

"My dear, I can always tell when my spices have been, shall we say, readjusted."

We walked a few more steps and then I stopped again. "Are you angry?"

Naomi pulled a twig from between her toes. "No, not really. I was just wondering what you were looking for."

I was just about to say, "The secret ingredient." But I didn't. Instead, I lied and said, "Oh nothing. I was trying to memorize them, so I'll know where everything is the next time we bake."

We walked through the back door of the house. Ruth was sipping coffee and looking through a phone book in the kitchen. When she saw us, she closed the Yellow Pages and said, "Today's the day! I've had it! And I won't stand for it another moment!"

Uh-oh, I took two steps backward. Naomi might not have been upset, but it sure sounded like Ruth was. My heart pounded faster than it did during church when the garter snake got loose. All I could figure was that Ruth knew I'd sneaked into the kitchen and snooped, and now she was sending me back to the home. I swallowed. My throat tightened. But then Naomi pulled me close as though she could read my thoughts. "Don't fret, dear. Ruth is finally going to take the car in for repairs. She just has a flair for the dramatic sometimes."

"Yes! Today we get a new radiator in that old heap. I can't have it boil over one more time. It's driving me nuts!"

"Good, good, Ruth," Naomi said.

The ticking of my heart eventually slowed back to its usual rhythm.

"While you're doing that, Wilma Sue and I will be making a cake for Ramona Von Tickle."

I looked at Naomi. "Who?" I asked.

"Ramona Von Tickle."

I shook my head. And I thought the name *Wilma Sue* was bad.

"The opera singer?" Ruth asked after she'd thought about it for a second or two. "The one who lives in the big house?"

Naomi pulled the cover off her big mixer. "Yes. She has a bit of stage fright, it seems. And tonight is opening night. I think this situation calls for cake, don't you?"

"Undoubtedly," Ruth said. "But make it a large one because well, you know, Ramona is quite . . . well, how shall I say this delicately? Large."

"Many opera singers are," Naomi said. "They must hold a lot of air in their lungs."

I didn't think that made any sense at all, but Naomi was a doctor and the expert on these things.

Ruth finished her coffee and the bowl of fruit she was eating. "I have no idea how long I'll be, and then I might go over to the shelter. So I probably won't be back until supper." Then she snagged the car keys from the peg near the door.

"Do take care," Naomi said. "And drive carefully."

I slipped off my sneakers and tossed them into the mud porch. Naomi smiled. "First things, first. Cornflakes."

"Right," I said. I grabbed a blue bowl and filled it with flakes. Then I dumped milk up to the rim and tapped down the flakes. "What kind of cake are we making today?" I asked as I chewed a mouthful of cereal.

"Pineapple upside-down cake. Ramona has been seeing things all turned around lately, so it makes sense, don't you think?"

I nodded. And then I remembered the funny spice. I looked up at the spice cabinet. "What's that funny spice in the little box, Naomi?"

Naomi made a terrible clang with the mixing bowls and said, "Oh, that. It's saffron, dear. A very expensive spice that comes from the crocus plant of the family *Iridaceae*. It comes all the way from Southeast Asia."

Cake

I swallowed a mouthful of cornflakes. "I opened the box last night and smelled it. It reminded me of hay. Seems to me that something that exotic should smell exotic."

Naomi laughed. "Yes, you would think that." She pushed the mixing paddle into the mixer. "But sometimes the most humble things can be the most powerful."

"Like pineapple upside-down cake?"

"We'll see. But we must get baking. Ramona is singing in —" she looked at the cat clock hanging on the wall, " — oh dear, six hours."

That seemed like a very long time to me, but maybe it's not for opera singers.

I finished my cereal and dropped the bowl in the sink. Next, I washed my hands. I scrubbed clear up to my knuckles like I was preparing for surgery. I hoped Naomi wouldn't mention that I didn't wash straight from the chicken coop like I should have.

Naomi and I assembled all of the ingredients: pineapple, butter, sugar, and eggs. I chose two large green eggs, the fancy vanilla, flour from a paper sack, baking powder and baking soda, salt, and buttermilk.

"Buttermilk?" I asked.

Naomi smiled. "Ahhh, for this very special cake. Yes."

I wondered for a second if buttermilk could be the secret ingredient. Maybe it wasn't really milk at all. Maybe it was—

"I'll need an extra three tablespoons of butter," Naomi said "And please get down that large container with the brown sugar. You can climb on the counter if you need to."

As usual Naomi beat the butter and the white sugar together first. I cracked the eggs, and she let me dump them into the mixture along with the fancy vanilla, which somehow smelled even better than it had the night before. We let that all mix together for a minute or so, while Naomi sang:

I've got peace like a river,
I've got peace like a river.
I've got peace like a river in my soul.

I was starting to feel my body sway to the tune just a trifle when I heard a knock on the back door.

"Goodness," Naomi said. "Who could that be? I wasn't expecting company."

Penny stood on the other side of the door looking a little like a mix between a lost puppy and a princess. It was the first time I'd seen her since the snake infraction. At first I wanted to tell her to go away, thinking she'd come over to get back at me. But then I remembered her sad eyes that day she hid behind her mother and the way she looked at the cemetery after church.

"Hi," I said in a very polite manner.

"Whatcha doing?" Penny asked.

"We're baking a cake," I said.

"Can I watch?"

I stepped aside and let her in the kitchen even though there was a part of me that wasn't quite sure. I'd need to keep my left eye peeled.

"Hello, Miss Beedlemeyer." Penny said it so sweetly that I thought she must have eaten a ton of cotton candy before she came over. "What kind of cake are you baking?"

Naomi turned on one of her bare feet. "Penny, how nice to see you. We're making pineapple upside-down cake."

"That sounds good."

"It's for Ramona Von Tickle," I said.

Penny sat at the table. "That crazy singer? She sings really, really loudly. I can hear her sometimes when I walk past her house."

Naomi laughed. "She does have a gift."

"What's next?" I asked.

"I think what's next is an apology, Wilma Sue."

"An apology? For what?"

"For the snake," she said, pushing her glasses farther up on her nose.

I looked at Penny, who was looking a little uppity at the moment.

"Oh, all right. I'm sorry I brought the snake to church and it scared you and half the congregation of the Bloomingdale Avenue Church of Faith."

Penny smiled with closed lips. And I figured that was that. Sometimes a girl has to do what's right even if it feels wrong.

"Good," Naomi said. "Now, you can sift all the dry ingredients together in that big red bowl."

Sifting was fun. I dumped the flour and salt, baking powder, and baking soda a little at a time into the sifter. Then I held the sifter over the red bowl and squeezed the sifter handle fast and hard. A small blizzard of flour fell into the bowl, soft and white. New snow.

But of course I had to sneeze right in the middle of sifting. And even though I turned my head away from the bowl, I ended up with flour in my hair. I even got some on Penny on account of when I sneezed, my arm jerked up and flour dumped out of the sifter. I looked at her sitting there with flour on her face and in her hair.

"You creep!" she squealed. "You did that on purpose."

"No I didn't. It was an accident. My arm jerked and—"

"You did so. Just like the snake."

Naomi set her big spoon in the mixing bowl.

"Now, now, Penny. It was an accident. And we don't call names in this house—or outside this house." She handed Penny a towel. "Just wipe your face."

Penny wiped off the flour and handed me the towel. She definitely had a scowl on her face that made my throat tight.

"Now listen, girls," Naomi said, diverting our attention, "here comes the tricky part. We need to incorporate the wet ingredients into the dry ones, but it must be done carefully. It's science."

I picked up the bowl that held the dry ingredients.

"How come she lets you do the mixing?" Penny asked. "My mother never lets me help. She says I'll ruin it."

"Would you like to dump a little of the dry mixture into the wet, Penny?" Naomi asked.

And I will admit that it made me mad. But I bit my tongue and watched as Penny tilted the bowl with the flour mixture into the mixing bowl.

"Whoa, stop," Naomi said. "Not all of it. This part is done in stages. Remember, slow."

"Let me try." I yanked the bowl away from Penny.

Naomi shook her head at me. Infraction number three? "Add just some of the dry ingredients and then some of the buttermilk."

I let a little of the flour mixture slip into the mixing bowl. Puffs of flour smoke blew up.

"Good," Naomi said. "Now give Penny a try."

Penny tilted the bowl and used a small spatula to help guide the flour into the mixture. "Like this?" she asked, feeling all proud of herself.

"Excellent," Naomi said. "You're a natural."

I took the bowl and did the same.

"Excellent," Naomi said again. "Now go back and forth like that until it is mixed well. On a very slow speed. You can't rush pineapple upside-down cake."

I thought what we did next was funny. Naomi took a large cast iron skillet and set it on top of the stove. She added all of the remaining ingredients: the brown sugar, the butter, and then the pineapple rings with a single cherry in the center of each, along with some of the pineapple juice. It smelled so delicious; I could have eaten the entire thing right then and there. But I did not see or smell anything strange, weird, out of the ordinary, or special. Just plain old ingredients in a plain old cake.

Next, Naomi poured the cake batter into the skillet and evened it all out with a spatula.

I've got joy like a river,
I've got joy like a river.
I've got joy like a river in my soul.

She opened the oven door and set the skillet inside. "Now we let this bake for about an hour and it's done."

"In the skillet?" Penny asked. "Who bakes cake in a skillet? It will never work."

"Of course it will," Naomi said. "Now why don't you two run along and play. I'll call you when it's baked."

I looked at Penny. I really didn't want to play with her.

"I need to check on the chickens," I said.

"Didn't you already tend to them this morning?" Naomi asked.

I gave her a look. A look that I hoped conveyed my thoughts. I was hoping Penny would not want to go visit the chickens with me and leave.

"Sure, go on and visit the birds," Naomi said with a bit of a sputter. "They might have a lot to tell you today."

I looked at Naomi as if she had just sprouted petunias out of her ears. She let go a sigh that smelled like brown sugar and sang:

I've got love like an ocean,
I've got love like an ocean.
I've got love like an ocean in my soul.

"C'mon, Penny," I said. "Let's go talk to the chickens."

Nearly all of the birds were out in the hot sun.

"Goofy birds," I said. "Why aren't you in the coop where it's cooler?"

"Chickens are dumb," Penny said.

"No they're not," I said.

I watched Florence give herself a sand bath. Eggberry pecked for a second or two and then skittered into the coop as though her tail had caught fire.

And it just might have. It was so hot.

"They smell," Penny said. "I don't know how you can stand it."

"It's not that bad," I said. "But you don't have to stick around if you don't want to."

She didn't say anything. So I kept talking to the chickens. "Now Florence," I said, "you really should give Eggberry more room and stop pecking at her. And Dottie, thank you for being considerate and giving Slowpoke some shells."

Sonny sprinted into the fray and everyone scattered.

"Want to hold one?" I asked Penny.

"Hold one? Really? Will it bite me?"

"Nah. Chickens don't bite."

"Okay," Penny said.

I set Dottie, since she was the biggest and fattest, into Penny's arms like a baby doll. "She's soft but also prickly."

Penny was reluctant at first, but then she lightly touched Dottie's feathers. "You're right. It's weird."

I saw Dottie's left eye give Penny a wary look. Dottie squawked and flapped her wings, and Penny dropped her on the ground where Dottie then exploded into a mass of feathers and sand and high-tailed it back into the coop.

Penny screeched, "Oh! I ... I *hate* your dumb chickens!" Then she ran off with her big Pippi Longstocking feet. I stayed with the chickens a little while longer to make sure Dottie was okay before I went back to Gray House. It seemed every time I thought I could like Penny, she did something dumb.

Chapter 10

Naomi was pulling the cake out of the oven when I went inside.

"It smells good," I said.

"It sure does." Naomi held the cast iron pan with a potholder and two hands. She set it on top of a hot pad on the counter. "We should let it settle and cool for a few minutes before we take it to Ramona."

"Okay." I sat at the kitchen table. "Penny dropped Dottie."

"She did?"

"I let Penny hold her, but Penny's dumb face must have spooked Dottie because she clucked really loud and fluttered her wings and then Penny dropped her."

Naomi laughed. "That happens sometimes. And Penny's face is not dumb."

"I never dropped one."

"It's not a contest, Wilma Sue. And right now we have to think about poor Ramona."

Another poor person. I knew from Naomi's voice that she meant poor in the sad way.

"Why does Ramona have stage fright?"

"I'm not quite sure," Naomi said. "But if I had to base my diagnosis on anything, I'd say it has something to do with that butler of hers. Sometimes he's more critical of Ramona than she deserves."

"Enough to make her afraid to sing?"

Naomi sat at the table and touched my hand. "Of course. Especially if he said something critical about her last performance. He attends them all."

"Why doesn't she fire him if he keeps making such snarky remarks?"

Naomi tapped her cheek. "That, my dear Wilma Sue, is a good question."

⁓⁓⁓⁓⁓⁓⁓⁓⁓⁓⁓⁓

Naomi left the cake in the skillet. She said it was still warm and best served that way. So off we went to make another cake delivery. This time we walked across the street and down a long driveway that led to a house I didn't even know existed. It was hidden behind tall evergreens. The house was grand. More grand than any house I had ever seen—except maybe in a magazine. Two large pillars guarded the front door, which had a brass lion's head doorknocker in the center.

"Go on, clap the knocker," Naomi said.

I laughed a little. What she'd said sounded funny. But I did as she said and heard a low, loud sound that seemed to rumble in every direction. We waited for a few seconds and then the door opened. There stood a tall, gangly man wearing a black suit with long tails and a yellow bowtie. He had slicked-back black hair and a nose that was so long I thought it might be a fake. His eyes were tiny and scary, and his chin came to a point. He looked like a criticizer.

He raised his pointy chin and said, "Good afternoon,

Miss Beedlemeyer and—" he looked at me and said, "And ... and ...?"

"Miss Wilma Sue," Naomi said.

"Oh yes, of course," the butler said. "Do come in. I shall inform the diva ... er ... Miss Von Tickle that you're here." Then he waved his arm and we walked into a huge room with a large black piano in the center of it, which was sitting under a crystal chandelier that hung from the ceiling like a gigantic spider. And there was a funny-looking, red velvet couch pushed up against one wall where a hairy white cat rested on a purple pillow. A huge staircase led to the upper floor, which was kind of like a balcony. The stairs were shiny and bright.

I sucked a deep breath. "It's ... it's amazing," I said.

"Yes, isn't it?" Naomi said. She seemed to be getting uncomfortable holding the cake.

A couple of minutes later, I saw who I thought must be the Great Ramona at the top of the stairs. She was magnificent.

"Is that her?" I whispered.

"Yes. That, my dear, is Ramona Estileeza Von Tickle."

Naomi looked up at her, and Ramona said, "Naomi, dahling, how nice of you to come!"

"Ramona," Naomi said in kind of a loud voice. It echoed around the room. "I heard you were having a bit of ... stage fright."

Ramona, wearing a long, diaphanous dress with pictures of peacocks all over it, started down the stairs. I loved that word. Diaphanous. It means light and delicate, silky, almost transparent. It was one of my found words. She seemed to glide as though her feet were inches above the ground. She swept the air with her hands. She had long, long hair that trailed down her back like a waterfall. Her eyes sparkled in the beam of sunlight that suddenly blasted through the window.

"It's *Die Fledermaus*," Ramona said. "I ... I cannot do it. Not tonight." She crossed the room in grand fashion, threw her arm across her forehead, and flopped onto the red velvet sofa, which made the cat screech and run.

"Go. Go now, Kitty," Ramona said. "I don't blame you for fleeing. My career is over."

Naomi shook her head. "It's worse than I thought. We mustn't waste any more time."

We crossed the huge room. Ramona looked up at us from her prone position on the couch. "I fear I am beyond help."

"Nonsense," Naomi said. "Why, you are the Great Ramona Von Tickle. *Die Fledermaus* is no match for your talent."

"But, but it's 'The Laughing Song.' So ... so difficult, but especially when the star does not feel like laughing. Oh dear, woe is me."

She actually said those words. Looking around her grand house, I couldn't think of anything she had to be woeful about. I could tell her about woe—starting with the lousy Crum house. I figured you could probably fit their skinny house into Ramona Von Tickle's bedroom closet. But I remembered Miss Tate's words: "Get along with everyone."

Naomi set the large skillet on top of the piano, since there really was no other place to put it. Fortunately, there was a pink doily on the piano. I didn't think Naomi would want to scratch the gleaming surface. Then she marched right over to Ramona. "Now tell me exactly what happened," Naomi said.

"It's Bernard," Ramona said. "He ... criticized my aria. He said my high C above A was ... was ... I cannot say the word."

"Flat?" Naomi asked.

Ramona let go a squeak. "That's it."

"And for that reason you can't perform?" Naomi moved closer to Ramona.

"Who can sing when her high C above A is gone? I can't get it back. And one cannot possibly sing 'The Laughing Song' without it."

Cake

"We brought you cake," I said. "Pineapple upside-down cake."

Ramona sat up straight. "And who, who is this ... this child?"

"This is Wilma Sue," Naomi said. "She's come to live with us."

Ramona touched my cheek. "Such a young thing and oh so pretty." She let go a big sigh that smelled like peppers, and then she said with such sadness that I wanted to cry, "Never become an opera singer. It's nothing but heartache."

"I'm not a good singer," I said. "But you are and you must sing. It's your talent, and I think you should sing and not give up no matter what Bernard says."

Ramona smiled at me, and I noticed she had large horse teeth and a large mouth. The better to belt out her arias, I supposed. "But ... but what if my note falls flat again? I could not abide such a calamity."

"It won't," I said.

Ramona swooned again with the back of her hand across her forehead. Then she looked straight at me and said, "But I cannot sing tonight. I have no ... no song in my heart."

"Nonsense," Naomi said. "Now, will you please ask Bernard to bring us four plates and forks, a knife, and a serving platter?"

Ramona sniffed. Then she pulled a purple hanky from her sleeve and sniffled into it. "Please go and ring for him. Use the bellpull over there, won't you, Wilma Sue?"

I pointed to my chest. "Me? Ring for the butler?"

"Of course, of course," Ramona said.

So I went to the bellpull—a long silk scarf suspended from the ceiling. I couldn't imagine how it would ring any bell. But I pulled it once, then twice, and within seconds Bernard was standing right next to me.

"You rang, madam?"

"Yes, yes," Ramona said. "Bring us four plates and forks, a knife, and, oh, a large serving platter."

"Certainly, ma'am," Bernard said, and then he shuffled off with silent feet.

Naomi went to Ramona and patted her hand. "Now, now, Ramona, I am certain you will be able to sing tonight. There is no better voice available. It is your song—"

"Aria," Ramona corrected.

"Aria," Naomi said.

Bernard returned with the plates and other items. "Shall I serve?" he asked.

I looked at Naomi. I could tell by the way she frowned at me that she knew I wanted to say something to Bernard about the way he treated Ramona. But I could also tell that under no circumstances should I say what was on my mind. So I held my breath for a minute to keep from saying anything.

"No, thank you, Bernard," Naomi said.

"Certainly, ma'am." Bernard said, stepping to the side and flinging his coat tails out like nasty crow's wings.

"Wilma Sue," Naomi said. "Are you ready for the most exciting part of making a pineapple upside-down cake?"

My heart beat like hummingbird wings. Here it comes. The magic.

"Yes," I said.

"Okay, now, Wilma Sue, you come closer; you'll want to see this."

I stepped closer as Naomi set the large platter on top of the skillet.

"What are you doing?" I asked.

"Flipping."

"Flipping? Flipping what?"

"The cake, of course," Naomi said. "I am going to turn the pineapple upside-down cake right-side up onto this platter."

Cake

I felt my brow wrinkle, and Ramona Von Tickle sighed so deeply the chandelier shook. Bernard craned his neck to one side.

Then in one grand swoop Naomi picked up the skillet with two hands and flipped it over. I closed my eyes. I didn't want to see that magnificent cake spill onto the floor. But when I opened my eyes, there it sat on the platter as perfect as can be. And Naomi stood there looking at it like even she was surprised it didn't fall and crumble. She adjusted it slightly, centering it exactly on the platter, and said, "Oh my, it's a thrill every time."

Then she sliced into it, and there we all sat with plates of pineapple upside-down cake on our laps. Ramona took the first bite. Then Bernard. And then Naomi took a bite. I waited to go last. You can never tell what might happen with cake. Ramona took a second bite, and as she did her cheeks grew rosy and her eyes bright. By the time we had eaten all of our slices, Ramona was smiling and laughing and so happy that she burst into song. I had never heard a voice so loud and so big. It took my breath away as she effortlessly reached a very high note. I shuddered inside. I thought her voice could fill the Grand Canyon.

"Ah, perfect!" Naomi said. "One octave above E. Now I suggest you eat another slice just before the opera tonight," Naomi said.

Ramona, who was still laughing and singing, only nodded.

"Don't you agree, Bernard?" Naomi asked.

A smile spread across Bernard's face. "Lovely," he said. "That was just lovely!"

"Come along now, Wilma Sue, our work is done here."

And off we went back to Gray House. We could hear Ramona singing until we got home.

Chapter
11

The next morning I went to see the chickens right away. It was warm and muggy, as usual, so no one could stay in bed very long unless there was air conditioning. And we didn't have that. Only a single, solitary white cloud hung in the blue sky. I thought maybe it had floated away from the others and couldn't get back to them—like a lost sheep.

I heard the chickens cackling and talking before I got there. They seemed upset. Eggberry was running around like mad, and Dottie was sitting in a corner of the pen looking frightened. The others were inside the coop.

"What's wrong?" I asked. "Did something happen?"

The chickens didn't answer. They kept bobbing and weaving as though something had disturbed them. It was possible that a hawk or a fox or a raccoon had maybe given them the willies, but their yard was pretty secure.

"Something must have scared you," I said. "But I'm here now, so you can all relax."

They calmed down and came near me as I tossed feed on

the ground. I threw a couple handfuls of fresh hay and some pellets and shells. There seemed to be a lot of feathers on the ground, and I was thankful I'd been reading that book about chickens. I knew a couple of the chickens were molting, which meant they were shedding their feathers to get new ones. I'd read that sometimes it could take up to twenty-four weeks for a wing to completely refeather. And a molting chicken is not a pretty chicken. Eggberry's neck looked red and scrawny, like she'd been fighting.

Next, I checked the nests. I found three eggs: two white and one brown. I'd also read that molting chickens don't lay as many eggs. The nests were dirty from the hens tracking mud and poop into the bedding, so I replaced the old stuff with new straw and shredded newspaper. I gave the coop a quick cleanup with some new hay. Ruth kept an old broom in the coop, which I used to sweep off the ramp. It was important to keep the nests clean.

All in all, the coop looked pretty good. I took the three eggs and was about to open the gate when I saw Mrs. Agabeedies walking toward me. The chickens cackled and scrambled into the coop like they didn't want to see her.

"Good morning, Mrs. Agabeedies," I said, wanting to get along. Only she was standing there looking all cross and pinch-faced as usual. I couldn't understand why anyone would want to be so cross all the time.

I held out the egg basket. "Three eggs this morning."

She did not care one iota about the eggs.

"Good morning, Wilma Sue," she said. And then she started in on it again—the whole thing about her being the church secretary and having a right to know everything that goes on in the church and parsonage.

"I trust we won't have another snake incident," she said.

I kicked at some cracked corn. "It was an accident. I didn't mean for the snake to get away."

She snorted through her nose. "Well, you never should have brought the nasty beast into the church to begin with. Haven't the Beedlemeyer sisters taught you anything?"

I was glad to spy Naomi standing on the back porch steps. "I think Naomi is calling me."

Mrs. Agabeedies turned quickly. "I didn't hear her, but I suppose you'd better go. If they had spent their days teaching and doctoring our own needy children, then perhaps—"

I took off running toward Gray House. I did not want to hear what came after "perhaps."

"What was that all about?" Naomi asked when I reached the back steps.

I looked back. Mrs. Agabeedies was strutting across the lawn toward the church.

"How come they let people like her work at church?"

"She does a good job of taking care of business, even if she is a bit of a—"

"Bigot," I said. "That's what Ruth called her. And now I know why."

"I was going to say *fussbudget*." Naomi went into the house and I followed her.

Ruth was still home, which was kind of surprising since she was always quick to get on with her volunteer work and shopping and such.

"I made French toast," Ruth said. "Hope you like it with syrup and sausage."

My mouth watered. "Thank you." I washed my hands and then sat at my place at the table.

Ruth set a yellow plate in front of me. "Enjoy!"

"Wilma Sue had a little run-in with Mrs. You-Know-Who," Naomi said.

I chewed some sausage and nodded my head. I couldn't swallow fast enough to get my words out. "She said you and

Naomi should have taken care of American kids instead of African ones."

Naomi patted my shoulder. "I know, dear. She has some twisted thinking. But don't you worry about what she says. Ruth and I know what we did was right before God."

"That's right," Ruth said. "We followed God's plan for our lives."

I looked at a little ribbon of melted butter moving around in the amber syrup on my plate. I touched it slightly with the tip of a fork tine, and the ribbon swirled off in a new direction. I supposed I might have been part of God's plan for the sisters. But that would mean God planned for me to be an orphan.

"Finish your breakfast, Wilma Sue." Naomi said. "And then I think we should take you to the store for some new clothes."

"New clothes? I don't need new clothes."

"Oh dear," she said. "Your underwear is in tatters. Plus, school will be starting soon, so I want you to have some bright new clothes."

"And you should have a Sunday dress," Ruth added.

"Mrs. Crum always gave me hand-me-downs. They were good enough ... good enough for an ... or—"

Naomi reached across the table and touched my hand. "What is it dear? Something the matter?"

My eyes filled with tears. I hated wearing hand-me-downs all the time. I used to wish that Mauveleen would buy me new clothes, but she never did. And now Naomi wanted to take me shopping, and it made me sad for some reason. I felt embarrassed that I was an orphan, that I was a hand-me-down kid. "It's just, it's just that I ... well, leapin' red lizards!" I stood up and slammed my hand on the table.

Naomi jumped. "Now, Wilma Sue, that's not—"

"Do you think it's easy settling into a new foster home and getting used to bigots, and girls who give you bloody lips, and chickens, and cakes that ... that do things? Well it's not. I don't want you to buy me clothes like I'm your ... your daughter or something. I'm just an orphan."

There, I said it. I sat down with a thud.

Naomi's eyes were about as wide as the chicken eggs.

"Now I certainly didn't expect that reaction from you, but ... but you are absolutely right."

"What?" I looked at her with my left eye.

"Of course it's hard to settle into a new house with two old sisters. We've tried to make you comfortable here, but I can see you need more time. We can shop another day. And as for your being an orphan, I would prefer it if we never, ever used that word again."

I pushed back from the table and stood. Tears spilled down my cheeks. I swiped them away like mosquitoes. "May I go outside now?"

"Of course you may."

"Thank you," I said. My heart was still beating like a bird's.

━━━━━━━━━━

My first stop after my escape was my bedroom. I grabbed my notebook because I had "the flash" to write. I looked out my window. Sweet Silver Maple stood tall and bright with yellow sunshine dappling through her branches. From the third floor I could see the church and the little cemetery and clear on down the path to the creek that ran alongside the property.

The creek was at the base of a steep cliff packed with trees. But one tree stood out. A weeping willow with long skinny branches stood like a regal queen. Her branches bowed low to the ground, their tiny fingers swiping the dirt and barely touching the creek water. The tree looked old, older than Naomi and Ruth, even older than Moses. From my viewpoint, when the breeze blew I could see a face in her branches that reminded me of a grandmother.

"I will call you Old Woman Willow of the Creek," I said. "Why are you crying?"

I opened my notebook and pulled out the pen I leave clipped inside of it. It was a pen I'd purchased when my fifth grade class visited New York. I'd bought it on Liberty Island in the Statue of Liberty gift shop. On the side were printed the words, "Give me your tired, your poor . . ."

I wrote:

Old Woman Willow of the Creek
you make me want to sneak
down to see you dressed in green
prettiest tree I've ever seen.

I clipped the pen inside, closed my notebook, and thought, *Why not? Why not visit her in person?* I hadn't ventured too far from the parsonage since I'd arrived at Gray House, and all of a sudden it seemed like a good day to explore, especially now that I wasn't grounded anymore.

Old Woman Willow was dressed in a wide green skirt that I thought could hide a thousand baby willows. She clung to the edge of the creek bed. Someday, and I hoped not too soon, her bed would no longer hold her roots, and she would tumble into the water and be swept out to sea.

I sat under the tree and listened to the sound of the creek tumbling over the rocks, some wide and flat, others craggy and big. They were the color of dirt but with glistening crystals. I sat with my back against the willow's trunk, opened my notebook, and read over my words:

This is what I know so far:
- The sisters are spinsters but that's not a nice word.
- They make cakes that make people feel better, and sometimes birds fly out when you slice into them.
- Penny Pigsworthy is not nice all of the time, but I still want to be her friend.
- I like the chickens, especially Florence and Eggberry and Dottie.

I added:

Mrs. Agabeedies is a bigot, and Naomi wants to buy me new clothes. NEW clothes.

I underlined the word three times.

Robins and sparrows flitted about the willow's branches. I thought about their hollow bones and how delicate they must be.

That was when Penny showed up wearing a pink dress, white sneakers, and pink bows in her pigtails. I smiled at the thought of Penny Pigsworthy wearing pigtails. They seemed out of place for her. I was certain her mother made her wear them.

"What do you want?" I asked. Then I threw a stone into the creek and listened to it *plunk*.

"Wanna play?" Penny asked.

"Nope." I threw another rock. It made a bigger *plunk* and a bigger splash.

"Okay. Suit yourself. Why are you hanging out down here?"

"It's a nice tree. I named her Old Woman Willow."

Penny laughed. "Why did you name a tree? That's stupid."

"No it's not. She's a living thing. All living things should have a name. And besides, she looks like an old woman with her head bowed down. From my window I can see a face like a grandmother's in her branches sometimes—if the wind blows right."

Penny touched the tree and then looked up into her branches. "I don't see a face. You're cracked."

"I am *not* cracked."

"Well there ain't no face in the branches, and this is just a dumb old tree."

There was no use in talking to Penny about it anymore. I think she liked to argue with everything I said.

Penny looked at me with bunched-up eyebrows. "Whatcha writing?"

I closed my notebook. "Nothing. Just thoughts."

"About what? That's stupid."

I practically laughed out loud. "No it's not. Haven't you ever felt it?"

She picked at the bark on the willow's trunk. "Felt what?"

" 'The flash,' the urge to get down on paper your innermost thoughts and feelings and worries. Or the urge to write about the way rain smells one way in summer and another in winter, and how it sounds like bacon frying when it hits the road. Or about how looking at a sunflower can almost take your breath away."

"You *are* cracked," she said. "I've never had a 'flash.' I don't like writing—especially about my feelings."

"You don't have to write about your feelings. You can write about your family or—"

"What about my family? I don't want to write about that either. My family is perfect."

I thought about what Naomi had said about Penny's mother being an orphan in the home.

"I know your mother was an orphan—like me."

Penny swallowed and I watched her eyes glisten like she was about to cry. Instead, she pulled herself up and squared her shoulders like she was bracing herself against a strong wind. "So what? She isn't an orphan anymore, and ... and neither am I."

For a second I stared up at her. I couldn't figure out why she'd said that unless ... unless sometimes she felt like an orphan. I supposed even kids who had parents, their real parents, could feel that way sometimes—all alone, silent like a snowflake. Maybe Miss Tate wasn't entirely correct. Maybe the most important thing wasn't getting along with everyone, but belonging to someone and knowing that someone belonged to you.

Penny picked up a stone. She threw it into the creek with as much force as she could muster. "If you don't want to play, then I'm leaving."

"Suit yourself. I'm going to sit here a little longer."

I watched Penny skip off toward home.

I wrote:

Penny is a funny person. I always think we could be friends, and then she runs away. I guess I ran away from Naomi and Ruth today. I got mad because they wanted to buy me new clothes. I'm not sure why it made me angry except that sometimes when a girl isn't with her real mother and her real father, it feels like the whole world is doing her a favor by taking care of her, like she's a burden. There's a lot to carry through life, but I think a girl should carry her own weight—at least I think I do.

Chapter

12

That night, Naomi and Ruth tucked me in. Naomi sat on the edge of my bed. "You were very quiet tonight," she said. "Is anything troubling you?"

"Can we help?" Ruth asked.

I shook my head. "No. I guess I just had a quiet night. That can happen sometimes, don't you think?"

"Sure," Naomi said. She patted my knee under the thin blanket. "We just wanted to make sure. You aren't sick, are you?"

I practically laughed. "No. I feel fine."

Naomi felt my forehead. "Okay, you look fine."

"Does she have a temperature?" Ruth asked.

Naomi smiled at me. "Of course she has a temperature. Everyone has a temperature. What you mean to say is, *Does she have a fever?*"

"Okay, okay, Dr. Beedlemeyer," Ruth said, sounding a little annoyed. "Does she have a fever?"

"Nope," Naomi said. "She just has the quiets." Then she kissed my cheek. "Good night."

"Sleep tight," Ruth added.

I waited until they were gone, and then I set my palm on the place where Naomi had kissed me. I left it there, maybe all night. I felt like I belonged to them.

The next morning I felt normal again. I washed and got dressed and wrote in my notebook:

> Naomi kissed my cheek last night. The only other person who ever kissed me was Millie, and I can barely remember it.

I closed the notebook and slid it back under my mattress. Enough said.

I found Naomi preparing breakfast. The kitchen smelled like bacon and coffee.

"*Mwauka bwanji*," Naomi said.

I tried to answer her in Tumbuka, but all I could remember was "bwino."

"Almost," she said. "You'll get it."

Naomi flipped six strips of bacon all at once. "Ruth is doing some studying. She started a new ESL class at the Life Center."

"ESL?"

"English as a Second Language. She teaches English to some Vietnamese women."

"Oh, I get it. Does Ruth speak Vietnamese also?"

"A little. You might not have noticed this, but Ruth is very smart—practically a genius. She also speaks French and Russian."

"Really? Wow. I thought only spies needed to know so many languages."

"Nope. She just always had a knack for it. She learns very quickly. Our father was a linguist. He studied languages and folk tales."

Cake

"Folk tales? Do you mean fairy tales?"

"Those too. He's one of the reasons we have so many books."

I broke off a piece of bacon and chewed it. Then I pulled a little fat off of another strip. "Do you miss him?"

"Sure, sometimes. He was a great man."

"I never knew my father. I don't even know his name. I don't think anyone does."

Naomi sat at the table. "I know, Wilma Sue. But you do have a father. A heavenly Father."

"You mean God."

"Yep. He's the best Father of all."

I swallowed my bacon and sipped some orange juice. "Can I have a cup of coffee?" I did not want to talk about fathers.

Naomi snorted air through her nose. "No, of course not. You are way too young to start drinking coffee."

"Okay." I laughed. "I'll go check on the chickens after I eat. Did you know they're molting?"

"Yes, Ruth did tell me that. The chickens look so ugly when they shed their feathers. But it's important."

"I'm glad we don't shed feathers," I said.

"Well, we do shed. Hair, skin."

I looked at my plate of eggs and swallowed a sour lump that had formed in my throat. Sometimes living with a doctor was a little weird.

"I think I'm done."

"Okay, dear. Hurry back from the chickens, though. We have another cake to bake."

"What's the special ingredient this time?" I tied my sneaker laces.

"Special? Oh, nothing new. The usual, I suppose, a little of this and a little of that."

"But I want to know, for cryin' out loud!" I had been living with the sisters for almost a whole month, and I wanted to be in on their secrets. It seemed to me that if they wanted me to be a part of their family, then I should know their family secrets.

Naomi dropped the bacon pan into the sink with a clang. "Wilma Sue. I would appreciate it if you didn't use that tone with me."

"I'm sorry, it's just ... it's just that I want to know."

Naomi pulled the flour sack from the cabinet. "What is it you think you need to know?"

"How you do it. How you bake cakes that make people ... sing and be happy, that make their fingers go straight and their chairs lift off the ground."

Naomi shook her head. "What makes you think it's the cake?"

I sighed.

———————

I ran down to the coop, stopping for a moment to visit with Sweet Silver Maple. It was getting to be late summer now, and her leaves were getting that look, like they were tired and waiting to burst into their autumn clothes before falling to the ground. "Soon," I said.

Then I went to the chickens and went about the daily routine. Eggberry was pretty molty—if that's even a word. But they all looked okay. So I fed them and checked the water supply and did all the necessary chicken chores. Most days it was a matter of routine. Nothing new.

On my way back to the house, I spied Penny sitting in the church cemetery again. She was perched on one of the tombstones and appeared to be plucking petals from a daisy or some such flower.

My first thought was to go find out why in the world Penny Pigsworthy spent so much time in the cemetery.

I turned back toward the chickens. Dottie was pecking at some corn. "What do you girls think?"

Sonny Liston let go a loud *cock-a-doodle-do* letting me know he did not appreciate being left out of the conversation.

"All right, you too," I said. "Should I go see what she's doing in the cemetery?"

The birds clucked like mad. I looked up at Gray House and knew Naomi was getting ready to make her next cake. I told her I would help, but I also had a feeling I needed to go see Penny.

I slinked toward the cemetery like a spy, hoping Penny wouldn't notice me right away. The large iron gate creaked when I opened it. Penny looked in my direction.

"Hey," I called, since I'd been caught in the act of sneaking. "What are you doing?"

"Nothin'," she hollered back. "Just sitting here."

When I was standing right near her, I asked again, "How come you're here?"

She tossed what was left of the flower, just a stem, onto the ground.

"Can't a person visit a cemetery?"

"Sure they can but who are you visiting?"

Penny swallowed and looked off into the woods. "Nobody." Then as if a lightning bolt had struck under her feet, she took off. All I could do was stand there and watch her run.

I shrugged and then I heard Ruth calling me from the mud porch of Gray House. So I took off running lickety-split too. When I got inside the house, Naomi and Ruth were standing in the kitchen discussing the next cake.

"Who is it today, sister?" Ruth asked.

Naomi pushed the large beater into the mixer. "Hortense Quill."

"The librarian?" Ruth said. "Come to think of it, she did look a bit piqued the last time I was in."

"She was?" Naomi said. "That could very well be because a person who comes down with a bad case of the gossips can begin to look a little . . . strange."

"The gossips?" I asked as I untwisted the cap on the vanilla bottle and took a whiff.

"Yes, yes," Naomi said, "and we must proceed gingerly where Hortense is concerned. She won't take kindly to us offering her cake."

"And you must never tell her it's because of her . . . her problem," Ruth said.

The gossips? I thought about the chickens and how they're always clucking and chattering and how they sometimes sound like women gabbing with each other. I'd think they had a bad a case of the gossips, but it was their normal chicken manners.

"Okay," I said. "I don't suppose it would be a good idea to say it right out loud to her. I never liked it when a Crum said something about me. Even if it was true."

Naomi and Ruth smiled at each other. "She's learning quickly, isn't she?" Ruth said.

"Yes she is," Naomi said.

Ruth finished her coffee and set the cup in the sink. "If you have everything under control here, I should be getting off to the Life Center. I have my ESL class first, and then I'm helping in the garden today."

"Garden?" I said. "I didn't know the Life Center had a garden." I climbed onto a kitchen stool.

"They do," Ruth said. "And it's a dandy. They are growing the most lovely zucchinis and tomatoes." She pulled a straw hat with plastic fruits around the brim onto her head.

"I'm glad you're wearing your hat this time," Naomi said. "The sun can be dangerous."

"You're a worrywart, but I know you're right. I should be home in time for supper." And with that, Ruth left the house.

Cake

Naomi and I started working on the cake for the librarian.

"What kind of cake are we making?" I asked.

"I thought a carrot cake would be just what the doctor—and of course that's me—ordered."

"Carrot cake?" I said. "Yuck. Who makes cake with carrots? Maybe rabbits and guinea pigs."

"Oh, my dear, guinea pigs cannot bake."

Naomi assembled all of her ingredients and utensils. "*Mise en place*," Naomi said.

"What?" I asked, looking at her kind of crooked.

"*Mise en place*. It's a French phrase that means 'everything in its place.' The Culinary Institute uses it all the time; it's the number one rule—after washing your hands, of course."

"Oh," I said. Then I went to the kitchen sink to wash my hands.

"This is a very involved cake," Naomi said. "It requires a lot of concentration."

Oh boy, I was certainly going to pay close attention today. I thought for sure I'd see the special ingredient this time. So I watched Naomi's every move very closely, like she was under a microscope. The first thing she did was grate three large carrots. But there was nothing fancy or special about it. All she had was a bowl full of orange by the time she was finished. Then she dumped a bunch of brown sugar into the carrots, which kind of made me sick at first. But it actually smelled pretty good. I would say it was . . . aromatic. One of my new words.

By the time we finished mixing all of the ingredients—and there were a *lot* of ingredients in this carrot cake—we had a lumpy but *aromatic* concoction of sugar, carrots, raisins, eggs, cinnamon, and even pineapple—which I thought was a little weird, but Naomi said it's what made her carrot cake so special.

My eyes grew wide when she said that. "Really? Pineapple?" I said. "Why is the pineapple so special?"

I thought she might let me in on her secret, but she only smiled and said, "All chefs have their secrets, and this is mine."

I know she didn't put pineapple in all of her cakes, well, except for the pineapple upside-down cake. So how could pineapple be special? I kept up my scrutiny while she mixed the batter and then dumped the mixture into the cake pans. But I didn't see anything out of the ordinary.

"So how come carrot cake is good for the gossips?" I asked finally.

Naomi shrugged and pushed the cake pans into the oven. "Oh, goodness," she said. "Carrots are really quite healthy; gossiping is not."

But I could tell that was all she was going to say on the matter because she went right to singing and rinsing the bowls and spoons:

I sing because I'm happy,
I sing because I'm free,
For His eye is on the sparrow,
And I know He watches me.

I licked some batter off the beater. It wasn't bad, not bad at all. I think I might learn to like carrot cake. It was a bit spicy, but not like Szechuan. That's what the Crums always ate. I hated it. But all the Crums thought it was the best. Naomi's carrot cake batter tasted more like I always imagined Thanksgiving would taste if I were surrounded by a mother, a father, sisters and brothers, aunts and uncles, cousins, and maybe even grandparents. Then I thought of Penny—out in the cemetery. I wondered if she had grandparents who visited her on holidays and brought her gifts and things.

Naomi pushed the cakes into the oven and then sat down at the table with a thud. She seemed to be covered in goo—pineapple, brown sugar, even a piece of carrot hanging from her nose, which she swiped with the back of her hand. "I'm bushed," she said. "We'll let the cake bake, and then we'll make the frosting. I could use a cup of coffee while I put my feet up." I watched her rub one of her bare feet. "Mixing carrot cake is a tiring job."

I sat across from her at the table. "I saw Penny in the cemetery this morning."

"You did? She was probably just visiting."

"That's what she said but who? Who does Penny visit?"

Naomi took a breath. "She didn't tell you?"

I shook my head as a queasy feeling rushed to my stomach. "No."

"Her father," Naomi said, looking me square in the eyes. "He … passed away when Penny was just a little girl. I believe she was about four or five years old."

I swallowed. A sudden rush of feelings struck me. I was sad for Penny but also mad. She never told me. She let me think her family was perfect. I was getting used to the way she was, or at least the way I thought she was, all uppity and snooty sometimes. A crybaby at other times. And now I knew there was a very good reason why people like Mrs. Agabeedies rushed to her rescue and treated her like a princess.

"Well…well…cockamamie!" I said. "It isn't fair. It is *not* fair."

"Of course not, dear," Naomi said. "It's never fair when a child loses her father. He was an Army officer, and he was killed in a helicopter crash."

"That's not what I mean." I banged the kitchen table so hard the saltshaker fell over.

"Wilma Sue!" Naomi said. "You'll make the cake fall."

"Sorry. But now … now I have to feel sorry for her but … but—"

"But what?"

"I don't have a father either. Or a mother. And nobody treats me like I'm special. Definitely not the Crums and even Millie sent me back to the home. Nobody really wants me." I looked into Naomi's eyes and saw that my last words might have hurt her. Of course she treated me special. She and Ruth did all they could to make me feel welcome. They made me feel like their own child. But still, I had no mother or father, not really.

For a reason I didn't quite understand, the way that Penny had become an orphan—a half orphan, technically, since she still had her mother—was different than mine. I always had the feeling that people, even Miss Tate sometimes, thought I'd done something to make my mother not want me. And that thought was hard to tame.

"Penny at least has her mother. Her real mother," I said finally. "I don't."

"That's true," Naomi said, sniffing the air. "I can smell the spices. I love the nutty brown spices, don't you?"

"Yes," I said. "But what about that? What about Penny having a mother and not me?"

"Poor Portia," Naomi said, righting the saltshaker I'd toppled. "Portia works very hard. And nearly every day—except Sundays. She cleans houses for people on the Main Line. Mrs. Agabeedies told me Portia comes home some nights so exhausted that she can't even make Penny's supper."

I had heard enough. Poor Portia. Poor Penny. Poor Mrs. Snipplesmith. Poor Dr. Mergenthaler. And poor Ramona Von Tickle. But nobody ever said "poor Wilma Sue."

"Maybe I'll go check on the chickens again," I said.

"Good idea. I think you could use a breath of fresh air. I won't deliver the cake without you."

I went out back but I couldn't even talk to the chickens. I watched them going about their business for a while, pecking, clucking, chasing each other; and I thought how simple it was to love chickens. I don't think any chicken ever thought, *Poor so-and-so*. To chickens, people were just people—no matter what.

Cake

The birds flapped and pecked and argued with each other just like always. Just like a family. I grabbed Eggberry and held her to my chest. It was like she hugged me back, but then she wanted to get down right away. I tossed some scratch on the ground and watched them gobble it down.

"Okay, girls," I said. "I'm gonna go visit Old Woman Willow for a little while. But I'll be back to feed you later. Probably leftovers from whatever we have for supper. Maybe spaghetti again."

I started down the path to Old Woman Willow. But when I passed Sweet Silver Maple, I saw Penny walking—actually it was more like marching—toward me. Only she wasn't carrying a stupid Barbie doll this time.

"Whatcha doing?" I called.

"It's a free country," she said with a touch of anger in her voice, like I'd been complaining that she was on our property.

"I was just asking," I said. "But suit yourself. I'm going down to visit Old Woman Willow of the Creek and ask her why she cries."

She laughed a kind of laugh that touched that spot in my heart where embarrassment lurked like a vulture.

"Want to go with me?" I asked, because something inside of me suggested that asking Penny was the right thing to do. "Even if you are in a bad mood."

"I'm not in bad mood."

"Yes you are. I can tell by the way you're walking."

"I am not. But I'll go with you."

I looked up into the sky. Some dark, bottom-heavy clouds were rolling in.

"Thunderheads," I said, pointing.

"Oh, do you think we should still go to the creek? What if it thunders and lightnings?"

"What if it does?"

"My mother would kill me if she knew I was out in a thunderstorm," Penny said.

"Yeah? The sisters probably wouldn't kill me, but I bet they'd want me to come home — and right away too. We have a little time though." I looked back up at the darkening sky. "I think."

"Come on," Penny said. She grabbed my hand, and we ran all the way to the willow tree, holding hands like we were best friends or something, like we had no choice but to run head-on into the storm.

And I never let go of her hand.

The wind kicked up. I could smell the creek, the grasses, and the tree bark. It was kind of a musty smell like the inside of my suitcase. Old Woman Willow bowed even lower as the breeze blew. She curled her branches inward like she wanted to take a stand against the rain.

"Isn't she spectacular?" I asked Penny, who was busy looking into the sky.

"What?" she asked as distant thunder rolled overhead.

"The tree. Isn't she spectacular?"

"Ahh, I told you before. It's just a dumb old tree." Penny was now back to her old self as though letting go of my hand had sent her back in time.

"Then why'd you come with me?" I asked.

Penny kicked a stone into the creek water just as some drops of rain fell. "I don't know. I think I'd better go home."

"But it's hardly raining yet, and I can still see spots of blue in the sky."

"Storms scare me," Penny said. "They make me want to hide under my bed."

"Oh, I like storms. I bet it's spectacular to hear one from inside Gray House with all of those rooms and the tin ceilings.

I bet Naomi will even bake something special—'Storm Cake' or something."

Penny kicked another rock into the creek, this time with a little more force. "I'm sick of hearing about them and their stupid cakes, especially stupid old storm cake. Whoever heard of storm cake anyway?"

A loud clap of thunder rumbled overhead.

"How come you never told me about your father?"

Penny looked at me like a startled cat. "Because you never asked. And besides, everybody in town knows about my father. He was a hero."

"A hero?"

"Yeah, he was a soldier and died in the line of duty."

"Oh, okay. But that still doesn't explain it." I watched Penny pick at the tree trunk. "You still could have told me when I asked who you were visiting in the cemetery."

She stamped her foot on the mossy ground. "Well, what did ya think I was doing there? Just visiting some dead people I didn't know?"

I remembered the times, back when I was living with the Crums, when I'd walked by the cemetery on my way home from school. I'd read the gravestones of people I didn't know, but I felt sad and missed them just the same. I sometimes wondered if I would see my mother's name or my father's, even though I never had a clue about them. I just knew my mother's name, her first name—Susan.

I shook my head. "I never read the stone. Was that his? The one you sit on?"

Penny looked away, off toward where the creek ran brown and tripped over rocks and twigs and branches. She tossed a chunk of bark into the water. "No, his is the one in front of where I sit. I never knew him much."

"At least you knew him. At least he wanted you. At least you still have your mother."

Penny's mouth twisted into a grimace as if I'd just said the worst curse word a kid could say.

"I better go," Penny said. "She'll . . . she'll kill me if I get home all wet and muddy. The sisters won't care if you come home caked in mud from head to toe like a mud monster."

"Don't splash in any puddles then," I said.

Penny took off while I stood near Old Woman Willow. I looked into her thousands of branches and tendrils as the raindrops fell harder and harder. I wanted to stay in the shelter of Old Woman Willow, but I knew I couldn't.

An extremely loud rumble of thunder made me run faster as I sprinted up the path. I saw Naomi and Ruth standing out on the porch.

"I'm coming!" I called.

"Wilma Sue!" hollered Ruth. She was definitely the hollerer in the house.

"I'm coming!" I ran harder just as a bolt of lightning split the sky over Sweet Silver Maple. "Don't hit her!" I said to the sky. "She's such a beautiful tree."

"I've got to check the chickens," I said as my foot landed on the bottom porch step.

"No, they're fine," Naomi said. "Come inside. We need your help."

"But . . . but I have to check on them."

"Wilma Sue!" Naomi hollered. "Do as you're told. This instant!"

But I didn't. I took off toward the coop. All of the hens were inside the little red building. I could hear them making clucking noises, but I didn't hear anything that made me think they were scared of the storm. The rain fell harder as I dashed back to the house and discovered why the sisters needed my help.

Chapter

13

Naomi and Ruth were running around like the chickens do when the sun is shining. They each had a pot or a pan in hand, and they were chasing drips from the ceiling in the dining room and near the crooked stairs.

"What's going on?" I asked over the sound of them slipping and crashing on small puddles and calling to each other.

"Over here!" Naomi said. "We've sprung another one."

"Grab a bucket, Wilma Sue," Ruth called, "and go check your room."

"My room? My room is leaking?"

"Go check," Naomi said. "Seems we've sprung a few more leaks in the Good Ship Beedlemeyer." Then she laughed and laughed like a hyena.

"I'm sorry," I said. "I didn't know. I'm sorry I didn't come right away."

Naomi stopped collecting rain buckets for a second and looked at me. "Next time, listen. You never know when a person might really need you."

For a split second, I felt Penny's hand in mine again.

I grabbed a plastic bucket and started toward the crooked stairs. I stopped halfway up and watched the sisters. They didn't seem particularly upset. In fact, they laughed as they set down a variety of containers to catch the rainwater.

Naomi heaved a huge sigh and flopped into her rocking chair. "That's the last of them."

But just as the words left her mouth, I heard a noise, more drips, and another leak appeared in the dining room ceiling. Rain dripped down the wall near the window. I raced over with my bucket, but it was hard to catch the water. So Naomi stuffed a towel against the baseboard.

"Horsefeathers!" I said. "This is crazy!"

"Yes, yes it is," Ruth said. "But it can't be helped. We can't afford a new roof."

"But this is nothing," Naomi said. "This is nothing like the rains we had in the village during the rainy season. Now *that* was some serious rain. Remember that, Ruth?"

Ruth nodded as she dumped the contents of a small purple pail—the kind kids take to the beach—out an open window. She closed the window and set the pail down to catch more water.

"But can't the church help?" I asked. "It's the stinkin' parsonage!"

The sisters looked at each other. Naomi said, "It would take a committee and fundraising."

"Oh," I said, not quite understanding what she meant. A few drops of rain fell on my head. I ran up the stairs to my room. No drips. I was happy about that. The roof over my room apparently didn't have any leaks. I thought about it for a second. This house had lots of roofs. I stood in the middle of the room and looked up at the ceiling. That's when I noticed the rain was letting up. It was no longer pouring down in torrents. It still pattered against the house, but it was definitely slowing down. From the window I could see the sky growing brighter as the dark, dark clouds moved away like lumbering hippos.

It wasn't right that the sisters should have such a leaky house and chase around like hysterical chickens with buckets and pots trying to catch the drips and harness the small waterfalls running down their walls. I sat on the bed with my feet dangling. No, it wasn't fair.

I wrote in my notebook:

> It isn't fair that the sisters should have so many leaks in their house. But it was kind of funny, and they did laugh a lot while they chased the drips. Naomi is right: thunderstorms are spectacular in Gray House. Penny ran home scared to death of getting caught in the rain. I worry about that girl. I wonder if Naomi will want to deliver the carrot cake to the librarian with the bad case of the gossips.

I found Naomi in the kitchen staring at the carrot cake on the kitchen table. It seemed to have been spared the deluge.

"Are you going to deliver it?" I asked.

Naomi looked bushed. She was sitting slumped on the bench, her hair was mussed, and she was breathing a little hard. I thought she might be sick.

"Are you okay?" I asked.

"Of course, dear, yes, yes, I'm fine. Exercise is good for me. I need to rest a bit, and then we'll take the cake to Miss Quill."

I sat down across the table from her. "You were right."

"I was? About what, dear?"

"The rain. Thunderstorms at Gray House are . . . something else."

Naomi slapped the table. "I told you. But one day—one day we'll get the roof fixed and they won't be quite so spectacular." She laughed.

I looked at the carrot cake. The kitchen still smelled delicious even after the storm rolled through. "Are you ready?"

Naomi sucked a deep breath. "As ready as I'll ever be. But I might need you to carry the cake."

"Me? But what if I drop it?"

Naomi waved a hand in the air. "You'll do fine. Miss Quill's house isn't far. It's that little house on the other side of the church property."

"I don't remember seeing it."

"You'd have no reason to do so until now. Let's go."

I saw Naomi's bare feet again. "Aren't you going to put on some shoes? It's probably muddy outside."

Naomi laughed. "No."

I shrugged and lifted the cake, which was sitting on a large silver platter, from the table. It was kind of heavy, but not so heavy that I couldn't carry it.

"Now just hold her steady and off we'll go. I think Hortense Quill will be thrilled." Then she stopped and thought a moment. "I hope she will be. You can never tell with gossips. They can be so defensive."

Naomi held the front door open for me, and I set off down the steps. I liked the feeling of helping—helping in a special way, not by cleaning toilets or scrubbing floors like at the Crum house. Not that those things aren't important. It's just that cake delivery seemed different. And besides, I was aiming to keep my left eye open this time. I was definitely going to catch the change, whatever it was, and be quick to point it out to Naomi. Then she'd *have* to tell me her secret. I was ready to see if Hortense Quill lifted off the ground like Mrs. Snipplesmith had done, or if her eyes grew into two bright lights like Ramona Von Tickle's eyes.

We traipsed across the yard, skipping over some puddles along the way. Then we passed behind the church, which looked empty and sad in the gray light of day. We walked around the cemetery inside its black wrought-iron fence. We walked and walked down a dirt path, and Naomi's feet got grimier and grimier, and my sneakers got soaked and caked with mud.

"I guess we should take off our shoes before we go inside," I said. Then I laughed. It wasn't like Naomi could take off her feet. The path curved a bit, and I could smell the creek, which was running right beside it. It was full and brown and running quick from the rain. I could smell dirt and ferns and rotting leaves that really didn't smell rotten, not like city garbage did—coffee grounds and orange rinds and pickled herring. It smelled clean even though it was rotting.

"Lookee there," Naomi said, pointing to the ground. "My favorite wild veggie, *Athyrium filix-femina*."

"What?" I said. "Felix who?"

"No dear, *Athyrium filix-femina,* fiddlehead ferns. I just love the way they curve and spiral and grow straight from the ground. Did you know they're edible? Of course you have to boil them twice to rid them of their poisons, but then I fry them with butter and garlic—delicious."

Poisons? No way I was going to eat them. I didn't care if she boiled them six times.

"Remind me to pick some on the way back," Naomi said.

Then I saw the little purple house. It was adorable, like a dollhouse with a porch and tall windows. It had a chimney that stuck straight up into the sky, not crooked like the chimneys of Gray House. And there must have been about a thousand bird feeders scattered about the property. Some hung from the porch and the trees; some sat on top of poles. I could hear the birds singing as we got closer.

"She must really love birds," I said. "That's terrific."

"Almost as much as you do. She can identify hundreds of species."

"Like Dr. Mergenthaler?"

"Kind of. Dr. Mergenthaler has a more scientific interest in birds. Miss Quill likes them because they're pretty."

I wondered who else in this town loved birds as much as I did. It was hard to imagine that someone who lived in such a sweet house and loved birds so much could ever get a case of the gossips.

I steadied the cake, as I'd almost tripped over a rock that was hiding under some mud.

"Ahh," Naomi said as we hit the stone path that led to Miss Quill's house. "There it is."

"What?" I asked, trying to follow Naomi's line of sight.

"The rain barrel. Miss Quill collects the rain and then uses it to water her plants. I'll just use it to rinse my dirty feet."

I nodded and steadied the cake again. I was glad we were finally at her house. The carrot cake was getting heavy. I waited while Naomi washed. I loved hearing the birds sing and watching them flit around from feeder to feeder. A hummingbird, no bigger than a small sausage link, flitted by. It stopped right in front of my nose. It was so close, in fact, that I could hear its wings beating like one long thrum. I knew from reading books about birds that a hummingbird's wings beat fifty-five times per second. I wished I had wings like that. The hummingbird paused for a second or two and then flitted off again.

"You must be special," Naomi said. "Hummingbirds don't visit just any old someone walking down a path."

"Maybe it was the sweet smell of the cake," I said.

"Nope, it was you," Naomi said. "Come on. Let's go find Hortense Quill."

We walked up the steps, and I knew Naomi was right about the hummingbird. I did feel like she'd visited me especially.

Naomi knocked on the purple door. "We'll give her a minute and then go on inside if she doesn't come to the door."

Just walk inside? That didn't seem like the right thing to do.

"Miss Quill gets lost in her work," Naomi explained, after seeing the look of surprise on my face. "But before we go inside, I must ask you to—" she pretended to lock her lips and throw away the key. "Don't say a word, not a single word, about her case of the gossips. We don't want her to know that we know."

"Why not?"

Naomi pushed a stray hair out of her face. "Think about it, dear. If we tell her we've heard she has the gossips, then would that not mean that we were listening to gossip ourselves?"

"I . . . guess so, yes, but . . . how did you know she has the gossips if you weren't gossiping?"

Naomi didn't answer me. Instead, she pushed open the front door and in we went, totally uninvited. My knees shook.

Naomi called out, "Hortense! Oh, Horrrrrtennnnnse!"

We waited inside the living room, which, let me tell you, was like a library. There were books *everywhere*, stacked from floor to ceiling against all four walls.

"She must be downstairs," Naomi said. "Let's leave the cake here." She set it on a table next to a statue of three penguins. It was hard not to touch the statue, to feel their feathers with the tips of my fingers.

I followed Naomi down the steps. I could hear a voice talking; I figured it was Miss Quill's. When we reached the bottom, I saw she was gabbing away on the phone to someone. She was sitting on a fat chair in a room that was also filled with books. There were books on shelves that lined every wall, stacks of books on the floor. One pile even reached to the ceiling. It smelled like pages, thousands of pages. I didn't think she'd noticed Naomi and me standing there.

"But then, and you just won't believe this," Miss Quill said into the phone she had cradled in her neck, "she had the *audacity* to say—"

Naomi looked at me and raised her eyebrows. I knew what she was thinking. Miss Quill was gossiping with whoever was on the other end of the phone. But we didn't say a word about it. Not a single word.

Naomi cleared her throat, and Miss Quill looked up without finishing her sentence.

I cleared my throat also.

"Excuse me, Lorna," Miss Quill said into the phone. "But I have company. I'll talk to you later." She clicked off the receiver and looked at us. And I am not afraid to say I felt kind of nervous. Hortense Quill did not look pleased to see us.

Even though she was sitting down, I could tell she was short. She had wide ankles and thin wrists and short black hair. Her glasses were pointy and glittery.

"Naomi," she said. "I didn't know you were coming. Did we have an engagement?"

"No," Naomi said. "I only wanted to bring you a cake."

"A cake? For me?"

"Yes," Naomi said. "Now, shall we have a slice?"

It seemed Naomi had dispensed with the niceties because Miss Quill was in dire straits. Dire gossip straits.

Hortense stood. "Well, aren't you going to introduce me to your young friend there?"

"Oh, yes, of course," Naomi said. "This is Wilma Sue. She is living with Ruth and me."

Hortense walked closer. My stomach wobbled. My heart raced. She grabbed my hand and pumped it up and down. "It's nice to meet you, Wilma Sue. I've heard all about you from Mrs. Agabeedies and Mrs. Gullie down at the bank. And of course I saw Portia Pigsworthy the other day at the market. She was—"

"Thank you. It's nice to meet you too. You have many books." I thought I should stop her train of thought before it crossed right into Gossip Land.

"Oh, I love books. Books are my life."

"I love books too," I said.

Naomi held up her hand. "How about a slice of carrot cake?"

"Oh, carrot cake," Miss Quill said. "I love carrot cake."

So I followed them up the steps and back into the living room. Naomi excused herself. "I'll get us some plates and forks and a knife to cut the cake."

Miss Quill flopped into a chair that sunk down a few inches when she did.

"So," she said, "Wilma Jo—"

"Sue," I said. "My name is Wilma Sue."

"That's what I said."

"No it isn't. You said 'Wilma Jo.'"

"Oh pish," she said.

Naomi returned with the plates and utensils. "Here we go. Let's all have a slice."

She cut the cake and the aroma filled the room. It even over-powered the musty book smell.

"It looks divine," Miss Quill said.

"Good. Go ahead and eat."

We all took bites and it was scrumptious. I didn't think I would like carrot cake but I did. It tasted like autumn.

"So tell me," Naomi said. "Have you heard any news?"

Miss Quill finished chewing her first bite of cake and set her fork on the plate. "Why yes, I was just talking to Lorna—"

"Go on," Naomi said. "Take another bite first."

Miss Quill giggled. "Don't mind if I do."

"I'm reading *Beowulf*," I said. "And a book about chickens. I think I like the chicken book better."

Miss Quill turned in my direction. She chewed and smiled at the same time. "Are you now? My dear, *Beowulf* is quite a tall tale." She coughed and then spoke in a loud, clear voice as though she were on stage, "Now Beowulf bode in the burg of the Scyldings, leader beloved, and long he ruled in fame with all folk, since his father had gone away from the world, till awoke an heir, haughty Healfdene, who held through life, sage and sturdy, the Scyldings glad."

Naomi clapped. "That was lovely, Hortense. Now go on, another bite or two of cake."

"You . . . you memorized it?" I said.

"No, no, only most of it," she said.

I was so impressed, I decided right there that I would finish reading *Beowulf* as soon as I could. It must be a good story if Miss Quill had memorized it.

The phone rang. Miss Quill rushed to answer it.

"Oh, noooo," I heard her say. "He didn't really say that."

I looked at Naomi and raised my eyebrows.

"This will take another slice," she said. And then she called to Miss Quill, "Please, Hortense, come join us."

"I'll talk to you later, Lucretia." I heard her hang up the phone.

"More cake?" Naomi asked. She placed another slice on Miss Quill's plate.

Miss Quill took a large bite. This time, from the corner of my eye, I thought I saw a wisp of orange smoke come out of Miss Quill's mouth.

I looked at Naomi, who was smiling. "Did you see that?" I whispered.

"Did I see what?"

"The orange smoke?"

Naomi waved her hand at me.

"How's your cake?" Naomi asked Hortense.

Miss Quill, who all of a sudden looked somewhat distracted, said, "Fine. Just fine. Moist. Delicious but ... but well I feel rather—full now." Then she burped and a large puff of orange came out of her nose.

"Look there," I hissed. But by the time Naomi, who'd had her head turned, looked back at Miss Quill, the orange cloud was gone. Nothing was left but the sweet, spicy smell of carrot cake.

"Good, good," Naomi said. "Now I'll leave the rest of the cake here. I suggest you finish almost all of it tonight and maybe have a bit more for breakfast in the morning."

Miss Quill nodded.

"And perhaps, in a day or so, Wilma Sue can come by so the two of you can discuss *Beowulf.*"

* * *

On the way back to Gray House, the sky filled up with dark clouds again. It rained a little bit but not nearly as hard as it had before. Naomi stopped and picked a couple handfuls of the fiddlehead ferns. "These will be delightful with supper tonight."

I didn't like the idea, but I carried a handful home.

"You really didn't see it?" I asked.

"See what?"

"Ahh, never mind," I said.

But I knew what I saw. And I also knew that no matter what I said, Naomi would act like she didn't know a thing. Not a blessed thing.

Chapter
14

"I'm going to get supper started," Naomi said on the way back to Gray House. "Why don't you go play for a while?"

"Okay," I said. "Why do you think Miss Quill likes to gossip?"

Naomi twisted her mouth and stopped walking for a moment. "That's a good question. Sometimes it's just a nasty habit. The tongue is a wicked thing, sometimes."

I swallowed because I remembered how I used to call Lola Crum names.

"But other times," Naomi said, "people talk about others because they don't like their own lives and discussing someone else's troubles makes them feel better."

"That's confusing," I said. "How come Miss Quill doesn't like her life?"

Naomi started walking again. "Now, I didn't say that. I think with her it's more of a habit."

When we got back to Gray House, I noticed the air was about as hot and thick and uncomfortable as ever. "I think I'd rather sit inside and read," I told Naomi when we reached the steps.

"That's fine too. It is a little muggy out here. But the sun will be setting soon, and it should cool off. I heard there is a cold front moving in tonight. Could be the harbinger of fall — wouldn't that be nice?"

"Sure would. I can't wait for the trees to catch fire."

"What?" she looked at me with a wrinkled forehead.

"Not really." I laughed a little. "That's what I call it when the trees burst into their different fall colors, orange and red like flames. Especially Sweet Silver Maple."

"Oh, okay. Yeah, me too."

I looked at Naomi's bare feet. "Do you wear shoes in the cold weather, when it snows?"

"Sometimes. In the snow for sure." Naomi pulled open the back door. "Now you run along to the library or wherever, and I'll get supper started."

The library, being on the east side of the house, was a little cooler at this time of the day than my bedroom, which was on the west side and directly in the sun's path about now. I read a few pages of *Beowulf*:

TO GUARD HIS HEAD HE HAD A GLITTERING HELMET
THAT WAS DUE TO BE MUDDIED ON THE MERE
    BOTTOM
AND BLURRED IN THE UPSWIRL. IT WAS OF BEATEN
    GOLD,
PRINCELY HEADGEAR HOOPED AND HASPED
BY A WEAPON-SMITH WHO HAD WORKED WONDERS
    IN DAYS GONE BY
AND ADORNED IT WITH BOAR SHAPES;
SINCE THEN IT HAD RESISTED EVERY SWORD.

Hooped and hasped? I put the book aside and picked up the chicken book.

This is what I read:

Most chicken eggs have a rounded or blunt end and a more pointed end, although some eggs are nearly round, while others are more elongated. An egg's shape is established in the part of the oviduct called the isthmus, *where the yolk and white are wrapped in shell membranes. An egg that for some reason gets laid after being enclosed in membranes, but before the shell is added, has the same shape as if it had a shell. Each hen lays eggs of a characteristic shape, so you usually can identify which hen laid a particular egg by its shape.*

I closed the book. The only trouble is figuring out which hen laid which egg. They always skitter off the nest before I get in there. I figured Dottie's eggs might be the fatter ones.

I headed out to see if anyone had made a nest deposit that day. Sometimes the chickens laid their eggs in the afternoon.

"I'm gonna go see the chickens," I told Naomi on my way through the kitchen, which was filled with the aroma of garlic.

"Okay," she said. "We'll call you when supper is ready."

I dashed out the kitchen door and headed for the chicken coop. The birds had come out after the rain and were pecking around in the dirt. It was so hot that the ground had mostly dried already, except for a couple of small puddles in the shadows. Dottie lumbered down the coop ramp and headed straight for one of the puddles. She gave me a look with her left eye first, though. She danced around in it a bit, drank some of the rainwater, and then felt the need to bother Eggberry.

Dottie and Eggberry were a little like Penny and me. Things always started out okay, but they turned very quickly into a fracas of some sort. That's what Mauveleen Crum called any debate or argument, a *fracas*. I mean, Penny and I could be having a perfectly nice conversation, and then all of sudden she'd jump up and run away or say something dumb that hurt my feelings. And there I'd be—like Eggberry watching Dottie scarf down all the cracked corn—wondering what I did wrong.

I checked the nests, and sure enough there was big, round, white egg in one of the boxes. Since Dottie had just left the coop, I deduced it was hers.

I snagged it from the straw. It was clean and perfect. "See that," I told Dottie. "Now I know which eggs are yours." I looked at Eggberry. I would guess her eggs were the more elongated, greenish ones because she was more elongated and ate more greens.

"Wilma Sue."

I heard Ruth calling for me at the exact same time that I saw Penny making her way down the street.

She raised her hand and waved. I waved back and waited for her to reach me.

"I can't play," I said. "We're having supper."

"Now? But I wanted to play." She pulled a Barbie from her back pocket.

"I can't."

"Wilma Sue!" It was Ruth calling for me again.

"I'd better go." I took a few steps toward the house and then stopped. Turning around, I said, "Maybe you can have supper with us." The words had just jumped out of my mouth. I didn't have a clue, not a single clue, why I'd said that.

Now, it was hard to know for sure, but I thought I saw Penny smile. "Really?" she asked.

"Why not? The sisters won't mind. You can call your mother from the house."

"Ah, I don't have to call her. She never cares what—" She stopped talking and then said, "Is that an egg?"

"Yes. It's one of Dottie's. I can tell because it's fat like she is. We're having fiddlehead ferns for supper."

Penny wrinkled her nose. "I guess it will be okay if I stay. My mother won't mind, but I'm not eating any fiddlehead ferns."

We walked back to the house and in through the kitchen

door. I smelled roast beef and potatoes. Mashed potatoes are my most favorite food. I could eat them all day, every day.

"Can Penny stay for supper?" I asked, handing Ruth the egg.

Ruth looked at the two of us and then at Naomi. "Of course. Did you ask your mother, Penny?"

Penny shook her head. "She won't mind."

Ruth held up the egg to the kitchen light. "Looks like a double yolk."

"No, no, Penny," Naomi said. "You need to call your mother and ask her permission. It's only proper."

Penny looked at Naomi as though Naomi had the unmitigated gall to suggest such a thing. *Unmitigated* was a word I'd discovered the night before, and I'd been waiting all day to use it. It means "absolute; not softened or lessened."

Ruth handed the phone to Penny, who took it into the living room. I could hear her talking and then she rushed back into the kitchen. "She said it's fine."

"Good. Good," Naomi said. "Now you two go wash up. Mr. Woolrich will be here any minute, and then we can eat."

"Mr. Woolrich?" I asked. "You mean that really big guy from church?"

"Our friend," the sisters said in unison. "And yes, he's the really big guy from church."

"Who's Mr. Woolrich?" Penny asked as we headed for the bathroom.

"You know, that big guy from church. He's really tall like an oak tree, and he has huge hands. I think he might be a giant, but the sisters won't say so for sure. You must have seen him there."

"There are no such things as giants," Penny said.

"There are too giants." I felt another argument starting. I rinsed and dried my hands. Penny did the same.

"You'll see," I said. "Just wait until he gets here."

I heard the doorbell ring and pulled open the door. Mr.

Woolrich looked even taller on the porch than he had at church. His head reached above the doorway. His hands looked bigger, and his feet were like canoes. His arms hung down so long that I thought they were probably taller than me.

Penny took three steps back. Her mouth opened like she wanted to speak, but no words came out.

"Hello," he said. His voice boomed like a tuba.

"Hi, come on in," I said, sweeping my hand toward the living room in what was probably a feeble attempt at grace.

"Jacob," Ruth called from the kitchen. "Come on in. Supper is almost ready."

Mr. Woolrich walked into the living room and headed toward the back of the house.

Penny grabbed my arm and hissed in my ear, "He ... he is very tall. But he's *not* a giant. A giant couldn't fit in this house."

"He is so, Miss Wisenheimer! He is!"

Penny shrugged and pushed her way in front of me.

"I see you're still having roof problems," Mr. Woolrich said as he ducked through the entryway into the dining room. Ducking seemed so natural for him. He must duck all the time.

Penny even made a quacking sound when he did it.

I couldn't help but laugh.

"Where do you suppose he buys shoes that big?" Penny asked.

I shook my head and looked at Penny's big feet. I stopped a wisecrack before it could leave my mouth. "Bet he has to have them made special."

"Yeah, probably. It must take nearly half a cow to make that much leather." Then she laughed, and I laughed with her. If only Penny could be this ... this regular all of the time. But something in my gut told me not to get too trusting of her, not yet.

A couple of minutes later, Mr. Woolrich came out of the kitchen. Ruth followed him.

"Now girls," she said. "Look after Mr. Woolrich while Naomi and I get supper on the table. Hopefully all of the drips are dried by now."

He did look like a man who needed looking after. His clothes were wrinkly, and I noticed when he sat down in the big chair that he was wearing one blue sock and one bright red sock.

"So, girls," he said. "Are you enjoying your summer?"

We nodded in unison. Like two bobbleheads.

"Good, good," he said. "School will be starting up soon enough for all of us."

"All of us?"

"I'm the science teacher at the middle school."

What is it about seeing teachers outside the school building that's so weird? It's like they don't belong in the real world. Not with us anyway.

"I don't like science," Penny said. "My mother says that science has no bearing on my life. All I need to do is act sweet and be pretty."

I felt my eyeballs roll around in their sockets. Even Mr. Woolrich kind of sputtered and snorted. I thought he was going to say something, but before he could, I said, "I like science. Did you know chickens have two eye systems? One left and one right."

Mr. Woolrich smiled. "I did know that, Wilma Sue. Did you know that garter snakes are born alive, sometimes twenty to forty at a time? The record is ninety-eight."

Penny looked like she wanted to throw up. I guess the thought of about a hundred garter snakes was a little too much for her, especially after that one Sunday in church.

Ruth came out of the kitchen drying her hands on her apron. "Soup's on," she said. "We have pea soup as our first course."

"Pea soup," Penny said. "I hate pea soup."

"Come on." I grabbed her hand and practically dragged her

into the dining room where the long table had been set like we were royalty, with fancy crystal glasses, two candelabras, and plates with gold edges. It was grand. Too grand for a Friday afternoon supper, if you asked me. "You never know what you might find in pea soup."

"Peas, probably," Penny said. "I hate peas."

"Is there anything you *do* like?" Mr. Woolrich asked.

"Yes," Penny said with a snarky edge to her voice. "I like Barbies."

"That's nice," Mr. Woolrich said. "But let's see if we can get you to like science this year."

"Sit, sit," Naomi said. "We made this soup with fresh peas and a ham hock Ruth got from Mr. Delight at the grocery store."

"It smells good," I said.

"Sure does," Mr. Woolrich said.

Penny squinted at the thick green liquid in her yellow bowl.

"But first we need to ask a blessing," Naomi said.

"Yes, yes. A blessing," Ruth said. She looked at Mr. Woolrich. "Would you?"

He nodded. Then we all bowed our heads and closed our eyes. Well, I kept one eye partially open as Mr. Woolrich began to pray.

"Thank you, Lord," he started. And then he said a whole bunch of words with fancy *thees* and *thous*, *mighty* and *majesty* and other words like *bounty* and *harvest* and *hands*. He even asked God to help Penny enjoy science and pea soup. And then we all said amen. Even Penny. But I think it was mostly because she was afraid not to.

I pulled out my small notebook from my back pocket and wrote: *"Unmitigated. Bounty. Harvest. Hands. Blessing."* I wondered for a second what connected them. Words were like that. They got connected. One word always leads to another word, which leads to another word, until you have whole sentences. Sometimes words are scattered and don't seem to make much sense. But I know that if I search real hard, I can find the connection.

I tasted the thick green soup. It ran down the back of my throat like a small river. It was good, smoky, and hardly tasted like plain old peas. Like all of the food at Gray House, it was the best pea soup—and well, the first pea soup—I had ever eaten. Even Penny liked it, although she was pretty slow to taste it. It took some extra coaxing from Ruth.

"Go on," Ruth said. "Naomi's soup is something special."

My antenna went up when I heard that. I looked around in my soup, but I didn't see anything unusual or special. I tried to be extra aware when I tasted it again. I let it sit in my mouth and tried to extract all of the different flavors. But since I had never eaten pea soup before, I couldn't be sure if I was tasting anything special. Or secret.

Mr. Woolrich ate every last drop from his bowl. I think he wanted seconds, but he also wanted to be polite. So he let Ruth grab his bowl and take it into the kitchen with the rest of our bowls. Next, she brought out a salad. It was a crazy salad in a huge wooden bowl with giraffes for handles. The bowl was piled to nearly overflowing with all sorts of greens like lettuce and spinach. Fiddlehead ferns stuck straight up, the way they grew in the ground with their little heads swirled at the end.

I passed on salad dressing and ate my greens raw—like I was rabbit or a hippopotamus. Penny dumped a lot of dressing onto her salad. Mr. Woolrich used a little, and the sisters both gobbled down their ferns like they were the tastiest morsels on the planet.

"By the way, Jacob," Ruth said as she chewed a piece of lettuce. "Wilma Sue has taken over quite a bit of the chicken care for me, so I can concentrate on my work at the Life Center."

I felt something tug at my heart. I straightened up, waiting to hear what she was going to say next.

"Did she now?" Mr. Woolrich said.

"Yes, and she is doing an excellent job. She's a natural poultry person."

I smiled. "I really like them. They're like my little friends."

"I . . . I held one, the big fat one," Penny said.

"But she got scared when Dottie clucked and dropped her."

Penny kicked me under the table. I didn't say anything. I reached down and rubbed my shin.

Ruth snatched our salad bowls, and then she and Naomi brought in the roast and the potatoes and the broccoli and more fiddlehead ferns—this time in a blue bowl, and the aroma of garlic wafted around us. Naomi set the roast in front of Mr. Woolrich. "Would you do the honors?"

He stood and everyone's heads followed him straight up almost to the ceiling. He took the large knife and the large fork in his large hands and said, "Of course." The roast seemed so small. His hands practically covered the whole thing.

"Will the chickens eat roast?" I asked.

Ruth laughed a little, like the question caught her off guard. "Oh, chickens will eat practically anything."

Penny was the first to get a slice of roast. She poked at it with her fork.

"What's the matter? Don't you like roast?" I asked.

"Oh, I like it well enough. It's just . . . it's just that I ate so much salad, and—"

There was a knock on the door. It sounded angry. Naomi rose to answer it. But Penny ran out of the room first—like she knew who was standing on the other side.

"Now who could that be?" Naomi asked, looking at me.

I shrugged. Before any of us could reach the front door, I heard Penny say, "Mother!"

Naomi grabbed my hand. "I guess she's here to pick her up."

"I guess," I said.

"Let's not be rude," Ruth said. "We should greet her."

"Maybe she'd like to join us," Mr. Woolrich said.

Portia Pigsworthy, who was looking a little distraught, said, "I have been looking all over the neighborhood for you." Then Portia looked at all of us, but her eyes finally landed on the sisters, who were standing close together with Mr. Woolrich behind them like a wall. "Why is my Penelope here?"

Now I was about to open my mouth, but I didn't on account of this was one of those situations that was better left to the sisters. I stood by Mr. Woolrich.

"She joined us for supper," Naomi said.

"She told us she called you and you gave her permission," Ruth added.

Portia looked at Penny and shook her head. "She never called me. I've been … been worried sick."

Penny looked up at her mother. "I'm … I'm sorry, I … wanted to stay, and I knew you'd say no, so I … I thought I'd be home before you got there."

Portia seemed to swallow a lump the size of tonight's roast. "I apologize for my daughter. I'll just be taking her home now."

Mr. Woolrich moved toward the front of the small group that was now crammed in the entryway. "Would you like to join us?"

This time I swallowed a lump, but I had a little trouble getting it down. Portia Pigsworthy at our supper table?

"Can we, Mom? It's really good food—even the pea soup."

Portia shook her head. "Not tonight, but thank you."

"If you're sure," Ruth said. "We have plenty."

Portia Pigsworthy looked like she wanted to cry. "No, thank you, perhaps another time."

"Fine," Naomi said.

I looked at Penny, who looked like she wanted to run away and cry. I wished she had hollow bones.

"But . . . but thank you anyway," Portia Pigsworthy said. She took Penny's hand. "Come along. We can discuss this further at home."

"See you tomorrow," I said with a hopeful lilt in my voice.

Penny shook her head like she knew that was not going to happen. The sisters and Mr. Woolrich and I stood there for a few seconds after they left.

"That's too bad," Mr. Woolrich said. "I wonder why Penny felt like she had to lie."

Naomi tapped her cheek. "I'm not a hundred percent sure."

We returned to the supper table.

"Well," Ruth said. "That was certainly unpleasant, but we shouldn't let it ruin our supper."

I picked at my potatoes.

"Correct," Naomi said. "As a matter of fact, I think it might have done some good."

I looked at Naomi. "Good? How was that good?"

"Perhaps now Penny and her mother will talk, and some necessary things will come out."

"Necessary things?"

"Yes," she said, digging into her potatoes. "I believe Penny and her mother have been living in a great sadness. Hopefully now they can begin to talk about it."

"You mean about Penny's father," I said. "Now I wished I hadn't said what I said to her."

"Yes," Naomi said. "That's one thing."

I poked around at my fiddlehead ferns.

Naomi set her fork on her plate and folded her hands underneath her chin. "What did you say to Penny?"

"I told her that my father . . . and my mother . . . were both . . . you know . . . dead."

"Oh dear," Ruth said. "Why would you say that?"

"It's easier. It's easier to say that than the truth: That your mother didn't want you."

"I understand," Naomi said. "But don't fret. You had no way of knowing about Penny's father."

My fiddlehead ferns swam in butter and garlic that was running into my mashed potatoes. I tried to build a dam with a piece of roast, but the butter still got through.

"The truth always has a way of getting out," Mr. Woolrich said. "It's hard to keep it dammed up even when saying it right out loud is painful. But I think Penny will understand why you fibbed."

"That's right," Naomi said. "Don't fret. Ask for her forgiveness and let it go."

The beef wasn't keeping the fern juice from spreading into my potatoes. So I pushed the mashed potatoes toward the edge of the plate.

"Sometimes it feels safer to rearrange the truth," Mr. Woolrich said.

"Now please, Wilma Sue," Ruth said. "Don't let this spoil such a nice supper."

"Okay," I said, still thinking about Penny and her mother.

"Cake?" I asked after a couple of minutes. "Should we bake them a cake? Is it their turn?"

Naomi patted my hand. "Not yet. All in good time. The fullness of time."

"Time isn't full yet?" I said.

Ruth shook her head. "Not yet, but I do believe it's getting there."

Naomi smiled. "The fullness of time is a marvelous concept."

Marvelous concept or not, it was one that I didn't understand, at least not entirely. I only knew that things happened when they needed to—somehow they always worked out.

Mr. Woolrich turned his head and let go a sneeze that rumbled the table. "Excuse me!" he said. "That was an unexpected outburst."

Ruth laughed. "And I think it was a timely one. Why don't we all enjoy our meal now? Penny and her mother will be fine—just fine."

"This is delicious," Mr. Woolrich said as he cut up a piece of roast.

Naomi smiled. "I hope it's tender."

"Butter," he said. "Like butter."

I ate a lot even though I was still chewing on what had happened with Penny and the fullness of time and cake.

After everyone had finished eating and retired to the library, Naomi brought out some coffee for the adults. It was decided that we would have dessert "in a little while." And that was fine with me because even after the Penny incident, I managed to eat so many mashed potatoes that my stomach bulged.

"Would it be all right if I went outside?" I asked. "I'd like to bring the chickens some leftovers."

Ruth touched my hand. "You go right ahead, Wilma Sue. We'll call you when it's time for dessert. Naomi whipped up a thunder cake."

Thunder cake? When did she have time to do that? But then again, Naomi was pretty quick when it came to throwing together a batter and baking it, and she always seemed to have frosting on hand.

"Okay," I said on my way to the kitchen. I took some of the meat scraps, mashed potatoes, and broccoli out to the coop. I passed by Sweet Silver Maple and stopped. Her leaves looked even more tired, and I watched one fall and swirl to the ground.

Yep. Autumn was on her way.

The chickens were still outside the coop. They usually went

inside around dusk. I pulled open the gate, and they came running. They knew I had leftovers. I put it all on the ground, and they went at it like thugs in a rumble. I learned that phrase from the Crums. Martin the Destroyer liked talking about the fights he'd gotten into. I cringed at the memory. I was sure glad I wasn't a Crum anymore.

"Enjoy," I told the chickens. I looked down the road toward Penny's house and wondered what might be going on inside. I sure hoped she wasn't in trouble, but I supposed that of all the infractions, lying is one of the worst.

"She needs a cake," I told Dottie. She had taken a scrap of meat off to a corner of the chicken yard. "I wonder if I can make a cake like Naomi does. I've watched her do it enough times."

Eggberry fought with Florence over a particularly fatty chunk, while Slowpoke, as usual, stayed off in the distance and reaped the rewards of patience and timing. Timing. Who's to say *when* it's the fullness of time? Penny needed a cake — that was for sure.

"Do you girls know her secret?" I asked the hens. "Do you know what Naomi does to her cakes?"

I took my notebook out of my back pocket and wrote:

I would like to bake Penny a cake. A fullness of time cake. Chocolate with chocolate frosting, rich and full.

The sky was finally turning that soft, steely gray, and I was kind of happy that night was falling. I yawned twice and decided to head back to the house even though Ruth hadn't called me in for dessert yet.

Naomi and Ruth were in the kitchen putting some finishing touches on our dessert. It wasn't tall, but it was very round and very large. The cake had gray frosting that flowed down the sides in billows, like clouds.

"Black forest makes the best thunder cake, don't you agree, Naomi?" Ruth asked.

"Oh, I do indeed."

Naomi was putting blue-and-yellow swirled birthday candles on the black forest cake.

"Whose birthday is it?" I asked. "Mr. Woolrich's?"

"No one's," Naomi said. "Must it be someone's birthday for us to have candles on a cake?"

I couldn't think of a single reason *not* to put candles on it. I helped carry a tray with plates and forks into the living room.

Mr. Woolrich smiled and nodded. "Well now, Naomi, that's some amazing cake."

"Thank you," Naomi said. "And now, Jacob, since you're our honored guest tonight, you get to blow out the candles."

And like the Big Bad Wolf, Mr. Woolrich blew out all of the candles.

"Did you make a wish?" Ruth asked.

He tilted his head toward Naomi. "Yes, yes I did."

Ruth picked up the large silver knife/spatula thing and made a slice from top to bottom. Then she made another slice and removed a large triangle of cake and rested it sideways on the white cake plate. She set a silver fork on the plate and held it out to Mr. Woolrich.

And that was when it happened. I heard thunder rumble over our heads, and then all of a sudden fireworks leaped out of the cake and swirled around the room. Ruth rushed to a window and opened it just in time for a smallish rocket to escape and burst into all the colors of the rainbow outside.

Mr. Woolrich laughed and laughed until the short display ended. "My dear, Naomi," he said. "You still make the most impressive cakes." They all laughed. "Pyrotechnics never fail to entertain."

And that was it. No one said another word about it. As if

fireworks exploding out of cakes was normal or something. I stood there looking at the three of them as Ruth handed me a slice. "How? How did you do that?" I asked.

Naomi chuckled. "Oh dear, it's all in how you mix the batter."

"It's just science," Mr. Woolrich said. "Just science."

I knew I could never make fireworks happen for Penny and her mother, but I needed to make a cake that packed as much of a bang if it was going to make them better like Ramona Von Tickle and Mrs. Snipplesmith and Dr. Mergenthaler and Miss Quill. But what?

The rest of the evening went along sweetly. Naomi and Ruth were all excited about sharing pictures and stories from Malawi. I learned an awful lot about the rainy season there, which, by the way, starts in November. According to Ruth, it smells like the deepest, dankest forest you can ever imagine.

"But," Ruth said, "all of that rain helps the villagers grow sweet potatoes and beans and peanuts."

"The rain is magnificent," Naomi said. "It could be as dry as ... as sandpaper one minute, and then the next minute you see it: The rain rolling in over the hills."

"You can actually see the rain coming?" I asked.

"Sure can," Ruth said. "A deluge hits and everyone scrambles. Except, I remember that one time when I saw that little girl, one of the orphans, standing outside in the pouring rain like she didn't have a clue."

"That's right," Naomi said, "until Leon, he was such a tiny boy when he came to us, he raced out there, took the girl by the hand, and brought her to shelter."

"Orphan? Are there orphans in Malawi?" I swallowed a piece of cake.

Naomi sighed. "Yes, dear, many, many orphans."

Wow, maybe *that* was why they took me in. Maybe. I would

need to chew on that a while. Everyone silently ate cake until out of nowhere Ruth said, "The rain brings out the *ngumbi*."

"The what?" I asked.

"Ngumbi," Naomi said. "African termites. At the beginning of the rainy season, they have wings and fly all over the place. They can get pretty thick at night."

"Yes," Ruth said with a chuckle. "In the mornings you'll see wings all over the roads."

"I understand they are quite a good snack," Mr. Woolrich said.

"A snack?"

Naomi slapped her knee. "You bet. The children love to pull off their wings. They snap right off. And then we fry them up over a fire and there you go."

"I bet they'd be good on ice cream," Mr. Woolrich said.

"They are," Ruth said. "And covered with chocolate. But mostly we ate them roasted, like peanuts with a little salt."

"I won't eat termites," I said.

"We don't have any here," Naomi said. "But you'd be surprised what you can do . . . and eat when the time is right."

There she went again, talking about time. It seemed just about everything with Naomi had to do with it being the right time.

"When will it be the right time to make a cake for Penny and her mother? I think they need one."

"Soon," Naomi said. "Very soon."

That wasn't good enough. I knew they needed a cake, and they needed it sooner than soon.

"Why did Penny say she called her mother when she really didn't? I think if I had a mother, a real mother, I would never say a lie about her."

Mr. Woolrich took a breath, "Sometimes people make decisions and act without considering the consequences. And this time Penny didn't think she'd get caught."

"That doesn't excuse what she did," Ruth said.

"Not at all," Mr. Woolrich said. "She should have talked to her mother and asked for permission. This was no oversight. She knew exactly what she was doing."

"Yeah," I said. "I hope she asks the next time."

"We'll make sure of it," Ruth said.

With that, Mr. Woolrich stood and said, "I really think I should be going now. Thank you for a lovely evening." He paused in the doorway and turned back toward the living room. His head was tilted so as not to touch the doorjamb. "I had a grand time," he said, and then he looked at me. "And it was a pleasure to spend time with you, Wilma Sue."

"Thank you," I said.

He winked at me. "See you in class."

We walked Mr. Woolrich to his car, which was quite compact and not at all what I thought a man his size would drive. But he managed to get into it without a problem; good thing the top was down. His head reached well above the windshield.

"How come he drives such a small car?" I asked the sisters after he'd driven away.

Ruth laughed. "He's something else, isn't he? He likes sports cars."

I yawned as Naomi took one hand and Ruth took the other. "It has been a lovely evening, hasn't it?" Naomi said.

"Lovely," Ruth said as we walked into the house. "But I think we should be heading off to bed, don't you?"

I yawned a second time. "Okay, but you don't have to tuck me in tonight."

"It's no trouble," Naomi said, looking toward the kitchen.

"I'm fine, and I might sit on the window seat and read for a while, if that's okay."

"She's a big girl, Naomi," Ruth said.

"That she is," Naomi said. "You go ahead. Read. But not too long."

I changed into a T-shirt and sat on the window seat holding the hawk tibia, it was smooth and whitish with dark places. That night the air was thick and warm, like it had been most nights lately. But that's the way it is in late August. There was hardly any breeze, and the little fan I had was barely cooling the room. I looked out at the sky. Thinking. Thinking like I did so many nights about the things that have happened, about my mother, about the Crums, sometimes about God and Beowulf's glittering helmet, and also about cake and what made Naomi's cakes so special—or seem so special.

But that night as the sky grew darker and the stars blinked into place, I also thought about why in the world Naomi said that Penny and her mother weren't ready for cake. What made a person ready for cake? If anyone needed cake, it was them.

Chapter
15

That Sunday at church I looked for Penny. She wasn't anywhere. Neither was her mother. Mrs. Agabeedies was there, and I asked her if she knew where Penny might be.

"I haven't seen her for a couple of days," I said. "Have you?"

Mrs. Agabeedies snorted. "Of course I have. I saw her and her mother just last night. They told me about the . . . the matter."

"Is Penny in trouble? Is that why she's not here?"

Mrs. Agabeedies adjusted her hat, which was bright red with a long feather. She looked like Robin Hood. "All I can say on the matter is that Penny and her mother have had quite a bit to deal with."

"Okay," I said. I went back to our pew and sat next to Naomi. "You were right. Mrs. Agabeedies said Penny and her mother are dealing with things."

"Good," Naomi said. She glanced over at Mrs. Agabeedies, who looked back but then turned away sharply.

"Maybe *she* needs a cake," I said, tilting my head toward Mrs. Agabeedies.

Naomi smiled. "I think you know my answer to that."

"In the fullness of time."

The service went as usual, but without any snakes to interrupt Pastor Shoemaker. He spoke about a Good Samaritan, and I figured Mrs. Agabeedies for a Levite.

That afternoon as I tended to the chickens and read *Beowulf*, I thought about Penny. I thought about putting on armor and going out against a huge monster like Beowulf had done. I thought about Penny and her mother and how much I wanted to make her a cake. It wasn't that I wanted to go against Naomi, especially after Penny just got in trouble for lying. But I just had to try and make a cake for Penny and her mother. Maybe it wasn't so much a particular ingredient as it was what came from Naomi's heart that made the difference. Maybe I already had what it took inside me—like in *Dorothy and the Wizard of Oz*. She had power in those ruby slippers all along; she just didn't know it.

I strolled past Penny's house a little later in the day hoping I might see her. And I did. She was sitting out on her front stoop with her Barbies. I waved. "Hi."

She looked up. And then she looked behind her at the door. Then she looked back at me. "You'd better go home," she called in a loud whisper. "I'm not supposed to play with you."

"Are you grounded?"

"Yeah."

"For how long?"

She shrugged. "Til she says I can go out."

"Okay," I said. "I'm sorry you got in trouble."

"Me too."

I went back to Gray House feeling sad for Penny. What she did was wrong, but something else was the matter. Maybe it was on account of her father. Maybe it was on account of her mother being an orphan. I stood near Sweet Silver Maple and decided right then and there to make a cake for Penny.

So that night, after I was certain the sisters were asleep, I crept downstairs to make a cake.

I imagined constructing something fabulous, something like Naomi would make. Twelve layers high with lots and lots of drippy frosting and maybe even a chocolate filling that would flow like lava when the cake was sliced. Yes. That's what it would take, a pink and chocolate volcano cake that oozed all of the goodness that I could put into it.

The kitchen was dark even though a wide beam of moonlight filtered through the window. I needed more light, so I flipped on the overhead light. The cat clock on the wall read 11:30. I had plenty of time to concoct my first-ever volcano cake before morning.

I assembled the ingredients as Naomi always did. I set canisters of flour, sugar, brown sugar, salt, baking powder, cocoa, and even a box of cream of tartar on the table. Next, I grabbed some eggs from the fridge, heavy cream, and five sticks of butter. All I was missing was a recipe. Naomi never used one, so I would have to bake by memory. I had watched her make so many cakes by now, I figured it was easy peasy, a piece of cake. Then I laughed at my own joke.

First, I measured cups of flour, making sure to level off each cup with a knife the way Naomi did. Some of the flour got on the floor, but I would clean it up later. I dumped the flour, two cups of sugar, six teaspoons of baking powder, and one quarter cup of water into the large mixing bowl. I cracked four eggs into the bowl perfectly. Then I started mixing. Flour flew around like a blizzard at first, but soon the ingredients turned into what looked like batter. I tasted it. Blech. I added some salt and three teaspoons of Naomi's expensive vanilla extract and then tasted it again. A little better. But it looked so bland, and I wanted Penny's cake to be pink inside and out—well, except for the chocolate lava, which I still had to figure out how to make. But it seemed to me that adding the lava would come later.

Naomi had prepared some strawberries earlier that day, so I grabbed them from the fridge and added most of them to the batter. I gave it a good mix and there I had it: pink batter.

I coated four cake pans with Crisco, rubbing the excess into my hands, and then I lightly floured each pan the way Naomi always did. I poured the batter, making sure to divide even amounts across all of the pans.

Then I popped them into the oven to bake. Naomi never set a timer, so I didn't either. She always said she could "sense" a cake's doneness and that when the aroma reached the library, she knew it was time to check the cake.

Now I had to make chocolate lava and pink frosting. I had enough strawberries left over for the frosting. But the lava would take some scrutiny. After a while I dumped nearly the whole can of cocoa powder into a saucepan with some melted butter, which I'd seen Naomi do once, some more vanilla, and about three cups of heavy cream. I heated it on the stove, and it started to smell amazing. When I tasted it, though, it was so bitter that it made my lips buzz. Sugar. That's what it needed. I dumped some sugar into the pan and stirred it all up with a wooden spoon. But the sugar didn't melt very well, and it made the lava gritty.

I set the lava aside and got to work making strawberry frosting. Frosting wasn't difficult and didn't take very long to mix. I left it in the mixing bowl and went to the library to check for cake smells.

Yep, I could definitely detect strawberry in the air. I went back to the kitchen and jabbed a toothpick into one of the cakes. It didn't go in as smoothly as when Naomi did it. I had to push a little hard, but the toothpick came out nice and clean. So using potholders, I removed the cakes and set them on the rack to cool.

Okay, so it wouldn't be twelve layers high, but a four-layer cake was still pretty impressive.

An hour later I had the cakes assembled and frosted when I remembered the lava. Now what? Simple. I took the long wooden spoon and created a hole that went all the way through the four cakes. Next, I poured the chocolate sauce into the hole, and then I plugged it up with more frosting and a big fat strawberry on top.

I flopped onto the kitchen stool and smiled. It looked spectacular.

The next morning I woke to a bright stream of light shining through the bedroom window. I watched it dance on the wall, but only for a second because I wanted to get downstairs to the kitchen and check on my cake—hopefully before the sisters got there. I didn't clean up my mess last night—and it was a doozy. But no, I could hear the sisters, and I could smell coffee and sausage. My heart beat like a bird's. This could very well be the worst infraction of all.

I pulled on my cutoff jeans and a yellow shirt, plus my red sneakers with no socks, and then I ran down to the kitchen. A plate of pancakes and sausage sat at my place. Naomi had made my pancakes in the shape of my initials—W. S.

Ruth said, "The chickens need tending first. And I'm bringing eggs to the shelter this morning, if you'd like to come."

"How come you didn't say anything?" I asked before stuffing the entire W into my mouth.

"About what?" Ruth asked. "Say something about what?"

Penny's cake stood smack-dab in the middle of the kitchen table. There was no possible way the sisters hadn't seen it.

Cake

"Yes, dear," Naomi said as she placed another sausage on my plate. "You must be more specific."

"My . . . my cake. It's sitting right here."

"Oh, well what would you like us to say?" Naomi asked. "That we had quite a mess to clean up this morning before we could make coffee and breakfast? That I told you it wasn't time to make the Pigsworthys a cake yet? That I am quite upset with you for using my ingredients without permission?"

A piece of sausage got stuck in my throat. "I'm sorry." Tears filled my eyes. This was definitely it. I could just smell Miss Daylily's Home for Children now—old and dank. "I was gonna clean up everything this morning." I sniffed. "But I slept too late. I really wanted Penny to feel better. I didn't want to wait any longer."

"Yes, well you really should have discussed it with us," Naomi said. "You should not have rushed out on your own and baked this cake without permission."

"I said I'm sorry." I felt syrup drip down my chin. I wiped it away with my finger. "I made it so she would be nicer and happier—except it probably won't even work."

"Work?" Naomi asked. She sat down at the table and stirred cream into her coffee.

"Yes, the way that your cakes work. Except I looked and looked, but I can't find the special ingredient. There must be something you put in the cakes to make them . . . do things to people."

The sisters looked at each other and then burst out laughing. Naomi even slapped her thigh.

"Fine, fine, Wilma Sue. You may invite Penny over for lunch, and we'll have your . . . your cake for dessert."

"I see you used the strawberries that I was saving," Naomi said. "I was going to make Pastor a strawberry, blueberry, raspberry surprise cake today."

"Why? What's wrong with him?"

"Nothing is wrong with him," Naomi said. "Except, well, he's been suffering from a bad case of stick-in-the-mud-itis."

I stood and pointed at her. "Blast it! See, he *does* have something wrong, and you *are* going to cure it with one of your cakes, and that's *exactly* what I am going to do with this ... this strawberry-chocolate lava cake."

"Lava?" Naomi asked.

"Yes, I poured a whole pot of chocolate sauce into the cake, and it will flow like lava when the cake is sliced."

Ruth laughed. Then Naomi laughed.

"Why are you laughing?"

"Well, you see, dear," Naomi said, "lava cake is very difficult to make. The baking process has to be done so precisely ... let's just see what happens."

"Am I punished?" I asked. "Are you going to send me back to the home because I baked this cake without your permission?"

"What? No, of course not," Naomi said. "We aren't sending you back to the home. But as for discipline? Yes. Ruth and I would like you to scrub out the trash cans. Then we want you to carry out all of the storm windows, they're leaning against a wall in the garage, and clean them with vinegar and newspaper. We'll need to put them in soon. And it's high time the chicken coop got some fresh hay and paper shreddings and some general organizing."

I snorted air out my nose like a bull. "All of that?" I admit I whined, but the discipline seemed whine-worthy.

"Yes, all of that," Ruth said.

"Can I still give Penny the cake?"

"I don't want it to go to waste," Naomi said.

"Good. She's grounded, but I'll see when she can come over."

"Okay," Naomi said with a chuckle. "But I hope it's soon. Lava has a way of turning into rock."

Chapter 16

It wasn't until around lunchtime the next day that I saw Penny. And she was heading straight for me. I was standing in the driveway with the garden hose and a bottle of Pine-Sol, cleaning out the garbage cans—including the one we throw the chicken mess into—and the bucket we keep in the chicken yard for water. It was a pretty awful job, but Ruth gave me bright yellow rubber gloves that reached to my shoulders and bright yellow rubber boots that reached to my thighs.

"Are you allowed out now?" I called.

She walked a little closer but not too near the cans or the hose.

"Don't worry. I won't spray you," I said. "Or your Barbies."

She gave me a wary chicken look.

I hoped Naomi would call me in for lunch before Penny asked me to play with her dolls. I got lucky because just as Penny started to say, "Wanna play Barbies?" Naomi called my name.

"Maybe after lunch," I said. "You're invited to eat with us— if it's all right with your mom."

"She's at work. She won't know."

"Yes, but … remember what happened last time. You'd better call her."

"I'll call."

We dashed up to Gray House. It smelled like Naomi had made grilled cheese sandwiches. My favorite. This time Penny really did call her mother, and Naomi even spoke with Portia on the phone.

"Thank you, Portia," Naomi said into the phone. "And don't worry, we'll take good care of her."

Naomi clicked off the phone. "Well, okay, she seemed a little … anxious, but it's okay."

Penny smiled. She actually smiled and then sat down at the table right across from me.

We ate grilled cheese sandwiches cut into triangles, creamy tomato soup, and milk. All in all it was a delicious lunch, but I could hardly keep my eyes off the cake. Naomi had moved it to the counter. So far it seemed to be holding together. No chocolate lava had escaped. I thought it smelled scrumptious.

We finished our meal, and Naomi brought the cake to the table.

"Now, Penny," she said. "Wilma Sue made this cake especially for you."

Penny looked at me and said, "Are there snakes inside?"

"No," I said. "No snakes."

"Well, I'm kind of full," Penny said.

I swallowed. "But, but you *have* to eat some," I said. "I made it just for you."

"That's what worries me," Penny said.

I laughed. "Oh, it's perfectly safe. It's strawberry-chocolate lava cake."

"Lava cake?" Penny asked. "How?"

"You'll see."

Cake

And then Naomi took her big machete knife and . . . she tried with all her strength to push the knife through the cake, but it wouldn't budge. She even tried to saw it, and still the cake was like granite. No lava flowed, no sweet aroma wafted around the kitchen. Only the smell of failure and disappointment. I wanted to cry while Penny just laughed.

Naomi jabbed the knife into the cake, and a small thick ooze of chocolate burped from the hole like hot tar. Now I couldn't help myself and I cried.

"But hold on," Naomi said. "We can at least taste it. Sometimes just a small taste is all a person needs." She winked at me.

"Yes, let's at least taste it," I sniffed.

Penny said, "Yuck!"

Naomi managed to break off three pieces of cake with a hammer and chisel. And there we sat with cake and lava rocks on our plates. I tried to bite mine, but it was too hard.

"No, thank you," Penny said. "I am not going to chip a tooth on your cake."

Naomi jumped up and said, "I have a notion. Let's go to the ocean."

"What?" I asked.

"Look," Naomi said, "these slices of cake are like icebergs. Maybe if we soak them in glasses of milk, they'll get soft enough so we can eat them."

"Ewwwww," Penny said. "Whoever heard of drinking a piece of cake?"

"Nobody," Naomi said. "We just invented it."

Soon we all had tumblers of milk with cake-bergs floating in them. We waited a few minutes until the cake started to soften.

"How much baking powder did you use, Wilma Sue?" Naomi asked.

"Only half the container."

Naomi smiled. "Oh well, that's probably what turned your batter into concrete."

Tears formed in my eyes again.

The cake-bergs softened and we all drank. Well, a little bit. It tasted pretty awful, and I couldn't blame Penny when she jumped up from her seat and spit hers into the sink. "That is the worst cake I have ever eaten," she said. "It's worse than cough syrup."

My lower lip quivered. I had worked so hard to make the cake, figuring out the ingredients, making the frosting, baking it, and . . . and it was a disaster.

Penny looked at the cat clock. "I'd better go. My mother said she might be home early today, a little after lunchtime."

"Okay," Naomi said. "You run along, dear." Naomi kept her hand on my shoulder.

I put my tumbler on the table and cried for a whole minute until Naomi wiped my eyes with her apron.

"It was a total fiasco," I said.

"Yes it was, dear," Naomi said. "But good can still come out of a total fiasco."

I looked at the cake standing there like a pillar with no lava, no goodness. It was good for nothing. Not even the chickens could eat it. And they'll eat practically anything.

"Let's just chalk this one up to experience. We'll dump it outside in the trash, and tomorrow I'll help you make another strawberry-chocolate lava cake. But first I have to make that triple berry surprise cake for Pastor. Ruth went to the farmer's market to get more berries."

And right on cue, Ruth walked into the kitchen carrying a tote bag filled with fresh fruit and veggies.

"Perfect timing," Naomi said.

"I guess I'll go down to the creek," I said. I wanted to write in my notebook, but I didn't tell them that.

"Have you finished your chores?" Ruth asked. She was eyeing the tumblers filled with chocolate cake.

"Nearly," I said. "I still have to put fresh paper and straw in the nests and refill the cans with feed and corn. And I'm nearly done cleaning the trash cans."

"Then that's what you should do first," she said. "Before the creek."

"Okay." I wanted to stomp out of the kitchen, but I was concerned that Ruth would add another chore to my list.

I passed Sweet Silver Maple and lightly touched her bark. "I hate doing chores when they're punishment," I said. I looked up into her leaves, so green and dense. I pulled out my notebook and wrote:

Sweet Silver Maple tree
Your leaves so green and bright
Will soon turn to flames
And fall to the ground.

I shoved the notebook back into my pocket. It didn't rhyme, but I didn't think every poem had to. It was almost a haiku, but I could never get that syllable thing straight. I pulled out the notebook again and wrote:

Practice haiku.

When I got to the chicken yard, I saw Penny. She was actually talking to the chickens.

"Hey, I thought you went home because my cake was lousy and your mother was going to be home early."

"Nah, I just said that. Can you play Barbies?"

"You should stop saying things that aren't true."

She stuck Hiawatha Barbie in my face. "Can you play?"

"No, I have to clean the nests. Want to help me? Then I'll play."

"Me? Inside the coop? It smells bad."

"No it doesn't. Come on. I'll show you. Put your dolls down."

I opened the gate, and Penny followed me into the coop. The chickens scattered because a stranger was in the pen. Sonny came near and gave Penny a peck on the shoe. She jumped. I laughed. Dottie clucked.

"Just be natural," I said. "They won't hurt you."

"Okay, but if they do, I'm going to . . . to bop you good this time."

"Gee whiz, okay. Now grab some of those newspapers over there and start shredding them."

I slipped on the pair of rubber gloves that Ruth kept in the coop and then scraped the old, nasty shreddings out of the box. I let them fall to the floor.

I turned around to check on Penny just in time. She took a step toward me with an armful of paper shreds, but her left foot caught in a hole in the floorboard. I meant to tell her to be careful, but then her right foot gave out. Before I could say or do anything, she fell—*BLAM!*—down to the floor on her backside, and right in the middle of the awful mess I'd just made.

She screamed. She screamed loud.

"Are you okay?" I asked. I reached down to help her up, but she pushed my hand away. "You wanted me to fall. You set this up. It's just another stupid prank."

"No, I didn't," I said. "It was an accident. I forgot to tell you about the hole in the floor."

She scrambled to her feet. "You did this because I hated your stupid rock cake. Ewww, look at me!"

Her shorts were covered with chicken poop and wet food, and wet paper shreds were stuck to her legs. She had chicken feathers in her hair, and I thought I saw some cracked shells on her backside.

I tried not to laugh. "I'm sorry."

"I'm telling," she said. Then she started crying.

"Look, it was accident. I didn't make you fall."

"I'm telling Naomi. Right now."

"No," I said. "Don't. Please. I'll help you clean up."

But it didn't help. She stomped out of the chicken coop and right up to the house.

I stayed close behind her, hoping I'd get a chance to explain my side.

Naomi had come out onto the back porch steps. "What's wrong? I heard a scream."

"Look what she did!" Penny cried.

Naomi asked, "What did she do?"

"She made me fall into that disgusting chicken ... mess and poop and whatever else. I think I even sat on an egg. Ewwwww!"

"I did not," I said. "She just slipped, that's all."

"What was she doing in the coop?" Naomi asked.

"She was helping me clean up so we could play Barbies together."

By now Ruth had joined us outside. "But taking care of the nests is your job," she said with a tinge of annoyance that wasn't lost on Penny or me.

"See? She did it because she didn't want to clean the stinking coop because you made her do it. And then she made me fall, and now I'm a mess, and my mother is going to kill me."

Naomi sucked air. "No, no, she won't kill you. It was an accident."

"It was not. And I'm telling my mother."

"Penny," I said. "Don't. Really. I'll wash your clothes." I felt my knees shake.

"No!" Penny said. Then she stomped down the back porch steps and all the way home. I was absolutely certain this was the worst infraction of all.

I stood there looking at Naomi and Ruth. They weren't saying anything. They stared at me with wrinkled brows. It was the first time I'd noticed the sisterly resemblance.

I thought of Beowulf as I stood there wearing yellow rubber gloves up to my shoulders and yellow rubber boots up to my thighs like armor.

TO GUARD HIS HEAD HE HAD A GLITTERING HELMET
THAT WAS DUE TO BE MUDDIED ON THE MERE BOTTOM
AND BLURRED IN THE UPSWIRL. IT WAS OF BEATEN
  GOLD,
PRINCELY HEADGEAR HOOPED AND HASPED
BY A WEAPON-SMITH WHO HAD WORKED WONDERS...

I waited for the upswirl.

"Okay, Wilma Sue," Ruth said. "I don't believe for one second that you did it on purpose, that you made Penny fall. But it was your chore to do — alone."

"I know, but she wanted to play stupid Barbies. I told her I would play with her if she helped me in the coop. She said yes. Then she got caught in that hole in the floor and fell. That's all. I didn't do anything."

I crossed my arms and took a huge breath, steeled against whatever upswirl might come.

"But Ruth is correct," Naomi said. "It was your job. Not Penny's."

"I know. I'm sorry. I didn't think it would matter."

Ruth puckered her lips and looked at the ground, like she didn't want to say what she was about to say. "I think we have to add another restriction," she said. "After you've finished your chores, you can stay inside the house and read. No going to the creek today."

I kicked a stone. "Okay."

"Go on," Ruth said. "Finish up with the chickens."

Cake

―――――――――

That afternoon the sun was high and hot. The air wasn't as humid as it had been, which made playing outside a lot easier. Or so I assumed, since I was stuck in my room with *Beowulf* and *Storey's Guide to Raising Chickens*.

The breeze that puffed my curtains felt good, and it smelled like sweet grass and honeysuckle. I could hear the cicadas in the trees making their songs, a round that started off far away and came closer and closer before swirling back like a wave into softness again.

I sat on the window seat. Old Woman Willow was looking at me with her grandmother's face. It wasn't fair. I didn't want to stay in my room anymore. I wanted to visit Old Woman Willow and feel the breeze at the creek and watch sticks trip in the water's current.

And that was when it struck me. I could squeeze through the round window and slip down onto the roof below. Then I just had to jump a short distance to the next roof and then on down to the ground. The sisters would never know. I could visit the willow and sit by the creek and be back in my room before supper.

I raced down to the creek. My plan was to read for only a few minutes and then get back to my room before anyone noticed. It felt good to sit with my back against the willow. I tossed pebbles into the water and listened to the creek babble as it traveled out to sea.

I opened *Beowulf.*

THUS SEETHED UNCEASING THE SON OF HEALFDENE
WITH THE WOE OF THESE DAYS; NOT WISEST MEN
ASSUAGED HIS SORROW; TOO SORE THE ANGUISH,
LOATHLY AND LONG, THAT LAY ON HIS FOLK,
MOST BANEFUL OF BURDENS AND BALES OF THE
    NIGHT.

Most baneful of burdens. I supposed I knew what that meant because that was how I'd felt for most of my life, getting passed from one place to the other like a too-heavy sack of stuff. I continued reading about the warrior Beowulf and his mission to defeat Grendel, the terrible monster. And I lost all track of time. Beowulf had just walked into the mead hall when I noticed an odd smell like smoke, and then I heard sirens. I jumped up, leaving the book beneath the willow tree, and ran toward the smell, the sounds, the smoke. It billowed into the blue sky, turning it gray. I ran and ran and stopped only when I saw the chicken coop on fire.

I could see orange and yellow flames shooting up out of the coop. Smoke wrapped around the little building like an ugly monster. Grendel had come to Gray House.

"Ruth! Naomi!" I ran harder and harder. Naomi saw me.

"Wilma Sue—there you are! Where were you?" Ruth asked. "Do you have any idea how this could have happened?"

Her tone made my stomach ache. "I ... I was down by the willow, at the creek. What happened? The chickens! Are the chickens okay?"

Ruth shook her head and put her hand on my shoulder.

"I'm sorry. I'm a little upset. We got everyone out but ... but Slowpoke."

I burst into tears.

Naomi pulled me close. "Now, now, dear. It's going to be okay. We can always build another coop."

"Slowpoke was my favorite."

The firemen trained a hose on the fire. It didn't take long for the flames to stop burning, even though it seemed to take forever. Now there was only a smoky, smoldering heap of wood and ashes. The smell was nearly unbearable.

I cried and shook like a sapling in a storm. It made no sense. "Why?" I cried.

Naomi shook her head and pulled me close for another hug. "We don't know, dear. Ruth saw the flames from the kitchen and called 911. We ran outside, but by the time we got the garden hose out, it was too late. Ruth managed to chase the chickens out of the yard at least."

I looked over at Ruth, who was wiping tears from her eyes. "All except Slowpoke."

"Yes," Naomi said. "The others, including Sonny, are inside the mud porch."

A fireman approached us. He was big and burly and smelled of smoke. "The fire is out now. I'd keep dousing it with water for a while, though. That hay can smolder."

"Any idea how it started?" Naomi asked.

The fireman shook his head. "Not yet. But if you want an investigation, you'll need to file a report."

"A report?" Ruth asked. "Don't you have any ideas?"

"Sorry, ma'am. It was probably the straw, the hot sun, someone passing by tossed a lit cigarette maybe. It can happen. Or we might never figure it out. I'm just glad it didn't reach that tree. The whole house could have gone up."

My heart raced. Sweat dripped down my cheeks from the heat still coming off the ground. Sweet Silver Maple. Gray House.

I stood there staring at the charred remains of the chicken coop. They were my responsibility—Naomi and Ruth had said so. They put me in charge of the chickens. And now look.

The small crowd of neighbors who had gathered—including Mrs. Agabeedies, who was clucking away like a chicken—now wandered off. Well, all except for Mrs. Agabeedies. She was making her way toward me, and my stomach hurt even worse. But she didn't even look at me. Didn't say a word. Nothing. Instead, she went straight to Ruth.

I moved closer and heard her say, "I'm certain we'll get to the bottom of this. Chicken coops simply do not burst into flames for no good reason."

"I'm sure a reasonable explanation will surface," Ruth said.

That was when I felt Mrs. Agabeedies's eyes bore into me. It was like she blamed me. Like I'd pulled a prank. Only I didn't. But that was Mrs. Agabeedies for you — as secretary of the Bloomingdale Avenue Church of Faith and Parsonage, it was her business to know everything that goes on.

I wanted Ruth to defend me, but she didn't say a word. She only grunted like a walrus.

I felt my eyes close like they did sometimes all on their own accord. It's as if my heart somehow knows before my brain does that I'm sad. I didn't move. I was too afraid to walk or run or anything. It seemed the best thing to do was just stand, with my helmet hooped and hasped. And that was when I noticed that the only neighbor who *didn't* come out to watch was Penny. Or her mother.

Naomi took my hand. "It might be best to get this mess cleaned up right away. We'll need to build a new coop now. And the birds need a place to call home sooner rather than later."

I looked at her. "How can you be like this? How can you be so ... so cold? Slowpoke is dead, the chicken coop is toast, and that Mrs. Bag-of-Wheaties thinks I did it."

Ignoring Naomi's calls, I ran off toward Gray House. I dashed up the stairs and into my room. Then I threw myself on the bed and cried.

A few minutes later I heard Naomi's voice. "Wilma Sue."

But I didn't want to speak with her. I didn't want to speak to anyone.

"Wilma Sue," she called again, this time walking into my room. "No one blames you."

I sat up. "Ruth does. I can tell."

"No she doesn't, dear, she's just upset. She loved Slowpoke also."

"But . . . but they were my responsibility. You said so. It's my fault. I should never have left my room when I wasn't supposed to. Maybe I would have seen something. Or stopped it from happening."

"Maybe yes, maybe no," she said. "But now is not the time to think of such things."

I sobbed into my pillow and felt Naomi's hand on the small of my back. The weight of it felt good, as though it held me together—hooped and hasped.

I turned my head like a swimmer and tried to look up at Naomi. I didn't want to move too much because I didn't want her to remove her hand from my back.

"This isn't your fault, Wilma Sue," Naomi said. "None of it."

I sobbed. "Yes it is. It's my fault that I'm an orphan. It's my fault that my own mother didn't want me."

Naomi turned my head. "Wilma Sue, that is not the truth. Your mother was seventeen years old. She couldn't take care of you. You had nothing to do with that. She did what she knew was best for you. She tried to give you a good home."

I tried to swallow, but it got stuck in my throat. I sat up a little bit. "It's not my fault?"

"No."

"Are you going to call Miss Tate? Do I have to go back to the home now? Please don't call her because I promise I didn't do it." I swallowed. "I brought the snake to church, and I . . . I might have even accidentally on purpose forgotten to tell Penny about the hole in the chicken coop floor. I sneezed on purpose and got flour on Penny, and I made a cake without your permission. But I didn't set that fire."

"I know," Naomi said. "I know. But like Mrs. Agabeedies

said, a chicken coop doesn't just spontaneously combust. Something provoked it."

I sat up all the way, feeling it was now safe to let Naomi's touch fall away from my back.

"Come on downstairs. Please. Maybe the three of us can figure this out together."

After a stop in the bathroom to wash my face, I joined Naomi and Ruth in the kitchen. Ruth was sitting at the kitchen table dabbing her eyes with a kitchen towel. I could hear Dottie and Florence clucking like mad in the mud porch.

"Oh, Wilma Sue," Ruth said. "I'm sorry I made you believe I thought you did it. I guess I have a lot to learn about being a mother."

I sat at the table and swiped my finger through the icing of what was left of the chocolate cake. "It's okay. I'm sorry too."

That was when the doorbell chimed.

"Oh dear," Naomi said as she headed for the front door. "I'd rather not have guests right now."

Ruth and I looked at each other and shrugged.

From the living room, we heard Naomi say, "Mrs. Agabeedies, what can I do for you?"

I looked at Ruth. She looked back at me. We both crept into the dining room for a closer listen.

"I thought you'd like to know that there was a witness to the chicken coop crime."

"Really? Who?"

"Well, I'd rather not say. But she or he unequivocally said that she or he saw Wilma Sue throw something with a flame into the coop, and then run down to the creek. Seconds later, the fire started."

My heart stopped beating as I felt Ruth's hand clasp my shoulder.

But I broke free of her grip and ran straight out the back

door and down the porch steps. I didn't stop running until I'd reached Old Woman Willow of the Creek. I looked into the sky, which by now was turning dark, and I wished with all my heart that I could sprout a pair of wings and fly. Fly away with hollow bones.

Chapter
17

I hardly remembered going to bed the night before. I only remember how quiet everyone was. We didn't sit out on the porch. Naomi didn't share stories from Malawi. I sat near my bedroom window with the small bedside lamp turned on, reading through my dictionary and looking for words that might describe my feelings and thoughts. I discovered *commiserate*. It means to feel sympathy for someone.

Finally, long after the moon had disappeared, my eyes grew so heavy that I climbed into bed and slept in my clothes.

The next morning the smell from the burned-down chicken coop was still strong. I saw the shell of it from my window. I also saw Ruth. She was out there with a shovel and some trash cans. She wore long yellow rubber gloves that reached to her elbows and yellow rubber boots with purple dots on them. But she wasn't doing anything. She was just standing there. I didn't bother changing into something clean before going downstairs. I didn't care if I still smelled like smoke or creek water or blame. It was all the same, moldy and stale.

Cake

Naomi was in the kitchen baking a cake. While living with the sisters, I had come to realize that she baked cakes whenever things were tough or whenever things were happy. She used cake to celebrate, and she used cake to commiserate (my newest word).

"Good morning, dear," Naomi said. "How did you sleep?"

"Not very well." I poked my finger in the cake batter—orange.

"How about some breakfast? Cereal? Oatmeal? Toast and jam?"

I shook my head. "I'm not hungry. I saw Ruth from my bedroom window."

"Yes, dear. She's waiting for the fire marshal."

"Fire marshal?"

Naomi poured batter into two round cake pans. She scraped the sides of the bowl with her spatula. "Yes. She managed to convince him to come over and see if he can find a clue. And Ruth cannot do a thing cleanup-wise until he's finished his investigation."

"How can he do that? Everything—" I sniffed at an unexpected tear, "—everything is burned." Then I swallowed at the thought of Slowpoke.

"They have their ways. It's very scientific."

"How come you're making a cake?"

"Oh," she said, wiping the counter, "just in case. You can never tell when you might need a cake. People can just show up sometimes. And it's always good to have one on hand."

"What kind is it?"

"I call it orange mellow macadamia."

"It smells good."

I finished a bowl of cornflakes while Naomi waited for her cakes to bake. She sang as she washed the dishes:

I've got a home in glory land that outshines the sun.
I've got a home in glory land that outshines the sun.
I've got a home in glory land that outshines the sun.
Way beyond the blue.

"Would it be all right if I went down to the creek?"

Naomi stopped washing and singing. "Oh, but you're still grounded, and you did sneak out yesterday."

I pushed a cornflake into the bowl. "I know. And I'm sorry. But I left Ruth's copy of *Beowulf* near Old Woman Willow."

"Okay, go on. But come right back."

"I will."

It was early, but the air was already hot and sticky. There wasn't a cloud in the sky or a breath of wind. I walked slowly past the church while keeping an eye out for Penny.

Then I saw her sitting in the cemetery, near her father's stone.

"Hey, Penny."

"Hey," she said. But she never looked at me. "I heard about the fire. Geez, my mom and I could smell it clear over at our house."

"I bet you did."

"What's that supposed to mean?"

"How come you told Mrs. Agabeedies that you saw me throw something burning into the coop?"

"Because you did."

"I did not." I felt my fists ball up. It was obvious now. The cake didn't make one bit of difference. "I should flatten you for lying like that. But the sisters don't believe you. They believe me."

"Well it's your word against mine. And like my mother says, they'd take my word over your word any day."

"Why would they do that?"

Penny jumped off the stone and put her hands on her hips. "Because my mother was an orphan, and she said nobody ever believed her."

"Leave me alone!" I hollered. I ran as hard as I could to the creek, way beyond the blue. The book was still sitting where I'd dropped it. I grabbed it and stood there looking at the rushing creek water. I knew I couldn't stay, but I stood there for another minute and remembered Slowpoke and how she liked to eat by herself and always managed to get the good stuff by being patient and waiting for the right time.

Then I said good-bye to Old Woman Willow and headed back to Gray House. When I got close enough, I saw the big black van from Miss Daylily's Home parked in the driveway. My stomach churned in an upswirl.

Miss Tate? I shoved Naomi's book into my back pocket. It barely fit, but I knew it was there. I closed my eyes and thought of Beowulf going up against Grendel and Grendel's mother. I ran up the steps and stopped at the front door. I pushed it open as quietly as I could, thinking I might overhear them talking. But I couldn't hear a thing. So I pulled myself up to be as tall as I could and went inside.

I found Ruth, Naomi, and Miss Tate, who was wearing one of her brown business suits and brown leather shoes, talking in the living room.

"Wilma Sue," Miss Tate said when she noticed me standing there. "It's nice to see you."

"Hi." I walked toward them, and it was like walking into a bad memory.

"Miss Tate is here to see how things are going," Naomi said.

I looked first at Miss Tate and managed a small smile. Then I looked at Naomi and Ruth. "Did you call her? Am I going back?"

"What? No." Naomi said. "Miss Tate came by for an impromptu visit."

"That's right," Miss Tate said. "So how are things going, Wilma Sue? Looks like I came at an exciting time."

I swallowed. "Things are going good. Real good. No problems."

"I'm sorry about the chicken coop," Miss Tate said. "Naomi and Ruth were just telling me—"

"I didn't do it!" I said. "I didn't set the fire. I didn't throw anything into the coop and run away."

"Whoa," Miss Tate said. "We're trying to figure out what happened."

"Yes," Naomi said. "The fire marshal was here a little bit ago. He said he couldn't be one hundred percent sure, but he's reasonably certain that the fire did not start on its own accord."

"Do you know what that means?" Ruth said.

"Of course, I know. But it wasn't me. It was not my accord that started it. It was not my infraction."

"Wilma Sue," Naomi said. "Settle down."

I sat down in the overstuffed chair, and Ruth settled onto one of the arms. She put her arm around my shoulders like a mama bird's wing. "We don't believe what Mrs. Agabeedies said is true," Ruth said. "But we do believe that we need to get to the bottom of this. To avoid further ... issues."

"I would agree," Miss Tate said. Then she looked right into my eyes. "How is everything else going, Wilma Sue? Are you making friends?"

It was difficult but I nodded. "Yes."

That was when Naomi jumped up and said, "Cake. How about a piece of cake?"

"That sounds lovely," Miss Tate said.

I got a little nervous on account of how I didn't know what might happen. I mean, if fireworks or birds or goldfish suddenly appeared in the cake, what would Miss Tate think?

Naomi brought the orange mellow macadamia cake into the living room.

"That looks delicious," Miss Tate said.

"Thank you." Naomi sliced into it, and the aroma of fresh oranges filled the room. The aroma was so strong that I almost expected orange blossoms to appear out of thin air.

Miss Tate took a bite. I watched, expecting pretty much

anything to happen. But nothing. I tasted the cake. It was so orangey. And the crunch of the macadamias was fun. The more I ate, the more peaceful I felt while sitting there with Ruth and Naomi—and even Miss Tate.

She told me that Miss Daylily was doing well and the Crums were still jetting around the world. But as I sat there listening, I could honestly say that for the first time ever the thought of the Crums went into my mind and right back out again. They were like birds now—birds that flitted away. And I was fine with that. I would have said this out loud, but I didn't. I only thought to myself, *I like my new nest.*

Miss Tate stayed for a few more minutes. She reminded Naomi that I needed to get a school physical and she's there if we need her.

"Thank you," Naomi said. "Wilma Sue is doing very well. We are all very happy."

"Very happy, indeed," Ruth said.

"Okay, then I must be getting back to the home," Miss Tate said.

We all walked her to the door and onto the porch. The chickens clucked loudly in the mud porch. Miss Tate pulled open the van door and climbed inside. I watched her back out of the driveway and onto the street. I waved once. Twice.

Ruth and Naomi went back inside the house, leaving me to watch until Miss Tate's van was long out of sight. Mission accomplished. I felt the book in my pocket, snagged it, and opened it to where I'd left off:

NOW, BEOWULF, THEE, OF HEROES BEST, I SHALL
  HEARTILY LOVE AS MINE OWN.

Chapter
18

I woke up extra late the next morning. Past noon. The sounds of voices outside woke me. I jumped out of bed, dressed quickly, and dashed down the steps and straight outside.

Ruth was standing near the chicken coop with Mr. Woolrich. They were just about finished cleaning up the rubble. The strong smell of smoke and ashes burned my eyes and nose.

"Morning, Wilma Sue," Ruth said. A pile of wood and wire sat on the ground. Mr. Woolrich held a large piece of paper, and he was pointing like he was directing a show.

"Morning," I said.

"You finally woke up," Ruth said. "We thought we'd let you sleep."

"Whatcha doing?" I asked.

"We are getting ready to build the new coop. Mr. Woolrich has the plans."

"Really? Can I help?"

"Sure you can," Ruth said. "We're waiting for Pastor Shoemaker to arrive. He used to work in construction."

"We helped on a lot of building projects in Malawi," Naomi said. "But we never built a chicken coop. The chickens went wherever they wanted to go in the village."

"Yeah, I bet this wouldn't have happened in Malawi," I said. "I bet no one would burn down a coop just ... just because." I stopped talking.

Ruth shook her head. "No. And if something like this had happened, the villagers had their own way of dealing with it." She snapped her fingers. "That's it! We'll convene a village council and put the matter before our elders."

"Elders?" I asked. "We don't have any elders." My mind jumped to *Beowulf* and King Hrothgar, who was too old to defend his people against the monster Grendel.

"Yes, we can ask Pastor, Mr. Woolrich, Mrs. Snipplesmith, and Dr. Mergenthaler," Ruth said.

"How about Miss Quill?" I asked. "And Ramona Von Tickle?"

"Sure," Ruth said. "They're all a part of our village. We'll call witnesses, and I bet that will help us get to the truth. And it will put our minds at ease."

I saw Naomi coming down from the house. She carried a tray piled high with sandwiches in one hand and a pitcher of lemonade in the other. I remembered the goldfish.

"I thought you could use some lunch," she said.

Then she spied me standing behind Mr. Woolrich. "Hi, Wilma Sue. Will you be a dear and run up to the house and fetch the paper cups? I left them on the sideboard in the dining room."

"Sure," I said. "But guess what? We're going to have a village council—just like in Malawi. And we'll have witnesses and elders."

Naomi set the tray on a stump. "That's a grand idea. Jacob will be our headman."

Mr. Woolrich lifted one of the sandwiches off the tray. "Me? The headman?"

"Sure," Naomi said. "You can announce the final verdict."

My heart raced like a sparrow's. I dashed up to the house and found the cups in the dining room, just like Naomi said. But I stopped short when I saw one of the drawers in the sideboard was slightly ajar. I looked inside and found the box of blue-and-yellow swirled birthday candles that Naomi had used on her thunder cake. The box was opened as if someone had recently been in there, or maybe Naomi had been doing some checking. I read the box: CONTENTS: 12 CANDLES.

There were only three left.

I took the paper cups out to the coop builders. Pastor Shoemaker had just arrived. They were all munching on Naomi's sandwiches, so they were very glad when I showed up with the cups for the lemonade.

"Naomi," I said, "do you remember how many candles you put on the thunder cake?"

"Candles?" she asked. "Let's see … twenty, I believe. I used one full box of twelve and eight from another."

"That's right," Mr. Woolrich said. "I remember because I blew them out. There were twenty."

"Why?" Naomi asked.

"Because that means someone stole a candle. There are only three left in the box in the sideboard, but there should be four."

"Interesting," Pastor Shoemaker said. "Save that information for the council, should we need it."

"I will."

We ate ham and cheese and turkey sandwiches with lettuce and tomato and drank lemonade until Ruth decided it was time to start building.

"Those poor chickens need a place to call home."

"Will they have trouble getting used to a new place?" I asked, swallowing the last of my sandwich.

Ruth nodded. "They might. And it's possible they won't lay

eggs for a few days. That's why I kept some of the shreddings and old straw that wasn't charred. It will make the new coop feel like home."

Soon we were hammering nails and Pastor Shoemaker was cutting wood and Mr. Woolrich was giving directions. But I kept thinking about the council.

"How will we get all of the witnesses to come? I mean, what if they don't want to? What if they don't tell the truth? What if we don't find out what really happened?"

Naomi patted my back. "So many questions. Don't worry, Wilma Sue. Everyone who needs to be here will be here."

"That's right," Pastor said. "I can do some convincing if I need to."

I took a deep breath and let it out slowly. "When can we do it?"

"Soon," Naomi said. "Very soon."

By late afternoon the coop was finished and the sun was setting, leaving ribbons of red and orange stretching across the sky like flames. The new coop looked very much like the one that had burned down. It had a long door, a slanted roof, and a ramp for the chickens to use. I suggested painting it purple.

"Good idea," Ruth said. "Maybe we can stencil some flowers and chickens on it."

"And you, Wilma Sue, can be the one to paint it," Mr. Woolrich said. "I'm beat."

"Sure," I said. "I'll paint. But can we have the council first?"

Naomi, who had gone back to the house a while ago, now called from the back porch steps, "I think it's quitting time!"

Ruth invited Mr. Woolrich and Pastor to stay for supper, but they wiped the sweat from their foreheads and said in unison, "No, but thanks."

Supper—spaghetti and meatballs—was quiet that evening.
I guess everyone was a little tired and maybe a little anxious.
But Naomi did talk about the council after supper, while we sat
on the porch and listened to the cicadas.

"I called a few people," she said. "Miss Quill, Mrs.
Snipplesmith, and Dr. Mergenthaler. They all said they'd be
happy to sit on the council. And we can do it tomorrow. The
sooner the better, I say."

I smiled. Even though those three didn't know what had
happened, not exactly, I was glad to have them. "What about
Ramona Von Tickle?" I asked.

"She must be performing somewhere out of town." Naomi
yawned wide.

"Oh, I would have liked to have had her."

"I'll call again in the morning," Naomi said.

"Speaking of morning," Ruth said, "I vote we all go to bed."
She shoved her knitting into her bag. Somehow the yarn and the
motion of the needles comforted Ruth.

"I concur," Naomi said. "Tomorrow is going to be a big day."

I couldn't help but yawn.

"Then it's agreed," Ruth said. "Let's get some sleep.
Tomorrow we have to turn the library into a courtroom—
sort of."

Wow. Suddenly I was scared. I knew I was innocent, but
there was a chance ... a real chance that Naomi wouldn't be
able to prove my innocence. And then what?

I must have fallen asleep while reading, because I woke up the
next morning with the light still on and the book about chickens
sitting next to me on the bed. Once I heard Miss Daylily say she
had to "shake the cobwebs out of her head." Now I knew what
she meant. I felt a little unsteady and unclear. I shook my head

hoping the cobwebs, which might have had some spiders hidden inside them, would go away.

Sometimes a girl can think too much. So I stretched and yawned and then it struck me—the council. Now if ever a girl needed a reason to get out of bed in the morning, it was that she was holding a village council in her house with some elders.

I got dressed, choosing—I thought wisely—to wear bright colors that made me look cheery and not like a fire starter. Although, when I caught a glimpse of myself in the bathroom mirror, I wondered if a bright red shirt might be the wrong color to wear after all. I changed into a black T-shirt just as I heard Ruth calling for me.

"Wilma Sue, breakfast is ready! Busy day!"

"Okay," I called back. "I'm coming."

Yes, black was definitely a better color for court.

Naomi had made French toast with swirls of cinnamon and a hint of vanilla—the fancy Madagascar vanilla—for breakfast.

"Now eat up," Ruth said. "This could turn out to be a very trying day."

The three of us ate our French toast.

"Just be truthful," Naomi said. "When you're asked to tell your story, tell the truth."

"And only the truth," Ruth said. "Nothing more and nothing less."

"That's easy," I said. "The truth is that I didn't throw anything into the coop."

"Good," Ruth said.

After the breakfast dishes were washed and put away, I helped Ruth and Naomi turn the library into a courtroom—a village courtroom. Mr. Woolrich came by to help. I was beginning to think he was the nicest man on earth. He had kind eyes and a soft way of speaking that made me feel comfortable—perfect, I thought, for a headman.

We hung gorgeous African weavings on the walls and set out the sisters' entire collection of carved African animals. My favorite was a large elephant that I had never seen before.

Next, Mr. Woolrich set up a kind of makeshift dais. That was his word for a raised platform. On it, the sisters placed three chairs that kind of reminded me of thrones. Mr. Woolrich said the platform was taken from the church, and it was normally used by the choir for concerts and children's programs. Then we set up enough chairs, which were also borrowed from church, for the elders to use. When the room was finished, it looked spectacular and bright.

"By the way," Naomi said. "I reached Ramona Von Tickle this morning. She and Bernard are coming."

"Good, good," Ruth said.

I asked Naomi if she was going to bake a cake for the occasion. She shook her head. "Not for this, dear. Some things are better off without a cake."

My heart sank. It seemed to me that if ever a cake was needed, it was here in this courtroom. "But how will the truth come out?"

She hugged me tight. "It's going to be okay, Wilma Sue. You'll see."

I pulled back a little and looked up into her eyes while she still held me. "I hope so because . . . because I want you to know I didn't do it, and I want . . . whoever *did* set the fire that killed Slowpoke to admit it."

"Then what?" she asked with a half smile.

"Then we can . . ." I didn't know exactly. "I don't know what we'll do, but at least we'll know the truth. And I can be set free and not get sent back to the home."

"But we already told you," Naomi said. "Ruth and I believe you. You are *not* going back to the orphanage."

"What will we do with the real perpetrator?" I asked.

We hung gorgeous African weavings on the walls and set out the sisters' entire collection of carved African animals. My favorite was a large elephant that I had never seen before.

Naomi stepped back and said, "Forgiveness is so powerful; it's like an ocean." She mussed my hair a bit. "It looks like we're finished in here. I think I'll go put on a pot of coffee for our guests. They should be arriving any minute now."

"Okay, I'll go check on the chickens."

I didn't think the birds were happy out in the mud porch. But Ruth said we couldn't put them in the new coop until it was painted and the nests were filled with straw and shreddings, including some that she'd saved after the fire.

"Today's the day." I picked up Eggberry. She snuggled into my chest. "We are going to find out the truth. We are going to find out who killed Slowpoke." She snuggled deeper.

Sonny, who'd been sitting in a corner, let go a loud *cock-a-doodle-do*. "That's right, it *is* something to crow about."

I set Eggberry on a hay bale. Dottie pecked at my sneaker. "I'm going to paint the coop tomorrow, and then you can all go home to your brand-new place."

I tossed some corn on the floor. I wished they could talk. The hens knew Penny, and they knew who lit the fire. I wished they could tell me what happened. "I'd better get back. The elders are on their way."

I stood on the front porch and waited. The air was warm, and the sky was blue with a few clouds. I could smell the creek as it mixed with what lingered from the fire.

Mrs. Snipplesmith and Dr. Mergenthaler were the first to arrive.

"Good day, Wilma Sue," Mrs. Snipplesmith said. "It's a nice day, isn't it?"

"Yes, yes it is," I said. She looked so much brighter than she had the first day I'd met her. And Dr. Mergenthaler, who was standing next to her, still leaned pretty heavily on his cane and his back was still crooked, but maybe it was a little less crooked. He seemed to move with less pain anyway.

"Do you still have that tibia?" he asked.

"It's on my night table," I said.

"Good, good," he said.

I led them to the library. Ruth took over from there and showed them to their seats, while I went back to the porch.

Next to arrive was Miss Quill, who arrived in style. She pulled up on a bright red scooter. I wasn't sure it was her until she took off her helmet. "Hello there, Wilma Jo!" she called.

"It's actually Wilma *Sue*," I said, "but hello."

Miss Quill set the kickstand on her scooter and put her helmet into a box strapped to the back.

She climbed the porch steps. "Gorgeous day for a trial."

My eyebrows rose. "Yes, I guess it is." I walked her to the library and then went back to greet Ramona Von Tickle and Bernard, who were just now walking across the church lawn. I noticed they were holding hands as they made their way down the path. He wore his butler's suit, and she was wearing a bright red skirt with yellow swirls. Her hair was piled so high on her head that it made her seven inches taller than Bernard. But he wasn't so tall to begin with.

"Hello," I called.

Ramona Von Tickle spread her arms. "HELLLLOOOOO!" she sang.

High C above A.

"That was lovely, my dear," Bernard said. "Just lovely."

Now that made my heart sing.

Next, Pastor Shoemaker arrived. He wore a dark suit and dark shoes, and, in my opinion, he looked like he'd come for a funeral. "Hi, Wilma Sue," he said. "Are you ready for this?"

"I sure am." I didn't need to show him the way to the library.

Then I waited and waited for Penny, her mother, and Mrs. Agabeedies. But it was Miss Tate who arrived first. I couldn't breathe for a second when I saw the black van pull up. I didn't know she was coming. I thought her work was done for now.

"Miss Tate," I said. "How come you're here?"

"Naomi and Ruth invited me," she said as she climbed the stone steps.

I swallowed. Suddenly this did not seem as simple.

"Okay," I said.

She walked past me and into the house.

I waited for a few more minutes, but the Pigsworthys and Mrs. Agabeedies still hadn't arrived.

Naomi called me inside. "Come on, dear. We are about to start."

"But not everyone's here," I called back.

"They will be." She stood at the door and waved me inside.

Miss Tate was admiring one of the wall hangings with Pastor Shoemaker. Mr. Woolrich was sitting on one of the thrones. He looked nervous. And his socks didn't match again.

The others were seated on the folding chairs, chirping to each other and sipping coffee.

I heard the door chimes. My stomach sunk to the floor. "Penny and . . ." It had to be.

Ruth squeezed my hand. "Don't worry."

But it was Mrs. Agabeedies. She wore a bright yellow dress with orange and brown sunflowers on it. She also wore large pointy shoes and carried a bag as big as my suitcase. She plunked it down on the floor.

"Thank you for coming," Ruth said to her.

"No need to thank me. As secretary of the Bloomingdale Avenue Church of Faith, it is my business to—"

"Of course it is," Ruth said. "Now you can sit here. We're about to get started."

Penny and her mother were the last to arrive. Naomi ushered them into the library. They wore matching outfits of pink and white with dainty white sneakers.

I tried not to make eye contact with Penny, but there was no use in avoiding it. It was like I had two eye systems that day. My right eye wanted to look one way, while my left eye insisted on looking straight at Penny.

"Now, before we get started," Naomi said, "I would like you to know that we are thankful for your presence here."

The copy of *Beowulf* sat on one of the nearby lamp tables. I opened it as a distraction and read:

MANY AT MORNING, AS MEN HAVE TOLD ME,
WARRIORS GATHERED THE GIFT-HALL ROUND,
FOLK-LEADERS FARING FROM FAR AND NEAR,
O'ER WIDE-STRETCHED WAYS, THE WONDER TO VIEW,
TRACE OF THE TRAITOR.

I sucked in some air and closed the book. *To view the traitor.*

"And so, without further ado," Naomi was saying, "Wilma Sue, will you take your seat?"

Since I was the accused, I got to sit up front.

"Wait," I said. "I . . . I forgot something."

"But Wilma Sue, we're about to get started."

"I'll be right back." I ran upstairs, grabbed the hawk tibia off the night table, and shoved it in my pocket. Hollow bones. Warriors. To soar like a hawk.

Naomi was speaking to the elders when I returned and took my seat next to Mr. Woolrich.

"I'm scared," I whispered to him.

"Don't be," he said. "The truth will arise out of the ashes."

Mr. Woolrich stood. "Let's begin. The elders call Mrs. Agabeedies to the stand."

Mrs. Agabeedies stood. I heard her make a noise like wind escaping from a tire. Then she made her way to the remaining throne chair. The witness seat.

"Please, sit," Mr. Woolrich said.

"Thank you," Mrs. Agabeedies said.

"Now then. Please tell the council what you know about the chicken coop fire."

She then proceeded to spew the biggest pot of lies and half-truths I had ever heard. She finished her story by saying, "I suspected that orphan—" she pointed at me "—was no good from the moment I set eyes on her. But when Penny—who we all know has had such a tragic life—told me she saw Wilma Sue toss a lit birthday candle onto the straw . . . well, then I knew for sure that this orphan was no good."

I swallowed hard and wanted to cry. I also wanted to jump up and holler at Mrs. Agabeedies, but Mr. Woolrich held my hand tight.

"Thank you," Mr. Woolrich said. "Naomi and Ruth, do you have any questions for Mrs. Agabeedies?"

"Yes," Ruth said. She stood and paced back and forth in front of Mrs. Agabeedies, and then she said, "You told the court it was a lit birthday candle. Would you please—for the record—write down the color of the candle?"

"Wh . . . what?" she sputtered. "I will tell you what color. It was a—"

"Now, now," said Mr. Woolrich in his big, booming voice. "She asked you to write it down."

My heart pounded, but all I could think was, *Good! What are the chances of them both getting the color right?*

Naomi handed Mrs. Agabeedies a yellow legal pad and a

pen. I watched the woman scribble something and give it back to Naomi.

Naomi briefly looked at the pad and said, "You may take your seat."

Mrs. Agabeedies stood, straightened her skirt and blouse, and then harrumphed back to her seat.

Naomi walked over to me and showed me the paper. I read: BLUE-AND-YELLOW SWIRLED. It was one of the birthday candles from the sideboard. I knew it. Penny must have taken it that day she stayed for lunch.

There's no way Mrs. Agabeedies could know that unless . . . unless Penny told her earlier. My heart pounded and pounded. I could feel it in my ears and wrists.

"And now," Mr. Woolrich said, "Penelope Pigsworthy, please take the stand."

Penny sashayed up to the dais like she was a movie star. She sat and crossed her legs like she was all grown up, and then she gave me such a smirk I could feel it in my chest.

Pastor said, "You claim you saw Wilma Sue toss a lit birthday candle into the coop, is that correct?"

"Yes," she said, looking at her mother.

"Tell the council, please, what color was that candle?"

That's when she sat up straight in her seat and said in a loud, clear voice, "It was blue-and-yellow swirled."

Mr. Woolrich stood and looked directly at Naomi and then me. "You mean like the candles on the thunder cake?"

I swallowed. "I think so."

That was when Mrs. Agabeedies opened her mouth again. "See. Positive proof that Wilma Sue had access to the candles in question."

I tried to swallow again. But I couldn't. Something felt stuck in my throat.

Chapter
19

I heard gasps and whispers all around me. I was dead for sure. They had their proof.

"That's what I saw," Penny said. "Wilma Sue threw it in the coop right on top of that pile of straw that's always sitting in the corner. Then she ran like crazy, really fast toward that stupid old willow tree she's always hanging around. The big one down by the creek."

I swallowed hard as tears ran down my cheeks.

"And then what?" Mr. Woolrich asked.

"I just ... I was just so—"

"Stunned!" shouted Portia Pigsworthy. "My daughter was so stunned that she just stood there, and all she could do was—"

"Now please, Portia," Mr. Woolrich said. "We are questioning the witness, not her mother."

"But she's right," Penny said. "I got scared so I ran home. And even after the fire engines came, I stayed home. I didn't stick around."

After that, Mr. Woolrich excused Penny. My stomach ached

so much I wanted to scream. She was making up the whole story, but she was also the only person who knew the truth. I looked at Ruth, who was looking at me.

Mr. Woolrich cleared his throat. "Now, Wilma Sue, will you tell us your side?"

"I didn't do it," I said. "I was down at the creek reading a book and visiting Old Woman Willow. I didn't stay very long, though. I headed back when I heard the sirens and smelled smoke. And by the time I got near Gray House, I saw the smoke too. I ran and ran and then stopped when I saw the flames and Ruth crying. The chickens were running all around, and Naomi was trying to get them into the mud porch. All except . . . Slowpoke."

"Is that your testimony, Wilma Sue?" Mr. Woolrich said.

"Yes," I said. "But it's not a story. It's the truth. I would never do anything to hurt my chickens."

Mrs. Agabeedies stood up and said, "But you have been known to pull pranks in the past." Then she spoke to the council members, "You all remember that snake she brought to church and that day when Penny fell in their chicken coop while helping Wilma Sue."

I glanced at Miss Tate. Her eyes grew wide. She hadn't known about the so-called pranks.

"Please," Mr. Woolrich said. "You've already had your say, Mrs. Agabeedies." He then called Ruth to the dais.

"Now, Ruth, please tell the elders how Wilma Sue cared for the chickens."

"She was doing a marvelous job. Just marvelous. She took such good care of the birds. I cannot imagine her wanting to hurt a single feather on a single bird."

"Thank you," Mr. Woolrich said.

Ruth went back to her seat.

Mr. Woolrich looked out over the village council. "I don't

think there is anything left to do but ask the elders to render their decision."

I looked straight at Penny. She smiled at me and then made another smirk. "Told you," she mouthed. "I told you they'd never believe an orphan."

"The elders will convene in the ... kitchen," Mr. Woolrich said. "We'll take a brief recess."

Ruth took my hand and led me outside. We said nothing. Not a single word. Naomi joined us and so did Miss Tate, but no one said a word until I said, "You have to believe me. I didn't start the fire. I love the chickens. I ... I love it here ... at Gray House. I don't want to leave. I don't want to go back to the home." I wrapped my arms around Naomi and cried.

Mr. Woolrich opened the door. "We're ready," he said. His voice was sad, solemn.

"That didn't take long," Miss Tate said.

We walked into the library, and Pastor spoke first, "Wilma Sue, please understand that this was a very hard decision to make."

Mr. Woolrich said, "Wilma Sue, please take the witness seat."

I climbed onto the dais like I was walking along death row. I sat and stared at ... at nothing.

"The elders all agree. We have no choice but to find you ... guilty."

My heart was pounding so hard, I thought it would pound right out of my chest. In fact, I wished it would. I started crying. "But I didn't do it."

Naomi took long strides toward me, and then she hugged me. "Don't you worry, sweet lamb, we'll set the record straight."

"No you won't," I cried. I looked out at the group. Penny and Mrs. Agabeedies were smiling so wide I thought their faces would break. "Not with those two in cahoots. They planned this."

"Maybe so," Naomi said. "But we will press on and find a way."

"Now what?" I asked, looking into her eyes.

That was when Miss Tate spoke up, "You will need to return to the home."

"Is that really necessary?" Naomi said.

"Please," Ruth said. "We still want our Wilma Sue."

"There was a condition," Miss Tate said. "And Wilma Sue knew about the condition when she came here."

"But I don't want to leave." Now I was sobbing so hard my hair hurt.

"I will return for you tomorrow," Miss Tate said, and then she turned away.

I did not feel like Beowulf. My helmet was not glittering. It was smashed and broken into a million pieces.

One by one the others filed past me and said how sorry they were. Even Dr. Mergenthaler. I pulled the tibia from my pocket and handed it to him. "I don't want this anymore."

That night was the worst night of my life. Naomi and Ruth and I sat on the front porch, and the sisters tried hard to make me feel better about the whole thing. They kept promising they would get me back.

"I'm sorry we did this," Ruth said. "We should have left it alone."

I hardly said a word the entire night.

It was hard for her, I knew, but finally Naomi suggested that we all try to get some sleep. But I knew it would be impossible. They tucked me into my bed and kissed my cheeks and forehead. Naomi sang me a song, and Ruth sat on the edge of my bed for a long, long time.

"There will be a way," she said. "There must be a way."

"It's okay," I said through my tears. "I'll be all right—I just know it. And you and Ruth will be okay, and the chickens will be okay."

"Sure, sure," Ruth said.

Then they kissed me again. Ruth sat in the chair, and Naomi brought up another chair from her room. "We won't leave you tonight," she said.

⁓⁓⁓⁓⁓⁓⁓⁓⁓

Soon I heard the sisters snoring. Light and even, almost rhythmic.

I couldn't fall asleep, so I sat on the window seat looking out toward Old Woman Willow and wishing she really was a grandmother who could come and take me—a real relative, a blood relative who had every right in the world to claim me and maybe even adopt me.

Then a breeze kicked up. It shook the branches of Sweet Silver Maple. As I watched, the wind seemed to lower the branches and create a stairway to the ground. I realized that I could climb out my window and walk right down the tree. I kept watching as the limbs snapped into place one after the other until I knew what I had to do.

I climbed out the window and set one foot on the top branch. It felt firm enough to hold a rhinoceros. I swallowed, sailed a few prayers toward heaven, and then started down the tree-limb staircase. To my surprise—although, maybe it wasn't all that surprising—I made it all the way to the ground. And the instant my feet got settled on the hard dirt, the tree shook and rolled up its staircase—*Bing Bang Boom!* Now it was my Sweet Silver Maple tree again.

I darted down the street toward Penny's house. The muggy air wrapped around me as I ran, trying to hold me back. But I kept going until I stopped right at her front hedges. The

Cake

Pigsworthy house was quiet and dark except for one window with a yellow light. I knew it wasn't Penny's room. Hers was on the side of the house. I crept into the yard and somehow alerted a dog down the road. He barked and yammered as I made my way like a ninja to the side of the small one-story house. I found Penny's window. It was low enough that I could hoist my way through it if the window were open.

But I thought better of just bursting in on her. So I tapped on the window, lightly at first, and waited. Nothing. I tapped a little louder. Still nothing. I waited and waited. The dog had stopped barking by now, but then an owl hooted and scared me so much that I stumbled backward, tripped over a rock, and landed on my rump. That was when I saw Penny. She opened her window.

"What in the heck?" she asked.

I put my finger to my lips and whispered, "Shhh. I need to talk to you."

"Go away," she said. "You shouldn't be here."

"Please. I really need to talk to you."

"No. Go away."

I got to my feet. "I just ... I just want to know why you lied. Why did you tell them I started that fire? You know I didn't do it."

"I didn't lie."

I swallowed as I realized my case was hopeless. There was no way in the world to get Penny to tell the truth.

"*You* did it, didn't you?" I said. "You started that awful fire that killed Slowpoke."

Penny sniffed the wind and looked away from me. "You can't prove it. My mother says no one believes orphans."

"Is that what happened to your mother? Did someone not believe her when she was a kid?"

Penny didn't answer.

Something behind Penny startled her. She moved away from the window for a moment, and then she turned back to me. "I ... I have to go. My mother is coming."

"One last thing," I said. "It doesn't really matter what you say. Naomi and Ruth Beedlemeyer love me no matter what. And they will fight to get me back."

On the way back to Gray House, the dark clouds returned and hid the full moon—mostly. I could still see the huge, yellowish platter in the sky. A few drops of rain fell as I picked up my pace to almost running. I hoped Sweet Silver Maple would lower her limbs for me again.

The harder I ran, the harder the rain fell now. It was like a deluge. A summer deluge. A sudden crack of lightning and a rumble of thunder caused me to jump and nearly stumble. I was getting wetter and wetter until I was certain I resembled a drowned rat standing in front of Sweet Silver Maple, asking her to help me get back inside.

Sure enough, the tree limbs unfolded once again. And the next thing I knew, I was safely inside my room ready to spend what was certain to be my last night at Gray House. Naomi and Ruth snored away, having no clue that I had gone to Penny's.

Chapter
20

The smell of Naomi and Ruth's morning coffee tickled me awake.

I saw my suitcase sitting in the same place I'd left it since my first night in Gray House. I knew I should pack, but I . . . I just couldn't. I had to believe that Penny would do the right thing. I remembered what I'd done last night. It couldn't have been a dream. It just couldn't.

"Wilma Sue," Naomi called, "are you coming down?" Her voice shook like a tree branch in the breeze.

I touched my stomach. I wasn't very hungry, but I went downstairs anyway. I wanted to spend every minute I could with the sisters until it was time for me to go.

"Miss Tate will be here soon. She called a little while ago, and she's on her way now."

I sniffed back tears. Nothing had been so painful as this. "Would it be okay if I went to say good-bye to Old Woman Willow and the chickens?"

"Of course, of course," Naomi said after a few seconds. She seemed distant and lost in thought.

⁓⁓⁓⁓⁓⁓⁓⁓

Old Woman Willow looked sad. Her limbs and tendrils hung low as though she was having a hard time recovering from the storm last night. I touched her bark and said, "Good morning," as cheerily as I could. "I've come to say good-bye."

A slight breeze blew and wiggled her limbs; a thin green tendril touched my cheek in the tenderest fashion.

"I don't suppose I'll ever come back to Gray House. I don't suppose I'll ever have a house again. I don't suppose I'll ever write another poem, or feed another chicken, or read *Beowulf* again."

Next, I went back up to Gray House to say good-bye to the chickens. They seemed to know I was leaving. Dottie jumped into my arms. I held her to my chest and cried. "I . . . I don't want to leave."

I heard the front door chimes. My knees shook and my stomach pitched like I was standing on the deck of a sinking ship in a typhoon. And I supposed that's exactly what I was—a tiny ship in a typhoon that was about to sink. Not a ship like Beowulf's. Miss Tate was here.

I slowly walked into the house, and I heard Naomi say, "We weren't expecting you."

It wasn't Miss Tate she was talking to. It was Penny and her mother. I could barely breathe. For a second I thought I could feel my bones. And they were hollow—almost like I could lift right off the ground and fly because I knew. In that terrible, wonderful second I knew why they had come to Gray House.

I took a deep breath and looked at Penny. Penny looked right back at me with her left eye.

I smiled at Penny, took another deep breath, and closed my eyes as I tried to give her all of the courage I could muster.

"I DID IT!" Penny shouted suddenly. "I started the fire in the chicken coop, but I didn't mean for it to burn down the whole thing and kill ... and kill ... Slowpoke. I only wanted the straw to burn, and I only wanted Wilma Sue to get into a little bit of trouble, not a whole mess." She flopped onto the sofa.

And in that instant I felt my heels lift off the floor. I suddenly understood why Mrs. Snipplesmith's chair seemed to rise in the air, and why Ramona Von Tickle's cheeks grew rosy, and why Dr. Mergenthaler's bones didn't creak so much anymore, and why Miss Quill had found better things to talk about. When you give love away, it comes back to you even stronger.

Portia Pigsworthy stood there looking at Naomi and Ruth, and then at me. She was stunned. I closed my eyes and tried to give her my courage. "I'm so sorry," she said. "She ... how could she have meant to do it? To burn down that little house? To kill that poor bird?"

I wanted to cry tears of joy but I didn't. Instead, I walked over to Penny. "Why? Why did you kill Slowpoke?"

Penny looked over at her mother and said, "I did it because you said no one believes orphans and ... and because I wanted you to love me. And because I knew that orphans make you sad."

"But I *do* love you," Portia said.

Penny threw her arms around her mother's legs. "I'm sorry, Mom. I'm so sorry."

I touched the back of Penny's head, and she said, "I'm sorry, Wilma Sue."

Tears ran down my cheeks. Naomi cried. Ruth cried.

That was when I heard the van pull into the driveway. "That's probably Miss Tate. But I don't have to go now, right?"

"Right," Ruth said as she rushed outside to greet Miss Tate. "I'll go tell her the good news."

I took a deep breath and let it out slowly.

Naomi smiled and took Penny's hand. "Your mother does

love you. Things have been hard since your father died, I would imagine."

Now Portia burst into tears. "It's been so hard. So very hard."

Naomi put her arm around Portia and pulled her close. "We will always be here for you."

Ruth returned to the living room with Miss Tate.

"Wilma Sue," Miss Tate said, "congratulations! I always knew you'd find a way to get along, after all it is the most important thing."

I shook my head. I looked at Penny and took her hand. I looked at Naomi and Ruth and even Portia Pigsworthy. "No. The most important thing is love. Real, true love, the kind that believes in you even when you might not deserve it." Penny tightened her grasp on my hand. "The kind of love that makes the other person most important."

Miss Tate wiped something from her eye. It might have been a tear. It might have been a speck of dust. "You are a very smart girl, Wilma Sue. I guess I might have forgotten how important true love is."

I dropped Penny's hand and went to Miss Tate. I looked into her now glistening eyes. "But you do Miss Tate, you love so many children at the home. Maybe you need more love in return."

"Oh dear, Wilma Sue," Miss Tate said. "I ... I don't know what to say." She patted my head. "How could one little girl know so much about ... about love?"

"Love and chickens and cake," I said.

Ruth clapped her hands. "Maybe Miss Tate needs a cake of her own someday."

"What?" Miss Tate said. "A cake?"

"You'll see," I said. "Some day you'll see."

Miss Tate laughed a little. "Okay, okay. Maybe one day. But for now I must report back to Miss Daylily. She'll be delighted."

Cake

We all stood there for a few seconds after Miss Tate left. We were quiet, until Naomi spoke up. "You know what?" she said. "I think we should leave Penny and her mother right here so they can talk. And we should go bake a cake."

"Is it time?" I asked. "Is it time to make a cake for Penny and her mother?"

"Yep," Naomi said. "It is definitely time."

I followed Naomi into the kitchen. Ruth said she'd like to go down to the Life Center, if no one minded. She wanted to tell everyone the good news. We didn't mind one bit.

"What kind of cake are we making?" I asked.

Naomi stood and pondered that for a moment. She tapped her cheek and said, "How about we try and create that lava cake?"

That sounded terrific to me.

We assembled all of the ingredients: Flour, sugar, eggs, salt, baking powder, and butter. I set out the mixing bowls and measuring spoons and spatulas. Naomi sang:

Showers of blessing,
Showers of blessing we need;
Mercy-drops round us are falling,
But for the showers we plead.

As Naomi's cakes baked, she mixed up some deep, luscious chocolate lava that she promised would flow like a river.

Penny and her mother stayed around Gray House all day. It was like they didn't want to leave. Portia even said, "I was in this house when I was little girl. I was the foster kid for a little while until . . . until I got sent back."

"You got sent back?" I asked. "How come?"

"Because my foster mother didn't believe me. She said I stole money from her when I didn't."

"I would have believed you," I said.

217

Portia still looked sad. "I'm sorry I didn't believe you and let Penny blame you for the fire."

Penny sniffed tears. "I thought it would make you love me more, Mom."

"No. Nothing can make me love you more. And maybe I need to prove that to you by being home more."

Naomi smiled and clapped her hands. "You know what this calls for?"

"What?" I asked.

"A party! I think we should invite all of the village elders over because they need to know the good news. And then we can celebrate!"

"Good idea," I said. "How about it, Penny?"

Penny smiled. "Yes. A party."

And so later that day, after the lava cake had baked and Ruth had returned home from the Life Center and all of the elders had gathered down by the chicken coop—which still needed to be painted—Naomi brought the lava cake outside.

Even Mrs. Agabeedies was there. She still looked pinch-faced, but at least she came. I knew the fullness of time would eventually come, and then we'd bake a cake for Mrs. Agabeedies.

Ramona Von Tickle burst into song with Bernard at her side. Mrs. Snipplesmith and Dr. Mergenthaler stood side by side, and Miss Quill, who Ruth had once described as looked piqued, was looking quite nice with rosy cheeks and quiet lips. She didn't seem to have much to say now except, "Thank you for inviting me."

Naomi sliced into the cake, which stood seventeen layers high with white marshmallow frosting and cherries all around it. "Now watch," she said. "This is the best part." The chocolate lava flowed out of the cake in a wide river, just like it was supposed to. Everyone applauded.

Portia got the first slice. She took a bite and then smiled. It was the first time I'd seen her smile since I'd come here. And soon everyone was eating lava cake and smiling and laughing and singing.

"Is this just like Malawi?" I asked Ruth.

"Well, kind of," she said.

Dr. Mergenthaler made his way toward me. He handed the hawk tibia to me. "You should have this."

"Thank you," I said as I shoved it into my pocket.

"Still wish you had hollow bones?" he asked.

I looked around at my village, my family. "Nah. If I had hollow bones, I'd be too busy flying over the continents. Just think of what I would have missed."

Glossary

Mise en place (miz ã plas) — (in a restaurant kitchen) the preparation of equipment and food before service begins

Nsima — cornmeal porridge, a staple of the Malawi people's diet

"Mwauka bwanji" — "Good morning," or "Have you woken up well?"

"Ndadzuka bwino" — "I have woken up well, have you?"

Ngumbi — African termites

Discussion Questions

1. Wilma Sue wished she had hollow bones like birds so she could fly. Where would you go if you could fly? What would you see? What would it feel like to soar?

2. Wilma Sue is sent to live with a new family. She was a little scared and worried. Have you ever had to go somewhere that made you nervous? What did you do?

3. Wilma Sue is accused of doing something she didn't do. Has that ever happened to you? What is the best way to handle it?

4. Naomi baked some very special cakes. But what was really important about the cakes? Was it their special qualities or was it something better?

5. Early in the story, Miss Tate tells Wilma Sue that the most important thing in life is to get along with others. Do you agree? Did Wilma Sue agree all the time?

6. Wilma Sue said that "timing is everything." What do you think she meant by this?

7. Penny Pigsworthy wasn't always very nice. Why? Can you imagine being Penny?